e for *Aria fo*

"A deeply felt and richly drawn novel about love, ...ourning, commitment, and community in a time of great challenge. *Aria for a Farm: Lean Together or Fall Alone* snares its reader on the first page and never lets go. A wonderful first novel from a new and authentic Midwestern writer."—Nickolas Butler, author of *Shotgun Love Songs* and *Little Faith*

"A farm story, a complicated love story, some skullduggery, and a history lesson about the Great Depression all wrapped together in this page-turning novel."—Jerry Apps, author of *Settler's Valley: A Novel.*

"An engaging story of the complexity of family ties and commitment to community that imparts a rich sense of place with the authenticity of a deeply felt memoir. While set in rural Wisconsin during the Great Depression, the theme of finding—or reinventing—one's place in the world remains timeless and universal."—Sara DeLuca, author of *Dancing the Cows Home: A Wisconsin Girlhood* and *The Crops Look Good: News from a Midwestern Family Farm*

ARIA for a FARM

Lean Together or Fall Alone

A Novel

Victoria Brenna

Eau Claire, Wisconsin

Aria for a Farm: Lean Together or Fall Alone

ISBN 978-1-7331087-2-0

Library of Congress Control Number: 2021902758

Editor: Elizabeth K. Fischer
Cover by Shawna Lou Creative
Cover photos of author's horses and Fick family barn in Clayton.

Attention organizations and educational institutions:
Quantity discounts are available on bulk purchases of this book for
educational purposes or fund raising. For information, please contact
Monarch Tree Publishing,
P. O. Box 387, Eau Claire, Wisconsin 54702-0387.
www.monarchtreepublishing.com
info@monarchtreepublishing.com

Dedication
I dedicate this endeavor
to my son BJ and daughter Anna and their spouses,
my husband George,
but especially to my four grandchildren
Max, Maya, Evelyn, and Lily
who are the hope and blessing our world deserves.

History, Music, Nature, and God

"Those who cannot remember the past
are condemned to repeat it."
George Santayana,
Spanish-American philosopher, 1863-1952

"Real understanding…comes from what we learn from
love of nature, of music, of man. For only what is learned
in that way is truly understood."
Pau Casals, Spanish cellist, 1876-1973

"I see in the melody of Nature, God….Music is the
manifestation of God, like everything else."
Pau (Pablo) Casals, Spanish cellist, 1876-1973

Acknowledgments

I am eternally grateful to those gracious people who read the drafts or parts of this novel and gave feedback for revisions. Janna Darna, the cobbler, was the gracious first; Joel Dresang, journalist emeritus posing as an actor in Milwaukee, kindly responded; Sara DeLuca, a fellow reader and author of several books, provided perspective; Eva Mewes, a retired farmer of decades in Menomonie, supplied a valuable check on accuracy; Kathleen McLean, a Twin Cities editor and word wiz, read twice and critiqued with a sharpened pencil; Judith Kepper, a Turtle Lake farmer and weaver, reminded me to tell my story; Nick Butler, author extraordinaire, mentored extensively; Jerry App, former instructor and present day icon on WI Public TV, blessed me with his reading. To all those generous individuals who gave their time to be interviewed, I extend my gratitude.

I am heartfully thankful for my editor Elizabeth Fischer, her trust in me, her collaboration, and her expertise in guiding me through the last revisions. Any errors are mine alone.

This is a work of fiction.

Table of Contents

1. He's Gone

Claudia walked into the farm kitchen. The house seemed the same but wasn't. Earlier that morning she'd left her father at the kitchen table mending harness and there he was, awl in hand, as if waiting to put in the next stitch. His head was on the table, face down. He never took a nap at the table. He wouldn't put his head down there. She picked the bridle from between her father's cold stiff fingers without looking into his face. She'd seen enough death to recognize it without staring into vacant eyes.

He wouldn't finish the leather. If the stitches were going to be put in, she'd have to do them. That was Dandy's only work bridle and she needed to finish the west forty field work. She kept her eyes and hand fixed on the worn brass buckle where the waxed thread still hung waiting to be attached to the smooth hand-stripped leather strap. Her father had worked the land and cared for their animals with attention and appreciation. She held the corner of the table for the comfort of the wood's stability.

Her grandparents' old-country mantle clock ticked away the minutes. That's why she'd come in. It wasn't like him to take so long.

A couple of hours ago she'd heard his voice. "I'll be out in a bit." Now silence. The noon meal dishes were rinsed and stacked in the sink; her hand touched the sun-warmed rim of the top plate. He wouldn't need supper. Would she? She wondered as she stared out the window at Dandy grazing in the pasture.

Claudia tried not to think too much. Go to town. Fetch the undertaker. She turned her father's head to the side so he would be more peaceful, less unnatural. Monday and the table was covered with the everyday tablecloth of green-and-yellow-patterned flowers on white where his head now laid. He never took a nap at the table. She wanted air.

She grabbed the bridle from the table, her eyes locked on the leather, and a piece of twine string from the hook by the door. As she left, the screen door slammed behind her, and she called to Dandy.

Claudia tied her broad-backed Belgian mare to the rail outside the mortuary in the one-church, one-tavern town of Turtle Lake. She stepped into the workshop, which smelled of turpentine, tongue oil, and varnish and began speaking.

"You gotta come out to our place. We need you," she paused then continued more quietly, "Not we, not any more 'we.' I need you."

The undertaker stopped his hammering on a bird's-eye maple coffin. She waited the minute for him to straighten so he could look up at her. She noticed that his cataracts were worse than the last time she'd seen him. She didn't know him well. *A bit of a strange duck.*

"Sorry 'bout yer troubles but you're out a piece," he said, reflecting on her choice of pronouns.

Yes, I know we live a ways out of town. She stood silently waiting.

"I mean… to get out to your place. It takes a bit a doing."

"I have my horse. We could hitch up your wagon." *Ours is full of seed waiting for me to get it in the ground.*

"Well," he scratched the gray stubble on his cheek. "Trouble is, I don't know as I can make the trip. My rheumy's acting up."

God Almighty. Am I going to have to try to load my father into the wagon myself?

"See, thing is, the health department says Doc or me gotta go out there and see the body afore you go messin' with it." He paused and scratched again, this time with the claw end of his hammer on the inner side of his upper leg.

"Trouble is, Doc's over Pigeon Creek way tending to a baby come too early."

Claudia closed her eyes, took a breath, and then continued in a quieter than normal voice, "What should I do then?"

"Yer just gonna have to wait 'til tomorrow."

What difference is one day going to make? Doc won't be back by then and if the undertaker can't make the trip today how would tomorrow be different? She civilized her reply in her mind so it could come out her mouth without biting off his head. That's one thing she'd learned living alone with her father out on the Wisconsin prairie with neighbors few and far between. You don't go bad-mouthing or sharp-tonguing anyone who you may need tomorrow to help put up a crop or put out a fire.

"Tomorrow my nephew from New York City will be coming on the noon train. He's takin' over the business, and I 'spect he can go out with you and take care of yer dad." This was the first anyone had mentioned her father. The sudden pain in her stomach was like being in the sun too long, running out of water, but wanting to just finish that last row of beans, as she realized that her father's dead body was waiting in their kitchen and would be there one more day in this heat. She looked around for a place to sit. The only open surface was on the beautiful eyes of the maple box much like the red oak one she would choose for her father. *Cripes, and I'm going to have to deal with some greenhorn from out East. If that doesn't just top the heap of manure I'm shoveling.* She stepped out the door onto the walk.

Down the street Ernie, a short, round, redheaded man, stepped out of his general store, broom in hand, to sweep the plank stoop. He saw Claudia, her head tipped back and her eyes shut tight against the sun's glare. Still holding the straw broom, he walked toward her past the shoe shop and jewelers.

"How you doin', Claudia?"

Claudia looked down at the moon-faced man as unbidden tears rolled down her cheeks.

"What's the matter?" He asked, leaning forward and inspecting her face. She brushed her tears and his words away with the back of her hand.

"It's the sun."

They stood facing each other with eyes averted.

"I went to get him. He was taking so long. It's not like him. He was gone."

"Where'd Francis go?" Ernie asked.

"What?" Claudia was confused.

"I haven't seen him in town today. Maybe he went to one of your neighbors," Ernie offered, then peered from Claudia's tear-stained face to the undertaker's.

He removed his right hand from the broom handle and touched her arm tentatively as if testing a pan on the stove to see if it was too hot to handle. His hand returned to the broom.

"Wish Vivian was here." Ernie glanced back toward his shop. "She won't be back until tomorrow, maybe Wednesday."

The morning's flies had lost their lethargy and buzzed around the two of them in the heat of the day. Ernie drummed the top of his belly.

"Maybe some of the other women folk in town could be with you."

Claudia shook her head like a tired, stubborn child told to clean up and go to bed. If Vivian were around she could sit with her. But those other busybodies? She had nothing in common with them except they all had to breathe air. *Ta! To think of listening to their chatter and trying to answer questions that had no answers.* She felt like she was floating away from shore, seasick in a battered boat. *Why did my father die? He was healthy. I wish Vivian were here. I want my friend. I want...*

"I'll call George's boys to come over and do your chores."

"No." Now she was firmly on the street again. "I can

manage. I'd be doing them anyway. Father's been busy mending harness he didn't get to this winter. George's boys have their own work to do. We should've had the last of our corn planted but that low west end..." Claudia started to drift off again. "Father was holding off until it dried enough. We thought this would be the year. It's been so dry. We planned to use the horses. He didn't like to use the tractor on that field. We need more cropland."

Ernie stood silent, eyes wide. This was more words from Claudia to him than he'd heard in a month of Sundays.

Claudia stared off thinking of the low corner of that field. This year was hot enough to dry it, and now this. She and her father had disagreed over the old hayfield. They had plowed and disced last fall, and this spring he said no to using the tractor. She had wanted to plant the field last week, but when she went to get the horses' headgear, it wasn't there. He replied he was fixing it. She had expected he had done the repairs this winter. This morning, she had wanted to hitch them up and he'd maintained, "No. This bridle isn't finished."

She had suggested using the tractor even though she knew he would never use the machine on that field. He warned, "The tractor will tear the soft ground all up." She had walked out and left him to it. He'd been contrary lately. They'd butted heads more this spring than ever before. Now she wondered if he'd not been feeling well. Maybe she'd missed something...

Ernie cleared his throat.

"Let me know if you need anything. I'll tell Vivian when she gets back." She barely heard his mutter as he turned to go to his store, "'My grief lies onward and my joy behind.'"

It was getting late in the day, and she still had chores, animals, and her father all depending on her to take care of them. She hoisted herself onto Dandy's broad back and let her friend lead them home.

On her way, she passed old man Meiser's farm, where rows of green corn and golden oats had once swayed. A magnificent barn had housed two dozen Guernsey cows when Mrs. Meiser was alive and their daughter and son were there to help. They were folks who kept to themselves. With the pressure of all the snow this winter, the middle of the barn had begun to sag. Claudia wondered how long it could stand before falling down like so many other abandoned barns, part of the dissolution of their way of life. Two farms in Bear Creek Township had already been lost to the bank. Folks couldn't make a living with crop and cattle prices so low. She was glad to see the sharecroppers had been planting their vegetables again this year on Meiser's land. Routine was comforting.

That night after chores, she avoided the kitchen and her father's body and paced her bedroom until dawn. She couldn't touch her father after he'd grown cold and stiff. It wasn't him. Claudia knew people who had prepared their relative's body at home. She could have buried a dead calf but not her father, not if she didn't have to.

This morning she couldn't avoid walking past his body on her way to milk Daisy, feed the chickens, and gather the eggs. She both wanted to shake him back to life and tuck him out of sight under a blanket. She resisted the desire to caress his shoulder. Then she stooped to pick up the pig's pail of scraps from yesterday's meals, scanty additions to the pig's feed—egg shells, coffee grounds, wilted lettuce greens for a salad that she hadn't eaten. She decided to hitch stout Molly, rather than the leaner Dandy, to the undertaker's open wagon that was set up for one horse. The three-mile round trip would require stamina.

The journey had taken less than half an hour but the late morning sun was already hot. In town she offered her mare water and stroked her. The sun burned the back of her sleep-deprived eyes, and she retreated inside the mortuary where she didn't have to wait long.

Just after noon, the nephew, an undertaker from New

York City, walked into his uncle's shop with too much assurance for Claudia's taste. *Typical of those Easterners. They think they know everything. Besides, he's way too good-looking, and how's he going to get any work done in those pressed cotton pants and that white shirt.* She smiled at the thought of him after a few days in this heat, his white shirt fast becoming yellowed from sweat and dust and wrinkled from exertion.

"This here's my nephew, Thomas Alexar." The stooped mortician swung his hand toward the tall man who was about Claudia's age. Thomas set his suitcase down and reached to shake her hand. The undertaker motioned toward Claudia, "This here's Claudia Nelson, whose pa I wired ya about."

Thomas gazed straight into her eyes, and she saw his were blue, as blue as she imagined the ocean to be. That's another thing; blue eyes are weak, she judged. He'll need to wear dark glasses. He won't be used to the sun, living amongst skyscrapers. The corner of her mouth turned up.

"I suppose we had better get out to your home and get your father settled back here as soon as possible." With that he took her arm and walked out into the bright sun without even a glance back at his uncle. His composure was unexpected, but comforting, like the assurance of being with her father.

They climbed up onto the bench seat of the open wagon with the coffin she'd picked out the day before in the back. The lid was just sitting with one nail tacked to hold it in place. The casket was of red oak, a favorite tree of her father's—hard, slow-growing, and stable. She remembered another time when her mother was still alive. Claudia didn't come up to her father's waist but had helped him plant the little grove out in front of their house. He had talked to her as they had carried water from the creek to each tree.

"You can depend on a tree to be there for you. Give you shade for three or four generations and then at the end it'll give you boards to make a house that'll last another three or four."

Claudia and Thomas talked little on the way out to the farm. Holding the reins loosely for Molly knew the way as well as she, Claudia willed the road ahead to pass quickly. She wondered if it would've been quicker to have switched out the shafts for a pole and changed the hitch of the mortician's wagon from a single tree to one of her double trees to accommodate both her horses. If both horses were pulling, the trip might go some quicker but would the time saved have made up for the time taken to switch the mechanism? She focused on the rhythmic clomping of Molly's feet and the song of the meadow larks in the fields. Peripherally, she noticed Thomas contemplating the newly seeded cornfields, the hayfields, which were still dark green from snow melt, and the mixed deciduous and pine woods that tended to separate the fields.

As they passed a field of tall golden grain, he asked, "What is that? The field seems ready to harvest."

"Winter wheat," was all she offered.

When she opened the farmhouse door, he removed his herringbone-wool cap with a visor which he put in his back pocket before checking the body. From his notebook he pulled an official-looking paper that he filled in with neat, precise printing. Her father was a big man, but the city gentleman stooped down, squatted a bit, and put one arm under her father's stiffened legs and one behind his rigid back. Thomas lifted the body and carried it to the back of the wagon where he'd already taken the cover off and smoothed the flannel cloth protecting the inner satin lining. He laid the body on its side so it would fit. Her father appeared childlike with his knees up.

She set the satchel of her father's fresh clothes in the back and got up on the buckboard next to the man from out East. The process had taken less time than putting a baby to sleep and somehow seemed as peaceful and content. Claudia knew from all the death and dying on the farm that what was lying in the back of the wagon was no longer her father. The red oak trees out front were more her father now than the inflexible gray flesh in the wagon.

The return to town was as quiet as the ride to the farm but felt less rushed, more settled. She appreciated that he didn't require her to make small talk or entertain or instruct. He had a relaxed, confident, gentle manner that steadied her.

Early that evening after unhitching her mare from the mortician's wagon and tying her up outside Ernie's general store, Claudia went in to talk to Vivian, the clerk and unmarried friend, who had returned from her visit to a neighboring town. The two women, one twenty-seven and one sixty-four, were unlikely but long-time friends. They sat in the rear of the store where Ernie, the proprietor, had his home. They made the necessary decisions over coffee, and then Claudia went home to another sleepless night. The next day, Vivian made the arrangements with the pastor, and folks came into the store to hear the news.

On Wednesday, Mrs. Johnson, Claudia's closest neighbor, stopped by the Nelson farm. She asked if the service would be at the church the next day. Claudia suspected Doris Johnson already knew, but firsthand information held greater power, more status in Bear Creek. Mrs. Johnson came with condolences and a small casserole and to hear the details from the horse's mouth. Claudia told her the service would be Friday. The visit was short, as were most calls to the Nelsons when Francis wasn't present. After Mrs. Johnson left, Claudia, uncharacteristically, lay down on the sofa and closed her eyes.

The knock at the door later was another intrusion. A shiftless, dirty man stood there, sheepish and stammering. *I don't want to feed him. Not today.* Head down, he mumbled he saw the mark and pointed to the fence post. A stick cat meant there was a kind woman here who would feed a man.

"My memory is failing me," he apologized, "but I

thought…oh, it don't matter. If I could just rest myself, I'd be grateful. Maybe a glass of water?" When she returned with a glass of milk which he drank down, he recalled, "The mark is faded, but I'm willing to do a bit of work."

She wondered how this skinny, old man could work without collapsing. She decided she would make him a sandwich. As she turned in the doorway, she saw Shep, her aging Border Collie mix, come from behind the house. He barked once, then sniffed the man's pant leg and allowed the man to pat his head.

"If you sit there on the steps, I'll be right back."

When she returned with a cup of coffee and a ham and onion sandwich, he sighed, "I recollect the woman was here back some twenty-odd years ago or maybe it was more. It's been so long since I left."

Claudia couldn't believe that could be, but the woman must have been her mother. Would her mother have fed a dirty beggar man? He would have been more than twenty years younger. Maybe he was cleaner then.

"Cleanliness is next to Godliness," her father had frequently counseled. He often followed up with, "Soap is cheap. There's no excuse for being dirty." Claudia had questioned him, "But, Papa, we are dirty from being in the fields." His gentle retort had left no question. "Being dirty is one thing. Good clean earth is God's creation, but filth is another thing. No one needs to stay dirty and smell like an animal."

She sat on the step of the porch—upwind of—but next to the hobo. Shep lay on the ground between them.

"What was the woman like? The one you remember being here," she asked. He told her about the woman who had to have been her mother, but he made no mention of a baby. Claudia would've been a toddler twenty-five years ago. She pressed for details.

"It's been a long time ago." He shook his thin, dull hair. "I had relations back then, but there was a falling out. I left for a fresh start." Claudia could not imagine this man as young only twenty-five years ago. Even if he was mistaken and it was thirty years ago, before she was born, he'd only be fifty or so now. His stooped, straw-thin body and brown crocodile skin bore tell-tail signs of working hard, living rough.

"I been a couple states over. Tried my luck at logging up north almost to Canada above Minnesota there. But the work is for those with more life left in 'em. Besides, it gets mighty cold up there and now most of the trees been cleared and younger guys can out-saw me."

"But the woman," pressed Claudia, "What do you remember about the woman?" He wiped his lips with the sleeve of his filthy, ragged jacket and Claudia regretted not bringing out a napkin for the man. She could've washed the cloth afterwards.

"A fried egg sandwich and a jar of the sweetest buttermilk." He seemed like he was remembering the taste by the way his lips moved around his mouth. He didn't have all his teeth. She wished she'd made him a sandwich easier to eat.

"She was quiet-like. Looked some like you but not tall and she had kindly blue-gray eyes. I stopped by on more than one occasion and she always had a little job needing done and a sandwich. Sometimes it was ham, sometimes a bit of leftover roast beef but always she put these bread and butter pickles on the sandwich. They was the best."

Everybody had said that about her mother's B&B pickles; they were the best. She'd won blue ribbons at the county fair. Claudia had been told by several women in town when they would compliment Claudia on her pickles, that they were "good but not like your momma's."

"But the kindness that sticks is she always made me a sandwich to take along. 'To tide you over,' she said. Those were some pickles."

They talked, Claudia steering the conversation to details

about her mother and the hobo remembering the food and the little jobs done. She gathered together to give him an old wool coat of her father's, a couple of flannel shirts, and two pairs of pants that needed to be rolled up. He washed at the pump by the horse trough, and he changed into a clean shirt and pants in the barn. She gave him a pair of Francis's widest suspenders to help hold the pants up. He gave her the pants he'd arrived in that were little more than rags, but he rolled up his old shirt and jacket and stuck them in his rucksack along with the newly acquired items. When she came out of the house with a sandwich, "To tide you over." He smiled.

Claudia could keep that much of her mother with her by giving something away.

2. A Funeral, a Field, and a Barn

The church, small and familiar, was a mile outside of Turtle Lake toward Bear Creek and not far from Clayton. Only five days ago Claudia and Francis had sat in their usual pew. She had listened a bit bored but had been comforted by the sound of the pastor's voice droning on. Her mind had been preoccupied with that field that wasn't planted. Today the pastor would be speaking about Francis, the field would still be unplanted, and what did it matter. She felt numb. She had done what needed to be done, taken his body into town, and made funeral arrangements. Thank God Vivian was here.

Today was prescribed motions and talking in a tunnel, none of it real. Only at home brushing Dandy and Molly could she breathe, feel the warmth of their bodies, and smell their sweet green, oatey exhale. Mrs. Johnson had brought over a beef and noodle casserole. Later Claudia realized she should have offered coffee, but she'd stood in the door mumbling until Mrs. Johnson left. Thomas and his uncle prepared the body and gave Claudia the wreath to hang on her door. She had only been to one funeral and never had to help with details. Her father would've known what to do, but he wasn't here. She preferred to follow, not lead, so she just did whatever Vivian told her to do.

The funeral that Claudia had attended was Mr. O'Brien, an elderly Irishman, whose family lived not far from the Nelsons, and that gathering had been "an Irish wake." The family and neighbors congregated at the home of the old man where his son and daughter-in-law and a bunch of rambunctious children all lived. The house was small but cozy and smelled yeasty. Claudia wasn't sure if the smell was from bread or children. Thankfully, the wake and funeral happened in late spring when the weather was warm. People spilled out into the farmyard and outbuildings. Like the others, she'd gone into the parlor to pay her respects. The body was laid out in his best clothes—a worn suit jacket and a pair of pants that didn't match—in a pine box on the only large table in the house. The dining table with a tarp and a cloth on top must have been moved to the parlor, which seemed more suitable than having the body in the kitchen. Surrounding and keeping the box cool were great chunks of ice on the tarp under the cloth. Claudia could hear the water dripping into the pails and buckets set on the floor at the table corners.

She remembered that as the evening wore on and the men drank more, the stories got more fantastic and elaborate. Francis had toasted the deceased and speculated that the man would be happy to join his wife and parents in the glorious beyond, but some in the clouds might not welcome the sight of his face. O'Brien had gotten into his share of "physical disagreements." The mourners joked that as he lay dying he wanted last rites by the priest on more than one occasion to be sure he'd "end up there with me bonny lass singing with the angels." His friends piped in, "Him who sang songs not fit to be heard by no angels, especially when he was in his cups."

"He should'a been confessing more than taking of the holy bread, but he was a good ol' soul and far be it from me to talk ill of the dead or ill of him. I won't be needing any ghostly night visits from him to remind me to keep me tongue in me head."

"Oh, he'd ne'er begru'ge ya the occasion fer a laugh."

"Why, likely he be the one to start the tale." The talk went on like that all night until Claudia told her father she'd go home and see him the next day.

The family and friends gathered around Claudia on this Friday acted nothing like the people at that wake and funeral.

Neighbors and acquaintances sat quietly, respectfully. Claudia and Vivian were the first to arrive and met the pastor inside the paneled doors of the church. Ernie with his two buddies Klive and Bruno, a couple of bachelor farmers, showed up shortly afterward. They had dug the grave the day before, and Ernie told Claudia they would be handy with ropes when the time came to settle the casket into the grave. With her husband Herbert ailing, Luella Eggert, a neighbor who lived south of Turtle Lake not far from the Nelson farm, did not come. One of her sons had brought a small cake to Claudia's the day before and mumbled his mother's condolences and regrets. Claudia noticed the Gilberts, the jewelers, had brought their pretty but shy daughter, Wilna. Their hands were warm and soft against Claudia's calloused palms. Mrs. Gilbert wore lace gloves despite the warm May day.

Vivian stood close to Claudia who could lean on Vivian even if she stood a foot shorter. Claudia hadn't expected to see Randy Rottman. He had made several small, short-term loans to Francis but wasn't what Claudia would call a friend. He arrived in a new Ford V8 Standard Tudor Model 18. He pointed out those specifics to all the admiring men standing around the spotless vehicle before the service began.

Randy shook everyone's hand and asked Ernie how the store was doing. Claudia knew Randy had provided the mortgage decades ago for Ernie to expand the store and its stock. Randy strode over to Claudia and smiled broadly into her face. He smelled of starched shirts and expensive hair cream and conveyed his sympathy. "I'm so sorry for your loss." His words didn't have the hollowness of a dried gourd but rather the sweetness of a Twinkie, a nutrition-less confection, which appealed to some folks.

The ritual began. Folks peered into the casket. Some paused and folded their hands. Others told her how well he looked. A few shook their heads. "What a shame, only fifty-six years old." There were whispers punctuated by moments of dull quiet and a few periods of bustling activity. Claudia relied on the pastor or Vivian to guide her. When she didn't know whether to sit or step forward, Vivian led her toward the pew or up to the casket before they shut the lid. At the casket Claudia felt anger rise in her stomach and ignite her face. She heard the intake of breath from the Mevissens and Fourniers in the front pews.

Claudia bent over and reached in to grab the rosary someone had entwined between her father's large, rough hands. *That doesn't belong there.* Claudia's thought pierced her numbness. She felt Vivian place her hand over Claudia's and hold it to her father's chest. She peered at her friend, and Vivian imperceptibly shook her head. They turned and the casket was closed. Later Vivian would tell her the rosary had been placed there earlier by an old acquaintance in memory of her mother's faith. Claudia had trouble remembering what happened next. Afterward, Mrs. Reuter would say how lovely the service had been and now Claudia's father and mother would be together for eternity. After the service, Randy encouraged, "Call me if I can ever be of help," and left in his big, shiny Ford with white sidewall tires.

They walked out to the cemetery behind the church where Klive and Bruno stood off to the side leaning on shovels, waiting to fill in the hole they'd dug. Claudia didn't hear the sentiments the minister expressed but when silence followed, she lifted a handful of dark dirt from the mounds surrounding the hole and dropped it onto the casket top. The deep brass bong of the church bell broke the spell. Ernie, hat in hand, quoted,

"'Bell, thy tone is cheerful,
When the bridal party
To the Church moves by! …
Bell, thy tone is mournful,
Tolling for the loved ones
Who departed are!'"

Following the service, folks drove the mile back into town to Vivian's house for the lunch. Maybe the group numbers dwindled because everyone knew Vivian was not a cook. George and Doris Johnson, the Nelsons' closest neighbors, and their two adult boys stayed. Hank was twenty-four. Vivian called him the handsome Johnson boy. Ethan was twenty-one and had been in the school choir. Vivian called him the gentle one. Claudia saw that Hank kept glancing at her and finally approached, touched his hand to her arm, and expressed his concern saying, "He was a good farmer." Mr. and Mrs. Polenski from Clayton stood with their son and petite, auburn-haired daughter, Rachel, who was a singer also but a couple of grades behind Ethan. Mrs. Polenski's perfume was cloying, and Claudia felt nauseous.

Pete and Anna Mevissen, who lived immediately to the east of the Nelsons, were building a new barn with neighbors' help. They came but had left their three young sons at home with their eldest, a daughter. Claudia shook hands and thanked people for coming. She didn't know what else was expected.

Francis would have put everyone at ease. He could be solemn and then smilingly tell the mourners that the deceased was in a better place and didn't they all hope to be there one day, too. His condolences were followed by the comforting talk of fields and relatives not seen lately who had come to town to pay their respects. With Francis people could get caught up on what was going on in town and the Country, who had gotten married, and what they were doing and where. He knew how to make a small group comfortable. But he was not here, and Claudia was vaguely and acutely aware of that.

At Vivian's, Claudia held a plate of food that she never touched. She nodded and shook her head when she felt it was needed. When the time came for her to be alone with Vivian, she was glad she had acquiesced to George and his boys doing her chores. Claudia allowed Vivian to show her into a room with a single bed where she put on a borrowed nightgown that barely covered her knees or arms, pulled the covers up, and fell asleep within moments.

Monday after her father passed away, she stopped to watch the sharecroppers work old man Meiser's field on her way to help at the Mevissens' barn-raising. Old man Meiser's property abutted the Nelson farm on one side but, because of the trees, couldn't be seen except from the road. The Meisers had been solitary people, even when Mrs. Meiser was alive. The modest house was a small square with attic windows that indicated a bedroom or two tucked under the steep roof. The barn, on the other hand, was a work of wonder, which had been built at the turn of the century when hopes soared.

The barn was a three-quarter wooden cylinder on its side. With an arched curve the barn rose to a lofty height of forty feet without visible interior supports like an eagle with wings spread wide hanging in the air. The barn was supported imperceptibly resembling the mysterious cathedrals pictured on holy cards. Folks wondered how that could be. Francis had explained to Claudia that the weight was distributed by the curved ribs that reached from the ground to the peak. In the same way, he'd told her, the curvature of the bald eagle's wings allowed the bird to hang on the air as if suspended.

A floor separated the loft from the lower portion, where the cows were milked in the barn, which was half sunk into the ground. The loft, filled with golden straw and sweet green hay, had in-the-floor trap doors left open for tossing feed and bedding down to the twelve Guernseys. The bovines' breath drifted up through the small square doors to keep the wooden ribs viable and flexible. The barn had changed considerably since being built three decades ago; it had begun to slump.

This spring whenever Claudia or her father had gone to town, they had seen the dirt farmers out working every day in the ten-acre front field of old man Meiser's property. The mother, father, and what appeared to be the mother's teenage sister, and the couple's young son were working the soil together. Francis and Claudia had speculated on their relationship. What looked like the grandma and a toddler sat under a tree or arrived at dinnertime bringing a basket and a scrap of tarp that was spread on the dirt where the toddler played. These truck farmers raised food for their extended family and sold the rest to the Amery grocery. In Turtle Lake they sold some of their surplus out of the back of their one-horse wagon to folks too old or too busy to have a garden or to those who wanted to put up a bit of something that they didn't have enough of in their own garden. Ernie bought tomatoes from the couple, and Ernie's wife, when she was alive, had canned those for winter. They could have bought commercially canned tomatoes, but Ernie Tomah wanted "good-flavored tomatoes for making goulash," and the dirt farmers' tomatoes "tasted like the old country, tangy but sweet."

They were planting potatoes on the Monday after the funeral when Claudia paused to watch. The father dug holes a foot apart with a spade, and the mother planted a piece of potato from a scrap of canvas pulled ahead of her by her adolescent son. His teenage aunt followed behind them burying the seed that would miraculously multiply into six or maybe even eight large white potatoes. Their rough, brown skin was so tender that the harvester had to be careful not to break the delicate flesh when tossing them into the wheelbarrow.

Father stood, then bent over the shovel, then straightened his body. Up, down, up, down, he repeated his motions. Mother and young aunt were perpetually stooped, arms moving rhythmically and steadily, mother from tarp to hole, aunt covering and hilling. Working their way down the row, each labored as their task demanded. The young son changed his motions and often incorporated some kicking of stones or tossing of earth clods into the air between his parents' verbal prods to return to the task at hand.

Later in the week on her way to the barn-raising, Claudia saw the family making neat rows for onion sets. The hoe dug in a line under a twine string marking each row that began and ended with a piece of stick cut to a point and pushed into the ground. The upright father walked backward while hoeing a row, the mother stooped while evenly spacing the small yellow globes into the shallow furrow, and her younger sister walked behind covering each marble-size onion.

The family in the field all wore long sleeves and hats whether sunny or cloudy, windy or rainy. During the following weeks, passersby noted what was being planted that day. They speculated based on the tools used and the phase of the moon. One week someone noticed the peas were up and reported the news at Ernie's store. Another saw them planting what must be long rows of string beans.

In previous years Claudia had seen that the farmers had "planted" poles five or six feet high, spaced every few feet for the climbing beans. She and her father preferred bush beans, even if you had to bend to pick them; they were more tender, her father asserted. The plan, they guessed at the store, was that the dirt farmers would plant the remaining section in corn and melons as soon as the ground warmed completely. In years past, they had planted companion plants for economy of space and benefit. Claudia had admired how the corn stocks shaded the melons so the vines would flourish. As the corn ripened and stocks withered the melons would soak up the sun and turn the rays into sweet flesh. She wondered, when she first saw this method, why she and her father didn't do that. Their pattern was set, and asking to change didn't seem that important. Already this year was extraordinarily hot and dusty and if rain came haphazardly, the sharecroppers' method would have merit. But her garden was already planted, and she wasn't going to change anything.

After a month of work that had started two weeks before Francis died, the Bear Creek neighbors had completed erecting Mevissen's barn on their two-hundred-eighty-acre farmstead. Now they would have a barn dance, the reward for lending a hand with the tedious but necessary work of helping your neighbor. No one could erect an entire barn on his own in a reasonable amount of time, so by mutual, unspoken agreement everyone in a farm community helped everyone else. When help was needed, people would be there whether for a barn-raising or the annual threshing or a sudden emergency. In theory that was how it worked. In a perfect world that is what would occur, but here at Mevissens, like everywhere, life was imperfect. There were the slackers who seemed to arrive for the free food and drink but tended to have sudden urgent needs at home that prevented their participation in the hard, dirty labor of actual work. There were those who worked but not the way the owner would like. There were the slipshods who shrugged, "That's good enough; it'll hold." To be fair, they were that way on their own farms, too, and that was why their farms were falling down around their knees after a few decades. Floors sloped, roofs leaked, doors hung agape crooked in their jambs. Claudia had been in several. It made her shake her head, on the inside.

This was no different. The Mevissens were the hard-working variety. Claudia didn't mind showing up with the rest of their neighbors to build their barn. A small stone barn was at their place when they first settled, but with their herd of milk cows expanding, they needed more space. They had been making do by rotating their Jersey cows in shifts into the low-ceilinged barn, which was dark and damp, but the Mevissens had been soldiering on, helping neighbors with their projects and putting off their own. At the beginning of April when a not-so-industrious neighbor told everyone at the grist mill that he was going to add on and needed help, someone in the mill made a side comment, "I'd rather get Pete Mevissen a decent barn than help that Johnny-come-lately."

Didn't take long for the idea to spread. Ernie'd heard from Bruno how the plan took shape—in a tavern. A couple of farmers drafted the notion in their heads over beer. That same night, lubricated by liquor, they pounded on Pete's door and told him their plan. Everyone liked Pete Mevissen, a big strapping German who walked tall but with a sway to his back like an old horse ridden too young and worked too hard. His wife, Anna, round like a German cached doll with several dolls within, fit comfortably in the kitchen and the barn, raising children and calves.

During the barn-raising, Anna had a hearty meal each noon for all the workers who showed up to help. The majority of the help were men but included a few boys, such as Pete and Anna's young sons who helped fetch pails of nails and files for sharpening saw blades. Claudia was the only woman. The community was used to her working alongside the men. Since her youth, Claudia had been tall and strong. In her class at school she stood out and above in height. Her father never doubted her ability, and no one ever questioned Francis's judgment. Their routine was set. The work had started before Francis died, and today he had been in the graveyard just over a week when Claudia was on a ladder holding a two-by-ten for Matthew Reuter to nail in place.

Later in the day she was on the floor with the end of a beam on her shoulder while Matthew was on the ladder with the other end setting the timber into place on one side of the structure. Claudia was lifting and walking forward. She stumbled. Under the beam's weight she and it would have dropped to the floor but Hank rushed over, leaned in close to Claudia, and together, shoulder-to-shoulder with the beam resting between them, they lifted up and handed the timber to the man on the other ladder, who put the beam into place on his side of the structure.

Pete and Anna's daughter kept the workers plied with hot coffee. At midday, Anna served a little light lunch of sandwiches and flemisers, fried and sugared bread dough along with plenty of the Mevissens' Jersey milk to wash it all down. Some of the men poured as much creamy milk as coffee into their cups. Even though his cows' cream, sweet and thick, could be whipped with a whisk, Claudia noticed Pete preferred his coal-black. His doe-faced, brown Jerseys didn't produce the volume given by the larger, black-and-white Holsteins, the breed the Johnson men favored, but the fat content was higher and made creamy yellow butter and rich ice cream. In fact, Claudia had gotten the cream from this farm to make Francis's favorite dessert, strawberry ice cream.

A little more than three weeks since work had begun, the barn addition was almost completed with a full-height loft to store hay and straw. Folks began to talk of the dance to be held in the new pine-sided building. As the boards dried they would shrink, and air would flow freely through the vertical spaces. When wind swept through the prairie, the breeze would fly through the building and not be tempted to catch the broad side and blow the barn over. The coming decades would find fierce winds testing barns as the gusts swept the countryside carrying topsoil and profits into the coastal seas or dumping them at the foot of mountains.

On that Saturday morning in the middle of May, Claudia finished chores, washed, dressed, had a bite to eat, then saddled Dandy. She could've walked the three-quarters of a mile but wanted the option of leaving quickly, alone. The dance started in the afternoon and everyone would attend. People who had been hammering and sawing for weeks, those who had stopped with food and returned to their own chores, and those who had disappeared for the duration, all came out for the festivities. Ned and Carl, Luella Eggert's sons who rarely left their farm, played fiddle and accordion, respectively, with an enthusiasm they lacked in sociability. As long as no one spoke much to them, they stoked and pumped away for hours until without any rhyme or reason, they put their instruments in their tattered cases and went home. Several locals had harmonicas, and Quentin, a reserved young man who worked at the railroad and delivered several barn beams for Pete, played a beat-up guitar. Each had his specialty and gave a song or music to the crowd for them to do with as they saw fit. Clusters of four or five women were chatting and tapping their feet. Men stuffed their hands into their pockets or the bib of their coveralls while those younger men in gangs of a few slung their arms over each other's shoulders. The children swung and pranced around until, exhausted, they fell to hay and straw bales brought in for seats. Makeshift tables were set up around the perimeter. Against the walls, children curled up on bales until parents dragged them reluctantly home to bed.

When fall came, Pete would fill his barn with a fresh crop of straw and hay from his oats and alfalfa that blanketed his surrounding flat fields. This night the aroma of newly sawn wood and plowed, spring soil filled the evening. Strings, reeds, and bellows mixed with guffers' voices, kids' squeals, and girls' giggling.

Through the open doors, wide enough for a team to pull into, Claudia saw Vivian walk up the earthen ramp, enter, and survey the area. Ernie, slower but right behind her, shouted greetings to a clutch of men with drinks in hand and waddled toward them.

Vivian walked slowly past a group of clucking women and approached Claudia. "You're the topic of conversation behind those women's raised palms."

"I wasn't paying attention," Claudia admitted.

"Listen, it's enlightening," instructed Vivian.

"What is a young woman, alone, going to do on a farm out there? It is unseemly," Mrs. Elsa Gilbert, the jeweler's wife, scowled.

"Well, I'd never call her young. She's an old maid who should've married when she was not so headstrong and could be bent to a man's ways," advised Mrs. Alice Polenski, whose daughter Rachel was eighteen, almost ten years younger than Claudia.

"Alice thinks Rachel would make the *perfect* wife for *any* successful farmer," whispered Vivian to Claudia. "As if marriage were the be-all-and-end-all of every female's life." Vivian humphed. Claudia had heard this perspective on more than one occasion.

Mrs. Doris Johnson joined the group of clustered women not far from the two "old maids."

"I don't know. I think Claudia can do it on her own just fine. She was doing most of the farm work since Francis had been slowing down. Besides, a man could do worse for a wife. She works like a horse. And look at that farm. Any one of our boys would be lucky to get that in the bargain."

Mrs. Polenski piped in, "That's fine if a man didn't want children. She's too old to have normal children, even if she can have any."

"Well," conceded Mrs. Gilbert, "she definitely has her work cut out for her."

Claudia and Vivian exchanged glances. Claudia turned away, but Vivian declared, scrutinizing the women unabashedly. "What folks say reveals more about them than it does the one they're gossiping about."

While the matronly women wagged on, the young folks danced and courted. Claudia knew she didn't fit the mold for young people, but a few young men were definitely interested in courting her. With liquor-enhanced courage, they asked her to dance and dragged her around the yellow pine floor while they sweated, ruddy-faced. Vivian, who was standing off to the side, reminded Claudia of what she might expect to become in thirty-six years, if she didn't at least attempt to mingle. She saw how effortlessly the young men got the young women to follow their clumsy attempts at a square dance or a polka. Many of those girls were more the boys' height and prettier than she was. She wondered why they even bothered to ask her out onto the dance floor.

Claudia watched a couple of boys, their eyes large, follow her every move. *Why can't they just dance and let me forget for a while?* Two country girls, one in a colorful gingham, the other in a pink checkered dress, stepped closer to several boys. The closest boy turned, considered the smiling girl in gingham, *cute as a puppy* thought Claudia, then turned back to stare at her on the dance floor with one of his buddies. *Why?* Finally the dance finished, and Claudia scanned for Vivian. Another group of girls was laughing and glancing over their shoulders to gauge the effect on the boys in the general listening area. When Claudia walked by, the girls had been discussing clothes and hair until the boys got closer to them, then the girls' talk shifted to who was keen on whom and which boy had a new cart or horse. *Did it never stop? This constant fixation on what you wore or owned? Was their only purpose in life to attract a mate?*

The few town girls in attendance wore satin or silk and primarily danced with the town boys who'd shown up. Claudia's dress didn't fit in with the country girls' gingham or the town girls' satin, or, for that matter, with any of the married women present who wore their church dresses with neat collars and padded shoulders like Alice Polenski or wide frilly fronts like Elsa Gilbert. *I don't fit in here. I shouldn't have come. Where can Vivian be?*

Claudia scanned the scene. Smiling Mrs. Gilbert and Mrs. Polenski were watching their daughters. Wilna Gilbert had kept her eyes cast down, but her friend Rachel had danced with Ethan Johnson. When Ethan returned to ask Rachel to dance again, she turned to Wilna, who blushed and barely nodded. Rachel Polenski led the way onto the floor for a polka with Ethan. His mom Doris, standing with Mrs. Gilbert and Mrs. Polenski, beamed. Claudia, not finding Vivian, stood closer to the group of women and further from the perspiring young men.

"Most men want a girl who will follow him and not try to be the boss," interjected Mrs. Polenski, and then she acknowledged, "Rachel's quite independent." Mrs. Johnson's smile faded.

Mrs. Gilbert broke the tension. "After years of marriage and children, a man can welcome the advice of a strong woman." Then, as if an afterthought, she added, "In the privacy of their home."

While the music was still playing, Claudia started to walk toward the door before anyone else asked her to dance but stopped when she heard Mrs. Polenski mention her name.

"Claudia looks like the type that might stand up to her husband in public." Claudia did not turn back to the women but stood listening.

She heard Mrs. Johnson add, "Maybe. With the right man, who knows? Claudia knows a lot," which prompted Claudia to turn her head toward them.

Mrs. Gilbert smiled with a lifted eyebrow. "There might be more than one boy here hoping to learn what a woman of her age might have to teach." Claudia saw Wilna blush at her mother's suggestion. Mrs. Polenski grimaced, but Mrs. Johnson smirked. Claudia was almost to the door when Thomas, the new undertaker, slightly younger than Wilna's father, came up and politely requested the pleasure of a short dance, which Wilna accepted.

In his crisp, white shirt and iron-creased pants, the new mortician seemed an unlikely candidate to last long in their town. Claudia had heard that this city slicker, who had helped his ailing uncle for a few days with Francis's death, had gone back to New York City where he still worked. He had returned this morning to assist with another death and help Doc with a burn patient. He was expected to be in town for the next ten days or so. She heard he was not staying in the boarding house that was next to the mortuary, but rather with his uncle in his home behind the business. Several folks in town had encouraged him to come to the barn dance. Claudia watched Thomas dance with Wilna, who was attractive but reserved. Her father was a jeweler, clockmaker, and watch repairer. *A shopkeeper's daughter was just what would appeal to an undertaker.*

Claudia was startled when the Johnson's elder son Hank, the one Vivian called the handsome son, sidled up to Claudia. She wondered if Vivian had left.

"Would you like something to drink? I got some bottled home brew," he offered. She grimaced, and he quickly added,

"Also brought some of our bottled root beer." She lifted her eyebrows, and he grinned devilishly. "I'll be right back. Don't move." He returned moments later with two bottles of cold sarsaparilla. Hank clinked the neck of his bottle to hers. "Here's to a good barn-raising." She nodded. After a few exchanges regarding particulars about the barn they'd both worked on, often side by side, Hank asked Claudia to dance. Although Claudia had little stomach for the ineptness of farm boys, she was glad of the distraction from thoughts of her father. At home she had enjoyed dancing to Tommy Dorsey's "Boogie Woogie" or "Marie" and Duke Ellington's "It Don't Mean a Thing" on the radio while making supper. She usually turned the dial to news when she heard her father's boots on the porch.

She enjoyed being led by a strong, deliberate man, unlike the boys who'd pulled and pushed her around the floor earlier in the evening. When a slow song came moments later, Hank took hold of her elbow and drew her out onto the floor amongst her neighbors and friends and the new mortician. She relaxed into the music and let her head rest against his head, which was just below hers. She didn't hear the comments but noticed the nods of approval from several observers. Mrs. Johnson smiled toward her son. When the song finished, Claudia excused herself to sit alone at a side wall. She liked the song, liked the dancing, and liked being held, but she had a guilty feeling she shouldn't be liking everything so much. She leaned her head back against the fresh boards she'd helped put in place.

Her back against the wall of the activity outside, Claudia heard the rising level of noise and knew there was trouble. A few others in the barn who heard the commotion dismissed the hullabaloo as "boys being boys" or "boys trying to act like men." Hearing the rise in volume, she thought the ruckus likely to end in trouble or a trip to see Doc.

Claudia wanted fresh air and walked out behind the barn. Two young men were fighting. She walked to Ernie, who was on the periphery. He told her the trouble had started harmlessly enough inside with boasts of strength and prowess, fueled by home brew. Then a few adult men, who should have known better, encouraged the two boys to take it out back where, uninterrupted, they could test each other. Soon the rowdiness attracted a small crowd, which formed a circle around them. With raised fists punching the night air, the onlookers were as energetic in their encouragement as the activity at the center of their entertainment.

"Hit him in the face. He thinks he's such a pretty boy with the gals."

"Come on. What are you? A girl? Fight!"

"Quit pussyfooting around and give him what for."

"Let's see what he's made of." The remarks were flung indiscriminately at whichever one showed any reluctance.

She saw torn shirts, dirty pants, and blood running from one boy's nose and from a cut above the other boy's eye. They were locked in angry battle, a crowded frenzy of energy.

She saw Thomas's blazing white shirt push between the two brown blurs. He was more than a head taller but weighed about the same as the bigger of the boys. He did not have the biceps of these two farm-hardened lads who were used to tossing hundred-pound feed sacks into wagons or wrestling yearling calves to the ground to brand them. Thomas had his arm across the chest of one of them to hold him back. One of the adults, Bruno, who'd been a vocal cheerer-on moments ago, stepped up and grabbed the other boy by the shoulders.

"Okay, that's enough, you two. What a way to act in front of our new undertaker. Ya want him to think we're a bunch of savages?"

The crowd dispersed into small groups. Some wandered back to the barn dance, others chose to go home with over-stimulated senses. Claudia walked to where Dandy was tied. Gathering up her reins, she put one foot on the bottom fence board, swung up and over onto her mare's back, and rode off into the dark.

3. Randy's Community Service

While Claudia was contending with her one-hundred-twenty-acre farm in Bear Creek Township, Randy T. Rottman—RT as Claudia and her neighbors called him—of Rice Lake had his sights set higher and wider. Randy was a money man, dealing in loans and property in two counties, his and Claudia's. Eight months earlier and sixty miles northeast of the town of Turtle Lake, the idea for a new football field and track had been discussed at the Kiwanis meeting in Rice Lake. Change was brewing for the country and the residents of each of these municipalities. Early May 1932 in Wisconsin was hot, but nothing compared to the Dust Bowl that would torment the country in the upcoming years. The electric tension in the air could be a storm with the relief of rain or a whirlwind of destruction. Like much of what was ahead for Claudia, relief would be hard-found.

Randy T. Rottman worked tirelessly on the Rice Lake project. He had helped fund the installation of bleachers at the homemade football fields in Turtle Lake and Barron. Everyone knew Randy. His city friends credited him with initiating the scheme for Rice Lake, while some noted he'd capitalized on another man's inspiration. His defenders shot back, "If Randy were only thinking of himself, he would've built the field when his son Andrew was the high school's star football player."

During the winter of 1931–32, Randy spearheaded the project: recruited the men to design it, enlisted those to solicit and compare construction bids, and engaged the persuasive to raise the funds. Every prominent business owner and many visiting "dignitaries" coming up to their lake cottages from Chicago wanted to contribute to what the newspaper column by Randy's guy called "the bright spot in a gray world." Randy's father-in-law was on close terms with those who were surviving and thriving the Depression and Prohibition. That spring as construction began, Randy turned his focus to mineral deposits in Polk and Barron counties.

Several years earlier a geologist working on a Polk County project had approached Randy as the person who could make things happen and turn a profit as well. Randy knew an ailing old man who owned land in the suspected deposit area, Mr. Meiser of Bear Creek, Claudia's community of thirty-five square miles of farms. In the spring of 1932, Randy funded the geologist's initial soil borings to confirm their suspicions and then he discussed options with Bill, his close banker friend.

Randy and Bill believed now would be the time to cash in on land while prices were low and people were desperate. The land could be held until the economy picked up, which inevitably occurred. They could mine the land, sell the minerals, and resell the property. When the old man passed away, his only remaining family, a son, would get something for the property that couldn't produce a crop that could be sold for enough to cover the cost of the seed and fertilizer. If this year was as dry as the year before, Randy and Bill would be doing Mr. Meiser's son a favor by taking the land off his hands, even at rock-bottom prices. By the end of April, Randy had finalized the deal, and the son grabbed the money and hightailed back to California.

Randy enjoyed a challenge, and overcoming one gave him real satisfaction. He was proud to have married one of the most beautiful women in either Barron or Polk County, where his business interests were centered. Penny Swetosti, Penelope to her father, was the daughter of a successful Chicago lawyer. Unlike the home in which Randy grew up, the Rottmans lived in one of the biggest houses in two counties where they did a lot of entertaining. Penny was heard to say, "It's our moral duty to help the less fortunate." She chaired the annual Fall Charity Fundraiser held at their home. Randy's clients stayed with the Rottmans rather than the modest eatery and rooms that Nora Fleming operated in Rice Lake. Before the new hotel had been built last year, the only other place to stay had been a decrepit motel that Randy refused to use for his out-of-town business associates.

Randy came by his snobbish character without the silver spoon. He was thin and his nose was overly large. Classmates who teased him about his name, Radolphous Tobias Rottman, were ignored with impunity by teachers who didn't think the incidents relevant enough to alert his mother. When they first arrived in Rice Lake, Penny had hinted at social gatherings that Randy's parents had named him after two ancestors who were among the first settlers in the new world but confided that Randy was too modest to want to discuss it.

These days Randy could buy and sell many of those taunting classmates from Illinois. He was a man who dealt in money, mortgages, and development. Times were hard all over the country. Land in rural Wisconsin was worth next to nothing because crops were worth nothing. If the farmers didn't have cash to spend, the merchants and manufacturers didn't have customers to buy their merchandise and products. Randy made small business loans himself or larger ones with the help of the bank. He facilitated greasing the wheels of entrepreneurs and keeping the economy moving. Most people in both counties had dealt with him directly or knew of him through someone who had need of his services. He'd buy up foreclosed land and rent the property back to the owners, or the people moved on. He told many thankful store owners and farmers that he was merely doing God's work here on Earth. Bill and Randy talked about their winnowing process of helping move the weak out of the way so the strong could thrive.

That is why in mid-May Mr. Meiser's land was put into

soybeans, which were fifty cents a bushel, double what corn would bring, and more logical than vegetables put up on shares. Henry Ford was turning soybeans into plastic steering wheels. Randy pointed this out to everyone he saw while driving his new "Ford V8 Standard Tudor Model 18, which was far superior to the model A 4-cylinder" that others drove. Soybeans were a risk but, as any banker knows, it takes money to make money. Randy could ship his soybeans to the South where there was a market. With the weather drier further south than the Midwest and crops withering in the fields, this fall's crop of beans from Bear Creek Township could prove profitable. Not even the corn, wheat, and oats that northern farmers had relied on could be sold for the cost of raising the crop.

Randy and Bill were having lunch at Nora's Restaurant on a perfect day in May. They finished their discussion of how to proceed with a farmer in Bear Creek who'd passed away leaving a mortgage that had been neglected the last three and a half months. Banks were closing; money was tight. Randy told Bill he thought the farmer's daughter might need a nudge in the right direction. They decided to let the debt ride for the moment.

"How is Andrew doing in his studies?" asked the banker as he cut into his juicy pork chop.

Randy poured more of the homemade dressing on his deluxe salad. "He's doing fabulous. His science professor contacted us. There's a project that Andrew was working on with another fellow, Bennet, who Andrew said dropped the ball, so Andrew is completing the assignment. He's in line to win the school science prize."

"Reason to be proud of the boy. He had a few hiccups in high school, but college usually clears those up. It's a make it or break it place."

"I wouldn't know. I got my degree at the school of hard knocks." Randy scrutinized the banker, who was intent on his blue plate special. "Andrew will probably be awarded the senior exemplary student award. He's still a star quarterback." Randy paused, set down his fork, picked up the napkin, and wiped his lips. "You know boys," he chuckled, "always needing ready cash for something. Andrew's no exception." Randy began eating again. When the banker continued scooping his mashed potatoes and applesauce together with the peas, Randy added, "I suppose you had the same requests—sometimes it's almost a demand—for money from your boy." He studied the banker.

The banker inspected Randy. "Our boy had a part-time job, but yes, they all need their allowance of cash for incidentals," and he went back to eating.

"Andrew hasn't time for a job. His schedule has him at practice or studying every minute." Randy stared straight at the banker. "To be at the top takes effort, as you know."

Nora, the restaurant owner, came by with a coffee pot in hand to top off their cups and interjected, "How was it?" Noticing the lack of remains on the blue plate special and most of the deluxe salad gone, she asked, "Room for any dessert? I have brownies with walnuts or a lemon meringue pie." The banker ordered the pie and Randy replied he'd pass as Penny would have a big supper waiting tonight, and he had to save room. With that he patted his flat stomach. The banker lifted his eyebrows and leaned back comfortably in his chair to make room for his copious belly.

Andrew Rottman would be graduating from the Massachusetts Institute of Technology in June. Randy and Penny had been unable to get their only child into Harvard or Yale but had liked the idea that the MIT campus in Cambridge was connected to Boston proper by the Harvard Bridge. They coveted the hope that plans for MIT to be absorbed by Harvard would occur so they could claim their son had graduated from one of the top schools out East.

Penny had written Andrew at least twice a month his

freshman year and regularly wired him money for miscellaneous expenses and received a couple of letters in return. During his sophomore year, his letters mentioned Bennett, a studious but unpopular scholarship boy, whom Andrew had taken under his wing academically and socially. During his junior year Andrew's letters referred to working late with his buddies, necessitating the purchase of beverages to sustain them, and a need for an increased "allowance."

When Randy inserted a note in Penny's letter for an explanation, Andrew wrote back, "That kid in out-of-date clothes, Bennet, he doesn't have enough money to go out, buy extras, and show a girl a good time. I've been giving him a little cash for a nicer jacket and to buy beers. Aren't you always saying it's our duty to help the less fortunate?" Randy told Penny to wire their son the money.

Andrew's letters to his parents for funds were accompanied by descriptions of accolades and possible job offers in a tight job market, if prizes were won. The Rottmans were eager to share their son's prospects and Penny wrote back, "Everyone in town is so happy for our darling Andrew's successes." Randy and Penny had bragged over summer vacation, in Andrew's hearing, that their son wasn't only a great athlete on the field but a fabulous mind in the classroom. Funds continued to be sent as Andrew requested.

At the beginning of his senior year he wrote his parents about the class-wide science projects that required extra funds. "I could be one of the contenders for the Senior Science Prize. The dean revealed whoever is awarded the prize is likely to be offered a lucrative job after graduation."

After Andrew's visit home during Christmas break, Penny overheard her friends conversing about Andrew's inability to discuss Shakespeare with them. Penny asked Randy why they were paying large tuition bills if Andrew didn't know his King Lear from his Macbeth. The next time one of her good friends was over, she made sure to display Andrew's most recent college transcript, all As and Bs.

In February when a request for fifty dollars came from him for "supplies," his parents became concerned. When questioned by Randy, Andrew replied, "That Bennet I've told you about, we actually started on the science project together. He has to work at a pharmacy to supplement the scholarship money because his parents couldn't afford to pay for tuition or the dormitory. I assumed the project we'd started, and he took on a less challenging one. He's been having financial troubles. I feel it's my duty to give a fellow student a leg up and help a guy out. I give him a bit of cash once in a while, seeding the water for when I need help on my project. That's what we do, right?" Randy began to read between the lines of his son's letters and the references to working late with buddies and needing to buy beverages. In Randy's opinion, an entrepreneur may choose not to boast in public of using others' talents to further his own ends, but the quality was definitely an asset to be cultivated.

When the next request came, larger than the last and less than a month later, Randy and Penny called their son. Andrew claimed he'd gotten a girl in trouble and needed funds to rectify the situation. Randy and Penny told him to marry the girl, that they'd love to be grandparents. He wrote a week later and informed them the girl had been mistaken but could they send at least some of the money to help ease her disquiet. The money was sent and no further questions were asked. Penny wanted to avoid an embarrassing incident during Easter like the one last Christmas when Andrew didn't seem able to respond to their guests' questions on classical literature. He stayed out East over Easter. April and May passed with regular payments of "allowance."

4. Chores—a Bull

For weeks on her way to the barn-raising, Claudia had watched the sharecroppers farming Meiser's land. Whether windy, blistering hot, or cold and damp, they were out there. On her way to church the Sunday after the barn dance, she saw no one working, which was unusual. Monday still no activity. Claudia wondered if someone in the family was sick. On such a beautiful day, she thought she'd see them out hoeing around the tender green plants as in former years.

Monday was typical in many ways and so strange in others, especially for mid-May. The barn was a sanctuary where Claudia retreated with the young heifer laying in a roomy, wood-slatted pen. Daisy, their six-year-old milk cow, was tied next to the pen while Claudia, on a three-legged stool, milked her. Daisy had freedom to move around, but with the pen to one side and Claudia milking from the other, she had the comfort of a defined space. Tabby came from the fields to wait his turn while Claudia pulled gently on Daisy's teats and the milk squirted rhythmically into the galvanized bucket. Tabby sat patiently to the side waiting for the warm stream Claudia, like her father before her, gave their cats as a reward for a relatively rodent-free barn. Shep circled twice, then lay in the corner, nose tucked into the curve of his tail. After the full milk pail was set out of harm's reach and the milking stool hung on its peg, Claudia opened the rear door so Daisy could go out and the horses could wander in from the fenced pasture and walk down the middle of the barn. The horses had their stall on the side opposite the pen and milking area. The stalls had wood-planked feed bunks her grandfather had built before her real memory began, but she could picture the way the set-up used to be from Papa's telling. In her grandparents' time, the barn had been a lean-to attached to the house. Her father often talked of his mother being upset when his father left the door open while milking the cows in the winter. The chickens, searching for errant specks of food, would fly into the kitchen where the woodstove crackled.

Her grandmother had been the one who'd helped cut the trees and slab the boards to construct the new barn. In the comfort of the now separate barn, Claudia felt her shoulders relax at the familiar warm smell of Dandy and Molly and of the hay and straw stacked in the loft above her. She climbed the wooden ladder into the beamed loft and forked down enough for the first-bred heifer in the pen. She was due any day by the look of her back end and bag, but Claudia couldn't be sure. Her father was not there to consult. She didn't want to take a chance of losing the heifer or her calf so she used some of her winter store of hay and kept them in the barn.

This heifer shouldn't be here now. By all accounts she should be grazing with the others her age in the field six months pregnant instead of ready to drop her calf. The few chickens roosting in the rafters hadn't roused themselves to go out and scavenge in the yard when she'd opened the doors. These few renegades were not layers but more like watch chickens. There were always a few in every hatch that somehow decided they wouldn't be constrained by fences or coops. After a few weeks, even Shep stopped trying to chase them into the coop. Everyone on the farm was resigned to the fact that these creatures were not bound by the rules of the roost.

Claudia breathed in the huff of the Belgian mares' breath and their comforting shuffle as she spread some straw. Their huge feet were the size of dinner plates. They were so careful to set their feet gently down that a child could play under them. The only time she had to be watchful was outside in mid-summer. If a horsefly or bee caught the old Girls unaware, they might kick a leg without looking first.

Inside the barn, they were calm and everything was predictable. Except this heifer. One time, for a couple of hours, the bull had gotten loose. But that was all it took, once. Everything could change so quickly. One mistake and the heifer was bred too early and going to calf any day. Claudia shook her head as if to get rid of a pesky fly and scattered a handful of oats to the few chickens pecking the ground of the barn. She forked the few cow pies from the heifer's pen into the wheelbarrow, which she tipped out the back where the pile grew to be spread on fields this coming winter before the snow got too deep. She loved the smell of cold, crisp air in the winter. Sitting up in front of the box and beaters of the manure spreader each winter, she would watch the horse's breath form clouds in front of her as their heads bent down in a gentle curve. Their huge necks and shoulders pulled with each purposeful step, and after they got up a steady speed, their heads lifted. Their manes would wave back from their necks, accentuating the curve and the grace of each step. She kept their manes trimmed with an old, hand-forged shears from some great uncle blacksmith about whom she'd heard stories. He had been strong and artistic. The mares' tails, bobbed shortly after birth to keep from tangling in machinery, needed a trim only once a year unless the cockleburs were bad.

She closed the door behind the Girls and watched their whisk-broom tails begin swishing at flies. Taking the milk pail with her, she walked to the chicken coop and let down the narrow, ribbed chicken run that opened the coop for the parade of clucking hens led by the cocky red rooster. Inside the coop, she reached under the few hens still setting in their nest boxes and placed the warm brown eggs into the straw-lined basket. She started toward the house, thinking of her father moving comfortably from task to task and sadly missed him leading the way while she followed. Alone, she had to be thinking constantly, and it got tiring. Everyone acted either like she was incapable or too independent. She stopped at the pump and trough with the windmill overhead and thought of old Scotty, who could find where water ran deep and true beneath the surface.

When she was little she had marveled at Scotty, the crooked old man with the Y-shaped divining rod. Papa had him come out to find water on the west forty, so they could put in a pump and the cows wouldn't need to walk all the way home to get a drink in the sweltering summer. Claudia asked how they could pay when they had no ready money. "Will we have to get a short-term loan from the bank or RT Rottman?" He'd explained, "They're walking off their fat and that poundage we lose at shipping time. We'll save more in meat in just five years than the second well will cost us." She missed his certainty that was dependable, like their water supply.

She felt something wasn't right. She stopped by the barn on her way to the house. In the pen the heifer, a soft brown Jersey Hereford cross, was standing hunched with her back arched. After switching from Jersey milk cows, descendants of his parents' herd, to beef cattle, her father kept a few cross-bred heifers because he liked the high butterfat. Claudia missed his contented sigh as he poured cream into his coffee, anticipating that first sip. The crosses with their yellow fat brought less at market. City customers preferred white fat on their meat and country folk favored white tallow for soap and candles. She saw the heifer strain, her back end bulged, a first sign of labor. This was going to be a long day.

She grasped the bucket filled with Daisy's frothy warm milk and carried it and the basket of brown eggs to the house. She heard Thomas greet the dog in the yard. His voice was as soft as a wool shawl in winter. Shep hadn't barked after the first time Thomas had stopped to see what life on a farm was like. Shep welcomed his presence so readily that often only the dog's body wagging in great curves back and forth signaled the man's presence. After Francis's funeral Thomas had returned to New York, but his uncle called him back when a woman in Clayton passed away. He would've left after that but once Doc found out Thomas had been to medical school, he asked him to stay and assist him with debriding wounds of two of his patients—one a burn patient and the other a diabetic with leg ulcerations. Thomas would be in Wisconsin until the wounds healed. She was grateful to have his help for a few hours between his other responsibilities. In the barn they checked on the heifer whose delivery no longer appeared imminent. After Thomas left as the sun was scorching the horizon, she walked to the pasture where the young heifers, not ready to be bred, were kept. The weather had been so dry that the pasture was cropped close and turning brown. She had debated on cutting wild hay from the ditches and feeding the cattle to get them through this dry spell of poor pasture. That's when she saw that the bull had pushed through the fence and gotten out of his pasture and in with the few young heifers. She'd have to mend fence tomorrow.

The next day she finished chores quickly. She'd had to break up the fight between her two roosters which ended in the demise of the older one. When she was collecting supplies to fix the fence, she heard a big John Deere tractor in Meiser's front field where the dirt farmers' work was being destroyed. Claudia ran down the road to see someone unfamiliar plowing up the field. *Who did that?* She wanted to go up to the man in the cab of that big tractor and say, "You can't do this. These people worked hard. Get off this land." But that was not her land, and she did not know the people who had worked the field. She was busy with her own responsibilities; she could hardly summon the energy to worry about someone else. Her own plate of troubles was too full. Besides, it wasn't her business. Papa had made that clear early on. Everyone had the right to mess up his or her own life. *Stay out of other people's business.*

She'd had her share of troubles this morning: the unpleasant sadness with the rooster, which she'd have to process after the fencing, and witnessing the destruction by the tractor. After gathering her supplies and walking to the pasture, she stared at the broad hunched back of the tawny-colored bull standing protectively next to a slender golden-brown heifer.

Claudia had been in the barn next to Bully hundreds of times. She had scratched his back as she stood on the bottom rung of the gate. She had walked through the pasture where he would be grazing with the cows. But she never had to physically make the one-ton animal do anything he wasn't inclined to do. He did not seem motivated to leave the young heifer and go with Claudia. The heifer was one of a handful Claudia and Francis had raised to add to their dwindling herd of a few dozen. Francis had sold more cattle last year than Claudia thought advisable.

Claudia would move the bull and repair the fence once and for all. Last year was bad enough when another heifer had been bred early, but not again. With Shep at her heels, she walked with assurance toward the animal she had known since he'd arrived as a calf four years ago. Pushing her wheelbarrow of fencing supplies, she carried a stick and a length of rope as she'd seen her father do, the rope to put through the ring in the bull's nose to lead him and the stick as gentle persuasion. She parked the wheelbarrow, picked up the rope and stick, and stepped across the downed fence. Shep had been sniffing the fence line with his head down. Claudia saw him dash off and noticed a darting, back and forth movement of a rabbit yards ahead of the ten-year-old dog and wished him good luck.

The grass crunched underfoot. The spring day was weirdly hot, yet the sky could fill with clouds and burst into a bone-chilling rain in minutes. Rain had fallen for a few minutes yesterday but the dirt was already dusty again. By the time Claudia closed the distance, the bull was facing her with his head down. She licked the salty perspiration that clung to her lip and stung her eyes. The wheelbarrow with the hammer and some rocks sat out of reach on the other side of the fence. She had intended to transfer Bully to his pasture, then tighten the four-strand barbed wire. She'd never considered how far from the safety of the fence her father had been when he went into the pasture, but the thought raced through her mind now as she saw dust rise from where Bully pawed. She heard his low rumble and responded as she had when he was a calf. She mooed to him. He charged.

She froze. She snapped her arm with the stick out in front of her and connected with his forehead before he ran over her, his broad legs straddling each side of her body. She lay there on her back stunned, grit in her mouth. Bully turned and sniffed at her and returned to the side of the heifer in heat. He sniffed and mounted the heifer before Claudia reached the safety of the field side of the fence.

She wanted to leave and go home. She hadn't been trampled, but she was bruised and shaken. The pasture, charged with dust, musk, and atmospheric electricity, could be left to the bull and his prize. But, the broken fence remained.

She grabbed the handles of the wheelbarrow and pushed across the uneven ground. The hammer, pliers, and wire staples clanged in the metal bucket and bounced as the steel wheel got caught in an old furrow. She imagined her ancestors coming to Wisconsin in their covered wagon, wishing to go fast enough to escape the mosquitoes and to keep from getting wheels stuck in the rutted mud paths that passed for roads.

She picked up the bucket of fence supplies and reappraised the area where Bully had pushed through, popping the one-inch staples and loosening the posts. She refused to leave the fence and let the bull win. For the next hour she pulled, stretched, and hammered. As she worked and felt frustrated, she imagined her ancestors' weariness as pregnant women bounced over rutted roads or trudged alongside the wagon to avoid the jostling of swollen insides. She envisioned them nursing crabby babies or feeding irritable toddlers after scavenging for wood and building a fire. Whatever their husbands got close enough to shoot would be hauled back for the woman to skin, clean, cut up, and cook.

She was so dog-tired she didn't think any of her female relatives would've stopped to cook and eat. She pondered her solution. *I'd shove a piece of raw meat in their mouths and let them suck on that.* Anyway, the meat probably contained more protein raw than cooked over an open flame.

The fence barbs bit through the glove right where she gripped the wire and pulled. She tugged the glove from her hand, and the blood streamed down just as it had when she'd slit the rooster's throat.

"Darn!" she exclaimed to the sky. She was not going to cry.

The rooster had been old and the younger one was attacking him. She was not just going to end its misery, bury the tough old bird, and waste the meat. No! She slit its throat, plucked it, and planned to stew the meat, which was soaking in salt water, that evening after fixing fence. He'd been a good rooster.

"I won't waste you," she'd promised.

In the pasture her hand bled into the ground, but she refused to sit down. Earlier that day she had known she was just on the edge because after chopping the head off the dead rooster she began to bawl. She had curled in upon herself, clutching the old bird to her chest. His magnificent red feathers had already begun to lose their luster. At least now she wouldn't collapse to the ground.

Shep returned with blood on his muzzle. He must have caught the rabbit before the animal found its sanctuary hole, or else Shep had dug the rabbit out. She thrust the loaded wheelbarrow over the humped soggy ground of the lower pasture. At least during fencing, the work would be unemotional and systematic. The wooden posts wouldn't bleed when she hammered the staples in to hold the barbed wire. She stretched the wire. The ropes and pulleys of the fence stretcher gave her the power she lacked and that George's boys seemed to squander in backyard brawls. It wasn't fair, she thought, that men had so much strength and women got stuck with common sense. Men wasted so much of their potential proving to each other that they had IT.

She wanted whatever it was that had allowed her father to kill a deer or an old rooster. She had tried to peacefully slit the rooster's throat. He was so old and tough and her knife must've needed sharpening because several swipes across his scrawny neck were needed to cut completely through. The blood needed to flow swiftly and freely for him to die quickly. She had failed. She had collapsed into the grass in the quiet solitude of her yard. She had been alone except for the red rooster dying at her feet.

All morning she had felt alone and incapable. She was the only one to solve the rooster problem. She couldn't resolve the sharecroppers' dilemma. And there was no one else to repair the fence.

But she was not alone.

The chickens, the cattle, and the weather were all there, and the father she had listened to for almost three decades echoed in her head. "They're all depending on you."

She would not let emotion wash over her or pull her down a black hole. She pushed away that morning's sorrow. The blood had soaked through her glove. She calculated how far it was back to the house and how much daylight was left. She wished she could send Shep, who was asleep under a tree, to fetch a bandage for her. She tore the bottom edge of her T-shirt and wrapped the cloth around her palm. The bleeding staunched, she returned to stretching, pounding, and wheeling to the next post. The bull was in with the heifers and had to be led into his own pasture once the fence was secured.

Encroaching clouds clashed and thundered as she pounded and pushed. Feelings of failure had left little room for attention to the bank of ominous clouds that proceeded a storm. The rain began just as her physical strength was depleted. She continued to fight posts, and the wire was now slippery in her bloody gloved hands. She stumbled across the softening ground, scouring for rocks big enough to secure the posts that had been loosened by the bull's efforts to get at the heifers. The thunder and lightning were so close, the sky so dark she wanted to get out of there, but she refused to let the rain keep her from finishing. That must have happened last year, perhaps the reason her father hadn't finished securing everything.

When she'd reattached the wire to the last post, the sun was down. *That better keep Bully in.* Maybe father hadn't noticed the wires had gotten slack and the posts loose. Any bull worth his salt would test a fence if the mood came over him or he had an itch, whether that itch was on his back or in the shape of a heifer on the other side of that barrier. But this is where brain beat brawn. She plucked the top wire like a banjo. *Yup, that was as tight as old man Meiser.* She just had to secure this last post with a few more rocks at its base in case Bully got the urge to scratch himself again.

She had already scrounged all the rocks outside the pasture and all those close to the fence. She had to venture deeper into the pasture, closer to Bully and his harem. As she bent down next to the post to push the last rock in at its base, she failed to notice the bull pawing the ground. With the thunder cracking above her, neither she nor Shep heard the bull's snorting. A moment earlier she had been out in the open. If the bull had charged her then, he'd have gored her or flung her repeatedly across the pasture. Thankfully she was next to the post when he felt she had invaded his space once too often. He stampeded toward her, his one-ton bulk hitting her bent-over body, his massive head ramming her and pinning her to the ground, the great horns on each side of her.

Shep had finally run to her side and was crouched inches behind her, barking hysterically, ears flat to his head.

The bull had knocked the breath out of her, but she was ungored. Turning her head and looking up into his face that as a calf she had held in her two hands, she saw the irrational flare of rage. His breath was hot and steamy. He lifted his head to ram her again or maybe to ram the outraged dog. The bull's horns tangled in the now taut bottom wire. She smelled his strong urine as he relieved himself in frustration. Pushing herself further into the mud while Shep dug at the earth next to her head, she crawled under the wire but not before leaving her shirt on the fence. She clawed her way for several feet, then stood and ran through the safety of the field without thinking, Shep close at her heels. The fence would hold, she hoped. But she couldn't be sure.

To consider separating the bull from the heifers now was pointless. Dark had descended and she couldn't see clearly through the sheets of rain. She stumbled. She wanted out of the rain and dirt and mud and off this farm.

That night lying in bed, she remembered she'd left the wheelbarrow, which by morning would be filled with water-soaked tools. Listening to the much-needed spring rain, she thought how useless the barbed wire and one-inch staples were against a horny one-ton animal. Vivian would call it irony that those cowhide gloves had failed to protect Claudia from the barbs that barely bothered Bully's hide.

She mourned the loss of her father and the loss of her feelings of capability. Shep had been there but unable to help. She was angry. She slept in fits and starts, waking to thoughts of chores left to do; mental lists of priorities; and jobs that had to be done or animals would die or be hurt. What about her? She cried into her pillow. Wasn't she an animal deserving of care, too? How could her father do this to her? How could he just up and die and leave her to do all this alone?

5. Calves, Chickens, Farming

Claudia couldn't stop her brain from running full steam ahead like the Soo Line train through the countryside. The temperature was eighty to ninety degrees every day, and in certain places there were several inches of dust coating every surface. Prices for cattle and pork were at an all-time low. Hogs were $2.85 per hundred weight while the price for an entire milk cow was $5.40. Her father had had the foresight years ago to turn from milking cows to raising beef. Today top cut beef was still only $4 per hundred at South St Paul. The radio reported daily the Minnesota stockyard rates. At those prices a farmer had to raise his own feed to make ends meet. The talk around town was of strikes at the creamery and banks closing.

She was trying to make life work on her own. Thomas seemed remarkable, but he might not stay. He might decide to go back to New York for good. She couldn't count on anyone or anything. Everything had changed or died. And what was she left with? The work. Those darn local boys wanted her just because she could work hard and had land and cattle to bring to the match. They smelled. She hated the way they stroked her when she danced with them. She had tried. She'd sat there on the hay bale after dancing, and Hank had rubbed her arm like he was sawing through pine. She was sure he would cut through her flesh soon if he just kept at it. He had that stupid smile slavering like a dog in heat ready to jump anything that moved. Did he expect her to succumb to his "gentlemanly ways" by scouring her like a piece of balsam wood to be shaped to his desire. What *did* he want? To have her drop a brood of kids to work his fields for him.

She wanted to go to bed with a sick headache like those

brainless girls at church Sunday morning who went to bed for a week with a hangnail or ingrown toenail. When she and Papa had had their cows, she milked when she had a fever, she shoveled manure day after day after puking with the flu, and she cooked a full meal at sundown after working in the fields since sunup. The work was never-ending and the same monotony over and over. The only thing that changed was the weather. One day would be dust storms blowing Wisconsin top soil into the Great Lakes or a rare east wind carrying dirt to the Dakotas. The next time snow could fall in June or rain could drizzle in January.

Now she was doing the jobs all alone, and she didn't even know why she was doing them. Why did she feel compelled to rise with the sun and work past its setting? Was it her dream too—this farm? Or just the habit left after her father died? And what was Thomas? A city dandy curious about rural life who would soon tire of its relentless monotony.

Confused by her flustered attraction to Thomas, she had talked to the Girls, Dandy and Molly, yesterday while she'd curried them. The lilac bushes to the south sent out a heady aroma that filled the space between the house and their pasture, so intoxicating she couldn't think straight. When she had seen Thomas dance with Wilna, she had become intent on circling the floor in a slow one with Hank. She knew her reaction was stupid. She brushed Dandy, pulling bits of twigs from her mane.

"It is more than his physical appearance," she had confided to the Girls. "Thomas has a smell. He is different. I know I don't have any real practice, but he stirs up feelings I've never experienced before. Even Shep noticed the first time he met Thomas." Claudia had finished currying Dandy and worked on Molly slowly from her neck across her back and down her withers.

"Shep thrust his nose into Thomas's crotch, which at first surprised him, but then he just ruffled Shep's head, saying,

'Checking me out, old boy?' Shep examined this newcomer and attempted to put his two front feet up on Thomas, but his old bones couldn't quite make the reach. That man bent down in city pants, lifted Shep's front legs, and held his paws." Claudia wiped the Girls with a mixture she had discovered that deterred flies. "I wouldn't have been surprised if he had danced with Shep. There is something about him that I am attracted to. Am I a moth who will be immolated by the flame? Am I foolish? Should I discourage him?" She had left the Girls in their pasture, not feeling any closer to understanding her befuddled responses but sensing relief seep into her.

The next day thoughts of the new man were put on the back burner as her heifer needed her. The two births, now and last year's, couldn't have been more different and so much the same. Seemed just like life in general, full of contrasts and conflict and complications yet so normal and natural and necessary. Last year, her father had been there to assist, but she hadn't needed him. Now she wondered how she could keep this heifer alive and save the calf. She didn't have her father in the field or fixing equipment in a shed if she needed help.

Claudia dreaded the thought of birthing the young heifer that had been bred too early. She wondered if next year she'd have another early pregnancy of a heifer too young and small for the undertaking. They usually waited to breed heifers until they were over two years old and large enough to handle birthing a large beef calf. The animal in front of her was a slight, pretty-faced cross, which Francis preferred to raise for milk. Despite her father's half-hearted protests, Claudia had purchased Daisy, a Jersey milk cow, from Pete Mevissen. Bully being in with the heifers might mean another early birth next year. Checking and fixing fence had been her father's domain, which she had assumed he'd done.

Vivian had told her on more than one occasion "to assume makes an ass out of you and me." The iconoclastic Vivian advised, "Take *assume* apart. The first three letters are what it makes out of the last three." When Vivian pointed to the adolescent girl and herself, Claudia blushed at an adult even alluding to ass, but Vivian had informed her, "It's in every dictionary, just like bitch. They're names for animals."

Claudia had assumed he'd checked the fence between the bull's pasture in the woods and the heifers in the lowland. There was one stretch of fence where the bull would stand and bellow. She would've remembered to check fence before this spring, but that wasn't her job. It was her father's, and he'd failed to live up to the standard he'd set for her. She was angry with him. As she got the block and tackle fence puller to help with what she knew would be a difficult birth, she cursed. He knew better than to let something slide.

"There was no excuse," as her father would often say to her. "No sense creating work. God gave us enough the first time around. No need to go back for a second helping." Then as he turned away, he'd say quietly, "Unless you're a fool or a glutton for punishment."

His dying as spring began and leaving his winter work unfinished put her in line for more work of which she had more than enough. "God gives each of us a bag of rocks and a bag of blessings," her father had told her on the rare occasions when she had complained. Her bag of rocks was too heavy to carry today. And it felt like her only inheritance were her father's words and his unfinished work.

The heifer strained and Claudia knelt behind her where the calf's feet had been protruding for far too long. She looped the rope around the ankles and secured the other end of the block and tackle to the post in the barn to maximize each pull. At every contraction, Claudia tightened the rope to augment the heifer's effort. She had been laboring hard for hours without effect. Claudia could see she was tiring and losing her ability to put force behind the pushing. Claudia secured the fence puller to maintain tension and with both her hands stretched the heifer's membranes around the bulge enough to allow her to pull the calf's head into the world of the barn.

Claudia put her fingers into the calf's mouth, swiped the mucus out, and gently slapped its face. The newborn mauwed a bellar that caused his mother to lift her head and bellar back. At the next contraction, the heifer pushed, and Claudia pulled. The calf slid onto the straw-strewn floor of the pen. Claudia picked up a handful of straw and rubbed the shivering, mucous-covered calf. Shep poked his nose under her arm to sniff the new member of the barn family. The heifer, now officially a cow or a first-calf heifer, lifted her head and mooed at the trio. A few moments and the calf stood, shortly followed by its exhausted mother. When Claudia was finally able to coax both to be upright at the same time, she held the calf's head to his mother's swollen bag. She squeezed the closest teat with her right hand, and, holding his head with her left, guided the two together. The calf's tail wagged excitedly when he felt the warm stream on his face, and he lunged toward his mom's milk supply. After several attempts, he managed to latch on and sucked but got so excited he head-butted the bag and the connection was lost. The three of them continued like this for the next hour until an exhausted Claudia thought new mother and calf had the general idea down.

Claudia loved her animals. Grooming Dandy and Molly soothed her, but lately she hadn't been able to give them the time they needed and she enjoyed. On Monday she hadn't gone to town because Thomas had stopped after treating Luella's leg ulcers. She had taken the break to brush and stroke the Girls, and Thomas had smiled at her, gently stroking the horses' flanks. When she'd clucked to the chickens in the yard and they flew to her, Thomas laughed, delighted. Watching them file up the slatted plank into the chicken house to be shut up for the night was so simple and ordinary. But he'd remarked, "You sound like a hen with your soothing prattle of "clucks" and "Good night, girls." At first, she'd thought he was teasing her, but the look on his face and the way he closed the door and said, "Good night, ladies," reassured her. They had stood in the yard listening to the horses chew grass, then sat on the swing watching the swallows swoop.

Saturday, when she next saw him, seemed a world away from that calmer Monday.

She hadn't woken up on the wrong side of the bed, but everything was going wrong today. Even Shep had left her alone and gone off to the woods where there was coolness. When she found the axe for slaughtering chickens, she discovered the edge had a gouge. Her father must have used the tool for something other than chickens and then failed to grind the head smooth, to be ready for the culling of old hens. She had pumped the grinding wheel and held the blade to the spinning stone, but as soon as she put any real pressure on the axe's edge, the wheel slowed. She didn't have the power or stamina her father had had. That's why he did that job. Or used to. *But, he hadn't, had he?* She gave up after her arm, bruised from fencing and being hammered by the bull, became too sore to hold the axe weight against the grindstone.

Before doing chores, she had started a compact fire in a shallow pit surrounded by a discarded metal wheel rim. The water in the big iron kettle, suspended on a hook at the top of a tripod of rods, should've begun to boil, but hadn't. She went to the wood pile searching for the right size oak that was dry enough so the fire would burn hotter but not so small to burn too quickly. She didn't want the water so hot that the skin pulled away in pieces; she wanted the water just hot enough for the feathers to come way after dipping the bird.

In the early afternoon she had not even gotten to the job of processing them. The hens had been cooped up since before chores and were becoming agitated, which made her nervous as she was the cause of their stress. She believed in a quick, peaceful death for her animals that were giving their lives to feed hers. Last night she had assembled the tubs, gotten the wood, and set out the canning utensils in the house. She hadn't expected to have to grind an axe or to sort the mixed-together wood, which she was careful to keep separated according to size and type. She couldn't remember, had they been in such a hurry last fall that they hadn't done the sorting and stacking like usual? When she heard Thomas ride up, she smiled. *Help. Good.* Her pleasure at seeing him made him smile.

"I was on my way home from Clayton debriding Luella Eggert's leg and thought I'd stop. What are you going to do?" Thomas asked.

She frowned. *Was he here to see what life on a farm was like?* She tugged on the apron and stooped.

"Can I give you a hand?" he continued.

She stirred the fire with a long iron rod. The infusion of air caused the wood to burst into flame and the water boiled. She picked up the short-handled axe and began swiping the cutting edge back and forth across the whetstone where the chip was still visible.

"I can't stop to visit," Claudia stated without regard to him. "I have to sharpen this axe in order to butcher these hens."

"Aren't those your laying hens? I don't understand. Why would you kill them?"

"I don't have time to explain. They're old and will die in a few years, and they're not giving enough eggs." She'd finished sharpening the axe and tested by carefully running the pad of her thumb across the edge. She set the axe on the stump scarred with years of hatchet marks. She glared at the sun, shook her head, and walked toward the house.

"But you have enough eggs. More than enough for yourself… and anyone who visits." Thomas followed her to the house entry where she removed a larger heavy canvas apron from a nail.

"Feed is not cheap. We always butchered when they got to this age." She took a deep breath.

"Why can't you just let them die of old age? They've been good to you."

"If you want to be of use, help me catch those chickens locked in the coop." She threw Thomas the apron and walked to the coop. He was still tying the apron when she came out with a hen held upside down. She laid the bird on the stump and efficiently whacked the head which separated from the body and fell into the galvanized pail next to the stump. The headless body ran around the hard-packed dirt. He watched. She went into the coop again, but he stood staring. She returned with another hen and removed its head. This was going to be a long process if she had to do it alone. She didn't need an audience. She wasn't a performer in a sideshow for some greenhorn from the city.

This time he followed her into the hen house. The room was dark except for the one, small window toward the top. He watched her and seemed to be genuinely trying to figure out how to be of help. The hens were agitated in the closed, stuffy space. She went low and slow. Her arm shot out, grabbed a leg, held the hen upside down, and she walked out. If he got the idea, he'd do the same, follow close behind, and they could get into a rhythm. She could hear the agitated cackling hens running around the coop to avoid him, squawking, and wings beating against the wall, then a bang, and he started coughing. Claudia entered and sighed. A dust storm of dry, broken fecal matter filled the coop. She stepped out into the air and light, and he followed, closing the door behind him.

"I tried to do like you, but my head hit the pole, and the chicken got away," he coughed and wiped his index fingers down his eyelids.

"Let them settle down," she spoke to the ground as she slapped the dirt from her canvas coveralls. In the yard the body of one of her Barred Rock, black-and-white speckled hens flopped around in the dirt. She had plucked and eviscerated one chicken and laid it in a large galvanized tub of cold water, while he'd been chasing her hens and hadn't even caught one. She grabbed another headless hen, dunked it in the kettle of hot water, and pulled off wet feathers in great handfuls. She set the hen on a small wooden table, slit from the egg vent to the breast, reached in, and scooped the entrails out. She tossed the guts into a pail and the heart, liver, and kidneys into a crockery bowl, which she covered with a dish towel. Soon that naked body lay cooling in the tub of water next to the first one. She caught, plucked, and eviscerated the remaining headless chicken. She regarded Thomas coldly, then walked into the chicken coop again. The sun was approaching the horizon.

After watching her several times, Thomas seemed to have figured out how to grab and connect with a leg. He went into the henhouse, captured a chicken after a little ruckus, and then brought it to her where she cut its head off. The blood drained out as it ran around, then she plucked and eviscerated it.

"I discovered if I go slower, fold their wings by their side, and hold them in the crook of one arm, they're calmer," Thomas offered.

Slower? Calmer? Are you kidding?

She considered the sun, trying to gauge how long each one was taking and if she'd have to do chores in the dark. Her motions became hurried—grab from him, chop, drain, dunk, pluck, eviscerate, and cool the bird down. She couldn't keep up with him and soon there were several chickens spurting blood and looking like they were having a frantic last dance in the yard of packed dirt and stubby grass. Thomas tried dunking hens or plucking feathers, but the thin skin on the breast tore as he pulled feathers, and he made a mess of the animal. She sighed heavily but never uttered a word, just kept working. After helping catch and attempting to clean several more chickens, Thomas was soon covered in blood and feathers. He looked like a bloody scarecrow. If she weren't so tired and in such a hurry, she would've noted how odd, almost comical, he appeared. Instead she went back to pulling the insides out of the warm body in front of her.

"Claudia," He urged. She glanced up. "Can't we do something differently? Isn't there a better way?"

"This is the way we do it. Papa did it this way and so do I." Her voice broke the air like lightning. She hadn't meant her words to come out so sharp. *But he didn't know anything about farming or cleaning chickens. Why couldn't he just help her?*

"There's got to be a better way to catch them and a less bloody way to do them in. Maybe a wire hook to catch their leg and maybe set them in something after their head is removed so they don't run around?"

"I need help, not chitchat."

She grabbed the bird by one leg from his grasp and turned back to the stump and hatchet. The hen was flailing again and squawking. Thomas strode off toward the horse trough and pump in the yard. She watched as he scooped water from the trough, leaned over the dirt, and scrubbed at his arms. *What was he doing, now?* She stopped to watch as he splashed freshly pumped water onto his face. He scooped up more water from the trough and scraped his broad hands down each arm. The dirt surrounding the trough was black with bloody water. She had beheaded and released the bird while he pumped fresh water to refill the tank. He continued to pump with fast, strong strokes. He quit when the water splashed over the sides of the trough. He stopped in mid-stroke and pushed the pump handle down slowly into position to hold the prime for next time as she'd taught him to do.

He was going home! She wanted to shout at him, but she couldn't shout at a man she'd known for less than three weeks. He didn't owe her anything. Not even an explanation.

She watched him hold the cast iron pump handle in his grip for a minute more, lift his fingers away, and gaze up at the sky. She saw a few wisps of clouds streaking the blue sky. When she looked back, he was gone. Dusk would be here soon.

She brushed the dust from the chicken yard off her coveralls. Darn dust, she thought. Darn man. Get off my legs. Get off my back. She was trying to do a job. Help or get out. Go. He could go back to New York if he was so darn smart. Go back and bury dead people. She had living things to feed. Him? He was nothing but one of the hangers-on. He was so slow. Papa and she would have been done by now. He was nothing but a hindrance. Why did she bother?

She didn't need a man. She didn't need anybody. She could do it alone.

As she did the evening chores by the light of a kerosene lantern, reality slid into the slot covered by habit. She'd been doing most of the chores alone for the last few years. She never realized until her father died, but she did most of the everyday things. He had just helped her. She worked in the fields side by side with him, but he did none of the house chores.

Now she had a helper who was more hindrance than help. Her day wasn't done yet. Sleep had to wait.

In the house she canned the dozen old laying hens she'd butchered that day. She had filled the sterilized jars with cut up chicken, a pinch of canning salt, and boiling water, tightened the lids, and set the jars into the pressure canner. She watched the gauge and adjusted the heat to maintain the correct pressure. Finally, the jars were processed long enough for the chicken to be cooked. As she waited for the pressure cooker to cool down, she ate some leftover pork from the icebox.

She'd done all the cooking, cleaning, and laundry. Her father had helped her harvesting the garden but often left her to do the canning alone as he had "machinery to see to." And now she was doing the stuff he did around the place: keeping machines going, greasing, oiling, repairing, fencing, feeding, and watering all the animals. After the pressure cooker had cooled, she removed the jars with wire tongs and set them on the table to be transferred down to the cellar in the morning.

She added cold water to the canning water she'd emptied into the sink and washed up, then went upstairs to her bedroom. She pulled her nightgown over her head and crawled under the top cotton sheet, exhausted.

She was coming to the realization that she was perfectly capable of doing it all. She just didn't want to. It was too darn hard. Right now, she didn't need them—Thomas or her father's memory—bugging her. She had things to do. Tomorrow was Sunday but Monday she'd go into town to the store. She needed things.

6. Women and Horses

In every small town there was always a store. Turtle Lake had Ernie's General Store but the person generally in charge was Vivian who, besides being the clerk, was the postmistress and had her own book collection that she loaned out. Over the years, Claudia was the beneficiary of Vivian's collection of books. When Claudia found out post offices and libraries were in separate buildings in big cities like Rice Lake, she asked Vivian why.

"Big cities keep everything separate. Even people become separate. Here we deal with things in general, which means just that—all the necessities of life: groceries, soft goods, hardware, a bit of banking, and mail." She didn't say, but Claudia learned later, that the general store provided a few of what Vivian termed "hindrances" such as hard liquor that Ernie sold from under the counter. Vivian knew how to manage business. Over time she had commandeered more shelf space from Ernie's canned goods for her books, and Claudia was grateful.

Once as a young girl, Claudia had overheard Mrs. Fournier and Mrs. Andersen, two country women, refer to Vivian as a spinster, and she wondered why they called Vivian that. Vivian had shot the women a glare and told Claudia within the women's hearing that "I never married but don't ever presume to refer to me as a spinster. I am too independent and well-read and have higher expectations than any of the men who had wanted to tie me to a stove and a brood of children with snotty noses and bottomless-pit bellies." Mrs. Fournier and Mrs. Andersen had left shortly after making their purchases.

Most of the time, Vivian hummed as she sold goods and stamps and made small loans and organized the store's books. But she came alive when that rare person ran a finger across the titles of her books. She loved to discuss books. As Claudia had waited for her father to get their supplies, she'd hear Vivian recommend a recently published book to someone who came in to buy groceries or stamps or make a wire transfer of money. Usually the person would respond with, "But Vivian, how am I going to get time to read between washing sheets and coveralls and gardening and canning?" Vivian would become deflated or exasperated.

Claudia had been enticed by Vivian to read at least one book every month ever since Claudia's mother taught her to read. At first there were picture books. Claudia recently asked Vivian about that. "Your mother asked me to order a few for you and then I kept them for other children when you lost interest and progressed to *The Secret Garden, The Emerald City of Oz, and The Story of Doctor Doolittle.* Then just you and your father were coming in."

Francis would bring his daughter every Monday to pick up the supplies for the week. While he sat at the counter next to the barrel of apples and the keg of nails and talked the farmers' trinity—cattle, crops, and weather—Vivian and Claudia would talk about their books. As a young adult, she discussed with her friend the decadence of the wealthy in *The Great Gatsby* and the damaged but strong characters in *The Sun Also Rises.* Both women believed in the revivifying power of nature. The last couple of years, Vivian had recommended Virginia Woolf, Edith Wharton, and Sinclair Lewis, but Claudia hadn't been interested.

After her father died, Claudia quit talking about books and began to talk about the problems on the farm, but Vivian had never enjoyed the challenges of farming. Mrs. Polenski once had the gall to ask her why she came west if she disliked so much about it. "Well, that is none of your damn business, thank you very much," was her retort, which made Claudia tell her she was in trouble for swearing. "If you never do anything worse in your life than that, you'll be doing well," Vivian had replied as she picked up the store ledger. "Besides, could you see me as a farmer's wife, married to a sodbuster?"

On Monday Claudia walked in not knowing what she wanted but hoping for answers to descend miraculously and for a settled mind that had eluded her. The Great Northern Railroad wall calendar of Blackfeet portrait illustrations by Winold Reiss was flipped to May featuring Morning Star, an attractive young Native American with thick, black braids wrapped partially in brown buckskin with a single, black-tipped white feather tucked in her raven hair. She appeared as solemn and serious as Claudia felt, but seeing Vivian happily cooing to her parakeet put a scowl on Claudia's face. This was not the first time Claudia had come seeking a soothing balm for a turmoil that roiled beneath the surface. As a teenager, she had dumped quandaries at the clerk's feet. Often Vivian only needed to listen, and Claudia could return home emptied and cleansed.

Other times Vivian would ask, "What's the matter?" Claudia might give her a strident "nothing" that caused Vivian to shake her head slightly and lift her eyes toward that God everyone knew she didn't believe in. Claudia had asked her about that, too.

"Most ignoramuses need something to hang onto. The majority of people don't know how to take responsibility for their own success and failures and have to either thank God for their good fortune or see calamity as punishment for their ill-chosen choices."

Claudia didn't want to hear philosophy or platitudes today. She wasn't sure she wanted to hear anything. She did know she had plenty to be upset about and she wanted to vent. Like pressure canning her hens, the venting mechanism released excess steam that built up when you didn't pay close enough attention to the heat from the wood or gas underneath. A certain amount of steam was normal, but excess could mean a mess.

When Claudia walked past Vivian, she saw a new book, *A Farewell to Arms* by Ernest Hemingway, laying open on the counter in front of Vivian. Claudia liked Hemingway, but she'd come into town at this time specifically because she could have Vivian's undivided attention. Usually no one came in the store during the noon hour as everyone was home eating and having a lie-down. People who worked from sunup until sundown, especially when days were long and hard, needed time to be still. Francis had cooled down in the shade of a tree, but many farmers, such as George Johnson, chose a dark room for even just a half hour.

Claudia grabbed a handful of nails from the kegs and filled a small bag.

Vivian closed her book.

Claudia walked back to the other side of the store, picked up a sack of flour, and plunked the bag on the counter. *Why didn't Vivian say something!*

Vivian reshelved her book.

Back at the grocery section Claudia grabbed a small sack of dried beans.

Vivian reached into the parakeet cage hanging between the shelves of canned goods and the counter. She tickled and stroked the yellow bird's head.

Was she invisible? Did Vivian only care about that handful of yellow feathers? Claudia walked the length of the store to pick up a new shovel handle. Vivian returned Percy to his bell-shaped wire cage hung from a shepherd's crook-shaped pole and began to refold the top flannel shirt and restraighten the bolts of fabric that were piled on the corner of the counter. Claudia crossed in front of Vivian toward the salt but didn't look up and mumbled.

"What's bothering you, girl? Just get it out!" Vivian exhorted to Claudia's back.

Claudia turned in mid-mumble, which grew in volume and speed as she talked. "…He's so arrogant. He hasn't lived on a farm. He doesn't know." Without being aware, her words rushed out like cows released after a winter's confinement, each pushing into the freedom of space and jostling to be first. "And it's no excuse that he isn't a farmer. He should just do things the way I tell him to. What does he think? I'm stupid? I've been doing this for years. My father and I have been butchering chickens for … what? … fifteen years? No. Longer. And he thinks he can tell me. He just walked off. I was so upset I left the door open and ended up chasing the last two hens around the yard. I caught the last one as the sun was setting and the water had gone cool. The fire had died. I couldn't keep up with all of it. I was alone cleaning old laying hens until sundown and still had chores and canning the hens left to do. I'm used to my father being there and then…" Claudia sat down on the cane-backed chair across the counter from where Vivian had perched herself on the high-legged chair that put her five-foot, two-inch frame in a commanding position.

Claudia's feelings changed like the recent weather—dust devils of confusion, storms of anger, and fogs of sadness.

"I was so tired yesterday, I didn't make Sunday service. I couldn't face all those people."

Vivian nodded, her lips pursed in a tight, commiserate line.

"I just wish my father were here. Maybe he could talk some sense into Thomas. Sometimes I worry maybe I'm wrong, and if my father were here, he'd be disappointed with me. I couldn't have gotten as much done this past week if Thomas hadn't stopped by and helped, and I hate having to rely on him."

"Your dad relied on you," Vivian reminded her.

"That's different. We were family," Claudia replied.

"It's not different, Claudia. We all rely on each other out here. There's no shame in asking a neighbor for help. You were more than willing to help at the Mevissen's barn-raising. Why I heard many saying you could out lift and out hammer most of the men. And you reached out to George and his boys to have them help with field work after your dad passed."

"But this is different. I can't repay Thomas for helping me like I can George." *Wasn't that obvious?* Instead, Vivian shook her head and gently slapped her hands to both sides of her face, her elbows on the counter.

"You remind me of your dad."

Claudia looked up eagerly, "How?"

"He was an exasperation of independence. Seems like he kept a ledger of owe me's."

"No! You're wrong…he trusted people to pay him." How could Vivian think her father would ever badger people to pay a debt they owed him?

Vivian persisted, "Not your dad being owed, but him owing. He never liked to be in anybody's debt. At least not for long." Claudia smiled.

"No, girl. That is no reason to take pride. Never wanting to be the one indebted to anyone was arrogance on his part. He had a stubborn streak and liked to believe he knew better. Take those chickens you're talking about. I was here in this store when you were nothing but a minute. He was complaining about how long it had taken to butcher them and the mess he had. Ellie Kasper was in buying canning lids when she overheard your dad. She asked him, 'Didn't he put those hens under a bushel basket to settle before he did them in' and 'Didn't he hang them up by their feet on a hunk of clothesline so the blood would drain out?' Well, your dad was so flustered all he could say was he never heard of such foolishness, hanging hens on a clothesline and under bushel baskets. He wasn't laundering them. He was butchering. Ernie laughed at that and Francis and Pete and George went back to their field talk."

Claudia felt more crushed than when she was twelve, and her dad without a word had taken the fifty-pound sack of flour from her. *Sure, I'd been struggling, but I wanted to be of use. I think I could've got the sack to the wagon.*

"When your mother was alive, she did the chickens. Your dad didn't bother with those things when she was here. Then when he had to take over, I think he kind of resented having to do the man's jobs and the woman's and got in a hurry to get the woman's jobs done. At least that's what folks say. But nobody would fault your dad. He raised you well. And he has made that farm successful."

Claudia suddenly remembered a time when she was very

young and particularly frustrated by the hassle of butchering and the mess. She had asked if they could maybe wait until dark when the chickens were more quiet, and her father's retort was quick, "If you think you know a better way, you're welcome to do it." He'd walked off to work on a piece of machinery needing to be repaired. At the time, she felt bad complaining when he worked so hard and she acted like a know-it-all. Now she could see that her father had been like every other person in town—overworked and doing the best he could at the time. She always thought of him as better than the rest of the men in town. Now she saw him as she saw George and Hank or Ernie, all hard-working but fallible men just trying to be decent and capable.

She thought of gentle Thomas and wanted to be with him and tell him they could try it his way. Ernie entered the store from the back room, which had a door that opened into his home behind the store. He saw Claudia and began, "Claudia, did you hear the one about the woman who was having the upper rooms of her house painted and she fancied that the painter was slacking on the job. 'Painter, are you working?' She shouted at the foot of the stairs. 'Yes, ma'am,' came the reply. 'I can't hear you,' the woman shouted. 'Well, do you think I'm putting it on with a hammer?'" With a chuckle Ernie patted the top of his belly. She smiled at him.

With her flour, beans, shovel handle, and sack of nails loaded, she thanked Vivian, who stood in the doorway. Claudia walked past Gilbert's attractively decorated brick jewelry shop where the clocks he repaired and sold ticked away the minutes and chimed on the hour. In the next attached building, a plain, clapboard-sided storefront, she noticed there weren't many shoes or boots in the store window. She couldn't see any movement at the bench where the shoemaker's last, an iron foot on a pedestal, stood. Hammers, tacks, punches, and nippers lay ready to repair or make footwear. The shelves were lined with different sized lasts, wooden shaped feet, and leather in browns and blacks of different thicknesses. She stopped at the next building, the mortuary. Thomas's uncle was working on a coffin. He told her that Thomas had gone out to debride the O'Brien boy who'd pulled a pan off the cookstove and burned his arms. Thomas's uncle said he wasn't sure when Thomas would be back. Claudia resolved to talk to Thomas. She rode home to weed and water the garden. She'd cultivate the corn tomorrow.

Thomas stopped by Claudia's farm after his call in Clayton removing the dead skin from Doc's patients. She disclosed she was open to listening to better ways to process chickens. He helped her muck out the barn pen. Normally this chore wouldn't be done in the early summer, but this springing heifer and her calf had to be kept in for a while to ensure he was nursing well. After dumping a wheelbarrow full of manure, Claudia forked straw down from the loft and spread the golden bedding in the pen around the heifer and calf. Thomas petted the soft brown calf between the saucer eyes. The calf jumped gleefully up and to the side; Thomas laughed.

Dandy and Molly clomped through the open door, blowing air out of their noses. Dandy put her head over Claudia's shoulder. Molly rested her sniffing nose in Thomas's hand. He reached into his pocket where he'd put a few sugar cubes. Claudia frowned but didn't say anything. She preferred the Girls to eat carrots or apples, but the carrots were barely sticking up in the garden between the radishes. There weren't many apples left in the fruit cellar, and Claudia had instructed Thomas they were for human use not horse treats. Dandy and Molly could wait, as the humans would, for the trees out in the orchard to set fruit. Her two horses were physically a matched set, both honey-colored with light golden manes and tails, but there the similarity ended. Even though they were raised together by mothers who were sisters, their personalities were wildly different.

Dandy, who arched her neck, raised her legs high, and set them down, almost ballerina-toed, should have been a sleek

Morgan show horse instead of a hefty work horse. Claudia had to hold her back by talking to her whenever she was teamed with Molly, who was plodding and durable. She could plow all day with steadfast consistency while Dandy started with high-stepping energy, then fizzled early and stumbled along.

A patient tenacity was necessary for Claudia to keep Dandy and Molly working together without Molly having to pick up the slack for Dandy as the day wore on. Early in the day she had to hold Dandy back so the mare wouldn't use herself up before lunch. Claudia talked to them constantly, sometimes with words, mostly with her hands. When they stopped to rest, she checked their harnesses to be sure there was no tension on the connections that could break equipment or blister the horses.

She had explained to Thomas that Molly was the furrow horse, the boss. "She's hitched on the left as I hook them up to the wagon or equipment. She ends up being on the right side when I sit up behind them."

"But she's not the boss," Thomas had protested after two weeks of being around Claudia and her horses. "Dandy drinks first when you stop at the horse trough. Dandy flattens her ears back if Molly tries to reach for a chunk of apple or clump of clover I hold out to them. Poor Molly has to wait and give Dandy the first opportunity."

"That's only in the pasture. Dandy is head horse in the pasture, but you can tell that Molly is a furrow horse. She knows. In harness, she's the boss. Watch her when Dandy tries to run. Molly will nip at her to tell her 'Slow down, we've got to last the whole day.' Molly's the born furrow horse."

Claudia felt comfortable today educating Thomas about farm life. "I didn't understand at first, and I would holler at Molly to quit snapping at Dandy. Then when Dandy would slough off later in the day, I'd have to holler at her to pull her share of the load. She could be a real stinker in the winter pulling a load of firewood out of the woods. By the end of the day Dandy walked just a step or two behind, so Molly had the bulk of the weight to pull with her chest and shoulders."

Claudia shook the straw around the pen until there was a golden layer covering the hard-packed dirt. "Once I figured it out, I quit hollering at Molly for snapping at Dandy when she was all feisty early in the day. I like Dandy's spirit. When I was young I pretended Dandy was my circus horse all prancy and tossing her head."

"Didn't your father tell you what the horses were doing?" Claudia looked as if Thomas had asked why her father hadn't told her the moon was made of blue cheese. Only later in bed did she explore why her father had never explained the horses' personalities to her. Her father could become a bit frustrated with them just about the time he would ask her to take over. He never seemed upset. He worked hard, and if she could help out by finishing up some field work that he'd been doing, she did it. He never complained if that made supper a bit late. She couldn't get supper started until after working in the fields and unhitching and brushing down the Girls. The mere thought of grooming them caused her to smile.

Thomas reasoned Dandy was a boy's name and referred to the horse as "he" the first time he petted her. Claudia couldn't help but laugh at the city slicker.

"I'd have thought an undertaker could identify the necessary body parts for an animal to be female or male." The tall semi-stranger had bent down to peer under the horse and rose with a blush that made Claudia ashamed at the cheap jibe.

"You'd think I'd look before I spoke and insulted a lady." With that he had patted Dandy's neck with a quiet, "Sorry, young lady," and Claudia bit her tongue before correcting him again, explaining that Dandy was eighteen years old, not young, but quite mature for a horse. She fell asleep recalling each day with Thomas in the few short weeks since they had met.

7. Washing, Working, Loving

The week flew by with house, garden, and field work and caring for the heifer and calf. Claudia had cultivated the corn, and the low field was planted with oats. After chores and weeding on Saturday, a day with some wind but no dust, she was hanging out clothes. The wash basket at her feet held her bedsheets and towels. Daily chores, like weekly laundry, were never-ending. She threw the handful of dishtowels over her shoulder and walked along the line stretching and pinning each towel to the next like brothers, hands on each other's shoulders.

To hang the sheets, she grabbed another fist of wooden clothespins from the bag on the line waiting there, like a dutiful wife. Her mother must have used an old dress to fashion the bag that hung on a makeshift wire frame like a held-open pocket. The yellow flowered bag trimmed in blue binding cord was scooped in the front like a woman's dress and hung from the clothesline by a hook much like a clothes hanger. Either her father fashioned the frame or perhaps her mother had made the entire piece herself.

She had never asked her father about something as simple as the clothespin bag. The dumbest things kept coming into her mind to bite her unexpectedly about him being gone. She felt more keenly the passing of her mother now. She had never thought about her father not being there to answer any question that she might ever have, whether about farming or family.

When she wanted to ask about her mother, her father seemed too busy working on a harness at the table or sitting in his chair reading the paper in the evening under the halo created by the kerosene lamp hung on the wall and later by the glow of the floor lamp. Oftentimes he'd be at his desk working on papers for the farm cooperative, and she'd think, "I'll ask him later when he's not so busy."

She closed her eyes. They burned. The sun was shining off the sheets that were blindingly white from the bleach. She arched her back, stretching out a kink, and bent to get the last item, a terrycloth bath towel that she shook loose from its wrung-out tightness. Thankfully they had the luxury of the Maytag ringer washer that swung around so clothes could be transferred from washer to rinse tub to a bleach or soaking tub without the back-breaking work of a washboard and tubs.

She loved to wash clothes and hang them out—clean and whipping in the wind. Today with the wind and sun, the dish towels, sheets, and her underthings would dry as soon as she finished hanging the last bath towel. She unpinned the cotton dish towels, folded and put them away, and returned to the washer where the second load, work clothes, was swishing back and forth. She lifted the cover off, leaned it against the machine, and with the wooden stick lifted the overalls up and fed them into the rollers, mounted on the swivel neck.

The water had cooled so the clothes weren't hot. She was able to spread the legs of the pants as she fed them into the rollers, which spilled them into the rinse water on the left side of the double washtubs. The right side still had bleach water that disinfected and removed the vegetable and fruit stains from those dish towels she had used for canning.

She debated on using the bleach water to wash the cupboard, but she had to get back to field work, so she pulled the plug, which emptied into a smaller hand washtub. She dumped the disinfecting liquid on the area where she'd butchered the chickens and the rooster. At the time she had sluiced the area with water, but she had noticed flies congregating. Bleach would kill the blood smell and disinfect the stump for next time. She wanted to finish up the field work today so Sunday could be a day of rest.

She wondered if Thomas was back and would stop out. She hoped so.

The Sunday was normal in many ways. She got up early, did chores, cleaned up, and drove Dandy and Molly to church. She met Thomas, not typical, but this was the second time he'd been there. They sat together through Pastor's sermon and the songs she loved even more since she heard them sung with Thomas's tenor. Her father, dead less than a month, had sung with gusto but not much precision. Her father relished singing like chewing on a good steak. Thomas approached a song as she approached a horse, firm and steady but slowly and aware of the surroundings. If others were singing loudly, he let his full voice carry like a wave blending with other waves washing over the pews to a swell at the altar. If the congregation was sparse and timid that Sunday, he sang with a stable but quiet reserve that kept Ernie and several others like herself on key. Last year had been easier when Loretta was alive and had played the upright piano. Loretta had played everything like a polka, but most folks felt real comfortable with polkas. As they exited the church they were passed a hand-made poppy in remembrance of those who'd served in the armed forces. Thomas put a donation into the can held by Mr. O'Brien Jr. whose father had been a veteran. After church Thomas rode with her in the wagon, his horse tied behind so that after having dinner and helping clean up, he could ride home. Jasper, Thomas's horse, was owned by his uncle, kept at the livery, and lent to Thomas for his use when he was in Wisconsin.

On their way to the farm they passed Meiser's field that the sharecroppers had planted but Randy had re-plowed and planted in soybeans, a crop not seen this far north. When Claudia had ridden by the field the past couple of weeks, she had seen what appeared to be rows going across the soybean rows. As weeks progressed so did the crops. There were peas growing up in east to west rows that the farmers had hoed and planted, and the soybeans were coming up in north to south rows that the big tractor and planter had set out. Even the potato hills came up despite the plowing and replanting.

Today Claudia contemplated the field and asked Thomas, "Do you think it is the resilience of the heirloom seed that allows the sharecroppers' plants to survive despite being plowed, replanted, and sprayed with chemicals?"

"I wouldn't know," Thomas replied. Claudia wondered. *Was fighting formidable odds a sign of resilience or futility?* She didn't have the time to consider further, besides the field was someone else's problem. She had her own.

They ate the chicken dinner with fresh peas and new potatoes, a treat she and her father almost never had.

"You dig those now, Claudia, you get two mouthfuls," Francis cautioned. "You wait 'til the plants have died, and you'll get two meals worth of spuds." The past week had been busy processing the old hens; cutting, raking, and stacking hay in the barn; and cultivating corn. She hadn't had time to make a pie, so they decided to take a leisurely walk up the hill before the sun set to see if any blackberries were ready. Berries in a bowl with Daisy's cream would be dessert.

They each took a pail not because they expected a lot of berries but because they discovered they carried their buckets differently. They both wanted their hands free for picking. Claudia tied her bucket to her waist, but Thomas chose to hang his from his neck just below his chest. When they got through the recently cut hayfield in the middle forty waiting to be put up and across the small slough, they climbed the rocky knoll through some brush to the south side where the first berries usually appeared. As they walked, their feet stirred the hay, releasing the smell of clover and alfalfa. They breathed in deeply and walked up the hill with Shep between them.

Claudia stood next to the thicket where the afternoon sun shown. "Oh, my, I've never seen so many so early." The berries were bright black thumbdrops on thorny canes. She wondered why the birds hadn't gotten them. They picked and ate, unaware that the sun moved from overhead to horizon.

"We have to stop," she declared but continued to pluck. "I've got to do chores and you have to get home."

"But look at all the berries left to pick. Dump your bucket and mine into my shirt." After church he had changed into an old flannel shirt of her father's.

"I'll head back to take care of your chores, and you can pick two more buckets of berries. The birds will get them all in the next couple of days, and you've got hay to put up tomorrow."

Her face scrunched.

"I've helped you enough times," he answered her unspoken skepticism.

Her face softened, and he unbuttoned his shirt and dumped both buckets, hugged her, and strode off down the hill with the berries. Shep, who'd curled up under the bushes after a romp, looked toward Thomas, then up at Claudia.

"Go ahead," she smiled and motioned toward Thomas. Shep, tongue lolling, clumped after his friend. She watched as Shep caught up to Thomas, who reached down with his free hand to scruff Shep's head. Claudia kept an eye on Thomas's broad T-shirted back as she picked berries, her fingers stained with juice. She watched the man and dog disappear through the trees, then reappear, striding across the field, and her bucket was half full. She realized she needed him to help her, but more—she needed him for his companionship. This intense needing gave her mixed feelings. She was licking her fingers when she saw him disappear into the barn. She wanted to cry, to suck the ends of her fingers. Sweet dependency. She depended on nature to provide berries. She depended on her dog and cat, her milk cow, and her chickens. Even her garden, cattle, and pig. Her relationship with Dandy and Molly was the closest to what she felt for Thomas. Her father had been one sort of companion. Dandy and Molly were another type. She had talked to them about her flustered feelings while currying them.

She had depended on all of them. But this was a different dependency. The interdependency between herself and her father just existed, and she'd expected the mutual benefits and challenges to continue. Then everything changed. She placed another berry to her lips. This part of the change was wonderful.

As the sun was setting behind the hill only the deepest thickets held their jewels. The birds would relieve them tomorrow. With the sun setting behind her, she headed home more directly through the cultivated cornfield. She could almost hear the corn growing as she walked the rows one bucket a bit in front, one a bit to the rear. She didn't want to break any of the leaves or stalks, which nearly brushed the bottom of her bucket. The crop looked promising. Fingers crossed the rains continue, she prayed.

Her arms and shoulders were sore as she dumped her buckets into her bread mixing crockery bowl, where Thomas had put his shirt full of berries. She got out the canning kettle and jar lids and put the water on to boil. Into another kettle of water, she put the jars to sterilize them. Into a third kettle of water she put two scoops of sugar to make a light syrup.

By the time Thomas came in with Shep, after feeding the pig, closing the few remaining hens in for the night, gathering the eggs, and milking Daisy, she had seven jars of berries processing in a hot water bath.

"Those berries will be a great treat next winter," he remarked as he poured the milk into a jar, which he set in the icebox. "With Daisy's cream we'll be able to have pie and whipped cream or just open the jar and pour the cream over them in a bowl. We'll eat like we died and went to heaven." His smile always started by crinkling the skin next to his eyes then erupting at the corners of his mouth. He delighted her.

She was so happy she wanted to jump into his arms—eggs, milk, and all. Why, she would make a custard and feed the creamy dessert to him this winter with those berries, and he'd wear nothing but that T-shirt that was no longer the sun-bleached white of six hours earlier. Then she realized he had said "we" and "this winter" as if they would be living in the same house doing chores. That picture felt so safe and right.

Just like with Papa. No, not like her father, she reassured herself. Safe and right like father, but this was exciting. Scary and exhilarating. She said nothing. Had they known each other only a month? The time seemed luxuriously long. They finished canning, reserving enough fruit for dessert for the next few days. They used the hot water from canning to wash up their scratched and sweaty bodies. There was no moon, and even though Jasper would know the way home, traveling in the dark was not safe on these rutted, back roads. A horse could stumble and go lame, which meant the animal would have to be shot.

"The horse will make it," he reasoned.

"That's foolish. You'll sleep in my father's room."

"But..."

"I'll set out a clean shirt and pants."

"I don't want to be a bother."

"You're not." She didn't look at him but went upstairs to set things out.

"I'll leave when you do chores."

The next afternoon Thomas stopped again. Claudia stood at the sink washing the breakfast dishes. Since her father had died, she'd gotten into the habit of letting the day's dishes accumulate until evening and washing them all at once. Today she felt the need to keep herself busy, and she didn't like the messiness in front of Thomas, whom she imagined had a spotless New York kitchen. Was he regarding her and the room with disdain? No, his eyes, primordial pools of crystal blue, were dilated in excitement. She turned back to the sink. He was talking, and her knees wouldn't let her hear his voice and look in his eyes at the same time. Her hands took over and her legs strengthened. She was finally able to hear his words.

"…extraordinary and I was thinking if you came back with me to New York City just for a week, maybe two, I could show you my city. The theater. Oh, Claudia, there is nothing like it. And the music." His voice was rapid, and she knew without looking that his large hands with the manicured nails were gesturing.

"Fair turnabout I call it," he added with conviction.

She said nothing. Not because she didn't have plenty to say but because her mouth was forming words that were fighting with her heart. Claudia stood studying the embroidered hand towel she had made one winter afternoon to remind her of the far meadow with its pale greens and yellows on wheat-colored linen. She didn't know who she wanted to win—her heart or the mouth speaking for her practical mind. Without thinking, her mind won.

"I can't. There's too much to do. Who'd do the twice a day feeding and watering of the chickens and pig? What if the cattle got out? The new calf and heifer need to be watched. I can't expect Vivian to drive out here or to keep Shep at her little place for a week or two."

"But, Claudia, I've thought that all through. It's all taken care of, if you want it to be. We don't have to leave right now. We can wait until things settle down."

"How? I can't just leave. What would my father say if he were here? He worked so hard building this farm up; I can't let him down. Not now. No one will know what to do if something unexpected happens. Like when Bully got out of the fence last year. That's how that young heifer got bred and had all the trouble birthing. He only trusts me. Someone else will spook him." She thought of the episode with Bully and turned her head away. Her bruises were all but gone, so she no longer needed to wear long sleeves in front of people. She hadn't told anyone. She felt ashamed that the bull had gotten loose two years in a row.

"Claudia," he reached out to her, slowly turned her to face him, and brushed her cheek with his fingertips that smelled of the hand talc he used. "If you'd rather not go, just say so. I'll understand. But I do think we can trust George and his two boys to ride over here and do your chores. They handle the unexpected things on their farm." With that he let his hand fall from where he held her elbow, as if releasing her gave her more freedom.

"We just don't have as many people dying here and able to pay for elaborate funerals like you're used to in the big city where folks have money to throw away after dead people. I can't have you spending your money paying those Johnson boys just so I can take a vacation for no good reason," she chided.

"I thought I was a pretty good reason. I like you. I like to watch you canning berries, caring for that calf, and working in your garden. I just want to spend time with you. You're always so busy here. I thought if I got you to myself for a week, we might actually be able to talk without you cleaning, cooking, or sewing at the same time."

She heard Thomas and the silent words underneath that couldn't be vocalized because of their irreversibility. She did not want to take the chance of being alone again if she insisted no.

"Yes," Claudia acquiesced. Thomas reached to take her arms in his hands and inadvertently brushed her breasts in his excitement. Claudia felt the heat within her rise like water from the pump, slowly and then with a gush, quenching and consuming. This heat, too, was as scary as fire on prairie grass or water on parched land.

The first day of June shone sunny, perfect haying weather. In the field Claudia sat on the iron seat above the dump rake behind Dandy and Molly gathering into windrows the new-mown hay in their best field on the east forty. The blend of grasses was drying to a sweet green smell and touch that she had explained to Thomas was perfect. The leaves of alfalfa were still on the stems, the purple clover flowers were young and tender, and the timothy grass was slender and green. On Sunday they had sat on the porch swing talking, on Monday she'd consented to New York and had cut this hayfield, Tuesday she'd put the couple acres of the middle hayfield up into the barn, but he hadn't stopped. He would be returning to New York for three weeks to help his old firm and "take care of some unpleasant business."

When she saw him drive up the rutted path in his 1928 Packard, her heart raced. *Had it only been one day since I've seen him?* She smiled to herself but kept right on until she and the horses reached the end of the field and the round of windrowed hay was complete. As she approached she had a clear view of the man who claimed any excuse to stop and see if he could help. He wasn't the handiest at farming, nothing compared to her father, but he meant well. His business with his uncle in Turtle Lake didn't give him a lot of cash but plenty of flexibility. He had told her how he had set aside money from Hagstrom's Furniture and Mortuary in New York City to supplement his more modest earnings here. But he used some of his savings to purchase a used car from a former client, which gave him more options for travel than relying solely on the train to get to New York. He ended up using the vehicle more in Wisconsin.

Thomas was leaning on the fender. The sun shone full on his square-cut jaw with the faint shadow of his dark blond hair where a beard would grow if he allowed it. She imagined him with a beard and maybe a moustache. No, his smile was too broad. He needed that openness of face for the delight to travel across. As her hands rotated slightly to pull the reins back a fraction, the horses came to a stop. They flicked their ears in Thomas's direction, then dropped their heads to the newly cut clover and alfalfa that would be their winter's food. Dandy blew air softly through her nose when Thomas stroked her forehead between her eyes and down her nose. He seemed to know she couldn't reach that shallow hollow on her head to scratch the eternal itch. In the pasture Molly and Dandy would use their teeth to comb and groom each other's flanks and necks in small bites of neat rows in paired unison. All animals sought touch to soothe, relieve, reassure.

Claudia fought the urge to put her hands on Thomas's chest, which reminded her of the expanse of her best hay ground: level, rich, dark soil. She, like her father before her, loved to reach down, grab a handful of the black loam, and crumble the soil between her fingers as she bent over to breathe in its season. Soil smelled distinct at different times, changing with the seasons. In the fall, the smell was dense and heady, but in the spring, the odor was of earth worms and icy potential.

Instead of placing her hands on his chest, she held a twist of hay to her nose and thought of him inches away. She imagined him laying her down in that sweet hay, stroking her as he'd been stroking Dandy with such attention to her preferences. She breathed in again and thought of being undressed by him. As she dropped the hay and lifted her head, she pulled her thoughts to a stop, with less ease than she had the horses.

He reached for her face and held her cheek cupped in his large hand now browned from the Wisconsin sun. He kissed her, and she opened her mouth without thought and leaned into his hand. He put his other hand on her back, and she felt grounded. The kiss traveled through her lips, ran in rivulets down the back of her neck, down across her shoulders, and onto her arms that of their own volition now held his shoulders. She was excited yet fearful of the unknown, yes, but more afraid of her reaction to the sensation. She had felt this sensation before. When she was a child, she had shuddered with the fear of jumping out the haymow door for the first time.

At a social gathering at the Johnsons, they were playing in the haymow, and the other children were jumping out the upper door unto a pile of loose hay on the ground below. They had teased her for being afraid until she finally jumped into the unknown and gave herself to the air frequented by barn swallows. Her arms flung back after landing. She'd turned her face to the swallows still in that space where she'd been. She ran up the earthen incline to the loft and raced the other children in the barn to jump again. She couldn't do it fast enough—again and again. Now she was afraid of that feeling, that lack of control over a desire. She opened her eyes, pulled back, and began to talk hurriedly.

"There is just this field then all of the hay will be done for a while. To put up, I mean. Into the barn. Then I suppose…New York," Claudia heard herself, thought of a chatterbox from town, and stopped abruptly. She glanced up and saw Thomas relaxed, his eyes, blue flames dancing. She fought the desire, the need, to hold him again, to kiss him back, to have him take her to the ends of the feeling she tasted and feared, yet wanted to explore.

"Watching you with the horses and then the way you smell that hay, I couldn't help myself. Is it okay? I mean, are we okay?" Thomas was speaking so quietly she divined his words rather than heard them, or maybe the blood rushing in her head had drowned them out.

"Yes, of course. Well, I'm finished enough here for today. Do you want to come back to the house?"

"I thought I might be able to help you with chores, and we could sit outside. Looks like we're heading toward a lovely end to a beautiful day." He winked, and she wrinkled her forehead then blushed. She didn't want to clarify that he couldn't stay the night, again. She wanted to savor the moments.

After chores, they gathered a supper of greens from the garden, cold ham from the icebox, apples canned last fall from the trees out front, and iced tea. They sat on the wooden swing hung from the front porch rafters watching the sun—golden orange and pink—fall like a ripe peach below the silhouette of trees on the horizon. Their talks had become so comfortable over the weeks.

"The hens seem less crowded on the roosts now that the older hens aren't there," he observed as he held her hand.

"I was thinking of putting that small five-acre field that was mostly in clover into flax. The farm journals say it's good for cattle and chickens." She breathed slowly and deeply.

"When would that be? I can figure my trips back East so I can be around to help you. The people at Hagstrom's are pretty flexible in their schedule. The only unpredictable part is if they get busy and need me in a hurry. Wouldn't it be great if they needed me when the Berlin Orchestra was in the city, and you could come with me to hear them?" She blanched, then blushed, and he rushed to reassure, "I know a very respectable, economical hotel where you could stay. The orchestra is unbelievable. You'd love it." They rocked slowly, watching the night descend.

She didn't trust herself. The feelings he stirred in her were stimulating, exciting, and powerful. She remembered Vivian's words Monday, only two days ago, "Once a reputation is lost, it can't be recovered." Claudia should've known Thomas couldn't spend the night, no matter how innocent it was, without someone noticing. She needed to hold herself back. She couldn't let the horses have their head or they would run themselves ragged or crash into something. Dandy and Molly relied on her to keep a clear head, hands steady on the reins to hold them safely back. Besides she wanted his opinion on cooler topics than those that plagued her dream fantasies.

"New York is the premier venue for opera and orchestral works," he maintained as he scratched the neck of the cat curled in his lap. Tabby purred, and Claudia sighed.

"We have music in the town square sometimes. My father sat on the town board. They used to deed land for a school or town square where anyone could picnic or gather to hear music or a speaker passing through." She wanted to tell Thomas about her father acting as a guardian, caring for the land, keeping it healthy and safe for her and for his anticipated grandchildren. Her father would never have tolerated anyone treating his land as if it were theirs and acting as if his land was public. That's why they deeded land for communal use. Her father had always been active in their community. But he followed rules in order that life ran tidily.

She could see Thomas was interested, but his love of music and his career were what caused his eyes to glow and speech to flow.

"Thomas, do you think property belongs to an individual or are we just guardians?"

"I don't know. Maybe it's like music. It belongs to everyone."

"But someone wrote the music. Doesn't the composition belong to that composer? Or to the people playing the piece?"

"I never thought about it. I just love listening."

"I sometimes wonder why some people have so much and others so little."

They both were flushed from being in the sun and their animated discussions of their separate passions. The air was warm and still even though the sun was down. The wooden swing creaked as they went back and forth, letting the echoes of their discussion settle in silence around their individual thoughts. The crickets were stroking their violin legs as the bullfrogs inflated their bellow-drum throats. The stars had pricked bright holes in the blanket-black sky.

Claudia became aware of the stroking of Thomas's thumb on her hand. His thumb was tracing her vein on the inside of her arm from her wrist up through and across the hollow of her elbow and then his hand drew down the length of her lower arm. She considered him and saw his head tipped slightly back with his eyes half-closed. She sighed and closed her eyes, completely centering her attention on the sensation. She let herself savor her responses. She noticed that when he brought his thumb up the inside of her arm a tingling coursed up her legs. Then as his hand encircled her arm and stroked down she felt the tingling in her legs turn to a warmth that flowed like honey on hot bread. She wondered about this feeling in her lower extremities when he wasn't even touching her there. Her attention shifted to where his lips and tongue gently outlined her lips' contours much as she drew circles on the ground. With just the slightest tension, he held her bottom lip with his.

In her mind's eye she saw Dandy grooming Molly with her teeth and Molly in deep contentment, ears relaxed, eyes closed, shoulders and legs cocked like a tap dancer leaning over his cane. She felt his tongue flick across her teeth, and she reflexively clenched them shut. His hands slowed the massaging of her back and shoulders, and his kisses returned to their lip-centered wanderings. She opened her eyes but saw his were still closed, and the desire to feel his face caused her to hold him as she had the baby foal's face. She loved the lines of the sleek foal. She felt almost as if she had helped sculpt his perfect features. She wanted to feel Thomas's lines and angles and see if that feeling of co-creating felt the same with him. It wasn't ownership. She never felt she owned her animals. More like the Girls were in her circle of care. She crooned, "My Dandy and my Molly" as a term of intimate connection and care as if she belonged to them. She was voicing her commitment to them. When she entered the barn, she greeted them with, "Hello, my Dandy and my Molly," almost as a low whinny, acknowledgment of a mutual trust. She wouldn't work them too long or too hard, and they would do their best for her.

His kisses slid down her neck into the pool of her collarbone, traveled the crest of the ridge, down to the swelling of the top of her breasts. On the quick intake of her breath, his lips settled between them. His face rested there, rising and falling with each of her breaths. He seemed content to remain there, and she gave herself to his leisure.

Soon they would make their predictable excuses to end the evening respectably. He had understood when she'd advised he'd better not stay overnight again. Each would claim the need for sleep and the demands of the next day, and each would go to their separate beds, Claudia upstairs and Thomas to town. Tonight, neither would sleep quickly or well. Each would be remembering, anticipating, replaying, and wondering. Each in their own way would be trying to release and savor some of the intoxicating tension.

8. Lover, Mother, Offspring

To give yourself in love, as a choice, to another was a risk. To love your parent or child was a given. Growing up, Claudia didn't think about affection much. She knew she loved her parents and her animals, especially Dandy and Molly.

As a child Claudia never questioned Vivian's situation in life. As for relationships in her town and township that she witnessed, the majority of people married and stayed in the area, or if single, the person often left. She began to wonder about Vivian's unique, unmarried staying power. Vivian was the only unmarried mature woman she knew. Once when Claudia's father had to travel for the cooperative and be gone overnight, teenage Claudia begged to sleep at Vivian's. That afternoon and evening, Claudia heard the whole story in answer to her whys. *Why come to Wisconsin? Why didn't you marry? Didn't anyone love you? Don't you have a mother, either?*

"I never intended to end up in Podunk, backwoods Wisconsin. I saw myself in a cultured life in New England with a career. A husband, if he were my equal, could fit into that plan. But then I met him. My parents were some of the more progressives in Ithaca, who believed all children—not just boys—should be well-educated. When I met my beau at Cornell University, I felt I could fly to Sage Chapel's arch on my breath alone." Vivian stared up to her kitchen ceiling. They were seated at her chrome table and chairs after their special dinner of chicken divan that Claudia had made while Vivian read the recipe to her. Vivian appeared to be remembering that time in the Chapel.

"British literature class was an elective for him, but for me it was pure heaven. I laughed reading the *Canterbury Tales,* and my gentleman would quote the "Wife of Bath" with a glint in his eye. We used to sit together on the bank of the Fall Creek reading our Shakespeare. Do you remember when we read *Romeo and Juliet* out loud, how you liked the way it sounded?" Claudia had nodded vigorously. When she tried to read the play on her own, she had stumbled over the language, but, with Vivian reading with her and changing her voice for the different parts, the story came alive in Ernie's store. Vivian even picked up a pitchfork when there was the fight between Vivian as Tybalt and Claudia as Mercutio, and Mercutio got stabbed under the fabric Claudia held acting as Mercutio's cloak.

"My beau was witty and intelligent, like you. One of the only men in my courses who had charm and class. And there were a lot of men and only a few of us women at the universities back then in the late 1870s. Things are different now. You, Claudia, could go to any number of colleges, if you wanted to. And, my beau was no strain on the eyes, either." Vivian had winked. "We were made for each other, a pair of matched driving horses, high-spirited and sleek, fast and temperamental. Two thoroughbreds. I was in love," she'd confided.

"Take notice when you think you are in love and your senses have flown out the window." Vivian had cautioned the young Claudia, but then elaborated on details that didn't discourage Claudia but made her more interested in the complexities of love.

"A rash comment from my beau one evening as we walked around Lake Cayuga gave me an inkling of his true nature. I did not allow his roving hands to unhooked my dress. He chastised, 'I thought all girls in British literature were emotional romantics from reading Byron and Keats, not stuck up prudes like the virgin Queen Elizabeth.' That comment caused me to take a pause."

"What happened?" Claudia had asked and Vivian said she'd tell the rest after they'd gotten ready for bed.

"The gentleman, who turned out to be less than a gentleman," continued Vivian as they sat in their nightgowns after brushing their teeth, "turned to a prettier but duller girl, not a university student, for his solace. I was mortified when I discovered through a mutual friend that he was seeing this other girl. When I asked him about her, he dismissed my fears, 'Oh, her? She's just a friend. I don't take her seriously.' But after that he was never around, had no time, and he no longer attended any of my classes. I thought I'll give him some time to come to his senses. I kept myself busy with science classes and a paper on nineteenth century American writers. But while I was busy reading and writing, he was occupied fiddling and fondling."

When Claudia had asked what that exactly entailed, Vivian had confided, "You'll know if it happens."

"I lost all interest in food and sleep and even my classes that I loved. I was obsessed—only wanting to hear him, to see him, to be with him. I was not myself. I was a top spinning aimlessly. My mother kept complaining that 'a man doesn't want a bag of bones in a sack, Dear.' I didn't care. I only went to the seamstress to have my dresses taken in because my mother kept nagging me. Nothing mattered because he wasn't around me or my classes. I thought it was over. Then he was always there. Every dance, every social or school event. Even though he'd lived in Ithaca, now he was always with her, the pretty shell-with-no-substance girl. My mother chastised me, 'Life goes on. There will be other suitors.'"

"That's the thing to remember," Vivian had advised Claudia that night. "Life goes on. He made a life with her, and I had to move on. The cute little holly homemaker became his wife seven months before their baby was born. I could have learned to live with most of my disappointment, but the sight of that cherubic little boy in ruffles being pushed in a pram by the two of them down my street shoved me over the hill and out into the Midwest prairie."

"I just had to get out of the pan and the fire before I turned to ash." Vivian had stretched out on the bed looking as tired as her voice sounded. "I could not force food down."

"But why choose Wisconsin?" Claudia had asked. She was grateful Vivian had not gone somewhere else but wondered what about Wisconsin could compete with the atmosphere, the social life, and culture of New York, which Vivian had been extolling.

"My mother's comment finally prevailed on me to make a change. No one would reduce me to a skeleton or strip me of the passions that fleshed out my existence. If I couldn't have the life I wanted with that moronic clout from my British lit course whom I loved, then I'd find my own life with or without love."

Vivian confided to Claudia that she hadn't informed anyone that she was leaving. She just got on a westbound train one day and when she got tired of riding, she got off and there she was, in Wisconsin.

"I wrote my parents. Yes, I had a mother and a father, and informed them that I was fine. They weren't too happy that I'd 'thrown my education away, to work in a store' but they loved me in their stiff-upper-lip New England way until they died."

A sleepy teenager up past her normal bedtime revealed to her older friend, "I'm glad you, at least, had two parents."

As Vivian had tucked Claudia under the chenille bedspread, she had reassured her, "Parents can't guarantee their child's happiness. Each of us must find our own. Sleep tight and don't let the bedbugs bite." Claudia thought that last comment was more like Ernie than Vivian. She thought that maybe Ernie was rubbing off on Vivian.

Loving a man, as far as Claudia was concerned, was a risk. Consider Vivian. But, yesterday she'd raked hay and today, because of Thomas's help, she'd gotten the crop into the barn. Sitting on the swing with Thomas scanning the neat rows of cultivated earth between emerging lines of corn sentinels, she didn't want to think about the complexities of love. The pink peonies under the lilac bushes were in full bloom, and the subtle, sweet scent was beguiling. Their talk started at dinner with food, then flowed to the porch with music. Claudia's right foot was curled under her while her left leg swung in rhythm to his voice. Shep had circumscribed a tight circle on the porch floor and lay within it. Tabby had curled up on Thomas's lap where he purred as Thomas stroked his head.

"The music is as complex as your soups. Each instrument has a flavor unique to itself yet when part of the orchestra, the combination becomes more." Thomas waited, letting the swing count out the beats to a measure in his head.

"I think if you got more people involved on the farm here to help you, it would be easier, better too," he continued.

She put her foot down and the swing jerked off balance. Tabby jumped down and ran toward the barn.

"Every farmer's got his own way, and my father and I had ours. You don't just have strangers come and start doing things on your land."

"I don't mean strangers." He tried to get the swing in motion again, but she now had both feet planted on the porch floor. "Look out there." He indicated the field out front. "You said your dad would sit here and say he could hear the corn grow."

She leaned back, and, as her feet lifted, the swing resumed its creaky song. "My father used to be out there working by the light of the moon sometimes, if there weren't enough hours in the day."

"Yes, he worked hard." He put his hand on hers and pushed back to give the swing momentum. "You work hard. Maybe too hard."

"Farming takes effort. My father did the work. I can do it."

"But I want you with me for a long time."

"You don't understand. Land is different. Not like other work. If Papa were here he'd tell you. He could make you see."

"But he's not here. It's just you and me." With that he put his feet down and went inside. The swing, released of his weight, swung aimlessly with Claudia at one end.

As a child, Claudia had been taunted. As a good girl, Claudia learned to control her emotions or hide them.

"Claudi's got no mama. Claudi's an orphan baby." The teasing often occurred at recess when the teacher was busy. Like chickens or pigs, the small group who hadn't been picked for a game of kick the can turned on the weakest in the group. "Suck your thumb, poor orphan baby."

"I'm not an orphan. I have a father, you dope."

"Who you calling a dope, you dumb girl," cried a scabby, skinny boy who was often himself a target of teasing. "You don't got no mama to teach you no manners. You're just a girl in boy's clothes." Which was true. Dresses were such flimsy material. Her father thought wearing one to school was foolish.

"Save that for church and good," was her father's tenet. "School is more suited to sturdy flannel shirts and dungarees." She had liked the comfort of the clothes she wore that were like her father's and was glad in grade school on cold days that she didn't have to wear those dresses and coarse, wool leg socks that wouldn't stay up.

She could've hung her head and cried when they teased her. They'd have laughed, but they also would've left her alone. But, she wouldn't hang her head. She wanted to punch that scabby boy in the face. She was stronger and could beat the snot right out of him, but then the teacher would call her a tomboy like that substitute had last year. The woman, hardly more than a girl herself, sniggered at Claudia. "Well, if you don't care that you'll be a dried-up old maid, honey, you just keep being a tomboy."

Claudia liked her regular teacher, who told her about different countries and people and gave her maps and *National Geographic* magazines to read when she finished her regular work. Later when this scabby boy and a gang of bored pimply roughs circled her in the prairie surrounding the schoolyard, she held her arms to her side and clenched her fists to keep from punching out at them.

The words rained down around her "orphan-baby," "girl-boy," "no mama, no mama." Soon teacher rang the bell and saved her from further torment. She learned at an early age not to rely on anyone to save her. But she had relied on her father and now that turned out to have been wrong, too. Teachers were too busy, fathers didn't notice, and even Vivian couldn't raise someone else's child. Claudia had also learned to go inside her head or a book to escape.

As a child, books had saved her more than once from the ghosts of mothers abandoning children and fathers who had more important things to do than listen to what she was thinking or doing.

She wondered if she had been too much for her mother. Maybe her mother had died because of her. Or had her mother really not died of influenza but run away? Was the gravesite on which they put flowers for her mother's birthday just an empty marker her father put up so Claudia wouldn't feel badly that she was the reason her mama went away? These thoughts haunted Claudia as a child and permeated her dreams as an adult. She had not been allowed to see or touch her mother after a certain point, and Claudia secretly hoped that one day, like the hobo, her mother would appear out of nowhere–maybe paler and older–but still her mother.

Thomas had left for New York the day following their off-kilter evening. He left two weeks ago and would not be back for another week.

Claudia awoke suddenly. She'd gone to bed expecting the night to be like most. Instead, she wrestled her sheets and blankets until she got up and made herself hot chamomile tea in the middle of June, hoping it would carry her into sleep. After another hour of tossing, she tried brandy, just a shot sipped. Finally, she felt the veil begin to fall, and she rolled into her sheet and awoke at the crack of dawn, literally. She'd slept through the storm, but the sharp crash from the falling oak branch woke her. She realized her inner alarm had failed to wake her.

She felt hot and sticky and her mouth tasted like paste. She vaguely remembered sitting as a child at the kitchen table with a gummy mixture her mother gave her of flour and water to use as paste to attach cutout catalog pictures onto old newsprint. When Claudia had put the flour mixture into her mouth, her mother had smiled and directed the toddler's fingers back to the newsprint.

Claudia hurriedly pulled her nightgown off over her head with one hand and stepped into her cotton coveralls with nothing on underneath except her panties. She didn't stop to wash or eat. Chores were waiting. Pushing the door with her left hand and pulling her rubber boots onto bare feet with her right, she didn't immediately see what was right in front of her.

The bear was standing. She would realize later that the bear must have been trying to reach the berry pulp she left on the edge of the roof for the birds. Her immediate concern was Shep who was deaf in one ear and might come upon them unexpectedly.

It was not clear who was more startled. Both females moved slowly, apprehensively. That seemed odd to Claudia. Why didn't the bear drop to all fours and run? They were so close to each other that Claudia could smell the milky fur on the chest of the bear. That's when she noticed the cub in the periphery of her vision, just at the edge of the tree line. She felt the perspiration instantly and wondered if the mother bear could smell the fear drop into place. Claudia's left hand remained on the door. Slowly she backed into the house, eye to eye close to the big black bear with her massive right mitt on the roof and her left down by her side. If those in heaven were watching, they might think this unlikely pair of females was about to dance, each with an arm extended. The bear dropped to all four of her legs. Then, bear safely on the ground and woman safely inside the doorway, she let out a howl that pierced Claudia and caused the cub to race to his mother's side. As they loped off, cub between his mother's front legs, the she-bear appeared to half carry the cub as she swept up the hillside into the trees.

Shep sluggishly came from around the corner of the house. Yesterday Claudia had had to feed him brandy to unhook the porcupine quills from his nose with a pliers. No wonder he hadn't smelled the bear. He only began barking when he registered Claudia's fear.

"That was close, old boy," she spoke into his good ear and rubbed his head to steady her legs as she bent down to sit on the porch.

"Did you ever see anything like that?"

Claudia shuddered to think of the consequences if the bear had decided she was a threat to the cub. The bear's paw spanned Claudia's face and could rip it off with one swipe of five ivory-daggered fingertips. She sat on the step of the porch. A couple of years ago while picking berries, she and a bear had chanced to be on separate sides of a thicket, and both had scurried in opposite directions discretely. The bear today and the bear of years ago may not have differed much in their personalities, but the presence of a cub needing protection brought out instinctual fury in today's Ursus.

Shep's head had settled onto Claudia's lap, and he began to snore. Claudia cupped the back of Shep's head, her arms around him. Claudia had seen mothers cup their infant's head with one hand while the other hand and arm supported the baby's body, which allowed them to gaze at or for others to admire their infant. Always the child could be pulled in close, cradled in the crook of both arms with baby's head in the bend formed by the mom's elbow.

She imagined her mother holding her. She pushed back into the slog of time to recover a memory. The image that she extracted was of a teenage girl, which Claudia knew was impossible for she was six when her mother lay dying from influenza. Her mother couldn't touch her child, who was held back in the doorway tearless. The pain and perspiration on her mother's face made the child unhappy. Young Claudia had loved to be held by her mother, but the room smelled sour and repellent. She retreated into the other room to find her toy tractor.

Claudia wondered if the reason she never felt a maternal urge to start a family of her own was because she never wanted to feel the pain she saw on her mother's face. She wasn't allowed near her mother the last few weeks because her mother had wanted to protect her. Had her mother felt the way the bear had? Had her mother fought death, lingering in agony for weeks trying to get well and return to being a mother? Claudia knew the bear would have attacked and even died to protect her cub. Maybe her mother finally died to take the source of contagion away and protect her child with her own death. As Claudia pushed up from the step, she woke Shep.

"Come on, boy. Enough wasting time. We're burning daylight."

9. New Experiences

Thomas had been in New York for almost three weeks and they were hungry to talk and touch. He returned to Wisconsin just to accompany Claudia and share in her experience of the overnight ride on a luxury train, the Atlantic Limited. She was excited but fearful.

Claudia felt like young Dandy turned into the Johnsons' pasture alone all those years ago when Claudia was a teenager.

Her horse had stood confused, ears flicking back and forth, nostrils flaring. When the stallion entered, she snorted and bolted. Young Claudia had led her companion into this fearful situation. Claudia had started to climb over the fence to go to Dandy to calm her but felt the arms of George's oldest son Hank grab her. She fought to pull away. She'd always been a bit afraid of the boy, the way he stared at her like a prize heifer on the auction block. All his for the right price.

"Don't. He'll trample you to get to her."

Claudia put her arms down and turned her back to him and the stallion. All around her the dust flew from Dandy's hooves in her attempts to get away from the stallion. Claudia fought the desire to put her fingers in her ears to stop the sound of her friend's squeals. She couldn't forgive herself for putting her mare in this position. She didn't want George's son to have sport at her expense, so her back stayed turned away and her arms and fingers stiff at her sides. She would have left, but her father's words hung like the dust around her head and smothered her with the screeching of the virgin filly.

"Don't leave that mare, Claudia. George's boys know horses and what to do, but they don't know Dandy like you do. Dandy trusts you."

Now on her way out East, Claudia had to trust Vivian and Thomas. Vivian seemed to know things of which Claudia never thought. Claudia wondered if Vivian had learned from books or from her years at Cornell University in New York.

With her carpet bag of clothes, Claudia had gone to Vivian for suitable accessories and advice. Between Vivian and the Johnsons, all the farm chores would be taken care of. She was only going for the weekend, but Vivian insisted that Claudia pack day-wear and evening-wear. Claudia's blue midcalf dress with the feather design and a collar with tie-like tails that knotted at her neck would serve for one day. Out of her round-topped, leather-strapped trunk, Vivian pulled a stylish felt hat with a modest feather that coordinated and demonstrated on Claudia how to tilt the hat jauntily on her hair. For the second day in the city, the two women settled on a church dress of yellow flowered print and a white Peter Pan collar, which Claudia had in her wardrobe. Claudia overruled Vivian's advice to order a new red dress from the *Sears and Roebuck Catalogue*, but she did order new silk stockings. Vivian acquiesced, "Yellow and red are your colors. Yellow shows off your smooth, tan complexion but red is bold and would be striking with your black hair. We'll have to make do with what I have in my trunk and your yellow dress, as you don't own a red one." She added soft, yellow gloves and matching shoes with a single strap to the pile accumulating on her bed. Years ago they discovered that despite their difference in height and weight, they wore the same size shoe—seven and a half B, which surprised both of them.

Claudia owned one tube of a pale rose lipstick, a compact of face powder, and a small pot of rouge, all items Vivian had given her as gifts. She tucked all these plus her full-length slip, girdle, silk stockings with a garter-belt to hold them up when not wearing her girdle, her panties and brassiere, and her good cotton nightgown into her heavy, carpet-sided bag that sat open on Vivian's bed. Her dress for the opera was hanging in a cloth bag of Vivian's.

A week ago Vivian had pulled from the trunk her coming-out-party dress made of coffee-colored silk. The seamstress had cleaned the dress, remade the gown into a modern style that rose to just below the knees in the front and touched the floor in the back, and fitted to Claudia's lean, muscled body. When Claudia had objected to the dress style with Vivian and the seamstress, "I can't walk around in a sleeveless dress that has a deep V neck." Vivian had pulled out a shawl from the trunk's depths. Unwrapped, the shawl still shimmered with shiny threads of gold and black woven crisscross in large diamonds through the bands of browns and yellows. The yellow shoes and gloves would serve for day and evening. Vivian had remonstrated, "You really should have elbow length gloves for the evening, but this will do on a budget."

That was Monday. Thomas returned to town on Thursday, and they left together on Friday. Claudia was so concerned about her own fears, she hadn't thought of how tired Thomas must be from the constant travel by train until she heard the ticket agent, "Leaving us so soon after you just arrived yesterday?"

Turtle Lake had two major railroad line crossings, the Omaha and the Soo. Thomas had purchased the tickets at the depot for The Atlantic Limited, the finest Pullman train in the northern United States. This Soo Line train was used primarily by businessmen traveling from the Twin Cities to the eastern states. He and Claudia could make the trip to New York in less than twenty-four hours without stopping in Chicago. Thomas selected that train for his trips back to work at Hagstrom's, always sleeping in his seat. They could have driven Thomas's Packard, but the train was more economical, and they would not need to constantly fix tire punctures. He'd cajoled her, "I want you to experience the train's premier dining and vestibule-style sleeping cars."

The train picked Claudia and Thomas up at Turtle Lake and deposited them in New York without fuss and as efficiently as clockwork, which puzzled Claudia. Her father had talked of the expense, hassle, and inefficiency of travel out of Wisconsin. He'd had little desire to leave their town and even though he was invited to attend farm meetings that would require overnight train travel or accommodations, he rarely went. He used the passenger train to conduct business in nearby towns when taking the horse and buggy was impractical. These last couple of years had been an exception. He seemed to have found many reasons to go to Rice Lake, which didn't follow his habit from a decade ago when they needed to be home twice a day to milk cows. When she was younger, they had dairy and slowly transitioned to beef cattle.

In her adolescent years milking cows, side by side with her father, she had heard the mantra often enough. "Cows get mastitis with unfamiliar hands pulling on them." Another time he counseled, "We have a responsibility to these animals that can't be shirked just because a person might like to take some time to get away. Besides, it'd be a foolish waste of time and money to have to stay in a hotel and pay for food when we've got better at home just by taking it down off the shelf and bringing it up from the cellar." She was confused by his haphazard logic because the older he became the more reasons he found to travel on farm business.

The train's mahogany-lined dining car had starched, linen tablecloths and sterling silverware. She felt sorry that her father had never had the time to enjoy an extended train ride. He'd have been surprised by the quality of the food and the service. The uniformed porter who served them had a towel over his arm and white gloves. He had a small hand brush, which he used to sweep any breadcrumbs into a small silver dustpan after the soup and bread course. On her first trip out of Wisconsin, Claudia observed and overheard things she had only read about.

Thomas had booked separate hotel rooms for them in

downtown New York in a modest but very pleasant hotel. Claudia didn't see any of the deprivations she'd read about— no bread or soup lines, no families starving in the alleys due to lack of work. The abundance she saw belied the newspaper's accounts.

At the hotel the doorman tipped his hat and the concierge offered to help with a carriage or taxi. After settling themselves, they prepared for the evening and met in the lobby. Claudia was excited, but Thomas was fidgety.

Claudia felt exhilarated and frightened by the noises and the lights. Tall buildings were lit all night, people were laughing and talking fast, and the city sounded as different as she imagined a foreign country to be. She remembered when they had trained Dandy and Molly. Going into town the first time, the horse's ears twitched, their noses snorted and huffed, their eyes were enlarged even with blinders, and their feet tapped restlessly on the stone street.

She felt the same mix of unease and excitement. Behind the reins she had tried to transmit through her hands and voice that she was in charge and would keep the horses safe if they just trusted her. She could hear that same reassurance in Thomas's voice and feel his light yet steady pressure on her arm as he led her down the street toward the restaurant that was lit up like money was no object. Since leaving the hotel, Thomas seemed to have relaxed.

He steered her gently away from where the menu was set up, and she knew he wanted to prevent her from seeing the prices, which she would have commented on. "Look what they charge for a steak! Why I'd be rich if I got paid that for my beef."

She felt and heard Thomas. "Let's sit here. Please come this way. It's quieter here." She flashed on Dandy, beginning to rear up, during her first trip to town alone with Claudia who was only sixteen at the time.

On that day she'd thought, *You're doing that to show me*

you're in charge. I like your strong will but I know better just now. Trust me and follow my lead. Like Dandy had for her, this evening she settled into allowing herself to be led.

At the restaurant, Thomas seemed relaxed, smiling, in his element. This was his city.

Claudia felt confused with so much silverware and dishes until she perceived the ease with which Thomas did everything. She found it easy to copy him. He ordered their wine with assurance. Their salads arrived in the shape of a bird. The carrots were cut long and thin and placed like feathered wings. Several different lettuces ruffled and interlaced like a nest and golden raisin eyes peered from a red radish head. Who would ever think to serve raisins with lettuce, carrots, and radishes? A seafood soup lacked the brilliant orange, green, gold, and red of the salad but the flavors were exotic like nothing Claudia had ever tasted.

"That white flaky fish is halibut," Thomas informed her as the young man in starched white set before her a gold-rimmed porcelain bowl and plate that were luminously thin.

She had read about shrimp but had never tasted one. When Thomas instructed, "And the pink and white ones shaped like Cs are shrimp and, of course, you know potatoes and carrots." She had wanted to assert, "I know." But she didn't really.

She put a small almost translucent white sphere into her mouth. "This one tastes like an onion but it's not the shape exactly."

"That's a scallion."

When there was just some broth left, Claudia wanted to pick up the delicate porcelain and drink the last drops. The others in the restaurant were so reserved and refined; she set her spoon down and sighed.

"You enjoyed it?"

"Delicious. I've never tasted anything like this before in my life."

"I'm so glad. Would you like to try something equally unique for dessert?"

Claudia was pulled back to the time when her father had first asked her, "Would you like to drive the Girls?" Is the sky blue? Of course, but she hadn't known what to expect then or now.

"I think we'll have the tiramisu." She heard Thomas through the swirl of exciting and new feelings.

Once the waiter left Thomas confided, "Even though they're known for their crème brûlée, your custard exceeds theirs."

After dinner they went to *La Traviata*. Now she was in this foreign opera house in a strange city. Standing next to Thomas helped. Maybe knowing Claudia was standing there helped Dandy. Reflecting back she hoped so. Later when the dust had settled in the corral and she heard George's son chuckle and poke her in the ribs, she turned to see Dandy standing, hind legs spread wide, her back end winking and the stallion's lips pulled back, curled, and neck extended. Then the stallion mounted her, and Claudia thought her strong young filly couldn't bear the weight of the large black Percheron. The stallion almost completely covered her slender golden Belgian body. That's when she saw it. She'd seen horses urinating, and the bull breed the cows. But the bull's pencil-thin appendage barely poked the cow. This was no pencil. With a mixture of fear and excitement, the teenage girl had been unable to pull away but had watched the unfolding with fascination. She had led Dandy over to George's farm knowing her filly was to be bred but not realizing what that would entail. Now in the grand opera lobby, she smiled at the memory. Scary things can be exciting, too. Thomas noticed her smile and took her hand.

Whenever she was anxious during the performance, Claudia focused on the sweeping curves of the stage and the balconies in dark wood with gold gilt or the light laughter and the rustle of programs and ladies' silk fans. Ears grown sensitive and sharpened by apprehension, she could hear the tinkle of the crystals on the chandelier. Sound and color washed around the people in their section like a misty spring rainbow.

She was breathing deeply, like Dandy, to settle herself as Vivian had instructed Claudia to do just days ago when she became nervous. She thought of how uncomfortable Thomas was with ordinary everyday occurrences like dust storms, slaughtering pigs, butchering chickens, and even conversations with farmers. To her those were just part of everyday life. This throng of perfumed, trussed, and laced women ringed and entwined with smoking, starched, and tuxedoed men was his world, and he moved as effortlessly in the city as she moved confidently on the farm.

Again, the circumstances reminded Claudia of Dandy, who had liked the breeding even within the unfamiliar situation. Claudia had admonished herself if she had been able to warn Dandy what to expect, then the encounter would have been easier. But Claudia hadn't known what to expect. Her father had known. But her father hadn't told her. Maybe it never occurred to him to tell her what the breeding would be. That's why he'd warned, "Stay with her; she trusts you." But he wasn't the one to take her, and now Claudia understood even if he'd taken Dandy, he wouldn't have known how to talk to her. With the knowledge she now possessed, she would have spoken to her mare about the fear, assured her that the incursion would be over soon, and confided that she might even like the experience. Claudia would have spoken quietly to relax and reassure her. Even if Francis had known how to calm Dandy, he wouldn't have thought it important to communicate that. Francis didn't explain or warn the horses of an upcoming puddle or low-hanging branch the same way Claudia did. "You baby those horses. They know you and trust you. But they are animals." His voice rang in her head. "You need to remember who is in charge."

Claudia wished she had known what to expect at the opera. Initially Claudia had felt out of her element. Such extravagance, yet the native New Yorkers she saw appeared so comfortable with the trappings. By the end of the night she would not even remember these uneasy feelings. In several hours, alone in bed, she would fall asleep. Like Dandy's body, her mind would be aquiver with new sensations. Neither Dandy's breeding nor Claudia's opera were inevitable; both were scary and lovely.

She cried even though she didn't understand a word of Verdi's opera. She felt like the orchestra was inside her chest. The strings were attached to her limbs, the drum beat on her heart, and the piano played up and down her spine and within her head. She felt the conductor held her life and death in his hands. At the end, his arms crescendoed for the final notes and the baton went down. A thunderous surprise of applause forced her to feel her spine take form again and air filled her tingling spaces.

"How did you like it?" Thomas asked before seeing the tears and leading her gently to the taxi, another first on this trip of firsts. They had walked from the hotel to the restaurant and from the restaurant to the opera. She sat in the taxi next to him cocooned by music playing in her head. She bathed in the newness of being chauffeured down a busy street in what should be the dark of night, though everywhere was brightly lit with street lamps, carriage lanterns, and passing vehicle lights. Thomas's arm was around her shoulders. With the rich food a still warm remembrance within her, she rested her head against his chest. Languid and lovely, flowing notes suspended in the depths, then a gentle voice drew her to the surface. "Claudia we're here." She realized she had fallen asleep in his arms in a strange city, in a strange car, and she didn't feel one bit strange but perfectly relaxed and peace-filled.

The next day after an excursion to see Central Park, Times Square, and the Empire State Building, Claudia and Thomas returned to Wisconsin. Thomas expressed his disappointment that the trip wasn't longer, and despite her desire to stay, she felt unease being away even for three days. Upon their arrival at the farm the next morning, they greeted the animals and did the evening chores, but Claudia left the unpacking and opening of mail for the next day.

Tonight, basking in the evening glow of their New York trip, they were tired but sat contentedly on the porch swing and watched the sun set in the late June sky. Neither had spoken in quite some time but neither was aware of the passing of time. Claudia was breathing in deeply, feeling the relaxed comfort and safety reminiscent of evenings such as this with her father. He might have had the newspaper in hand or not. She could almost smell the sweet, slightly bitter driftings from his pipe. Yet she was glad Thomas did not smoke. She blamed tobacco for her father's shortness of breath those last years. Who knows, maybe smoking contributed to his death. Thomas had smoked cigarettes but quit after assisting on some autopsies. The contrast between a smoker's black and gray lung tumors and a nonsmoker's smooth pink lungs was enough incentive, he'd confided to her.

She became aware of the sound of something familiar, a recent familiarity, reminding her of stories she'd read of ballrooms and women in belled skirts swishing with partners in crisp white and formal black. Claudia imagined herself in that crowd of elegant sophistication, among the women of precision coiffures, and felt out of place. She'd overheard her father at Ernie's store once dismiss the fancy women in a magazine as *idle*, nothing to do all day except be attended to. She had agreed with almost everything her father had said, but she loved to have someone give attention to her hair. She had held inside that feeling of disagreement with her father. Sitting on the porch, dreaming of dances, she remembered her mother. A mother brushing her toddler's hair.

Claudia loved to have her hair brushed—one clear memory of her mother which she played continually to keep the remembrance alive. After her mother's death Claudia would occupy herself playing on the floor of the general store while her father got provisions. Vivian had seen the snarled nest of hair and offered to "play beauty shop" while the menfolk talked. Vivian tried to tame the tangle of curls for the little motherless girl whose father didn't notice and probably didn't know how to brush through gently. Young Claudia had relaxed into the hair-brushing like taking a warm bath. With each stroke memories rippled down her of tender patient hands, cotton flour-sack house dresses, and a muslin apron hung on a nail by the kitchen door. Claudia would close her adolescent eyes, and if Vivian didn't talk, Claudia could imagine her mother, not Vivian, brushing the hundred daily strokes she recommended every lady should give herself to keep her hair healthy and shiny.

The music pulled her back to the ballroom in her mind, and she realized the melody was coming from Thomas. He was humming. She put him into her mind's picture—tall, handsome in tails and a simple-cut shirt. She'd seen frillier shirts on their trip to New York. She tried to envision what she was wearing in her evening daydream, but it kept shifting. First, she visualized a white dress. She looked like a bride and didn't like that. In her mind's eye women with long blond ringlets displayed themselves in pale blues and pinks. One with an auburn chignon was arrayed in peach. Then she noticed a woman in a pale green dress, the color of a Norway pine or maybe maple leaves in a spring rain.

She couldn't see the woman's face. Claudia willed her own face to be there and for the woman to turn toward her. She imagined a shade of green more like wood moss at dawn. The dress transformed in her mind from a multilayered taffeta to a single layer of silk with a sheen that changed hue as the light caught the swirling folds like moss catching sun rays through whispering leaves. The bodice, she viewed as the woman turned, was as simple and elegant as the scooped back had been. Small delicate rows of shirting pleats encircled the woman's waist like a ripple that Claudia wanted to touch. The man she recognized as Thomas clasped the woman's waist with one arm and held her hand in his other hand. He was leaning down to hear what she was whispering. He was smiling into her face, which was grinning but unnaturally so, too broadly, and her eyes had a calculating sparkle. Claudia pulled back her mind's eye. That was not her face! She must have jerked because the music stopped, and the vision vanished.

"What's the matter, Claudia?"

"Oh, nothing."

"*La Traviata* just popped into my head. Then I remembered a dance in Manhattan that I'd been to several years ago. The women's dresses were every color of the rainbow. They were like hothouse flowers amongst a sea of us penguin men."

Claudia wondered if he had danced with the woman with the calculating eyes. She went from easy enjoyment to worried apprehension. She had enjoyed New York immensely but what was she thinking. She couldn't compare to or compete with the sophistication and glamour of his colleagues. She wanted to get up but was held by Thomas's hand on hers and his questioning look.

"Do you want that pie now?" she started to stand.

"I want to kiss you," he admitted, the slightest pressure on her arm. She felt the muscles in her legs, which had been tensed to push her up and out of the swing, relax. She sat back into the swing and closed her eyes. Thomas's lips didn't touch her lips as she expected. He often did something unexpected, which was disconcerting but exciting. He started on her cheekbone just under her eye, then between her eyes, across, and down the other cheek below her ear and dotted the line of her jaw with kisses like connecting the dots in a child's picture book. She heard his vibrating breath and the hum became *La Traviata* again.

She envisioned herself in the green silk gliding across the marble floor carried on air by Thomas's arms under a chandelier in a room of soft light, silk gowns, and satin wallpaper. A conservatory of scents surrounded them: magnolia and lavender, citrus and musk. Then she distinctly tasted a brandy richness that was almost buttery. Thomas was kissing her mouth, his tongue tentatively touched hers. She sighed. Butterscotch. He often had a brown paper sack of lemon drops or horehound in his pockets. "A habit after quitting cigarettes," he informed her when he handed them out to children. She felt herself kissing his neck as he had kissed hers.

She felt so companionable, like Dandy and Molly. She kissed him. His shirt unbuttoned in a V where his skin was smooth and smelled of his New England milled soap. His hands were on her back under her blouse massaging in slow gentle circles up to her shoulder blades then down in long strokes to her waist where he held her and gently squeezed the tops of her hip bones. She realized she had her hands gripping his biceps that were flexed from massaging her. A thought, which she'd had more frequently recently, popped rudely into her reverie. No, this was not right, not what she should be doing. Shouldn't she be giving herself on a bridal bed to a local farmer who would take care of her as her father had?

There had been young farmers full of potential who her father had "happened" to invite over to examine a piece of land or new equipment and who "happened" to stay for supper.

Her father would conveniently encourage, "You young people sit out on the swing. I'm tired. I'll just sit here with my pipe and the farm journal."

Those boys were awkward, fumbling, dirt under their nails. She always felt disloyal to her father when she didn't want to hold their grease-creased hands.

But being with Thomas felt so right. She wondered how that could be. Her father wouldn't want his daughter to go gallivanting off to New York, dancing in ball gowns and sipping champagne. She was a farmer's daughter living in rural Wisconsin, square dancing in barns, and drinking beer. She'd held hands with the few farm boys her father had over to the house. They were her age or a few years older, but she knew as much about farm animals, equipment, and crops as they did, and she tired of farm talk. She spent enough time talking the farmer trinity with her father; it was her lifeline with him. Those farm boys knew next to nothing of Shakespeare or Faulkner, much less Chaucer. Most of them were pulled from school by the eighth grade to help full-time on their farms.

Sitting with Thomas on the porch swing, discussing the opera, kissing him, Claudia felt intoxicated. She felt how she imagined electricity flowed to turn on the lights or how she'd seen a lightning strike travel one stormy night. The bolt struck a tree, raced across the ground, then with a crack, a bush burst into flame and was consumed in a flash. The sensation from his arms traveled through hers down her back into her legs but not before starting a small brush fire in her groin. She wanted to be consumed but not quickly like the bush she'd seen. She wanted it to take until the sun burned out. They stayed at the swing until the cold night air lifted them upstairs toward her room. Being in her room was not a first. They'd sat on her bed studying family photos she kept in her dresser drawer.

They couldn't go to her father's room where Thomas had stayed that time when he'd helped and it got late. They couldn't do what they were going to do in her father's room. Her father's room with the lingering smell of pipe tobacco and his wooden boxes of change, fence staples, and odds and ends held too much of his ghost. She wanted only Thomas. She needed his smell, his touch. She needed to be expiated of her father and her obsession with him. She needed to atone and be absolved. She had had to please her father, cook for him, clean, care for him, never thinking of her own needs or desires, never seeing herself apart from him and his dreams, never separate from the land and the farm. This night was to be only for her, her desires, her pleasure. She sensed Thomas wanted only to please her. He was the knowledgeable one in this field, not an expert, maybe, but certainly more experienced than she was.

She thought of those clods of dirt boys and their limited knowledge as Thomas led her up the stairs. Thomas and she often discussed literature, or he'd recite poetry to her in the evenings as they sat together. But not tonight. She pushed thoughts of the past out of her head—past expectations, past duties, past memories. This was her time. Her head spun with her father's tobacco, ballroom dancing, fumbling farm hands, and Thomas's wandering sparkler kisses. She felt light-headed, almost like forgetting to eat. Soon she would forget everything except the exploration of the topography of Thomas and his fingers awakening the far reaches of her hills and valleys and her recognition that the tropics were more than photos in the *National Geographic.*

10. Debt

Claudia had returned from New York to the chores. She had missed Dandy and Molly and Daisy and Shep and Tabby and the remaining laying hens with their chicks. She didn't even mind slopping the pig. She did mind the mail that held unexpected and bewildering news. While still dark, Thomas had left for town after their lovely evening together. If he were still here, she may have spoken of the letter's content, but probably not; financial matters were private in her family.

The formal letter was from the Rice Lake Bank saying their farm was in default of a mortgage taken out by Francis Nelson that was due and payable immediately. Claudia grabbed the letter and went to saddle Dandy. Shep, whining, walked around the horse as she cinched the saddle.

"Quit that!" She snapped at Shep. With tail between his legs and head staring back at her, he left. She headed to town to talk to Vivian. Claudia was upset. No! She was angry. Why hadn't she been told about the debt? Why was a mortgage taken out? Why hadn't her father spoken to her?

The ride to town took Claudia fifteen minutes, but that was enough time for her to review the unexpected news and raise questions about her assumptions. The past—her father's unvoiced expectations, her loss of her mother, and someone to confide in—kept pulling at her. While in New York and last night, she had had several hours free of the past even if that freedom was at the cost of today's reality weighing her down. She had lived with her father on their farm without many traumatic worries and they always shared their farm decisions. Or, so she had thought! He obviously hadn't trusted her to confide some big problem that required a substantial amount of money. What was she going to do?

Now, she felt disloyal to him for liking a lifestyle of which he wouldn't have approved, and she felt angry and betrayed. She would have to confront RT, the one who held the paper on the debt. She would have to make a trip to Rice Lake. She needed Vivian's advice.

Ernie was on the front porch of his store sweeping as his two buddies, Klive, a lanky Irishman, and Bruno, a barrel-chested Dutchman, sat in wooden cane-backed chairs playing checkers on a barrel top.

"Howdy," they nodded at Claudia.

"Which travels faster? Heat or cold?" asked Ernie of no one in particular. "Heat," he answered himself, "because you can always catch a cold." Claudia gave a perfunctory "Good Morning" and pushed through the screen door of the general store.

"What brings you to town? How was your trip?" Vivian climbed down from the ladder that ran on a narrow track mounted on the highest shelf and traversed the length of the store. Percy cooed from his cage as Vivian passed, and she cooed back. The June calendar page behind Vivian was of a black-hatted, red-kerchiefed Indian with long, thin braids named Heavy Brest. *That's me, debt weighing on my chest.*

Claudia motioned to the back of the store. "Can we talk in private?" Vivian walked to the back room that divided the rear of the store from Ernie's living quarters.

"Pretty Boy!" Percy called to the two women.

Claudia held out the letter typed on bank letterhead. "Why didn't my father tell me he needed a loan? And why was I informed by letter? Why not tell me in person?" As Vivian read, Claudia continued shaking her head and pacing.

"It was taken out two-and-a-half years ago, which means my father's been paying on it. I thought I always knew about our payments. It's not like him." She sat down on a box labeled "Kitchen Gadgets for Every Woman's Needs and Convenience." *How could their life of partnership on the farm be true if he hadn't trusted to talk to me about a need for a loan and what it was for?*

"Maybe it slipped his mind?" offered Vivian who was perched on a gunny sack of rolled oats. "The need may have come up unexpectedly, and maybe he didn't want to bother you. You've been occupied doing more and more of the field work the last couple of years."

"Occupied?" She jumped up and began pacing. "I've been running around like a chicken with my head cut off trying to keep it all together while he's been absent-minded and distracted." She didn't say, *and not pulling his share of the load,* but she suddenly realized that was her belief. She stopped pacing when she was turned away from Vivian. If her mother were here, instead of Vivian, could Claudia have uttered those words against her father to her mother?

Instead she offered, "I wish he'd mentioned something." Claudia stuffed the envelope in her pocket. "What will I do? I'll have to sell the young breeding stock or some land. Maybe I can refinance the debt? My father wanted the new livestock to improve the herd to increase production and the market value of our stock. We can't sell our breeding stock, only the mature offspring. Our beef sales are what buys seed and pays the land taxes. And we can't sell land because we need the land to feed the stock. I sell one and don't have the means to keep the other." With that she sat back down on the crate. "I'll have to go talk to RT. There is something…sticky about him."

"It's not unwarranted." Vivian's face stiffened, and she shifted on the sack. "You were so distracted about those chickens and Thomas that I didn't say anything when I found out about RT buying old man Meiser's land after he died. In the excitement of assembling your wardrobe for New York, I forgot to mention RT's involvement in your neighbor's field which happened the middle of May, after the sharecroppers had most of the planting done."

"The sharecroppers have rented that field for the past five years. What happened?" asked Claudia.

"The family, believing the son of Mr. Meiser would honor

their agreement, had finished planting and intended to harvest this fall. Their down payment had been made as usual, and the balance would be paid after the harvest. Meiser's son either didn't know about the agreement or hadn't honored it and sold the land to RT."

"Why didn't RT honor the agreement?"

"He obviously thought he could make more money planting the field in soybeans. What makes me mad is how he handled the situation. RT sent one of his young "prospects," who wanted a job after high school graduation, to give the down payment back to them. Of course, the family couldn't have afforded to buy the property outright after Meiser died. Now they had lost the seed and almost a month of labor, and here was this glorified teenager too full of himself shaking an envelope of cash at them."

Vivian related the conversation to Claudia as she had heard it later that day when the young man came into the store to get a candy bar before heading back to Mr. Rottman.

"'Here, Mr. Rottman owns this land now,' the young man declared to the sharecroppers.

'But we planted,' the father of the family replied, as he stood there, hoe in hand in the planted field.

'You ought to be happy. The old man didn't have anything in writing. I wouldn't give you anything, but Mr. Rottman is paying you what you paid old man Meiser,' that young upstart had the nerve to say to his elder.

'But it's too late for us to plant elsewhere, even if we could find land and work it up.'

'That's not Mr. Rottman's problem.'

'But that,' the farmer pointed the hoe at the blossoming peas, sprouting beans, hilled potatoes, and neat rows of onions, 'that is what feeds our family.' And this nincompoop kid is relating all this to me as if this is something he is proud of. He goes on to tell them, 'Go to a store like the rest of us and buy your food. Take this money and go to Ernic's.' As he's relating this to me he had the nerve to smile, proud to have told the family to purchase their food here. Can you believe the audacity?"

"Everybody's got problems. At least I have enough food to eat," admitted Claudia.

"A few days later the farmer's wife, alone, came in to buy beans and rice," confided Vivian as she stretched her back and pushed off the sack of rolled oats. "I talked with her. She revealed her husband had turned away, but she took the envelope of money before following him and the children. I knew he was humiliated. How would you like to explain your situation to a boy half your age and in clothes twice as expensive as yours? No, thank you!"

Claudia straightened her long body off the crate. "If anyone was going to have to confront those sharecroppers it should've been RT himself."

"You have good reason to think of him as unsavory. Go talk to him. You don't need to do anything except get information. Keep your options open. Maybe you can come to some terms with RT, even though the loan is in default."

"How can it be in default by several months? RT must have known about the delinquency the day of Papa's funeral." Claudia stood towering above Vivian but peering intently into Vivian's face. "Why not talk to me then?"

"Give the man a little credit." Vivian's face softened. "A funeral is not the right time to talk about money owed." Vivian raised her left eyebrow and scrunched up the corner of her mouth in a question not intended to be answered.

Claudia breathed an audible sigh, raised her shoulders, then exhaled slowly, lowering her shoulders. "I wish we weren't in this fix."

The two women entered the main part of the store from the backroom.

Percy squawked emphatically at their return, "Pretty Boy!"

As Claudia walked out the screen door, Vivian called after her, "It isn't 'we' anymore. It's only 'you.'"

She turned to Percy, "Yes, you are my Pretty Boy."

Claudia stepped from the discussion of debt and labor lost into the playfulness of gents. All three men looked up. Ernie addressed Claudia, "Can you tell these two nondairy fellows how long cows should be milked?" Claudia stood dumbfounded.

"The same as short cows," he stated and all three men snorted. "Wait, I got another one for you." But no one expected her to stay.

On her ride home, she pushed the debt out of her mind. She would take care of that tomorrow. The countryside was dotted with little homes nestled into farmsteads that were similar—fields of crops, pastures, clusters of trees, and a garden patch; yet different—the variety of grains raised, their native language and customs, and the houses: clapboard, brick, log, and there tucked into the woods was one of sod. The three men on Ernie's porch represented first- and second-generation immigrants from different countries. Ernie claimed to be Bohemian, but Claudia never knew if he was bragging or making excuses. Most frequently he claimed to be Czech.

Klive had confided to her his parents came from Ireland but met out East on the streetcar his da was driving that his mam rode daily to her job cleaning a rich woman's home. They came to Wisconsin for the chance that fortune had denied them in title and pedigree in Ireland.

As she and Dandy passed a German family's house, she thought of Bruno, whose family came to Wisconsin for equality and better prospects but also for the comfort of fellow German settlers.

In less than a generation these differing folks had swapped stories and techniques, shared food and labor, and gained an appreciation for their differences and their similarities. Even in her short life, she'd witnessed immigrants who'd arrived speaking different languages but quickly learned the common jargon of cooperation.

People were constantly on the move: immigrants from Europe, migrants from Mexico, and frustrated pioneers heading further west for escape and opportunity. Maybe someday she'd want to move. No, she loved her farm. She'd make sure she kept her land and her animals.

The next day after chores, Claudia left Dandy at the blacksmith's where there was a livery and boarded the train to Rice Lake.

Traveling through the countryside to the city and gazing out the window, Claudia pondered the inequality of chances different people had been given. RT was prospering, but so many farmers were failing, not to mention small businesses. She counted the numerous rundown farms and dilapidated barns on this relatively short train trip. Could all these barns have been abandoned as a result of hard times? Why didn't people try to save them? She could see wash hung on a line at one house. The barn next to the home had begun the first swoop in its decline.

Barns with swayed backs reminded her of old horses or cows that sagged in the middle as if their joints had given way. Crouched on the ground aging cows that could no longer push up their back ends knelt, then leaning forward would push up to stand. Claudia had seen more than one old woman copy that procedure to rise after sitting on the floor.

These barns had lost their elasticity. Like an aging cow or a woman's elbows and knees, the barn's wooden ribs, the skeleton upon which the siding and roof could hang, had lost its strength.

Vivian once told Claudia that bodies were made up of ninety percent water, and plants were primarily water. A tree could bend with the wind because its limbs were flexible from the water flowing through it branches. Moisture was no less important, Claudia reasoned, for the wood's integrity and flexibility once cut and fitted into place in a building. Abandoned houses and barns deteriorated, weakened, and collapsed when people and animals were no longer in them breathing, exhaling vital moisture and body heat. Maybe animal body moisture permeated a building, saturated it like smoking a ham to preserve it or marinating a piece of meat. The life occupying the space soaked into and transferred from the people and animals to the wooden beams and planks. The accommodating shelter allowed the animals and people to conserve their moisture and heat from the elements. The symbiotic relationship between living trees and plants and animals and humans was no less important than the connection between the homes and stables and their occupants.

Life sustained life. Living organisms had to work together to stay upright and alive. Without animals or humans in the building, there was no life, no breath, no moisture to fill the wood's pores. Overly dry wood became susceptible to rot and insects.

Vivian had explained the delicate balance of plants and animals to Claudia when she was younger; plants take in carbon dioxide and give off oxygen, while animals take in oxygen and give off carbon dioxide, a symbiotic relationship. Claudia had been pleased to think her father and she had been part of that subtle equilibrium by planting trees and bushes around their farm. As Claudia thought of her unpleasant mission today in Rice Lake, she savored the thought of discussing with Vivian the comparison of barns to living creatures. They hadn't had a philosophical discussion in a long time.

The train pulled into the Rice Lake Depot, and Claudia switched gears from philosophy to practicality. She first went to the banker hoping to make arrangements to continue the mortgage under her name but on a repayment schedule she could afford.

The banker counseled her, "I wish I could, but the board has a standard and a single woman doesn't fit the profile.

These are troubled times. Get someone to sign for you and guarantee the loan, or sell off some land, then we could reconsider. Maybe Randy would be willing to help."

Randy Rottman's name was on the bank letter, and she knew that was where her father had gone when he needed to borrow short term. On the train trip here, she had considered the possibility she may have to negotiate with RT.

People in Claudia's small town regarded the Rottmans, from the nearby city, as upstanding citizens who were seen at public gatherings, attended major social events, and stood up to pledge for good causes. The Rottmans had secured the money to put a smaller version of the proposed Rice Lake athletic field in Turtle Lake and in Barron. The bleachers bore the Rottman's name in red block letters below the town's team name.

The most recent time her father had to go to RT, of which Claudia had known, was the winter of 1928-29 for the purchase of the Highland heifer calves and bull calf to enhance their herd's bloodline. Not many cattlemen were familiar with the hardy breed from Scotland, but Francis had read about their ability to thrive on grass while surviving severe weather conditions. With all the dry years and poor crop yields, he believed an influx of this new blood could benefit his beef cows. RT Rottman had taken a risk on the new cattle, had funded the endeavor, and made a profit on the deal, but that was the cost, as Francis had disclosed, of having to borrow money. That is why they tried never to have to borrow large amounts. She couldn't imagine what had caused her father in May of 1929, five months before the October 29th crash, to take out a mortgage of three thousand dollars, which was half the value of their property in 1929. After the crash, land values fell by twenty dollars per acre, which meant their land was worth twenty-four hundred dollars less. In 1932 their farm was worth only thirty-six hundred dollars, which was not enough collateral to cover the original debt if land prices continued to plummet and interest rates soared. Even with Francis making monthly payment for two and a half years at over six percent interest, the balance due on the loan was only slightly less than the 1932 value of the land held as collateral.

Claudia felt a mixture of shame and anger as she walked from the bank to RT's office. She had been rebuffed by the banker and now had to convince RT she was not a financial risk. She was ushered into RT's mahogany-lined office with the overstuffed leather chairs and a sofa along one wall. He sat behind his desk, a slab of polished wood, in a high, stuffed, swivel chair from some exclusive catalogue. The chairs in front of his desk were beautiful but low, and Claudia was forced to sit to the front of one as if perched there. If she sat back into the chair she was tipped back and felt like she was looking up into RT's face. She chose to sit forward and perch like Vivian's parakeet on her owner's finger.

"So, what can I do for you, young lady?" Randy laced his fingers behind his head and leaned back.

"I received a letter saying that there is a loan in default on my property." To Claudia's words, Randy nodded, pursing his lips knowingly.

"Why didn't you tell me the loan was due, and what it was for? Why wait two months before sending me a letter?" He smiled at her words, his lips compressed in a straight line.

"I don't understand. How can there be a mortgage on the property? My father and I paid off the loan for seed and cattle."

"This was a private matter." He imparted the word "private" as if even her hearing the word somehow violated the brotherhood of men.

"But I'm responsible. I need to know what I'm repaying."

"If your father had wanted you to know, I think he would have told you." *There. His finger was on the sore. Why hadn't her father told her? What was he hiding and how could any of her life be what she thought, if this part wasn't what she thought?*

RT pushed. "Maybe your father didn't want to bother you with the particulars. Maybe the best thing is to respect his wishes, make good on the loan, and move on with your life."

"I can't make good on this debt without knowing what it's for. Besides I'd have to sell my land or my animals."

Randy came around to the front of the desk and sat on the edge. She could smell the starch in his white shirt and see the glint of gold cufflinks as his hand whisked like a carnival conjurer in front of her to rest on his knee.

"We can take care of this without causing you any more trouble. I'm sure I can find someone to buy that land. You can get married and settle down. Let one of our local boys take care of you like your dad did." He smiled as if that were the solution to all her problems. The solution for which so many thought she should settle.

"You can even keep the house. A little dowry, like." He leaned forward conspiratorially, "I know things have been getting a little out of hand lately, and you've had to rely on a lot of help. It's only understandable. You alone. Out there. A woman." The last comment pushed the bruise so hard she couldn't feel the pain. Only the resolve. She wanted to get to her feet but he was so close.

"I want to know the particulars! I have a right to know!" She hoped her voice held more force than her upbringing allowed her to show.

"There is no law requiring me or anyone to disclose that information. The agreement was between two men and a bank, and it was at your father's request that the matter remain private. There was no need to register the documents until his death or, in the event of, his default on the loan. Besides, both deeds are in your father's name, not yours." He straightened his back and lingered. Lifting an eyebrow, he continued pausing frequently to punctuate his words. "Unfortunately, both untimely events have occurred, which necessitated the bank in filing the mortgage with the Office of the Register of Deeds so the lender could pursue satisfaction of the debt. There. Does that satisfy your curiosity, Miss Nelson?"

Curiosity! Miss Nelson! If I were a man, I'd cut him down. I hate needing to be nice because I may require his services. I have to get out of here, or I may say or do something I regret. Claudia couldn't stand up without being chest to chest with him. She pushed the chair back and almost fell as the legs caught in the thick carpeting.

"Thank you for your time, Randolph." She accentuated his formal name. *There. No buddy Randy. Not even the initials by which we refer to you. You insignificant, pretentious snob.* "How long do I have?"

Randy stood. "There's no need for this. We're all friends. We all have to help each other in a small community like ours." *That was pushing it. Turtle Lake was not their small town. Let him claim this city, Rice Lake. Bear Creek is mine, and he can't claim our town or township as his just because he does business with us. And he is not my friend.*

"As your father's only living heir, the law gives you one week to make good on the entire loan, but it needn't come to that." RT pronounced the words beguilingly. She wanted to slap that hand he was extending to her as she reached the door. Being her father's daughter, she shook it. As soon as she was outside, she firmly rubbed that palm down the cloth of her dress-covered thigh. She was glad to be going home to do her chores.

11. Macy

Back in March the Lindbergh baby had been kidnapped. Everyone from President Herbert Hoover to the corner shop girl was talking about the fifty-thousand-dollar ransom demand to return the curly-haired, twenty-month-old son to his adoring aviator parents at their New Jersey home. People stopped on the New York City street to read the newspaper headlines at the corner newsstand. Many couldn't afford the price of a loaf of bread, much less a newspaper. New Yorkers on their way to their offices and shops passed men standing in soup lines. On the docks at sunrise men loitered hoping to be one of those chosen to unload or load ships that day. No one was untouched. Rather than face their wives and children, three years ago this coming October, previously wealthy stockholders and owners of successful companies jumped out of windows to their deaths after the stock market crashed. Within hours they'd gone from financially secure to bankrupt.

Thomas had grown up as an only child of elderly, doting parents and gone right from college to study medicine at Syracuse Medical School in New York. After the sudden death of his parents and the settling of their affairs, he was left unexpectedly with few resources to continue his studies. He put his medical knowledge to use, working for a successful undertaker associated with a furniture company in New York, which allowed him little free time. He believed in being attentive to his customers, and his employers welcomed his experience.

Three years ago when he first arrived at Hagstrom's Furniture and Mortuary Emporium, Iris and her ill husband became Thomas's clients and purchased a living room and bedroom set to update their apartment. On this cold and icy first day of March 1932, Thomas was finalizing the paperwork for the funeral of Iris's husband who had recently passed away. Their niece Macy Jergenson, a slow-spoken girl with sparkling blue eyes, had come in a week earlier with Iris to pick out a coffin and was accompanying her today. Macy's drawly walk called to mind a circus horse with exaggerated gait that accentuated the roll of hips and muscle. She was beautiful but not a beauty. Her attractiveness was not natural but carefully cultivated like a hothouse orchid.

Iris, a stalwart woman who'd supported the suffragette movement, was not shocked when her husband passed away. "He'd been sick for some time, and as you know, we began our arrangements when he could help with the decisions. But I have been grateful for the company and distraction of Macy's visit."

Thomas was holding the door for the two women when Macy stumbled on her way out of the shop and fell against Thomas who steadied her. She cradled her ankle, and he insisted she sit for a moment in the reception area. Seated comfortably, she suggested her aunt continue without her.

"I'll just rest my ankle here, Aunt Iris. You go on ahead to take care of the other errands and I'll meet up with you in a bit." The childless aunt regarded her niece narrowly, then the bewildered young mortician. Iris shook her head slightly.

A few moments of silence followed. They stood: the aunt pensive, the mortician blushing, and the niece's eyes averted but intent. The aunt nodded.

"I will gladly escort your niece to your home, which is not far from here, if convenient for you. You could proceed immediately to your other errands unencumbered by her injury," Thomas offered. Macy smiled, resumed her seat, and rubbed her slender ankle above her calf-skinned petite shoe. Aunt Iris thanked Thomas, gathered her handbag, and held her skirt to leave, shaking her head at the handsome mortician and her niece.

Thomas fidgeted. "I will talk to my manager for permission to leave the floor before my usual time. I'm sure he won't mind. I've never left early before." He rushed his words, left the vestibule, and returned several minutes later blushing profusely. His boss had remarked, "A young woman? Why of course, go. We seldom get a single marriageable woman in here. Take your opportunities where and when God provides them."

When Thomas suggested a small horse cart to prevent further injury to her ankle, she hesitated with a cross between a pout and a slight grimace on her face.

"Does it hurt?" He held her elbow.

"I can bear it with your help. If a cart would please you that will be fine." She was quietly demure. He hesitated. She added, "I am usually taken in carriages." He hailed a carriage and they proceeded to her aunt's apartment where the doorman opened and held the carriage door, while Thomas rushed to the other side to help Macy out and into the elegant stone building.

They progressed from this meeting to weekly lunches, invitations to attend church, then daily outings that Thomas and Macy shared. Neither knew who was being led down which path until it was too late.

Thomas had never eaten out as much as he did that March and April with Macy. Occasionally, he ate at the corner lunch counter, but usually he made his own lunch and had his sandwich and a piece of fruit at work, neither of which would be suitable for a Southern girl like Macy.

On their first dinner together at the end of March, he suggested a modest restaurant.

"My only desire is to be with you tonight. Whatever would please you, will please me." With that she gazed up at him and placed her small, gloved hand on his arm. He decided on a more upscale restaurant that would cost him as much for that evening as he normally spent in a month. But Thomas had never met anyone like Macy before. He could not quit thinking about her.

That April marked the third year Thomas had been working at the Hagstrom Furniture Store and Mortuary when the tickets to see the opera *Aida* came unexpectedly. The banker, who'd denied a small loan to Thomas after his education abruptly ended, entered the mortuary.

"I'm called out of town suddenly. Some problem with an affiliate bank in Buffalo. I need to leave on the eleven o'clock train." The banker paced in front of Thomas. "I have these tickets for tonight's performance at the Metropolitan Opera House. You were kind to Sarah last year. She mentioned you enjoy the opera. My sister is a strong woman, but her husband's sudden heart attack was difficult for all of us. She expressed just last week how she appreciated your support." Three years ago, the banker, seated solidly behind his desk, had spoken in two short sentences when he denied Thomas the setup money for his own business on his arrival in New York.

With a generous urgency Thomas had hoped for but never received with the loan request, the banker thrust the envelope with the two tickets at Thomas. "You have a way that women understand. I see that now. I can appreciate its place."

He pumped Thomas's hand in farewell as he left waving off Thomas's "thank you" as if it might attach to the banker in some unsavory way.

Thomas brushed his coat with care before meeting Macy on the second Friday evening in April. When he stopped to pick her up she wasn't ready, which meant that they missed the opera's opening, but she was not distressed by their tardiness.

In their seats, she kept looking around at the others intently as if studying a textbook. While Thomas read the program, she held hers in front of her, but she wasn't considering the booklet. She was peering over the paper, studying the people.

On stage Aida lamented her dilemma. Would she be loyal

to her Ethiopian father who had crossed the border to defeat the Egyptians or pray her love, the Egyptian General Radames, was victorious? Macy didn't glance at Aida or even at Aida's rival, the enraged Amneris. She stared at a woman two rows in front of them who was dabbing at tears with her lace hanky. During scene two, Macy fidgeted numerous times. She kept examining her hands and the small ring over her gloves.

In the opera house lobby at intermission, she smiled at all the women in their finery and the men smoking cigars and gushed, "Isn't it wonderful. So… touching. I have to keep my composure so as not to smudge my makeup." She laughed and looked around the room. Thomas smiled and breathed a sigh.

After the theater, she suggested that they stop at a speakeasy. "It's quite late," Thomas offered.

"But we're having such fun, aren't we?" She countered. So they stopped at a club.

"Why didn't they speak English?" She asked about the opera in the carriage on the way home. "How do you understand what's going on?"

"I'm sorry," he apologized. "I should have found a synopsis for you. During medical school, I was invited to *Rigoletto* and didn't understood a word of Italian, but my benefactor had given me a synopsis on our walk to the Opera House. Next time if I'm unfamiliar with a piece, I'll get the summary." Macy was gazing out the window.

"Why didn't they pick a prettier woman for the main lady? There are so many women with gorgeous hair and makeup and jewelry. With all the beautiful people in New York City, you'd think one could be found who could sing and wear a gown without looking like a sow tied with a ribbon around the middle," Macy blurted out.

"A sow? I hadn't noticed the soprano's size," Thomas apologized. He had closed his eyes as the soprano reached the high notes, sustained them, and tickled the last breath out of the air during the aria. "I'm sorry you didn't like it."

She turned her attention to him. "No. I had a delightful evening with you and all the beautiful people and dinner. Thank you."

The next day at his work, he asked a married colleague, "Do you always understand your wife?"

The man had shrugged, "What's to understand?"

Regardless of the opera experience, Thomas and Macy's relationship seemed mutually equitable.

Thomas received a letter from his mother's only brother, whom she adored but didn't see much after marrying and moving from Wisconsin, saying he would like to sell his business to his nephew. The telegram from his widowed uncle arrived the third Friday in April, "Need you immediately Stop Please come Stop Urgent Stop."

He sent a return telegraph reluctantly. "Arriving Sunday Stop Only three days one client Stop." He didn't mention that he had no desire to take over his uncle's business in an area devoid of culture and a dearth of music or theater. He could be gone for a while, especially since management had hired a young man fresh out of business school to work in the store. Thomas and Macy were having their biweekly lunch date when Thomas brought up the trip.

"My uncle is ailing and would like me to take over his business in Wisconsin," Thomas disclosed over lunch. Macy continued to pick at her salad, ate the canned pear but left the lettuce. She didn't touch the spam on her plate.

"Is there something wrong with your lunch?"

"No, I just feel a bit queasy lately. It usually goes away by afternoon." She set her fork down. "Are you thinking of going?"

"I don't want to live or work there, but I think I owe it to my mom's only living relative to give him a hand." Thomas finished his egg salad sandwich and wiped his lips.

"You are still taking me to see the new film with Clark

Gable and Jean Harlow, aren't you?" Macy asked with that cross between a childish pout and a sexy grimace.

The following night they went to see the drama *Red Dust* about a man who ends up carrying on with two women while hunting big game in China. With thunder cracking and the jungle steaming, Clark Gable inevitably had a scalding affair with both Harlow and Astor on screen.

Off screen afterward, Macy entreated Thomas to take her to Delmonico's for a cocktail. Then later, she begged, "Let's see if anyone we know is at the speakeasy," and grasped his elbow with giddy abandon. Several clubs and half a dozen drinks later, Thomas was tipsy. Macy often left her drinks half-finished and insisted on moving on to the next place. Thomas, very aware of the cost, finished each of his. They ended up at a club just down the street from his rooms.

When Macy pleaded, "I'm so tired. I don't feel well. Couldn't I just lie down a moment?" Thomas guided her to his bedroom. Macy considered the sparsely but attractively furnished room. "I feel lightheaded, maybe sick, and constricted." She began to slip out of her dress but got stuck with her head and arms entangled in rayon. Thomas helped her lift the dress over her head, and her breasts pushed against him. They kissed. He wrapped his arms around her, and she rose up on her sling-back shoes in her lacy slip with the pool of blue and pink rayon at their feet. He lifted her. Her shoes and dress remained on the floor, but he gently laid her on his bed.

"Maybe if you rest a moment," his voice husky, his breathing short and quick. "You'll feel better." He straightened away from her.

"No," she protested. "Don't leave me." Macy reached for him with her slender white arms and pulled him toward her. She unbuttoned his shirt slowly and ran her delicate hands across his bare chest and sighed softly. Thomas held her against him tightly and felt the heaving of her small firm breasts, which she had released from her brassiere. He did what came naturally, and, when he finished, they slept soundly.

The next morning, Macy was gone before Thomas awoke or his landlady had risen. He didn't see her for several days, and when he did stop by her aunt's apartment, he was informed she wasn't available.

The next time he saw her, two weeks later, was after he'd received a second urgent request from his uncle. Thomas was tentative, solicitous, and awkward around Macy, and she was reserved but poised, self-assured. Neither spoke of that night.

"I don't want to go, but I feel obliged. I'll be back within a week." He fully intended to do just that—help his uncle, then return to New York to resume his real job and create a family by marrying Macy Jergenson.

Macy was nonchalant. "I'll miss you, but you'll be back soon. We can talk then."

The first Saturday in May after burying a fifty-six-year-old farmer who'd resided just outside his uncle's town of Turtle Lake, he returned to Macy who had news. "I think I'm pregnant. I know it hasn't been that long since we were together, but I'm as regular as clockwork."

Thomas proposed on the spot even though he had regretted his behavior that night last month, and she rose on her tiptoes and accepted his proposal with a kiss. He was a man who assumed responsibility for his behavior; he was a gentleman.

His uncle's third telegram cited another very sick person in the Turtle Lake area who was dying and implored Thomas to return as soon as possible. He arrived the morning of the barn dance and was convinced to attend as the invalid had temporarily rallied. Thomas ended up staying for ten days and helping the local doctor.

When he went home to New York the fourth week of May, he arrived a day earlier than Macy expected, and he decided to surprise her. She was walking out of her aunt's apartment arm in arm with a tall, handsome, expensively dressed man. Intent on each other, they didn't see Thomas at the end of her block, and the attractively dressed couple stepped into a taxi. The next day when he had been expected to arrive and had arrangements to meet her, he mentioned in passing that he had seen her the day before.

She looked indignant then burst into tears. "Are you spying on me? Don't you trust me?" He spent the next few minutes reassuring her as she murmured amidst tears that she had been forced to accompany a distant relative of her aunt's.

"I'm sorry. I'm uneasy. It's my problem. I've been helping my uncle, this doctor, and…this farmer." He turned away from her, but she was already taking his arm and walking toward the park.

"We could talk about the plans for our future," he offered hesitantly.

"Not now," she announced. "Let's listen to the music in the park. You'll have to go back to work after lunch, and I have some appointments to keep."

"I promised my uncle I'd return for the last week of May," he revealed tentatively.

"Okay." She found a bench, which he dusted with his handkerchief.

"I'll be back June third," he promised. He unwrapped their sandwiches, but she was intent on listening to the three men playing their instruments for spare change. During his three weeks in New York that June Thomas attempted to meet with Macy, but she employed various reasons for her absences. He was content to accept her frequent excuses and used the time to work at Hagstrom's setting money aside to bring Claudia back to experience a different world, New York. He'd gone to Wisconsin to accompany her there and back on the train. He intended to return to Hagstrom's to work most of July. Hagstrom's newly hired store worker had married and left to join his father-in-law's business. Thomas was willing to work and save money.

He arrived in New York the last day of June

unannounced. He had not written, telegraphed, or phoned to tell Macy of his return this time. He had not planned on being back in New York so soon, and he had not planned on staying in Wisconsin so long. He had not planned the last two months. He was inhabiting the place in which he found himself. He wasn't considering the roots his actions were planting nor the consequences of abruptly pulling those roots out.

At the last moment Thomas had decided to catch the Chicago Northwest Express to New York even though he would be arriving early the next evening too late to work or call on Macy. When he was walking from the train station, he decided on a whim to stop and purchase a last-minute ticket to a play or concert to settle his mind before going to see Macy the next day. He had decided he wasn't the gentleman he purported to be; he was going to break the engagement.

Everything changed at the concert where fate intervened and made the choice for Thomas. He arrived as the curtain opened. He relaxed into the velvet-cushioned seat for a couple of pleasant hours before he'd have to confess to Macy the next day that he would support her and the baby, but he could not marry her; he did not love her. Claudia would have to decide where her priorities lay. She would have to move on and quit wallowing in her grief and problems.

At intermission, he heard the unmistakable, impatient, high-pitched giggling of Macy. She was in the fourth row center with that same "distant relative" but in a fairly intimate posture, whispering into his ear with her gloved hand caressing his chin. She was wearing her blue dress with the tight bodice and narrow waist. If she were indeed pregnant, she would be three months along and unable to conceal her condition in that dress. He left the theater without talking to her, his boss, or anyone. He went straight to the train station to return to Wisconsin. No one even knew he had left Wisconsin or that he had returned a day later.

12. Weasels and a Gift

Claudia hated the animal. She couldn't understand how Thomas could say he didn't even know what a weasel was. Conniving people were referred to as weasels. Didn't everyone know how sneaky and evasive a weasel was? He had come back to Wisconsin with her on Monday morning after their dreamlike escape to New York, but she hadn't seen him in the past week. She supposed he was helping Doc or maybe someone had died.

She'd returned home to the letter informing her of the mortgage due and fieldwork. She'd only been gone three days, and this past week had been hectic; catching up, taking the futile trip to the banker and RT, and trying to consider all ways to solve the outstanding debt. Conflicting emotions vied for space—a demanding worry over money, caring for her animals, and dealing with crops on one side, while entrancing music, enchanting food, and a seemingly worry-free city seduced her on the other side.

When she awoke the morning of the Fourth of July, a week after their return, there were so many feathers in the small henhouse where the chickens were confined at night that they appeared to be molting. But they weren't. When she saw one of her remaining laying hens drained of blood caught in the chicken wire surrounding the henhouse, she knew. Somehow a weasel had gotten through the wire and into the henhouse. She was agitated and angry all during chores. She should be cultivating the corn today, picking and canning green beans, not spending a chunk of the day trying to keep her remaining five hens safe. The chicks were nowhere to be seen.

Instead of going to the garden to weed, water, and pick, she trudged to the shed to gather a bucket of the necessary tin, wire, nails, and hammer to fix a coop.

She had already filled several inch-sized holes when Thomas arrived as she was poking wire into a hole so small she couldn't get her thumb in the space. She had pieces of tin and several nails scattered on the ground and was pounding with a vengeance over the areas where she'd jammed wire.

"Can I help?" he inquired.

"I can't see how." She sat down on the hard-packed dirt of the enclosed yard surrounding the hen house. He squatted next to her.

"What can we do?"

"Nothing. That's what's so frustrating. I've done everything I can. I lock them in at night. I've covered every hole bigger than a pencil. Did you know that those weasels can fit their body into a hole half as big as they are?"

"How can that be?"

"I'm not sure, but I've caught a stupid one in a trap baited with fresh liver. I couldn't shove his body in the hole he got through, but he did. I think its skeleton can collapse in on itself."

Sympathy resting on his face, Thomas put his hand out to set on her arm.

"It makes me so angry! I do everything I'm supposed to do, and it's never enough. Look what happened! He got one of my hens!" She banged the ground next to her with the bucket. He removed his hand.

"He's just being a weasel. It's not his fault he likes the taste of chicken as much as we do," Thomas offered.

She jumped up, grabbed the bucket, and pushed her hair off her face with the hand clutching a hammer.

"He doesn't eat my hen. He chews off her head, sucks the blood out, and leaves her body lying there." Thomas reached for her arm as she started to march past him.

"I'm sorry," he offered.

"Why? You didn't do anything. It's just life, like you said. He's just being what he is, a weasel. Like the deer eating my apple trees are just being deer. Like Bully getting out and breeding the heifer. I know it. But why? Why?"

He shrugged his shoulders and scrunched his mouth in resignation. "It just is. We have to let it be." She let the bucket drop to the dirt. "I don't want to. I don't want to accept it. I want it different. I can make it different, if I could just figure it out. My father would be able to figure it out."

Silence and dust hung in the heat rising off the bare ground from the noon sun. She felt so vulnerable and unsure. She turned toward him and let the hammer fall. Her father wasn't here and she was beginning to see that her father hadn't always been there the way she had thought. Thomas took her in his arms. She was relieved he didn't say, "But your father isn't here." The tools and wire lay scattered on the ground around them.

"Reality is not a pleasant prospect," admitted Thomas. "In fact, it's quite painful, even if facing it is necessary." She let herself be held, his hands squeezing her shoulders reassuringly, and listened but halfheartedly. She wished she were sitting up behind the Girls cultivating between the rows of short green stalks, the sun warm on her back, and didn't need to think about how to get this darn loan refinanced or settled.

"I had a friend in New York who was a bit sneaky. Like a weasel. I tried to handle the situation with care, but I was the one expecting my friend to be different. I thought my friend was a certain kind of person and proceeded to act on those presumptions and expectations. My friend was just doing whatever was necessary to stay alive in the best way possible within her means. People don't always realize the consequences of their actions on others. Sometimes people need to take drastic steps just to keep themselves safe or to get out of a bad situation."

Claudia couldn't spend any more time doing nothing. She

broke from his arms and began picking up the pieces of bent metal and loose wire she'd been using, trying not to cut herself but jamming them roughly into the pail she used for working around the farmyard.

"I know." She hoisted the bucket onto her arm and a small part of a roll of wire screening onto her shoulder. "I have to just let it go." He reached to take the roll from her as he had tried to help other times. This time she allowed him and let her arms drop. The pail clanged as it fell off her arm and spilled the contents onto the hard-packed dirt.

Claudia scrabbled at the ground, retrieving bits of wire and nails. "I have to pick all this up. If one of the hens or Shep or Tabby found a piece, I would have an expensive vet bill at best and a lost animal at worst." She cut her finger on a sharp corner of metal sheeting and dropped it in the bucket. She couldn't afford any vet bill, or the taxes for that matter, much less the seed for next year or the feed for this winter. The crops were withering in the daily sun and wind.

"I'll pick this up." Thomas set down the roll of wire and began to put the pieces back into the pail. "I thought my friend was one kind of person and reacted to her like that and did things I regret now, but we were both following the path we thought was best. But then things changed for me."

Claudia was shaking her head. "I don't care." She sucked her bleeding finger. "I want to understand, but I don't want to try so hard. They are what they are. It just doesn't matter."

They walked without further words into the house after putting the supplies and tools away in the shed. Thomas left to file paperwork, and Claudia stated she was going to cultivate the corn. After seeing how shrunken the weeds and the corn were, she decided instead to pick and can whatever beans there were.

Claudia hadn't expected anything for her birthday, which was like any other day. One year she made a cake for her father's birthday, but he'd eaten only a small piece, saying he wasn't really hungry for cake. She tried to remember how Thomas even knew her birthday was July 8th.

He presented her with a gold, foil-wrapped gift so thin that she felt uncomfortable even opening it. She unwrapped slowly, as if the box held something unpleasant. It was beautiful and soft, delicate. A cashmere scarf. Why would he think that she would want something so impractical; where on the farm would she have occasion to wear such an extravagance? And how much had it cost him? Claudia's consternation must have shown because she saw disappointment wash down his face.

"It isn't something I could use." *What I could use is several thousands of dollars.* Immediately, shame flooded through her.

"That's the point, Claudia, for you to have something you wouldn't buy yourself. I wanted you to have something special. Not everything needs to be practical."

"But where would I ever wear it? If I needed it, I can buy it myself. I mean, I appreciate the thought and the idea but..." She thought of the few gifts her Papa had gotten her—a pocketknife when she turned eleven. She had felt proud he had trusted her enough to buy her a grown-up tool. Sure, Vivian had given her a nightgown of satin and lace that she had worn until the cuffs rode up at her elbows and the hem rose to her knees. But that was from a woman, an "almost mom."

This was impractical, expensive, and from a man who wasn't a family member. Was he frivolous with money? Did she *really* know him? She didn't even feel comfortable enough to discuss the looming money problem, yet she had felt comfortable enough to go to an opera and sightseeing in New York with him. What was she thinking?

She set the gift on the edge of the table and put her hands in her lap. Thomas lifted the scarf from among the filmy tissue and settled it gently around her neck. A subtle dark claret red thread ran through the deep bronze and gold of the scarf.

"You deserve to have a gift without it being practical. Besides, it is useful. You can wear the scarf to church, to keep you warm." With that he picked up her hands from her lap. Claudia raised her head like a puppet whose arms and head moved in unison. Her eyes were brimming with angry tears.

She was not angry at Thomas, she realized, but at herself for feeling like this and for crying. She hated to cry and hated to be seen crying. Mostly she hated that she felt like this—that she didn't deserve a useless gift, a gift that was so soft and thin and luxurious she wanted to stroke it. Her fingers were used to her materials: burlap, canvas, and sturdy cotton.

The scarf's physical weight was light on her. Even here in her kitchen it made her feel like a lady. It lay on her like a lie. She could smell the store it came from, rich and exotic, not Ernie's store, not even from the catalogue. This smelled of city women in high heels and furs. That's why it was wrong. She pulled the scarf off more slowly than she wanted. She didn't belong in a scarf like this.

"Thank you, Thomas. It is lovely and thoughtful of you." He didn't reply. He was gazing toward the oil lamp hung on the wall. Was he thinking about the upcoming month of work in New York? Her hand set the item back in its nest of tissue. She removed the steaming hot kettle from the stove and poured the water into the sink, then raised the pump handle and brought it down once. A short stream of water from the cistern ran into the sink where their coffee cups and cake plates waited. She stood in front of the window above the sink, her hand still on the pump handle, contemplating the pasture and fields.

The small frosted cake Thomas had brought would have been enough. They had enjoyed the cake's lightness. He called the smooth, firm frosting marzipan, which she repeated in her head to find in her cookbook, planning to make sometime. Later she would see the recipe required an almond paste which she had no idea how to make, buy, or order.

They had sipped their coffee and eaten the cake with delight, chatting and enjoying the break from routine and thoughts that could wait. Outside the window, she saw large birds circling in the sky. She couldn't determine whether they were eagles or vultures. The day had been spoiled, Claudia thought, when Thomas had pulled the slender, wrapped box from under his jacket on the chair. All of it was too much. She plunged her hands into the sink. She pulled them back. The water was hotter than she expected. She usually paid closer attention.

13. Rottman's Football Fundraiser

The football field fundraiser, managed by Randy and Penny Rottman, was held at the Rice Lake Eagles Lodge the Friday following the Fourth of July. The summer season was well underway, and the city council, on which Randy sat, had arranged for fireworks that evening for the locals and seasonal vacationers alike. They'd hoped to attract Chicago travelers to the benefit. They would discharge fanning displays of scintillating colored stars, punctuated by M80 booms, and fiery eruptions of red, yellow, and green shooting rockets over the lake to the oohs and aahs of the folks seated on the grass hoping for a cooling breeze off the water. The weather was volatile—hot and unpredictable, much like the economic climate of the state and country. If the poor were asked, they observed fortune was arbitrary. If the rich were asked, they believed things were a bit unstable at present.

Everything was changeable. Land prices that had consistently appreciated now plummeted as farmers lost their land when at market they received less than the cost to raise their crops and animals. Change would soon become the constant.

The production and consumption of hard liquor had been outlawed. Despite Prohibition, beer with a low alcohol content was legal to drink in Wisconsin, and moonshine was produced in backyards and woodlots. There were no teeth in the enforcement of Prohibition as of 1929. Soon, Prohibition throughout the country would be changed, too. The average Wisconsinite thought politicians were fickle and capricious.

Prohibition didn't cause anyone to go thirsty that summer or at the Eagles Lodge fundraiser. The chief of police was out of sight. Randy and Penny had separated at the Lodge's entrance to divide, conquer, and crack any nuts that were tightfisted with their dollars. They were priming the pump for the live auction to be held shortly and were encouraging everyone to raise their bids on the silent auction items. Golf clubs and porcelain vases were set up on the tables around the perimeter of the wood-paneled room. Men in dark suits and women in semiformal dresses gathered in groups clutching drinks and balancing petite plates. Some leaned over the side tables adding their names to auction items they didn't need or even want.

Penny had been making the rounds in the banquet room to all the locals and a few men with cabins on the larger lakes who had plenty of disposable income. Those with money who hadn't lost everything in The Crash were able to scoop up land and businesses on the cheap and eventually reap the profits from others' misfortunes. An attractive middle-aged man with a younger but equally enticing woman on his arm entered the main room from the lobby. Penny glided over to them, motioning a server with a tray of drinks to approach.

With warm familiarity, she kissed the man on the cheek, "Tony, how good to see you. What an unexpected delight! Did you come up from Chicago for our little Do?" She glanced at Tony, but her eyes lingered on the stunning blond on his arm. She offered drinks from the tray to Tony and his friend each choosing a cut-crystal glass. Tony put his manicured hand around a weighty old-fashioned tumbler holding an inch of deep amber, and his friend slipped her fingers around a long-stemmed wine flute as sleek as herself that held a liquid as drained of color as her platinum hair.

"We came up to stay at the cottage. I thought I'd stop and see what you were up to. Bill informed me about your shindig, and I thought I'd check in on my old high school classmates." Tony eyes went from Penny's hair, down her dress, and ended with her shoes. "You've done quite well for yourself." She tugged slightly at her dress and extended a hand to Tony's companion, "Hello, I'm Penelope Rottman. Tony and I went to school together with my husband Randolph."

"Randolph!" Tony drew himself slightly back, eyes wide, and studied her face. He made a slight nod. "Excuse my poor manners, this is my date, Bridget." Tony and Penny relaxed into a conversation of past classmates. She mentioned how much certain members of their mutual acquaintance had already contributed toward the fundraiser.

Bill and his wife approached their small group with drinks in hand. The copious man held a small plate of assorted hor d'oeuvres from which he periodically plucked and popped a delicacy into his mouth. Tony made the polite introductions. Penny made her excuses and slipped over to talk with the father of the young man who'd delivered the sharecroppers' rent. She approached the man as his wife left him to go to the restrooms.

"John, how good to see you! Your son has been invaluable to Randolph." She touched his arm and leaned in conspiratorially, her green eyes flashing brightness. "We need good men to keep this Country going. You and your contributions toward the athletic field are examples to our young people of community service and the rewards of Christian living. Our success and prosperity demonstrates God showering his blessings on us. I saw your name on several silent auction items, but you'll need to go back. I'm afraid some other good soul thinks they are more deserving. That painting of the eagles over the river would make a wonderful statement in your home and please your wife." She lightly squeezed his arm and tipped slightly forward, revealing a lovely, tanned cleavage. She smiled, left his side, turned to another more prominent man, and began her pitch again.

As Penelope left, he, like many of the men present, wished their wives would, or could, wear hip-hugging, breast-caressing designer clothes like the tight red, shimmering outfit Penelope was wearing. Watching her sway and dip around the room, several men felt like kids in a pastry shop who'd enjoy putting their hands around her puff pastries and giving a squeeze. John adjusted his trouser leg and went to get a plate of those tiny, bite-sized delicacies he saw circulating the room, but he upped his bid on the painting Penelope mentioned before he left the area. She smiled at him from across the room as he signed his name to the sheet under the large oil painting donated by a local artist.

The banker and Tony had been watching the staging of events. They, like many men, secretly thought and fleetingly feared that Penny was a bit of a crotch cruncher, but they continued their sticky attraction to her because they enjoyed the eye and nose feast.

"Penelope's social skills match Randy's shrewd business sense," commented Bill as he selected a bacon-wrapped bite from his plate. "He may believe he can corkscrew his way into heaven, but he does get a lot done in our community and the surrounding small towns while he greases his own wheels."

"I'm not sure Randy Rottman believes in a heaven. I think the only life that exists for him is the here and now." Tony proceeded to tell the banker of a time when Randy was working for his soon-to-be father-in-law and closing a deal on prime development property. Randy secretly had a contingency agreement that allowed him first option on another parcel of which his father-in-law wasn't aware.

Tony swirled the last of his alcohol and tossed the liquid heat to the back of his mouth. "Granted, his father-in-law came out as good as he'd expected, but Randy resembles a bottom-feeding fish, smoothly, quietly blending into the background doing what is expected." The paunchy banker stood listening intently. Bill's wife had left their group and joined two other women in her social circle held at bay by Randy's charm.

Tony continued as the two men studied Randy, while Bridget stood impassive. "But when Randy sees the opportunity, he can change tone and demeanor to become the unobtrusive piranha gobbling up property and resources in the mass accumulation of whatever strikes his fancy. He wasn't content to be a small fish in his father-in-law's big pond in Chicago."

"He's considered a big fish here." Bill finished the last of his hor d'oeuvres, pressed his finger over the smoked salmon flake on his plate, and stuck the morsel in his mouth.

"You should have seen him in grade school—a gawky, skinny kid with a long, thin nose too big for his face." Tony removed another drink from the salver of a passing young server, and Bill put his now empty plate on the server's tray. Randy had a triangular form—wide shoulders narrowed to a small waist and firm derriere.

"He definitely grew into the nose, and the women seem to like him fine. My wife plays tennis and golf with him and his wife. She said his swing is forceful, and he hits with accuracy," imparted the banker. Tony compared Bill to his younger, more fit wife.

"I'm not much for either of the activities. I'm too busy." Bill thrust his shoulders back.

Randy's group of laughing women, of which Bill's wife was the one closest to Randy and laughing the hardest after Randy related some little tale, were obviously enjoying Randy's attention. Randy put his hand on the arm of Bill's wife and on the arm of the woman on his other side and begged to be excused. "I can't monopolize the attention of you lovely ladies. I have to allow some of these other men a share in your delightful charm and wit."

With that he turned and walked to the wife of a current client with whom he had a deal in progress.

Watching his former classmate work the room, Tony admitted, "He turns his warm beam of attention onto every woman and ignites their libido. He had to learn at an early age how to circumvent a woman's power." The banker peered quizzically at Tony, who paused, considered the banker then proceeded rapidly.

"His mother was a control freak, a passive manipulator. As a kid, I was in their house several times. She conveyed to him nothing was his fault. If a problem existed, the setback was because the teacher or the other kid didn't appreciate her son's creativity and uniqueness. Yet I heard her constantly telling him he didn't do things the way she wanted. I think she was a frustrated old biddy, and he figured out flattery got him more ground than going against her."

Tony stepped out the side door. Bridget was busy listening to Randy in a small cluster of fans. A cloud of cigarette smoke encircled Tony as the heavy door closed behind him. He waved his hand and saw Penny, her long, lithe body leaning against the building, head tipped back exposing her smooth-as-milk neck, her right leg bent, and her scarlet high heel swinging on her seamed-stockinged toes. She saw him, and her eyes hardened. She straightened herself, planted both feet firmly on the ground, and crushed the cigarette under the toe of her shoe.

"Well," he announced in surprise. "I never knew."

"Neither does Randy, and I want to keep it that way." She fanned her hand in front of her face to dissipate the remaining smoke curls, and her eyes softened once again.

"He doesn't know?" inquired Tony.

"I think he does, but, if he never sees me, I never have to admit it."

"What does he care if you smoke?" They had started to walk out under the sprawling oaks that surrounded the Lodge.

"Unladylike, not befitting people who care about their bodies, their community, and the image presented to others." She arched her back in a cat stretch and gazed up at the stars. "How many do you think there are?"

"I haven't a clue." He studied her rounded hips under the clingy red fabric. "But not enough to outshine the one in front of me." He ran his eyes up her torso, passed across her red lips, then landed on her emerald eyes.

She peered at him.

"I could take Bridget home with an excuse to return to the Lodge on business," he offered.

"I have to get inside to insure the auction goes as planned…and my life with Randy and Andrew. They may not be perfect, but I don't need perfection. I do want and have stability." She revolved away from him and started back to the Lodge door. "Be sure to come back and bid on that weekend getaway at Stout Island." She turned and stared pointedly at him, "You'd love it, whoever you take."

146

14. A Bear Story

Claudia had kept the incident of the bear to herself. The Monday after she had gotten the scarf as a gift from Thomas, she went into town to purchase more canning salt and lids and twine for bundling her oats. She wanted intelligent, female conversation. Vivian was sorting mail when Claudia entered. Ernie was nowhere in sight, and the only one other customer left shortly without a purchase.

"Mrs. Andersen didn't need anything?" asked Claudia.

"She came in to see if there was any word from her brother who'd gone out to California, but no letter." Vivian, perched on her high-legged chair, swept her hand across the remaining mail strewn on the counter. Percy was swinging slowly and rhythmically. He kept his target eyes on his mistress. Claudia liked Percy and his vocalizations, but he rarely sang when there were too many people in the store. When there was a lot of talking, he would sometimes chatter. His talk was unintelligible, but Vivian claimed she could understand him. If Claudia listened carefully, she recognized Ernie's buddies—Bruno's deep bass cadences and, even though the words weren't clear, the lilting clip of Klive's voice. For the moment Percy was silent and seemed to be listening to them.

Vivian expounded on the poor Chinese farmer's life in *The Good Earth*, her latest read. Then Claudia confided, "I had a visitor last week. A bear." Without going into too much detail, Claudia disclosed her fear at the encounter.

"Oh, I need rat poison and some kind of smoke bomb. Something for varmits to scare them away." Vivian got down from the high-legged chair where she was sitting, working on next month's supply order. She stepped up on the wheeled ladder hung on the side of the tall shelves and climbed to the top where they stocked the poisons and traps, high on a top shelf out of the reach of curious children.

"What's the problem?" Vivian's thin hand brushed at her tight graying curls. She peered down at Claudia and reached for poison.

"I've got something under my one shed. Hole is as big as a prize watermelon. Seemed like a woodchuck, so I waited until I thought he was gone, and I filled in the two holes and patched the rock foundation, but now he's gone to the other side and chewed a board lose from under the stoop."

"Sounds too persistent for a woodchuck. Maybe it's a rat. Have you thought of using a trap?" Vivian rolled further down to where the traps were hung.

"I'm not sure I want to do that. What if Shep or Tabby put their noses into the contraption even with my best efforts of making it inaccessible to them? Poison I can put down the hole at night and cover out of Shep or Tabby's reach."

Vivian rolled back to the poison and brought down the box with the illustration of a rat with skull and crossbones below the rodent.

"I'll be gone for a day or two. I'm going to look into getting a loan on my cattle," Claudia conveyed quietly.

Vivian set the box on the counter, moved to her parakeet's cage, opened the door, put her hand inside, and stroked Percy's head.

"If that's what you want to do." Vivian continued to gently ruffle the budgie's head feathers as he cocked his head side to side, so she could reach all around his neck and head with her index finger.

"Traipsing to Rice Lake is not what I want to do. What I want has nothing to do with anything. This is what I need to do." Claudia snatched up the box of poison, canning lids, and salt and laid the correct change on the counter. "Besides, not everyone gets to do what they want to do. Some folks have

148

to just eat the dish that is served them." Vivian arched her eyebrows but didn't say a word.

"I know what you're thinking," Claudia declared over her shoulder as she left. "'We make our own life.' Well, that's fine to think, but it doesn't always work."

"Whatever you say." Percy stepped off Vivian's finger onto the perch, and Vivian pulled her hand slowly from the gilded cage.

As she left, Claudia heard Ernie emerge from the back room where he'd been busy prying open crates of hardware, but Claudia didn't think much of his presence until she returned to the store later. She'd been so agitated earlier that she'd forgotten the twine for binding her oats. The neighbors were hoping to thresh later next week.

Ernie was joking with reserved Klive and boisterous Bruno who'd stopped in to pick up their mail. Ernie continued as Claudia walked in and over to Percy's cage next to the counter where Vivian had set the twine.

"Did you hear the one about the bohunk to his neighbor the Pollock?" Ernie asked his buddies. "No? He says 'Do you know the difference between a bathroom and a parlor?' The Pollock says, 'No.' 'Then remind me not to invite you to my house.'" Ernie placed both hands on his abundant belly and laughed while hands, belly, and chest bounced with each chuckle. Claudia, who was feeding Percy a seeded cracker, ignored him. She was cocooned from worry by the man's carefree chatter.

"Did you boys hear about the visitor Claudia had out to her place?" She could feel a tease coming on. Ever since she was little and had come into the store with her father, Ernie liked to tease her. Afterward he had usually offered her a striped peppermint stick from the jar on the counter. She hadn't been teased by him since the death of her father.

"Are you sure it was a black bear that visited you the other day?" Ernie queried. She considered him and his two buddies, wondering what he was talking about.

He smiled and turned toward Claudia and the parakeet, "Maybe it was a Hog-Thorny Bear?" She viewed him blank faced. He spread his feet wide, hands on his hips, and began. She'd find out later from Vivian that Ernie had heard the ballad after landing in the United States, had memorized the tale, and dramatized it earning himself several free meals with folks hungry for entertainment on their way west.

"I call the attention of each merry blade.
Be still as a mouse and let nothing be said.
I'll sing you a song it will please you to hear,
How lately two men had a fray with a bear."

Claudia watched him extend his arms to include those present as the "merry blades." But on the next two lines he pointed with exaggerated emphasis to his two buddies who were listening and smiling in anticipation. He made a somber face when he described the men.

"It was one Tabor Coombs and Sam Esterbrooks,
They were not very handsome but quite clever folks.
'Twas on Turkey Mountain, I think it was there,
They had such a terrible fray with the bear."

On the last line he drew his stubby neck into his hunched shoulders and held his arms close to his sides, hands in front curved forward, fingers like claws, in imitation of a fierce bear.

"One evening as they were returning from work,
'Twas through the thick forest so dreary and mirk,
Said one to the other 'I'm not without fear
That ere we reach home we shall meet with a bear.'"

Ernie made mincing steps and widened his eyes in feigned fear. Claudia, who was used to Ernie's antics, watched interested but confused.

"With these apprehensions and while they were fresh
They heard a loud clambering noise in the brush.
The dog he did bark and erect stood his hair,
And both cried at once, 'Behold, there is a bear.'"

This last he imparted with such gusto that Percy started up a squawk unlike his usual chatter chorus to Ernie's stories. Vivian cooed to him and Claudia reassured, "It's only Ernie; it's okay," but she began to wonder if he had heard about her episode with a bear. Vivian wouldn't have betrayed her confidence. When would Vivian have had the opportunity? Claudia dismissed her fears. Ernie was just being Ernie.

Ernie stretched to his full five-foot, six-inches and brandished an imaginary axe.

"'Tis the nature of bears to slaughter for pelf,
But seeing two rivals look worse than himself,
He sprang to a hemlock and at them did stare,
Then with great dexterity, up went the bear.

"Then straightway to chopping, our heroes they went,
To cut down the hemlock, it was their intent.
He bowed his long head, his tail waved in air.
The tree tumbled down and the dog caught the bear.'"

Ernie pretended to fell a tree and then proceeded to act like a dog, flinging his head side to side as if attacking something. Ernie was spreading the yarn before them like a banquet tablecloth. Claudia had the uneasy feeling that she was the main course.

"The dog from the battle soon fled in defeat.
The bear in the forest soon made a retreat.
Then homeward these two old farmers did steer
To pluck out the quills of the hog-thorny bear!'"

Claudia couldn't believe her ears. How had Ernie known that she'd confronted a bear and Shep hadn't saved her? Then she remembered this morning when he'd stepped from the backroom. She felt a hot flush begin at her neck. Ernie threw his head back and laughed. Bruno and Klive followed their laughter with such slapping of backs and grabbing of shoulders they would have fallen if not supported by each other. Claudia would've been glad if they'd landed on their backsides and had their attention diverted.

The two women regarded each other. Ernie did have a way of spinning out a good story even if she was the source of the joke.

He turned to the two women. "Are you sure it was a bear, Claudia?" Then he turned back to his friends, "Maybe it was a Hog-Thorny Bear?" Ernie teasing her was torment enough, but then his two friends started in.

"Now don't feel bad, Claudia. See here these two farmers, men with axes, were abandoned by their dog and left to deal with a Hog-Thorny Bear," Klive piped in, intending to reassure.

"When was it your old Shep had that run-in with a porky pine?" Barrel-chested Bruno elbowed Klive. In a whisper loud enough for all to hear, he added, "About the same time I reckon. Can she tell the difference between a bear and a porky pine?"

That was it. As if she didn't have enough on her plate, she didn't need to be reminded that she wasn't up to the task of taking care of or even recognizing a threat. Claudia pulled open the screen door and walked out with her twine roll under her arm as Vivian's hand reached for her, and Ernie began his plea, "It's only a joke."

Only a joke? Her life felt like a joke. *Wasn't he the joke?* The wagon and her supplies bumped along the state road that had been recently graded, so the holes weren't as deep, and she didn't need to watch so carefully to avoid them. She let her mind wander.

Ernie claimed to have come over on "the boat," as if it were the *Mayflower*, hidden in a sack of veg. As a child she had pictured his round balding head sticking out of a burlap bag amongst potatoes, carrots, turnips, and rutabagas. *He wouldn't want to be far from food.* Sitting on the floor of his store, she had heard Ernie tell a few friends at cards how the voyage to the new country "really" happened. The captain of the ship lost to Ernie in a card game, and they'd settled on passage to America to wipe the debt clean. The captain had probably listened to so many of Ernie's jokes and stories that he agreed to take Ernie on the ship just as entertainment. She for one was tired of his good-natured humor, his head thrown back laughing, hands and forearms resting on his bowl belly, which was swathed in two yards of stark white cloth hung from his almost invisible neck, the apron tied at the back of his tremendous tummy. She was tired of his optimism.

Ernie claimed to have lived the high life at the start of the voyage, eating nightly in the captain's room. The greater the expanse of sea between the ship and Ernie's home, the more remote the captain became, until Ernie had to pull his own weight by swabbing decks with the crew. Ernie recounted he hadn't minded. He was getting bored drinking rum and playing cards all day. He'd been a frisky young lad.

She turned off the state road, down the town road that had not been graded. *Why had Ernie left his own country, whatever country that was? Had he seen an opportunity to leave a land of upheaval and change to come to a country that promised much to many? My great-grandparents did that years before Ernie.*

Her father had told her that the year Ernie arrived, the century had turned, and he had put on different surnames and precise country of origin as if trying on clothes. Had he been a Jew or a Cossack or just a peasant or had there been a youthful run-in with the authorities? Political unrest throughout Europe caused borders to shift. Her father had told her they were fortunate to have been born in America. *Maybe Ernie had had to leave because of girl trouble.*

Not just anyone could arrive in Wisconsin with only his wits and determination and succeed. But Ernie had. Claudia had to admit that much.

He'd started up his store in an old shed that doubled as his home and turned the shop into a thriving, if modest, business that served the community. He obtained a small mortgage from RT after he married a Native American woman and turned the shed into a proper store with his home in the back. He even got the post office job for which everyone was grateful. Marriage had settled him. While Ernie punctuated life with playfulness, his wife glided quietly in the background. Ernie had gotten quieter after his reserved wife passed away three years ago. As a teenager, Claudia had heard the women whisper that the loss of several babies by miscarriage tended to silence a woman or drive her mad. Ernie's wife became quieter and more withdrawn as the years had passed, but she'd never seemed crazy to Claudia, although she kept to herself in proportion to Ernie's gregariousness. By Ernie's attentiveness and gentle manner toward her when she came from the recessed rooms where they lived behind the store, town folk remarked how much he doted on her. At community potluck dinners she brought either a wild rice and wild mushroom hot dish or a tomato noodle goulash. Sometimes both.

Once when Mrs. Johnson had advised, "That's not necessary, Mrs. Tomah," Ernie had maintained, "I had a hankering for goulash, and the Missus had already gathered the spring mushrooms, so you all get the best of both worlds."

While she was alive, he had compensated for her silence by being more talkative but less audacious than when he was single. Now his humor had tempered, swinging from sentimental to superficial. Claudia tired of being the butt of his jokes, but by the time she had put the horse and wagon away, her mind returned to bundling oats, canning, and poisoning a varmit, and left off speculating foolishly and feeling sorry for herself.

15. Claudia to Her Papa

Oh Papa,

I never thought I'd ever be running the farm alone. I never expected you to die. Well, not until you were old, until we both were old. I didn't think much about it. We were busy. When you wanted me to like one of the neighboring farm boys, I thought you wanted grandchildren.

You wanted a legacy, a name, and a farm. You wanted me safely married to a capable man strong enough to work hard, take care of me. I work hard, but I don't have your passion, your drive. I love this place because you loved it. I lie here wanting Thomas beside me, not George's son who kissed me like a nursing calf.

I pretend to be so strong and competent and confident. I'm scared I will lose this farm. You saved it through the stock market crash and now when things should be easier, I can't make ends meet, and I work all the time. I'm not sure I want the farm to succeed. If I fail I could leave and start fresh somewhere else. Like that hobo. I should have had him stay, had him help me for room and board. I've made so many mistakes. Maybe I should find mother's people in Massachusetts or go west to California like the Meiser boy.

I think you would like Thomas. He's a good worker. He doesn't know much about farming, but he can learn. I don't think you'd approve of him for going to the city constantly, spending money like water, and going out to eat at the drop of a hat. I can't help that I like his attention. You were proud of what I could do and that I read books, not just newspapers. I don't need to drive a team or fix machinery or repair buildings to impress Thomas. In fact, he worries I might get hurt. He likes me for me.

Thomas likes to do what I do, but he doesn't care about the land. He was just as happy showing me New York. Oh, Papa, I can't help myself. I like New York. I think you would have if you had let yourself just relax and enjoy a big city. Not think about the cost. I didn't. Well, a couple of times I tried to discover the expense. I wanted to know, but Thomas steered me away from seeing at the restaurant. Later, Thomas whisked the opera ticket away, so I couldn't see the price. He revealed knowing the price would interfere with the enjoyment for me. I'm not that tight, am I? We are careful. We come from people who are not foolish with money. Thomas says thrift is good but taken to an extreme is arrogance. How can that be?

I asked him, and he smiled that smile that says, "I like you too much to spoil this moment." I can almost hear him, "It's not my job to change you. I love you just the way you are."

He's said that to me, Papa, and I believe he means it. He loves me just the way I am. Me, who nobody can please.

I think I know what he meant—that thrift could be arrogance. He once revealed to me about overhearing a man in the store who wouldn't pay Ernie the ten dollars for the implement he wanted. Ernie tried to explain about the cost of steel and shipping, but the man went on about his hard labor and how many bushels he had to sell and how he could wait and get it cheaper when he went to St. Paul to see his brother later in the month.

Thomas believed the man was arrogant to think his labor and his time were more valuable than Ernie's. He believed the man was judging Ernie to be a cheat to charge more than the St. Paul store. I had not thought about what was involved for Ernie to have to pay someone to bring his supplies from St. Paul and then to keep the implement oiled and polished at his store and what if the tool broke and he...Oh, Papa, why does it all have to be so complicated? Everything was so much easier when you were here.

I don't understand why you took out a loan. What for? You must have had a good reason. Why didn't you tell me? Did it slip your mind? What was going on this last year? You weren't yourself. There are so many things I need to talk to you about.

Why did you die? I don't understand. You weren't sick. Were you? Why didn't you go see Doc? You seemed distracted but not ill. You should have said something. After examining your body, Doc and Thomas told me you must have had a heart attack. How am I supposed to manage? I'm stuck doing all the work alone.

I worked side by side with you. I put up with you making all the major decisions, even the ones that should have been mine. You manipulated me to your way and only allowed me veto power. I'm so angry I'd like to shake you back to life. Everything was for you and the farm. I don't think you appreciated all I did.

I finally have someone in my life who treats me like a woman, who loves me for just being me without having to earn that love. He calls me beautiful. I've never been beautiful. Too tall and too muscular. A tomboy. In his arms, I feel beautiful, protected, and peaceful.

I only wanted to be loved, for you to tell me I was worthwhile. I'm so angry I could spit tacks. I want to break something, anything, just to hear and see it destroyed. That would feel good. And I would not clean up the mess. I am tired of cleaning up after you, and now I won't ever have to again. I'm glad to be rid of your greasy equipment parts, your coat dropped on the chair, the stubbles from your shaving left on the edge of the wash bowl.

I'll never have to get your opinion or permission. I'll buy an expensive dress if I want, even if we are in debt. Who cares about money, anyway? It didn't safeguard a future. It didn't protect or keep people from leaving when you least expect and have done nothing wrong. How could a child in need of a mother have done something so wrong that God would take my mother from me? Now you're gone, and Thomas has gone back to New York.

I don't want to end up like old man Meiser's daughter!

I want to crawl into bed and pull the covers over me and keep the world out.

Papa, what am I supposed to do?

16. Old Man Meiser's Daughter

Miss Meiser had given up her prospects for a life of her own to care for her father after her brother left them high and dry. When their mother had died the summer of 1919, the Allies and Germans had just signed the Treaty of Versailles. World War I was ended, and Mr. O'Brien Sr. had returned with his lungs gassed while serving in France. But a smaller war of wills had begun on Meiser's farm years before the ramifications reverberated to the present for Meiser and O'Brien.

To keep the two dozen Guernsey cows milked and the house going took all three of them: father, daughter, and son. Mr. Meiser believed his son would eventually take over the care of the farm, and his daughter would take over the care of him. The taciturn son, like his father, avoided conversation, but did not follow his father's desire. Instead at the age of twenty he took off in 1921 for California without a word, only leaving a scrap of paper, "No more manure. No more milking. Sunny California here I come," tacked up to one of the round posts supporting the loft floor in their cavernous barn. The father insisted that he and his daughter carry on as usual.

A few years passed, the miserly, recluse father became sick, and the bulk of the chores and the household burdens fell on the daughter's shoulders. Miss Meiser suggested they hire one of the Johnson boys to help. Mr. Meiser refused to pay someone for what they could do themselves. He struggled to help her but spent more days in bed than in the barn.

Vivian called that irony, as he had always spent more in time and money on the barn than the house. The house was no great prize. Although he never expressed his bias, he showed by his purchases and use of time and energy that the barn, where the money was made, was more important. The house was just a place to eat and sleep. And in truth, the couple and their two children did spend most of their day and evening in the barn. As time passed, the increasingly frail Mr. Meiser spent more hours in the merely adequate house.

When father and daughter weren't able to keep up, they sold all but a dozen cows, which included eight milking cows, three dry, and one that shortly thereafter died of milk fever after a difficult calving. When she came in from chores one day, Miss Meiser found her father sprawled on the stairs on his way to the outhouse. He had refused her attempts to move his bed to the first floor. After she cleaned him up, he demanded she carry him up the steep, narrow stairs to recover in their bedrooms under the eaves. She tripped in the turn of the landing and fell, cushioning her father, who fell on top of her.

He convinced her the injury was superficial. They didn't need to go to the doctor or bother him to make a house call. After two days her pain convinced him she needed medical help. They bounced their way in the buckboard to see the doctor in Turtle Lake, who immediately sent for an ambulance to take her to the Rice Lake hospital. Her leg was fractured. While in the hospital she developed an infection and died three weeks later at the age of twenty-seven.

In 1925 after his daughter's untimely death, Mr. Meiser sold all but four of his cows to pay for the medical bills. He tried to milk the four remaining cows. The milk hauler picked up his one milk can, but the milk check he got barely covered his scant expenses. Then came a godsend. In 1927 the sharecroppers who had noticed the fallow field out front stopped and asked to rent it to raise vegetables for their family, for sale, and for Mr. Meiser's use. They came to an arrangement that satisfied both parties. The dirt farmer's wife brought enough dinner to drop off some for the old man each time they came to work the field. Mr. Meiser sold his final four cows, which were so thin and boney they stumbled up the ramp into the knacker's truck. The weak bovines would only fetch a cutter-canner price, good for tinned beef stew and canned soup.

Shortly after that, a letter from the son in California crossed postmistress Vivian's counter and was delivered to Mr. Meiser, who dictated a response. Folks speculated times must be hard even in golden California, for the son was thinking about coming back. The son never responded after learning his sister was dead and his father ailing. Only when the attorney found the son's letter, after the old man passed away, was he able to trace Meiser's only living relative, who was more than happy to sell the farm to Randy Rottman.

The barn, which hadn't been full of cows for over ten years since the son left, had only four cows in it for two years, and then nothing in it for five years. In those years the loft hadn't had enough hay or straw to warrant the trap doors being left open for frequent access. Little to no moisture or heat escaped into the loft. The barn dried out like a desiccated beetle.

Although the house was in desperate need of repair, Randy offered it to the O'Brien family, who had lost their farm but could rent Meiser's house with the little money they were able to salvage from their foreclosure. Mr. O'Brien Sr. had passed away, but his son, daughter-in-law, and their seven young children moved into Meiser's small, three-bedroom home.

17. The Other Woman

The short train trip transported Claudia from Turtle Lake on the Minneapolis Sault Ste. Marie line to Barron where she transferred to the Chicago St Paul Minneapolis and Omaha line to Rice Lake. Threshing would start next week. She had a window of time for this trip midweek.

Claudia's first visit to see the banker and RT had been unpleasant and unsatisfactory. If they would not refinance the current loan amount, she would have to reduce it. She would appeal to the cattlemen to whom her father had gone. She had been to the city numerous times with her father to negotiate the sale or purchase of cattle or occasionally the bulk purchase or sale of grain or feed. She wished she had gone with him as an adult, so that she would know better what to do and how to do it.

She had made arrangements to meet the man her father had dealt with for years. Out of her usual coveralls and boots, she wore a lace-collared dress, light sweater, and heeled shoes. When the man shook her hand, he leered into her face and across her chest, which was level with his. With a firm grip he pulled her hand close to his side, forcing her to step into him. She tried to extricate herself, glancing around his workspace for relief. The looks and whispered exchanges by several men were no comfort. The only female she had seen was a drab receptionist in the front office who was typing madly. Now Claudia was deep in the bowels of the high-ceilinged building that smelled like the inside of Ernie's World War I foot locker.

"Well, haven't you developed into quite the woman!" The man was just younger than her father. "No pretty *little* thing anymore, are we?"

Claudia's face turned red.

She tried to summon her earlier confidence, painfully aware that she was without anyone to cushion, insulate, or protect her. Were businessmen always like this? Or could this man feel her vulnerability? She needed him. Claudia felt the alert that was instinctive to her horses. They put their ears back and their nostrils flared around people who set their nerves on edge. Dandy or Molly often alerted her to a fox in the brush or a human of less than savory character. She pulled her hand away forcibly, and the man stood straighter, stiffer, and unsmiling.

He resumed his seat behind his metal desk, busied himself with papers strewn across its surface. "You wanted to discuss a sale and repurchase in a year or so?"

"Yes, I need cash immediately. A slight unanticipated cash flow problem. Temporary." Claudia pulled up a folding chair and sat across from him as he shuffled and scribbled errant notes. Her father's firm words came back to her from recent years.

"The business isn't a two-person job. What's most efficient, makes the most sense, is for you to stay home." Had her father wanted to protect his young adult daughter from the unwanted attention of men like this? She had remained home and done chores. He had gone alone, and if "negotiations didn't go as planned" he would stay overnight, talk again in the morning, and return later the next day. She straightened her back and pulled the front of her light sweater close together.

"The farm is doing very well. We just, I need to get through…"

The cattleman interrupted her, peering directly into her eyes, "I'm afraid a single, inexperienced lady is not a sound financial bet. If you want to sell outright, we'll give you the going rate for poundage."

"But I'm talking about our breeding stock." She thrust her back upright and leaned forward. "Not some cutter-canner I could ship locally." She clutched her hands in her lap. "If I could sell some cows, or even heifers, now and buy them back in…"

Again, the man interrupted and this time, with a paper in hand, he stood to deliver his words of dismissal.

"We are not a bank. We could afford to be flexible when we were dealing with a man like your father. A man we had a business history with. We could take a risk with him. Here's the paper you need to sign, if you want to sell. We can give a little, considering the quality of your father's cattle. Let me know how many and when. I'll have a cattle jockey get them." With that he sat down and picked up his phone. She didn't want to leave the matter at that. She needed to eat and think.

Claudia stopped at a near-by gas station and asked for Nora's Restaurant and Rooms. Her father had talked about a "dinner room." As a teenager Claudia had imagined her father going to a room that had dinner set on a special tray waiting for the occupant. Her father described the place as a small diner with a few rooms to rent at the back and a couple of rooms above where the owner lived.

"They no longer rent rooms. Salespeople stay at the new hotel," the gas station attendant informed Claudia. "The diner owner remodeled the couple of rental rooms in order to expand the restaurant." The attendant gave her directions to the diner, "which still has great home-cooked food."

Only last year her father had stayed overnight in a "dinner room." She had assumed that was the same place he always lodged. Now she wondered where her father had stayed. He would not have been happy staying at the fancy hotel, which appeared to be about three years old. She walked past it down several blocks to the yellow-and-red diner with chrome trim that resembled a railroad dining car.

Claudia's stomach was rumbling, and her feet protested against the dress shoes. She wished she were at home eating her food and not thinking about selling their cattle. The enticing aromas coming from this unpresuming, yet tidy, establishment were unexpected. Long, narrow yellow boxes planted with red geraniums underscored windows framed with pulled-back, ruffled curtains. When she walked through the screen door, Claudia saw a chrome-edged, rose-and-gray linoleum counter. Five rose-colored vinyl stools swiveled on stainless steel columns attached to the floor at intervals down the length of one side of the counter. A few tables covered with ironed tablecloths were placed around the room, each with four matching wooden chairs. A middle-aged couple was seated at one of the tables, and a man was seated at the counter on one of the stools. He swiveled to gawk at Claudia when she entered. The short, gauzy curtains around the windows were light gray with rose-colored butterflies. Claudia was reminded of a meadow she passed once where two children with butterfly nets ran laughing.

The woman who came out from the kitchen wiping her hands on her apron was not pretty. She was beautiful in the way a fresh loaf of crusty bread is—substantial and comforting. Her rosy glow was constant not just from her oven-warmed kitchen. The sleeves of her cotton blouse were rolled up, revealing firm, healthy arms and slender hands. Her simple, straight skirt was attractive but not frilly. She was a woman into whose arms a person could relax.

"May I help you?" The natural ash blond set a glass of water on the counter. Her smile caught Claudia who reflected the courtesy back. The woman tipped her head, and Claudia nodded imperceptibly.

She indicated Claudia's forehead. "I have a soup from my garden that would ease those lines of concern."

"Yes. And bread?" She would eat and be revived. When the attractive, curvaceous woman with wavy hair returned, she offered a sturdy Buffalo-ware bowl steaming with fresh vegetables and chicken and a burgundy-trimmed white plate to match with a wedge of light rye bread. Claudia released a barely audible sigh. As the soup loosened Claudia's tensed muscles, her tongue relaxed. Later she would reflect that the conversation they shared might have been one she and her mother could have had, if her mother had lived.

"What brings you to our little corner of heaven?" Nora Fleming, the owner, asked.

"I'm here to sell some breeding stock and..." she hesitated, then continued, "have all but sealed the deal."

"We have a lot of folks that come to town to make deals about animals or land. Some meet right here."

Nora dressed gracefully but not like the ruffled femininity favored by women in most small towns. This woman with her wavy, off-blond hair softly pulled up and off her face had an air about her that Claudia found appealing, confident, and assertive without being aggressive. Claudia observed Nora's face closely and saw she was about her father's age. She wore cosmetics but appeared natural. Unlike the powdered and rouged Sunday ritual of women at home, this woman's daily toilette included a cosmetic and hair regimen that wasn't fussy or artificial. Makeup to this woman was as routine as scrubbing her fingernails. Claudia watched as she moved among her customers resting a hand easily on the back of a chair, coffeepot in her other hand ready to refill. She talked with Claudia about her back garden of herbs and soup vegetables, and Claudia talked about hers and how to keep potato bugs at bay with a mixture of soapy water and cayenne pepper.

Nora glided between tables and the entrance to the kitchen, which was separated by the counter with its tall stools. The women back home who were striving to be attractive looked paper dollish in their catalogue dresses. Their hair was spit curled under a net on Saturday. Powder and paint were a carefully applied mask worn for Sunday church and dinner then scrubbed away.

The man at the counter, whom Nora addressed by name, finished sipping his coffee before saying he was going home to supper. Overhearing the comment, Claudia realized she had begun her day with breakfast but had not had dinner, so this was a late dinner, early supper for her. Another man, upon entering, smiled at her before sitting down and ordering meatloaf and mashed potatoes, the special of the day. He set a salesman's case down on the floor next to him, put his brown felt hat on the table, and sat in the chair so that he could watch Claudia seated at the counter. When their eyes met he extended some pleasantry to her, and she reciprocated politely, but briefly, then returned her attention to her soup, bread, and coffee.

Nora and Claudia talked between customers. When she finished her meal, Claudia was reluctant to leave the comfort of the diner and go to her hotel room. She ordered the pie, lemon meringue, ala mode. The crust was flakey. *I bet she makes it with lard, not Crisco.* The filling tasted of fresh-squeezed summer, a welcome memory. When the small restaurant crowd left, Nora sat down next to her.

"I can understand why my father chose to come here after his business. I came with him when I was younger. Later, I'd stay home, do chores. Sometimes he would stay overnight to finish business." Claudia's eyes traced the lines on the ceiling. "Now, I'm doing the business." She turned her attention back to Nora.

"Was it just you and your dad?" Nora inquired.

"My mother died when I was six."

"Where did you say you were from?"

"Bear Creek."

"Oh, my gosh, I think I know your dad. Are you Claudia?"

"Yes. How do you know my name?" Nora picked up Claudia's bowl and plate, her eyes on the dishes in her hands, and carried them to the kitchen, a room partially hidden. Claudia heard water running into the sink.

"Did my father eat here?" Claudia called toward the kitchen.

"Yes," the single word came out slowly as Nora reentered

the dining room and resumed her seat next to Claudia. She regarded Claudia directly, calmly. "Why are you here? Did you come here to eat because Francis came here? Why didn't he come?" She leaned forward expectantly, distress on her face. "Nothing's wrong with him. He's not sick?"

"My father died over two months ago."

Nora put her hands to her mouth, as if stopping her own mouth would prevent Claudia from telling her the truth of the last few months, as if the words not being spoken would keep the facts from being real.

Nora didn't need to say that she and Claudia's father were more than casual friends—a relationship was obvious from her grief-stricken face. Slumped, Nora asked, and Claudia answered. There was quiet in the small restaurant. Outside the sun was setting. Only a few cars passed by, and a rare horse and buggy clomped down the cobbled street.

"Your father was a wonderful man. I feel I know you. Is that too familiar? He enjoyed talking about you. I think he sometimes wanted a woman's perspective. He missed your mother."

"How long have you known him?" Claudia wondered why her father never mentioned this woman who was obviously a good friend.

"I feel like I've known him forever, but we've only known each other five or six years, and almost three years that we have been close." Nora pressed her hands down her white apron. "Your father was an exceptional man. In these hard times for him to share his good fortune with someone like me, a nonfamily member, was so generous. He made keeping my restaurant possible. I couldn't handle the situation alone, and, even though the amount wasn't substantial by banker's terms, it was beyond mine. And he was so kind to personally take the matter to them and arrange the final details. He is…was a good friend." The sun had set, and the street lights were lit. Claudia was tired, weary.

She wondered what good fortune Nora was referring to,

but she did not feel comfortable questioning a woman she had just met, even if she was becoming aware that this woman and her father were more than ordinary friends. Nora interrupted Claudia's thoughts.

"I knew from our many conversations over the past few years that you were an only child, and your mother passed away when you were quite young, and your father raised you alone."

Claudia was silent. A whole side of her father had been revealed—a woman, a wonderful woman who shared time, conversation, and maybe more. She never knew.

Had there been any indication that her father had been living a life of which she was unaware? Claudia wondered if she had missed something. She was angry that he had not confided in her, not even shared this woman's friendship with his daughter. Why hadn't he at least mentioned Nora?

Back at the hotel lobby Claudia ran into the salesman whom she had seen at the restaurant. "Get your business done?" he asked.

"Yes, thank you."

"Nice place, that restaurant. I always stop when I come through this way. You by yourself?" She gave him a blank look, then started to walk away.

"What room you staying in?" he pressed. She regretted being so friendly earlier. The town seemed different from the last time she was here with her father almost fifteen years ago. The place definitely felt different. Her key in hand, she rapidly climbed the stairs to her room and locked the door behind her.

She lay spent in the clean sheets. This exhaustion was different than being tired from plowing all day. After working the fields with the horses or the tractor, she felt her sore back and shoulder muscles, but that was a tiredness that sleep cured. This was an exhaustion she had never felt before her father died. Brain-tired. That was the only thing she could think to call the feeling which was not the pleasant brain-tired newness of New York. She was in the Wisconsin countryside where she had always felt secure. This day had stressed every mental muscle. She was glad the door had a chain and bolt, which she had fastened. The sheets smelled clean but more antiseptic than sunshine.

On the train ride home the next morning, Claudia studied the papers the cattleman had given her and mulled over the conversation with Nora. What good fortune had her father come into a year or two ago? She had not remembered any particularly significant influx of money. They had bought the breeding stock, but that was several years ago, and they had borrowed and repaid that loan. She could not think of any good luck. Her father had been distracted this past year, not finishing the leatherwork, not talking to her about the loan that was now in default. And for what had he borrowed so much without talking to her? They did not discuss every small, short-term loan for seed or lime, but those were repaid in short order and for significantly less than this.

Like a thought she had known all along, but her mind could not fathom because it did not coincide with her vision of her father, the answer fell into place. *He borrowed the money for Nora to save her restaurant and do the remodeling and announced it to Nora as a gift "because he'd come into a sudden windfall." Typical of him to want to share his "good fortune." But with a complete stranger? But Nora wasn't a complete stranger, if he'd known her for more than five years, and they were obviously more than friends the last few.* To Claudia, Nora was a stranger. *How dare he do this—and to me! I have a good mind to take the train right back and tell that woman to sell the restaurant and pay me back, so I can tell that cattleman I am going back on my word. I haven't signed the paper yet. I am not selling the best of my breeding stock. Let that woman sell her livelihood. Why should I have to lose mine?*

There was no good fortune. It was betrayal. A betrayal of the trust she thought she and her father had. And now she had to pay the loan on Nora's restaurant. *But, was that the cause for the loan?* She would never know the truth. The only man who knew was dead. *Unless RT knew.* Claudia would find out.

Claudia chided herself for being so thick. How did she not realize yesterday that the loan was, of course, for Nora? *What is wrong with me? I have too much to do to waste time being stupid.* She should've stayed in Rice Lake, too late to go back today. Upon her arrival in Turtle Lake, she purchased a ticket for the next day, went home to load the hay she'd raked before her train trip, and get it into the barn. The hay wasn't the best quality but all she had available. She didn't want a much-needed rain to come and spoil her animals' food. She had to make hay while the sun was shining. *Ha, ha. The sun shines every day lately. Now if I just had enough hay to make.*

Claudia called on Randy at his office, and she could hear the eagerness in his voice. She suspected his buddy the banker had informed him of her attempt at refinancing and maybe he even knew that yesterday the cattleman had refused to work with her but would only give her cutter-canner prices for her custom breed of cattle. Or maybe she was being paranoid. Randy was only interested in land, not cattle, which meant he wanted her land. *He's not going to get my land, but I am going to get some answers.*

The exchange with Claudia was shorter than Randy had expected. She stood eye to eye with him. "I demand to know for what my land was being held as collateral. For what purpose did my father borrow three thousand dollars?"

"Please sit down, Claudia." He motioned to the low-seated chair in front of his desk. Claudia remained standing. He put away his smile. "As I've told you before, this was a private matter between your father and me regarding *his* land.

He didn't want you involved." She flinched despite her resolve not to show him any weakness.

"But I am involved. I'm responsible to pay."

"Yes, as part of the estate you are now responsible. You were informed in writing that a mortgage was in default, and you chose not to resolve the debt immediately. You have received the benefits of your father's sound decisions, and now you are responsible for the others." He was doing it again—telling her that her father was a foolish man who had made an unwise decision. *So, my father had invested in Nora's restaurant, but RT is refusing to say it aloud.*

"I didn't choose not to pay off the debt. That is what I am attempting to do. To resolve it! Why didn't someone tell me that my father had been making payments but hadn't made any for three months before he died?" Claudia persisted.

"As I explained last month, the law does not require us to notify anyone whose name is not on the deed and you, dear lady, were not listed nor were you consulted by the deed holder, your father. When it became imperative, you were notified."

"What are my options?" Claudia's arms were rigid at her sides, and increasingly she was having difficulty staying composed. "Couldn't I find another bank with which to refinance?"

"Considering that two of the banks in your area have closed completely and that the current interest rate is sixteen percent compared to six percent when I made the arrangements with your father, do you think refinancing is even an option for you?"

She had inquired at other banks and they had admonished her that no one was lending because no one was making payments on current loans. Those with savings in banks were withdrawing their money in a panic before the banks closed their doors, and the account holders were left high and dry with nothing. She had counted on a personal relationship and past history to matter for something.

With more confidence than she felt, she plowed on, "I have an offer from a cattle dealer, my father has done business with before, to buy some of my cattle."

"I've spoken with that gentleman. You could go back there today to see for yourself, but they are currently not paying the price he offered you. With a glut of unwanted cattle right now, I don't see things getting better soon." He leaned back, rested against the desk, stretched his long legs out in front of him, and placed his hands behind him on the shiny surface.

"I would be happy to find a buyer for your farm, or I can fix things so you could even stay in the house and keep enough land for a garden patch. I'll take care of the rest. You won't need to worry about a thing. I am happy to help, if you will just let me." His smile had returned. He acted as if he held all the cards, and she needed merely to pick one of them, and everything would be fine. *Take that rigged deck of cards and stuff it where the sun don't shine!* Instead of those words, she was her father's polite daughter, but she wondered how far that would take her.

"No, thank you." She shoved her hands into her pants pockets and walked out. Randy stood there with his mouth open. She hoped he would catch a fly, but he wasn't going to trap her.

On the train ride home, she considered her options. There hadn't been a payment made since February. She would have to find a buyer for some of her cattle or find someone to loan her some money to make payments on the debt until she could refinance, or she'd have to sell out. On the back of the cattleman's papers she scribbled an advertisement for her Scottish Highland cattle to put in *The Farm Journal* and *The Drovers*. She'd even put something in *Hoard's Dairyman* and every farm trade paper. No one was going to hog-tie her into an impossible situation. She would figure some way out.

18. Nora

Black Friday had yet to occur but most days prior to October 29th were dark for the average laborer in Wisconsin in 1929. Even when the Stock Market crash was behind them, the fallout of the Depression hung in the air like soot from city factories before they closed. The atmosphere was so oppressive that folks felt suffocated without even venturing outside.

Times were hard for everybody. Nora approached her banker in January of 1928 when she was having difficulty paying for supplies. She put her diner-house up as collateral. Her trouble continued when she started to give a cup of coffee and sandwich to guys down on their luck and hungry in exchange for chores around the diner. By June she was unable to keep up the payments and went to Randy, the man who brought his real estate and banking clients into her diner. He was successful even in these hard times. He knew about money sources and he knew her. Surely he would help her.

Randy was happy to help with a little personal loan. "No need for formal papers among friends," he had assured her.

People started coming in not to order lunch or dinner but to ask if she had any work that needed to be done. Or a man might come in to buy a cup of coffee for a nickel, pay with pennies then nurse that cup and her refills until the few folks having lunch left. Then the man would strike up a conversation that turned to "I'm a bit short of work." Or "I got laid off at the factory, what with The Crash and all."

Occasionally, one went right to her heart. "I've got a wife and kids. I work hard. Do you have any odd jobs? I'm not particular." She would find a job that could be done but also could have waited, or she could've done herself. The man in his eagerness did the sweeping, carried out trash, and peeled potatoes lickety-split. She returned to Randy more frequently in order to keep the bills paid.

Randy, being on the Rural Electrification Board and a school board member, brought fellow members in for coffee and clients in for lunch. He signed his name on the bill for the food, and occasionally he put a client up in the rooms she rented out by the day or week. When he received the bill in the mail from her, he would write, "applied to loan" and mail the receipt back to Nora, who knew she should say something. Often the monthly bill of Randy's was quite high, but how could she complain when he was so good to her.

The payment she made to him was a fraction of what she owed him monthly. She was getting further and further in debt and couldn't turn the corner. Her generosity to those worse off than her was not helping, but how could she say no to someone who looked like a scarecrow chasing scavengers off some field and begging for anything, willing to do whatever. How much did a couple of slices of bread and a sliver of meat or cheese cost? Egg salad was inexpensive but could only be spread so thin.

By the winter of 1928–29 word must have gotten out to the tramps on the train line that her place was hospitable. She had only so many doors to oil or roofs to mend or carrots to chop, not enough work or food for all the hungry and homeless. Most folks had tightened their belts and were bringing lunch from home or going home for lunch.

Every laborer, lumberman, teacher, and secretary was so glad to just have a job that they did not mind eating their own lunch. Truth be told, Nora's biggest customer most weeks was Randy treating clients. She thought of those clients as her guests because they brought no income, yet the grocer and farmer still counted on cash as payment each week.

Almost monthly she was in Randy's office needing a bit of cash to carry her through until things improved. Randy never made a big deal but just smiled, patted her shoulder, and reassured her. "Don't worry, Nora. You are an asset to our community. We need women like you." She walked out assured that funds would be there to pay the next delivery of beef or milk or produce.

When he came unexpectedly to the diner midafternoon in September of 1929 while she prepared the evening meal for her boarders, she became worried.

"I was told by the powers that be that our situation here is not tenable," he announced standing with his hat still on. Outside was brisk, and snow heavy with dust blew in the streets. She urged him to sit down and got him a hot cup of coffee and a slice of warm coffee cake with butter. When she set the plate in front of him, his hat was sitting on the table and his wool coat hung on the back of the chair, not on the coat rack where he hung them when he brought in clients.

"I don't understand."

"It's not me, Nora." He sipped slowly at his coffee, as if he had all day. "I'm fine with our arrangement, but the bigger banking system seems to think you are not a good financial risk." She had thought the same thing lately. How could she continue in these economic times? People were lucky to even have a job. She knew many in their wider community who were being foreclosed on. She had had a letter from a second cousin saying their son who had been away at school had to return home to help run the business as they had to let their hired help go.

"I'll need more collateral." He forked the buttery, nut, and cinnamon coffeecake into his mouth delicately. "The diner and boarding house are just not worth that much these days." He waited to give his words time to sink in. He used his fork to break away more cake and place the tidbit into his well-formed mouth. *He was very good looking, but she wished he would just get to the point.*

"There are vacant buildings in town to be had for a song. And, as I'm sure you are aware, there just is not as much call for going out to eat." *Boy was he preaching to the choir.* She felt like a failure.

She remembered her father declaring her, "You're a girl. You better marry well." She wondered what her mousey mother had thought of that premise. The irony was she had married well when she was just out of school, and the union still ended poorly. Her husband was one of the first to lose everything before he suddenly, tragically died. He had not wanted to burden her with the financial matters, so she counted herself lucky to end up with their house after paying off creditors. She should not be worried about her father and mother, who were both long dead, but she could feel the spirit of her father shaking his head as if he had known all along.

"What should I do? What will happen next?"

"You need to find someone to put up some collateral or you'll have to cash out the debt by selling," he replied as if that were the easiest thing in the world.

Where would she find help or cash? She had no family close by or well off.

That was when providence seemed to intervene. Claudia's father had eaten at the diner and rented a room occasionally when he came to town. The week after Randy had given her the ultimatum, Francis came in and commented on the lack of customers on a bright afternoon at lunchtime. Nora sat down across from him as she so often did when the lunch crowd had dissipated, and they lingered over coffee talking. After she had unburdened herself, she felt calmer, and Francis appeared happy and expansive. He reassured her that he had ready funds to alleviate the situation. This would be to both their advantages, for him an investment; for her a gift. He would go to the banker whom he knew vaguely from other community business.

She expressed reluctance at a "gift," but he intimated he needed to find a place for these ready funds, and this would be perfect. The partnership would mean he would have to come to town more often to check up on his "investment," and he gave her a wink. She uncharacteristically blushed. She was feeling more vulnerable than she had felt in a long time. But in the upcoming weeks, a lighter heart proved an invigorating cure that prompted her to tell the next down-on-his-luck man to help her give the place a fresh coat of paint.

She and Francis discussed their plans. "A new hotel is going up this spring," Nora informed Francis when he visited her in February of 1930. "An investor from out East has a chain of hotels and thought the Midwest held potential, so he's building a branch in Rice Lake."

"I think we would be wise to take the space used for renting rooms and remodel to expand the restaurant." Francis was excited. "All those construction workers will need three square meals. They'll appreciate your cooking."

"Why don't I keep the rooms while the workers are here. They'll need a place to stay and the only other place is that rundown hotel. Then this fall when they leave, we could expand the kitchen, and maybe I could hire someone to help me."

"You have a good head on your shoulders. Yes, let's do that." For a while Nora's restaurant did well while the men constructing the hotel had work. After the hotel was completed in the spring of 1931, they were initially busy, but then everything went slack again. She wondered how that hotel investor had avoided financial ruin when her dead husband and numerous folks lost their homes and businesses. She had heard that it took money to make money, but she also believed that hard work could overcome tremendous obstacles. Her perseverance had proven her correct. Good people like Francis help people like her. What goes around comes around.

Then in mid-July almost two-and-a-half years after Francis had taken care of her debt with the bank and Randy, Francis's daughter had walked in, and Claudia had seemed unaware of any influx of spare money. Maybe her dad and she did not talk about money. Nora thought that unlikely as Claudia seemed similar to her, capable and intellectually savvy. Nora could not worry about somcone clsc right now. She had inventory to consider and meals to plan.

19. Thomas and the Birds

When Thomas first visited the farm that third day in May, he commented on the multitude of birds and wanted to learn their names. Claudia chose to ignore his ignorance of the most common species.

On his next visit less than two weeks later he blurted, "I love birds. Some New Yorkers are bothered by the pigeons and their pervasive droppings. I like to feed them stale breadcrumbs in the park where they swoop down in great flocks around little children. The cooing birds are unperturbed by squealing toddlers or their scolding nursemaids."

The first day he came to help with barn chores, Claudia was touched by his excitement at seeing a scarlet tanager flit by. "Look at that small red bird. Why he's more brilliant than a silk scarf flung around a *Vogue* model's neck." That description pleased her. Later in the week when he came to see the new calf, he pointed to an indigo bunting. "Perched like a sapphire on a birch branch," he'd observed. "She's the partner jewel to the scarlet tanager." He'd been so pleased.

"I haven't seen one in a while. Both are becoming rarer," she'd noted as they walked across the yard.

"They appear so out of place in the countryside," he'd observed. "Their colors are flamboyant."

"When I was a child about this time of year, the indigo buntings would migrate in flocks, a small iridescent blue cloud."

"The bluebirds," he pointed to the dusty round bird and his dowdy mate, "are more obvious occupants of a farm." Claudia loved the shy bluebird, the minstrel of the farm.

They watched the numerous varieties of sparrows. "Have

you noticed each has a unique song?" She hadn't, but she listened and was amazed.

"What is that stately, distinguished bird?" He was pointing to the hooded, marauder blue jay who raucously squawked.

Claudia humphed, "That is the Randy Rottman of the bird family, a blue jay. They are brash, impressive, but ruthless. They attack smaller song birds, will mimic a hawk to scare other birds away from a food source, peck at other birds' eggs, and sometimes won't feed a fledgling that has wandered outside the nest. The parent lets the baby shriek forever."

Claudia pointed to the top of the cedar tree where the other hooded bird, a tweeting cardinal, perched. "Now, he is stately. He and his mate, which is difficult to distinguish from a cedar waxwing, are sweet dispositioned birds that sing lightly while the jay's screech pierces the air. But wait until early next spring when the red-winged blackbirds are mating. This year you just missed their singing back and forth like a call and response song in church." She recalled his voice at church and wondered what bird he most resembled.

When he returned to the farm at the end of May, he noticed a nest hung like a sack swinging with the breeze in a poplar tree. Gazing out the kitchen window as he dumped the blackberries into a bowl, he marveled at the bright orange and black bird that flew in, its three to four light notes ending on a questioning high note. Later that evening swinging in the porch swing, she reflected on how the round-headed oriole laid her eggs in a basket nest where hatchlings were lulled to sleep by gentle winds rocking their pouch of woven prairie grasses and soothed by the rustle of poplar leaves.

The next day he announced he was purchasing birdseed and asked if she had a feeder.

"I've seen one somewhere in a shed or the barn. My mother used to feed the birds, but we got too busy, and my father removed the feeder, which used to be mounted on the end fence post not far from where the bluebird house faces east." She pointed, and Thomas reasoned, "I'll bet your mother wanted to see the birds from the kitchen window." Claudia nodded, speculating on her mother's pleasure as she washed dishes and prepared meals.

"I can imagine your mother watching the birds collect bugs and worms to feed her babies as she cut carrots and onions to feed her family." The next day he didn't stop, but after his calls the following day, he met her out cutting hay and brought the sack he'd picked up at the feed mill. Back at the farm he filled the feeder, which he'd nailed to the post, with a selection of sunflower, millet, cracked corn, and thistle seed. Claudia shook her head. He'd paid more per pound for that seed than the cost for feed for her chickens or Daisy or the pig or what she could get for oats or corn if she had sold them instead of using them for feed.

After the feeder was filled, the birds began to come. The first birds to flock to the feeder were the tiny goldfinches. While back in New York, Thomas had bought a bird book and was eager to share his knowledge with Claudia. "I know that one is called a purple finch even though the color is more reddish than purple." Slate juncos with their trills, black and white chickadees, and sparrows in varied diversity vied for space, flitting, and hovering in the air while many waited in the branches of the cedar tree for their turn.

One day at dinner they saw all the birds fly away in a great hurry, and before long the gang of blue jays appeared. They quibbled amongst themselves for prized spots at the feeder, once they had dispersed the other birds. They were the bullies of the bird feeder.

"I want to go out there and shoo them away. They are so messy, too. They fling seed right and left, scattering smaller seeds to the ground in their greed. They only want the oily black sunflower seeds." Claudia nodded but went back to the dishes. "Look, they hold the seed between their feet and crack it with their sharp bills." She savored his delight. Seeing her farm through his eyes was refreshing. Once the jays had their fill, they flew off in a flurry as big as their entrance. In seconds the different varieties of songbirds returned.

When he noted, "The jays' antics proved my first impression of them incorrect," she responded with, "If you judged by first impressions, you'd think the docile-looking, sweet-sounding cowbird was an amiable bird. The brown-headed cowbird lays her eggs in other birds' nests to be raised. She parents like some lazy, rich wife who hires a poor woman to nurse and raise her children out of sight and sound of her high-society friends."

The week of her birthday, he related how he'd heard a great hammering and wondered what the source was. He scanned the area until he located a dying white pine at the edge of the yard toward the wooded pasture. "I watched and listened. The hammering was definitely coming from that tree, but I couldn't see anything. I walked quietly and slowly to the side, so I could see the back of the tree, and there was the biggest wild bird—other than a turkey, duck, or goose—that I'd ever seen. A great red hood topped a white-and-black body. With a beak like a railroad spike, he pounded the bark of the pine so that pieces flew off like chips from a lumberjack's ax. The tailored bird paused and tipped his head to the side as if listening. Then the hammering resumed. My guess is that there were larvae crawling just under the bark, which the bird was eating." She examined the bird book he held open. "A pileated woodpecker. Can you believe it?" He had a child's enthusiasm and even the behavior of one. "I wanted a closer peek so I snuck up, but he flew off." Thomas spread his arms out full length, "That's his wingspan." Claudia smiled at his exaggeration and informed him that an eagle had a bigger wingspan and several hawks had wingspans equal to those of pileated woodpeckers.

After their trip to the opera, she attributed Thomas's fascination with the myriad birds that populated the farmyard and woods of Claudia's land to his love of music. He loved the chick-a-dee-dee-dee of that aptly named bird, as lighthearted and pleasant as sun falling through new leaves. He became so enthralled that she would find him observing birds instead of stacking wood or hauling water to the animals.

Claudia did not mind. She would find the pail he'd set down after he'd offered to fill the pig's water trough but had gotten sidetracked by the sound of a delicate gargling that bubbled and mimicked the brook falling over rocks. He discovered the song had been coming from the brown-hooded black cowbird, the parasite bird she had disparaged.

Claudia was at the woodpile gathering an armload to carry to the house wood box, when he came to her, excited. He bent to help her. "I found a clutch of baby pheasants running through the meadow behind their mother." Another time he described a sight she'd come to regard as routine— the tom turkey's reddish-blue head held up like a question mark, but pulled close to his body, his beard thrust from his chest hanging to the ground in the pasture, his tail fanned in full Thanksgiving display, his puffed body turning slowly, and his skinny legs strutting carefully. In the woods where the tom's attention was focused, a drab petite hen was pecking at the ground in feigned disinterest. To Thomas the abundance of bird life was all new and that enchanted Claudia.

The smallest and by far the most brazen bird in the yard was the jenny wren, whose call was as quick as her wings. The little house she guarded was one Claudia's father had made as a Christmas present for her mother along with several bluebird houses. She had warned Thomas that if he walked too close to the wren house, the little bird would fly in front of his face and scold him for the affront. He chuckled at jenny's pluck when he ventured too close. Her courage was in inverse proportion to her size. But the first bird to be seen, whose arrival announced spring, was the gently chirping robin red breast. The round as a housewife, big-eyed bird hopped about in the damp grass in the mornings, head cocked to one side, then down her head would go, stabbing the ground, slowly extracting a long night crawler, and snapping it in her beak. Her sky-blue eggs in a tidy little nest were discovered tucked under an outbuilding eave or sitting in the crotch of a crabapple tree. Claudia knew where they favored, but Thomas had a keen eye and found one tucked under the eave of the house on one of his first visits to her farm.

Claudia confided to Thomas that her favorite song was the mourning dove's drawn-out whooo. "Almost like an owl's who—long and sustained. Not a barred owl, which asks, 'Who? Who cooks for you?' When Papa pronounced the mourning dove's name I thought he said 'morning' because that is when I heard her, but she sounded so sad that when I saw the spelling I realized her name suited her." Claudia's least favorite was the shiny black crow's ubiquitous caw, caw, caw over fields and trees. Thomas found the birds' plain, straightforward strut and sermon humorous. "The crow reminds me of a self-appointed, Bible-thumping preacher I'd see in New York, swaggering the streets with self-righteous religious fervor."

On a door frame arch in a part of the barn that wasn't the main traffic area but close to the old silo, dates had been marked in carpenter pencil. The wood jamb had two sets of dates for each year going back over three decades. The first dates in the set were various days in April and the second set were scattered between August and September. One day in July, they were in the barn, and Thomas asked Claudia, "What are these dates?"

"Those are the dates when the barn swallows first appear and when they depart." Claudia touched the marks. "I never noticed that my father forgot to mark the past couple of years."

20. Randy and Francis Transact

In mid-1929, Francis went to the banker who held the loan on Nora's restaurant. Earlier that year Francis had invested his ready reserve of cash on a new breed of hardy cattle he believed would revitalize his herd and be sought after by beef farmers throughout the Midwest. But hearing Nora's distress, he felt compelled to see if he could give her a helping hand. Banker Bill referred Francis to Randy, who was handling the arrangements with "the Fleming woman." Francis went to see Randy, who was not his favorite person, but Francis liked Nora Fleming. He had known Nora for a while, thought he'd like to get to know her better, and this might be the opportunity for that to occur.

Francis walked into Randy's Rice Lake office that smelled of furniture polish and woolen rugs over highly waxed wooden floors. The two men shook hands. Randy waved his hand in a wide sweep across his desk and toward the window where two plush leather armchairs flanked either side to indicate Francis should feel welcome to sit in one of those rather than the stiffer shorter chair that sat across from the billiard-size mahogany desk.

Randy inquired about field work with the extreme weather and Francis's cattle. Francis was curious how Andrew was succeeding at sports and school. After a few minutes of pleasantries, the two men got down to business.

"How can I be of service, Francis?" Randy crossed his long elegant legs at the knees revealing argyle socks that matched his silk tie. Francis briefly wished he'd wiped the dust off his shoes in the outer room while waiting for Randy to "finish an international call."

"I have an investment opportunity in town here but am a bit short of the funds required. The arrangement would be a partnership of sorts. She owns an establishment in town but is unable to secure the necessary mortgage to cover improvements for her to continue. I believe you know the widow Mrs. Fleming."

"Yes, lovely woman. A credit to our little community." With that Randy rested his elbow on the arm of the stuffed chair and rested his chin in the V formed by his hand and contemplated the street one story below him.

"My financial history of short-term loans with you," continued Francis who glanced out the window also, "and the fact that my farm is owned free and clear should speak for themselves." At the words "my farm" Randy's eyes returned to Francis. Randy responded so quickly and eagerly that Francis thought Randy's reaction was a testament to Francis's own solid reputation in the community. Randy stood and turned his head away, plucked the ironed hanky from his breast pocket, and wiped at his mouth.

"Let me just write up the mortgage papers for the amount you feel is needed to ensure the project is done right. Better to have enough ready funds to complete the work. I know you are a man of integrity and foresight. I trust your judgment and know you would want to do this up right, something you and the city can be proud of."

Francis pondered the information of a mortgage becoming common knowledge and having to explain to Claudia. Easier to deal with this just between himself and Randy.

"This friend of mine, as you know, is a proud and independent business owner, and I would like to remain a silent financial partner."

They spent a few minutes on the papers at the desk that mirrored the two men's faces back at them as they wrote in numbers and terms and the farm's description as security.

Randy assured Francis, "No one need know. The

mortgage can be signed and dated but does not have to be recorded at this time. The lien would have to be registered in order to settle your estate in the unlikely event of your death or, unthinkably, if nonpayment occurred for an extended period of time."

Francis preferred to deal in cash and had never carried a mortgage. He'd done short term loans but never had to secure them with his farm, but this was significantly more money than he had previously borrowed. On the trip home his excitement mixed with a tinge of dread. He would avoid Claudia that evening. She would notice that something was different in his manner. His excitement preoccupied his mind until he was going to sleep, then that hint of dread resurfaced.

He was foolish to sign the papers using his farm as security on the restaurant. But, he'd never defaulted on a previous loan. His new heifer calves could be bred next year. They'd drop their calves the following year and within a few years he'd be back in the black without having to bother Claudia or Nora with the particulars. He'd pay the interest only at first so he had breathing room. Nora had mentioned a new hotel, which meant the restaurant would prosper. He could approach Nora, if he had to, about the specifics of the loan after she was getting more customers. Or maybe Claudia and George's son would marry and join farms. He could marry Nora, and they could live at the farm and hire workers for the restaurant and manage the enterprise as a retirement nest egg.

Anything was possible. He didn't need to worry. He'd taken out loans before when things were tight. If a crop didn't get harvested before a bill was due or if a harvested crop had to be held to get the best price, sometimes a short-term loan was a necessity. He knew Claudia had always understood that the vet wanted to be paid after a visit, and seed had to be purchased regardless of whether ready cash was in hand. He'd never had a problem paying the loans back quickly in the past. He wouldn't now. Of course, a mortgage was not a short-term loan. He didn't want to bother Claudia or Nora with details or discussion. He'd take care of everything; he always did.

As Francis lay in bed, he preferred not to think of Claudia but to think of that September afternoon spent at Nora's after his visit to Randy. He'd walked into the diner with his hat in his hand, a smile on his face, and good news. At first Nora seemed perplexed and kept shaking her head slowly back and forth at his news that he had the solution to her problem.

"I shouldn't have bothered you with my troubles. You can't give me money. These are hard times. You need to keep a little cushion against the unexpected. We are friends, but you have your own responsibilities."

That's when the concocted story of a windfall of money came out of his mouth before taking full form in his mind. Her perplexity changed to disbelief then relief.

She jumped up and hugged him. "I can keep my diner? Oh, Francis, you are a generous man to share your windfall with me. I will pay you back when times get better. I know things can't get worse." She didn't question him about the particulars of this "sudden windfall." He appreciated her deferential manner to trust him and not pry. For now, let her think he had an inheritance or successful agricultural dealings with his exotic cattle. She confided she could breathe easier without the thought of losing her diner and her livelihood. He was glad he could come to her aid.

They spent the rest of the afternoon talking about remodeling and their trust that the economy would pick up soon. If they could all weather the storm, work together, and lean on each other, everything could return to normal. Everyone just had to hang in there, trust President Hoover to do what was right, and keep working hard. Times were tough but couldn't get much worse.

Why bother this beautiful woman with feelings of obligation? He loved to see her face without those worry lines on her forehead. Even her posture was more relaxed. She was a superb woman, hard-working, compassionate.

That afternoon they spent talking, he'd seen her tuck a sandwich into the hands of a rough-looking man who'd cupped a mug of coffee as if warming his hands at a fire. The man's moment of contentment reminded Francis of evenings sitting in front of the woodstove at home with Claudia.

The man's jacket hadn't been very substantial. He'd sat nursing his coffee until late.

"He's one of my regulars," she quietly explained. "He stops in on the days when he can't find work. He buys a nickel cup of coffee and warms up a bit. I don't know, but I imagine from the clothes he wears that he sleeps in them. God only knows where." Francis's face had remained serious. As if she needed to justify giving away food free when she was in financial trouble, she confessed, "I can at least give him the occasional sandwich."

But that's what he liked about her: her generosity, her calm spirit, and her can-do, make-it-through attitude.

21. Threshing and Fighting

The day was pleasant but hot, ninety-four degrees at 11a.m. where they sat on plank benches under the trees in the Johnson yard. Thursday, the twenty-first of July, in Detroit, Michigan, the temperature was more moderate, men wore suits and women's dresses had sleeves. The Hudson Motor Car Company rolled out two thousand of their new Essex-Terraplanes in hopes of stimulating the economy by providing eight thousand jobs. Amelia Earhart Putnam, renowned aviator, christened one of the steel-framed vehicles in front of dignitaries seated on folding chairs and a hopeful crowd of thousands standing. The photo published in papers two days later would mark the similarities and difference between those in Detroit and those on the farm: both hopeful but one complex group was money-centered and the other simple gathering was labor-centered.

In Johnsons' farmyard the men sat four on each side of the rough tables made from sawn boards nailed between cutoff stumps acting as table legs. Shorter stumps served as legs for the benches on which they sat in their bib overalls and rolled-up sleeves. Thomas was in work clothes but wore a belt rather than the ubiquitous suspenders or bib overalls worn by most of the farmers. Thomas sat cheek to jowl with Hank, who was next to Matthew Reuter, the farmer to the south of the Johnsons. Matthew had come over to help with the threshing at the Johnsons and had helped with Claudia's few oats and the Mevissens, who would return the favor to the Reuters, but Thomas wouldn't be obliged to go. He had returned from two weeks working in New York to help Claudia and her close neighbors for a few days before going back to Hagstrom's. She hadn't asked him to help, but after mentioning it to him on her birthday, he'd responded eagerly, "I wouldn't miss this chance to learn what threshing is all about."

Thomas was unaware of the potential dangers lurking in this bucolic farm scene, but Claudia knew. Farm accidents were regular occurrences. Scan any church meeting or barn dance; count the missing fingers, men with permanent limps, those with a hook because a hand had been given to a corn picker in an attempt to unclog gear-binding stalks. A plugged corn picker was almost impossible to clear unless the implement was in motion and impossible to extract the stalks without using hands. Everyone on the farm, even Claudia, wore scars from machinery edges and hot stoves. One glance at a threshing operation with spinning wheels and long looping belts driving grinding gears, and an accident seemed inevitable.

"Odd to be eating dinner this early," Thomas observed to the eldest of the Johnson boys. "The women could barely have finished the breakfast and lunch dishes." Thomas had learned from Claudia that the noon meal was called dinner, the evening meal was supper, and any meal break between, whether at 9 a.m. or 9 p.m., was called lunch. Claudia kept her head down and held the corner of her tongue between her teeth to keep from explaining why they were eating now.

George's son Hank shrugged and helped himself to the platters piled with slabs of bread, cheese, and meat. He slathered fresh-churned butter yellow as a prairie sunrise onto his plank of bread out of the oven that morning and stacked cold roast beef and creamy cheese made at the Mevissen farm across the road from the Johnsons. Claudia used Daisy's cream for their daily butter and in coffee but got cheese and cream for ice cream from the Mevissens.

Hank continued building the perfect sandwich by grabbing two thick hunks of ham set down on the table by the shiny, rosy-cheeked, apple-shaped Mary Reuter with her gap-toothed smile. Hank didn't glance at Mary but directly at Claudia and asked if she'd pass him a bowl of her bread and butter pickles and her long spears of dills that were her contribution to the annual meal. She obliged and gave a half smile. Everyone knew Claudia would work with the men and wouldn't be expected to bake the stacks of bread loaves or the dozens of pies needed each day to fuel this horde of threshers who ate as hard as they worked. Claudia glanced at Thomas, who was looking for somewhere to wipe his mouth. He was used to Claudia's cloth napkin under his fork.

"Where are the napkins?" he inquired just as he saw George opposite him wipe his sleeve across his face after downing a glass of lemonade, drinking his second cup of coffee, and shoveling in peach sauce. Sauce, he had learned, was the term for apples, pears, or wild plums canned late each summer. He called such delicacies *preserves.* What they called preserves, he called *jam.* Hank glared at Thomas and wagged his head.

Staring at Thomas, the Fournier and Andersen boys exchanged elbow pokes and chuckles enjoying a laugh at his expense, but Claudia remained silent, which wasn't the first time today. Earlier when he'd asked why they bundled the oats first and didn't fork them in loose to save time, the men in the field had doubled over with laughter. Claudia wished he hadn't blushed, which only encouraged them. She silently gave him credit for refusing to look down or away. He had merely smiled and given a half-shrug.

Claudia had not made eye contact since she sat down kitty-corner from him. She had avoided him when the bell called a halt to the work that had begun shortly after early chores. A huge breakfast had been eaten at dawn. When Thomas spotted Claudia later, he confided that six months ago he would have imagined only lumberjacks devoured such meals. As she glanced at him now, plates of pie wedges were being set down by girls hardly tall enough to reach the tables while other youngsters were continually filling water pitchers. Mrs. Johnson, her face glowing with perspiration, came from the kitchen with a coffee pot to refill every empty cup. Mrs. Reuter was in the kitchen already washing dishes. Doris Johnson would return the favor by helping Carolina Reuter tomorrow when the crew went to harvest the oats at their place.

Most of the older men were still sipping the dregs of their coffee when they heard the machines start up. Some of the younger men, not so young as to be held back by fear of reprisal but not old enough to have experienced reality's bite, seized the opportunity to prove themselves and get work started. Later the men in the field understood the boys had been careless. The details didn't matter. Fault wasn't assigned. They were boys being boys. Machines plus boys equal accidents.

One of the boys, really a man but acting like a schoolboy, was attempting to adjust the tension on one of the belts of the behemoth threshing machine. *Oh God, trouble.* He was the redheaded one who had teased Thomas in the field earlier. During dinner the boy had been fooling around near the gears of the equipment. Claudia had felt Thomas's attention on her and knew he was debating on cautioning the boys at the machine. Her steady gaze had stilled him from comments about the laws of physics and the law of averages. She had thought his comments would probably be ignored by the farmers. Having him here was difficult enough without having him provoke sarcasm and ridicule. He had remained silent. She recognized her judgment had been wrong, again.

Now, peripherally, they witnessed what had been a premonition earlier. The redhead, tired of his job forking bundles from the wagon onto the conveyor, decided he was ready for more challenging work. His pant leg had gotten caught and pulled him into the gears that churned relentlessly regardless of fabric or flesh. He screamed like a pig that had been caught by his back leg trying to escape the butcher's knife. They saw fear turn the cocky young man into a vulnerable boy. All the other men, close at hand, were above and couldn't see. As Thomas ran to the boy, he stripped his shirt off and began to rip it in two. He balled up one half and pushed the cloth into the gaping hole and used the other half to bind the quickly soddened scarlet ball to the boy's leg where the gear had ripped a gash. Claudia knelt beside him away from the machine. "What should I do?"

"Push on this." He grabbed her hand to hold the cloth on the wound. He stripped his belt off, cinched the leather on the boy's thigh above the wound, and then relieved the bloodied Claudia. Thomas held pressure on the wound all the while holding the boy with his other arm as far as possible out of harm's way of the still whirling drive shaft. Claudia's heart was racing. Hank and George, closest at the time, had stopped the machine, but all the parts took a while to quit moving. The screams had caused action. Pete Mevissen had wedged his pitchfork into the machine's jowls as Matthew Reuter grabbed the controls. The long looping belt running from tractor to thresher finally stopped completely.

The sun had set before they were able to piece together the different perspectives. The women spoke of the screams heard all the way in the house after the machine grinding had slowed and come to a halt.

The Fournier and Andersen boys were quick to tell how everything had been so normal, all going as usual. "He mustn't have paid attention."

When they were all safely in bed, the redheaded boy stitched and in a morphine stupor, they all understood one thing. Doc's comment made that clear. "He shoulda died out there. The main blood supply was hit." They all knew the truth, which Claudia whispered to Thomas as he held her in his arms that evening.

"You saved his life."

"I just did what I know."

"But none of us knew to push so hard. You tied so hard it

almost cut off all circulation to his leg." Thomas gazed down at her, touched her cheek gently. "That's the idea."

She didn't want to go to bed. Her muscles hurt; her head hurt. She knew the next day would begin with breakfast well before sunrise. What few oats there were this dry summer had to be threshed while the weather held. They all hoped much needed rain would come soon. They had lost the better part of a day today. One man less wouldn't ease the load. She needed to talk to Thomas–but not now.

She breathed in his smell. He always smelled clean and male but so different from the smell of her father or the other men. Ernie smelled like detergent or the making of beer and he was always prattling on with some joke or story. George smelled of sweat, cigarette smoke, and machinery grease and never complimented his wife. Many of the farm boys, such as Hank, had the sweet aroma of feed and cattle. A tang of animal and work and food radiated from them filling the space. Some smelled raw and untamed, others emanated a settled and seasoned quality. Lying with Thomas, she breathed in his scent—fresh, new, different. Almost exotic. Thomas was exciting yet comforting. A contradiction both fascinating and unsteadying. She didn't like feeling off-balance. She had the same feeling at the opera. Her nerves had been on fire. She'd felt unhinged, languid, out of control. She'd felt—unmoored.

Only in the morning when she woke did she realize she'd fallen asleep in his arms. He must have carried her, clothes and all, into bed, covered her with a quilt, and gone home.

The next morning after chores before threshing continued, she went to town. She couldn't go to New York. She had to tell him in person before he left. She pushed the horse and herself. She should be at Reuters to help with their forty acres of grain, although they wouldn't be upset. Her few acres of oats required less time to thresh than getting the wagon and thresher there.

He was alone in his uncle's tidy home behind the

mortuary. Claudia handed him the ticket that he'd purchased weeks ago for her to meet him in New York for the July 30th, Saturday performance of Sibelius.

"What do you mean you can't go?" Thomas stood above her.

"I have urgent business to take care of." She retorted as if that should be reason enough, and she set the ticket on the table. "You can transfer it for your ticket today."

"But I already have our concert tickets purchased and our rooms reserved. I don't understand what could be so important that you can't take a weekend away." He backed away from her and pushed the ticket to the edge of the table in her direction. Claudia felt she and the ticket were somehow tainted.

She was mentally scrambled trying to unravel money problems, not wanting anyone to know and blame her, and she was tired after several days of threshing. Tuesday the threshers had done the Fourniers' and Andersens' small plots. Then they'd started on Pete Mevissen's and finished on Wednesday. Thomas had helped Wednesday with her insubstantial oats and yesterday with the Johnsons, and she should be at Reuters today. She and her father had always helped.

"Why can't you get a refund or exchange them for another time? It doesn't seem that big of an inconvenience to me." She nudged the ticket closer to his side of the table. If he only knew what she was dealing with, he'd see that his problem was insignificant by comparison. He was drumming his fingers on the table, eyes on the ticket. She wished he'd stop. Her head hurt. She knew she could solve the debt problem somehow, and everything would be fine again. He turned away from her. The drumming had stopped, and she sighed. "I just need time."

When he turned to face her again, his face was flushed and his dancing blue eyes had turned to darts, "An inconvenience?" He shot at her, "Do you think a twenty-hour train ride to come back here to visit you is convenient? The concert is in nine days! It can't be rescheduled."

"Visit me? You don't come here to visit me! You're here to take over your uncle's business. Don't tell me that I am the reason or cause for your *inconvenience.*" He must need someone to blame and she was the target.

"I came back this time to help you thresh," he responded quietly.

Thank God, she hadn't confided in him about her financial troubles. She could imagine how he would hold that over her head.

"You said you wanted the experience," she spat back. "Well, you had it. Don't blame me for your choices." She spat the words knowing that only because he had been there had the boy's leg, and possibly his life, been saved. "I didn't ask you to come back. No one made you return."

He beheld her, and she couldn't believe the sadness on his face.

"I've asked nothing of you either here or in New York. I wanted to treat you to *La Traviata*, and I want you to hear Sibelius. If that isn't a commitment that deserves an honest explanation for this sudden turn of events, then I don't know what to say except I've been candid with you. I think I deserve the same respect from you." He was correct. He had been generous and honest to a fault. But could she trust him with knowledge of her precarious financial situation?

His face went blank and hard and his eyes cold. "Yes, I think you're right. You need time. Time to figure out what is important. And I obviously am not on that list of yours." He reached for the ticket, then stopped. "You have no idea what I've gone through because of you. I'm going to leave this here." He picked up the train ticket, opened her hand, and placed the ticket on her palm. "Use it or don't. Write, and let me know your decision. Please decide soon, in case I need to make other arrangements." With that he picked up his suitcase, held the door for her to exit ahead of him, and began walking past the boarding house toward the depot to await his train. She looked down at the ticket, then up to the man. A strong part of her wanted to try to catch him, explain about her father and the debt, but part of her resented that he didn't just trust her, and she didn't want to make a scene on Main Street. People all too soon would hear about her inquires to get financing. She watched as he turned the corner without a glance back.

On her way home, she decided that two days away wouldn't change the course of events for her financial situation, and she definitely could use a break from physical labor and a distraction like the otherworldliness of the big city. Unfortunately, she'd be obliged to the Johnsons again to do her chores.

22. New York Again

Late summer and her hay was in the barn along with the oat straw. Threshing was finished, and her oats barely filled the bottom of the metal cylinder oats bin, enough for seed but not much to grind for feed. She'd gotten caught up with the garden such as it was, and jars of pickles and early tomatoes lined the shelves.

Claudia had taken the train to New York City, or the Big Apple, as Thomas called his bustling city. Much of her first trip had been a blur, relying on Thomas to guide her through the crowds and confusion. This time she was alone. As she walked from the train to the main hall of Grand Central Station, the sizzle of sausages and fried potatoes that vendors dished into cardboard containers made Claudia's mouth water. Thomas would meet her at noon under the train station clock. In the arched and domed terminal, she seated herself on the wooden bench which was comfortable enough. The gold and turquoise cathedral ceiling towered several stories above her. Light flooded through the mammoth windows at the end and those high on the side walls and fell on the crowds of people walking quickly to catch trains or greet arrivals. She focused on the clock at the center of the building, which could be seen from all four directions. Awareness of the debt weighed on her like a yoke, but she had done all she could with the banker, RT, the cattleman, and ads in the farm journals. She needed space to consider what to do next. Thomas had made the arrangements for this second trip right after their first trip. She consoled herself, don't think, don't make waves. She focused on now and where she was.

Grand Central Station was like another land. People ranged from pale colors to shades of brown and yellow to black as night. Rushing past her were men wrapped in white cloth ending above their sandals, turbaned women in a color explosion of loose dresses, and children clutching their almond-eyed parents. Unfamiliar languages of countries at which she could only guess, bounced around her. Many spoke English, but she understood little. She sat feeling like she was waiting for a cow to begin labor. She wanted to be active; inactivity made her uncomfortable. Mucking out the barn was preferable to sitting here unable to do anything. Limbo was what Vivian called it, being impotent.

She overheard three men—"hedging, bear, bull market"—as they walked by in their pinstriped suits carrying briefcases. Even in their strange language and appearance, they were appealing to her, exotic. When they smiled as they strolled past with long-legged assurance, she tipped her head and returned their smiles.

She noticed the cracks and calluses on her hands and wished she had udder balm to rub into them. That would be something practical that she could do rather than just sitting.

"They also serve who only stand and wait," Vivian used to say to her when Claudia got antsy while waiting for her father. By the time she was an adolescent she had explored every nook and cranny of Ernie's store. Vivian could no longer distract her into examining some implement the way she had when Claudia was a child while her father talked farm. As an adolescent, if she and Vivian weren't discussing a book, she was bored. Later when she became interested in the farm, she listened in on the men's conversations.

Now she eavesdropped on the talk in this "strange country." New experiences excited her but at the same time made her apprehensive. She was confident in a field behind a horse or on a tractor. Here she felt like she either wanted to escape or withdraw into herself. She stared at the many-sided clock and waited for the next minute to click forward. She examined the people and breathed. They really weren't so different from her; their casual smiles or looks of indifference were similar to Vivian's or RT's. She felt her clothes dated her. She didn't see anyone with a flower, print dress like hers. The clothes here were confidently exotic or bold in black, white, and steel gray.

Thomas saw her before she saw him. "You look like you belong here, in the city."

He smiled, picking up her carpeted bag, and held his arm in a crook for her to hold. She realized she must appear more relaxed than she felt.

That evening the concert and dinner were wonderful once again, despite the lack of familiarity.

He requested a wine by type and year. Their salads had unique vegetables. She'd never heard of artichokes, which tasted as foreign as the waiter sounded. For dessert they had what at home she called custard, but Thomas called crème brûlée with a thin hard crust on top that was sweet and caramelly. Thomas ordered them an after-dinner drink. She didn't understand how this restaurant could procure alcohol, yet here was a small glass of an almost clear liquid that tasted of pears and summer, which made her head go light and bubbly. She glided back to their hotel with Thomas guiding her. Her feet never felt the cobbled stones.

When Thomas dropped her at her room she felt dreamily relaxed and couldn't get the key to fit in the lock. He reached down and put his hand around hers, guided the key to the hole, inserted it, slowly turned it, and gently twisted the knob. With his hands on her hips he held her from behind and guided her through the doorway and to the bed. The next thing she remembered was waking up in bed with her nightgown on, but something was wrong. Her head felt funny, swirly, and then she realized she was still wearing her underthings. She usually slept with only her underwear, and she was wearing her brassiere and garter belt under her nightgown. With a rush she realized Thomas must have taken off her clothes last night. She could vaguely remember feeling ticklish as he'd removed her shoes and unrolled her stockings from her legs and feet. She flushed at the intimacy of that action.

They had had another fabulous evening of music, food, and Thomas's city friends.

The next morning they went sightseeing, then returned to the hotel to rest before an afternoon that Claudia hoped would be equally as wonderful and a distraction from farm worries. They were talking to the concierge when Claudia saw Thomas give his attention to an attractive, older woman checking into the hotel. He turned his head away and ushered Claudia to the elevator more quickly than she cared. She stretched out on her bed, and he went back downstairs, saying he needed to talk to the front desk but he'd return in a few minutes.

He came up from the main floor and suggested rather abruptly that they cut their visit short and return to the farm on the afternoon train.

"But we were going to go to the Statue of Liberty," Claudia protested.

"Yes, but we can save that for the next time, a reason to return."

Claudia was confused. She resigned herself to going home and taking care of the debt. Perhaps this change was for the best, she mused.

While they were packing their suitcases, Claudia could see Thomas through their open doors across the hall from each other. He gathered up his clothes, haphazardly packing them regardless of clean or soiled. Usually his clothes were folded neatly, every shirt's sleeves crossed over the chest. Claudia folded the gloves borrowed from Vivian in tissue and tucked them in next to the dress and shoes she had worn the evening before.

As Thomas and Claudia were checking out, that same woman Claudia had glimpsed earlier stepped off the elevator and walked right up to Thomas. She was smiling.

"Hello," she exclaimed. Thomas had Claudia by the elbow. The bellhop had not yet picked up his suitcase and her bag.

"You must tell me everything that's been going on with you." The well-dressed, well-preserved matronly woman appraised Claudia up and down slowly, considered Thomas, and arched her eyebrow appreciatively. "And I have news of a mutual friend that I think will be of interest to you." Thomas, usually so polite, failed to introduce the woman. She presented herself as a client who had met Thomas when her husband died after a lengthy illness, during which her niece had come to stay with her. With that the small matron grasped Claudia's bare arm in one of her satin-covered arms, hooked Thomas's with her other, and led them into the lounge for a cocktail. After they were seated in a leather booth in a quiet corner, Macy's Aunt Iris began.

"You know our mutual friend, my niece Macy, is married." After a brief glance at Claudia, she tilted her head and stared at Thomas as if she'd eaten the parakeet before the cat even knew it was out of the cage. Thomas blushed. Claudia could see the blush even in the dim light and felt the leather turn cold against her bare arms.

"That's good news," Thomas mumbled with the conviction the parakeet owner would say after learning her bird was eaten quickly and had not suffered a lengthy illness.

"She married a physician, and they live in the kind of house Macy always thought she should have—large and showy. Her gowns and jewelry suit her taste and display his success. She was one of his "accomplishments," like his horses. He built his estate and stables and fashioned the perfect wife." She cocked her head and stared knowingly at Thomas.

Claudia, who has been listening to the aunt, turned her attention to Thomas. He had his shoulders slumped and his hands open across his thighs. He peeked up and broke the silence. "I hope she has what she wants."

"She got what she wanted, but I'm not sure she got what I would want for her. Her mother, God rest her soul, would be proud of how she bettered herself." The matron sighed. After a few awkward minutes, Thomas made the excuse that they needed to catch a train. Claudia was confused at the matron's remarks and Thomas's almost guilty reaction. She had questions but the bustle at the train station provided no opportunity to ask them. She thought once they were settled, they could talk. But the trip home for Claudia was confusing. Uncomfortable silences followed even more uncomfortable remarks, all going nowhere. Like the dust on the wheels of the train, time passed as a swirl of directionless motion.

They hadn't gotten a sleeper car like they had on her first trip. Instead they had decided to do as Thomas did on his trips—they would sit and sleep in reclining seats which were less expensive and comfortable enough.

The entire long trip she was bewildered and frustrated. She didn't understand why they'd left in a flurry. Obviously, Thomas knew this woman Macy and her Aunt Iris, but why was he was acting so strange. Why didn't he talk to her? She hadn't seen Thomas since he'd settled her into their ticketed seats. He stated he needed to walk and had disappeared. He returned just as she was drifting off, and when she awoke, he was fast asleep and only stirred at the clang and whistle as they entered the Turtle Lake Depot. He got his car, and they drove in silence the few miles to the farm. She didn't know how to begin the questions without sounding like a shrew. They were both exhausted. They stopped by the Johnsons to say she was home. He dropped her at her farm saying he'd see her tomorrow. As she went through the motions of evening chores, she felt her father's words ringing in her ears.

"I told you people without strong ties to the earth don't have a sense of principles. It's not their fault. They just have no moral grounding."

But that's not true, she had protested to her father's voice in her head. Thomas was very grounded and decent. At least that's what she had thought. *Who was this Macy?*

"It's an honest day's labor that gives a person fiber, substance, integrity. Working with your hands and body gives you a connection to the earth and to animals. It keeps you in the rhythm of life."

Thomas was in the rhythm of life. He was intimate with the process of living and dying. He was gentle and cared deeply about her and her animals. *Didn't he?*

"Being out in God's creation, working, builds character. Without character you are a shallow being, no better than a beast." The voice of her father rang accusatively in her head.

Thomas had character, and no one would ever think he was a beast, but he didn't love her land the way her father had been dedicated to it. Thomas could easily move back to the city and never miss her farm.

"Living off the land keeps your mind clear on what is right and just." Her father may never have verbalized those exact words but that is what she heard every time she felt drawn to anything other than what her father would approve.

She had enjoyed New York. The music and food were incredible. Yes, she had perfectly good meat and potatoes at home, but to sit and be served, no overalls hung on a hook to remind her of chores to do or manure-clad boots waiting out on the porch was a relief. At dinner she had enjoyed music playing and being waited on by men in crisp white shirts, ties, and creased black pants. She felt relaxed and content in New York with Thomas. His blue eyes had sparkled warmly while champagne bubbled cool in her glass. *Why had he insisted on leaving so abruptly?*

She could feel her father shaking his head, disappointed that once again she had left her chores for a neighbor to do, so she could go traipsing across the country, burning up wood and coal on a train trip for no good reason. But she did not hear him say the words she wanted an answer to—"and with a debt to be resolved." *There, that's the real reason for my misgivings and my failure to confront him on the train—guilt.* She had betrayed her father and the farm. A debt hanging, and she'd been off galivanting. But she had done what she could. She hadn't gotten a response to the advertisement in the farm papers for her breeding stock. She consoled herself that only two weeks had passed. She assuaged her guilt.

Thomas had assured her that she was the reason to take another trip: she deserved a break, she got sick from overwork, and she had lost her father. He wanted to treat her to experiencing the opera and concerts that he loved. She chided her father's ghostly whispers.

Now the gauzy specter of a young New York City woman named Macy hung between Claudia and Thomas.

The next day after a more restful sleep in her own bed, she ruminated on all that had transpired. She was so angry with Thomas, she wanted to scream at him. How dare he not tell her he had had a girlfriend before her? Why act so strange? Had he been intimate with her? Every week they had talked for hours, and she thought they'd confided everything. She had trusted him. After everything she'd been through, finally she felt she could relax into loving him, trusting him. She had opened herself like a delicate bluebell, and he crushed her like a farmhand in a field. No more. She would make sure of that. Never again would she tell anyone her thoughts and fears or worse, be intimate with him, letting him see and feel his effect on her.

She had allowed herself to go toward that place of loving him completely. She had reveled in the luxury of loving Thomas, being with him on her porch swing or seated at the opera. They would lie there; she enjoying him pleasuring her and rising to his need in equal measure to satisfying her own. She had been allowing herself to begin to live this wonderful womanly sensual play of theirs. She would rather face Bully than risk the hurt of being betrayed by Thomas.

Her temper, like the weather, had not cooled in the twenty-four hours since she'd last seen him. When he came up the drive late that afternoon, she was pulling weeds in the garden. He walked in through the gate, and she belted out, "What was she to you?"

"A close friend," he pulled the gate which clanked shut.

"Why not tell me?" she glared at him, shielding her eyes from the setting sun.

He began making excuses. "I thought it didn't matter. Why did I need to bring it up? It was over. It didn't mean anything. I was naive. That was nothing like what we have."

"Then why didn't you tell me about her? Why hide it?" She yanked at the weeds that had grown tall in less than a week.

"I didn't hide it. I just never said the exact words. I tried to tell you the day that you were working on weasel prevention."

"You were ashamed. That's why you wanted to leave New York so quickly." She put her hand up to block the sun when she looked up at him.

"You're right. But not for the reason you think." He moved so he stood blocking the sun. His shadow fell on her, which protected her from the bright light but prevented her from seeing him clearly. "We were engaged, briefly."

"What?" she stood up. "When?"

"Well, I proposed to her that Saturday after we buried your father," he offered sheepishly.

She couldn't believe the words. "You mean while you were interested in me, you were engaged to her?"

"No!" he rushed, then slowed. "Well, yes, but the next two months being with you, watching you, helping you, I realized I didn't love her."

She braced her dirt-covered hands on her hips. "But you were engaged to her! Was she the unpleasant business you had to take care of?" She stopped then scrutinized him. "Was she having your baby?"

"No, that's where you're wrong. At least, I think you are." He offered a deflated buoy to a sinking ship. "It was only once, then she claimed she was pregnant, but she wasn't, I don't think."

"That's why we had to leave in a hurry. You didn't want to confront her Aunt!"

She went back to her knees. *If I stay standing I will slap or punch that man.* She chose a verbal assault instead.

"I'm just another one of your women. How many others have you had?" She ripped at the weeds and accidently pulled up a struggling tomato plant with them. "Oh, I forgot. You're from New York. New Yorkers are sophisticated, unlike us country bumpkins." She stood again, holding the tomato plant and weeds together.

She worked herself up so her mouth outran her brain. "New Yorkers share their love with many. That's the way life is out East—fast and easy."

She stepped to the side, so the sun wasn't full in her eyes, and she could see the hurt she wanted to inflict. She tossed the dried vegetation to the ground.

"No attachments. High rollers out for fun and games." She knew the accusations weren't true. She knew she was saying them to hurt him. She wanted to cause him some of the pain she felt, but, when she glared at him, she knew she'd gone too far. He appeared deflated.

But she couldn't, wouldn't, take the words back. *Is everyone I love going to lie to me?* Her father took out a mortgage without telling her. Now she had to figure a way out. She couldn't trust anyone but herself. The words to Thomas couldn't be sucked back in and swallowed. They hung like great, dark vines wildly clinging to the branches of their psyches, preventing movement. Only patient methodical untwisting of the spiraled tentacles could free them both from the snarled mess and even then the debris would entangle their feet, inhibiting passage forward.

"It's okay. I'll leave." He opened the gate, not looking her in the face. "I wasn't meant for this." His gaze rested on the dog she knew he loved as if it were his own. The two males stepped out of the garden.

"I made my bed. I made poor choices, then I tried to do what I thought was better for me even if I was abandoning Macy who I thought was pregnant. But then that wasn't true," his voice was despondent. "I was a fool."

Shep whined at his feet, and Thomas bent to touch his shaggy head.

"Don't touch him," Claudia stepped forward as if to join them. "Don't touch him or me. I don't need excuses. I don't need you. I need an honest equal."

He hung his head and turned to leave. The tall man, reduced to slumped shoulders on a bent frame, walked away. Shep started to follow. Claudia grabbed Shep by his collar.

"No!" She shouted to Thomas's back, and Shep began to howl. Thomas left without turning around. He never saw that the ramrod stiff woman had tears raging down her cheeks.

23. Claudia and Hank

Three days after her fight with Thomas, a violent storm came up. The day before the storm Hank had driven by with a honk and a wave. Today she wondered how their farm had weathered the winds last night.

Claudia was not sure if she liked Hank, but she was becoming aware that he was interested in her. When they were younger he had teased her, even though she was older and had towered above him. He, like most of the boys in school, was awkward and full of bravado. She had been provoked by their antics to get girls' attention and had walked away for fear she'd punch one of them and receive more verbal abuse. If she hadn't been so incompatible, maybe she could reach out to her neighbor whose farm was kitty-corner across the road. She was not going to ask Thomas for help. She'd become too dependent on him, he wasn't very handy, anyway, and he'd proven he wasn't trustworthy. She didn't want to ask anyone to help her.

Lightning had ripped across the night sky with the windstorm last night, and Claudia's roof, which had been leaking ever since the last storm, needed repair. This morning she'd tripped over the bucket she'd set in the kitchen in case rain would come with the wind. But no rain came, just the howling gusts that left more shingles in the yard. She dropkicked the bucket in her hand but not hard enough to dent it. At her side, Shep jerked at the crash close to his good ear.

After chores she went up the extended ladder and climbed onto the steep pitch. Her body swayed, and the trees next to the house lost their shape and started to waver. She extended her arms to embrace the roof in front of her, squashed her chest to the shingles, and pressed her eyes shut. After a few deep breaths, she allowed her eyes to open. As long as she didn't look down she was fine, but every time she had to place her foot on a different section of roof she had to watch her feet, which set her head spinning. She went down on all fours until she could stand to survey the next section of roof for damage.

These old Norwegian houses had valleys and dormers and nooks and crannies, each steeper than the other. She had brought a piece of canvas, several laths, and zinc roofing nails to tarp over the kitchen and pantry where the worst area of the leaking had been. Now she could spot at least two sections on the northwest side where the shingles had blown off. Through the spaces between the exposed boards she could see down into the attic. She tacked the canvas over the largest exposed part and backed to the ladder leaning against the edge of the two-story home. Once she was on the ground, she sat with her head between her knees until the spinning slowed. That's when she heard him or maybe felt his presence.

"You okay?" inquired the male voice. She peered up and saw genuine concern. She nodded, accepting Hank's extended hand.

"How bad is it?"

"Not so deep as a well nor wide as a river, but 'twill serve," she quipped from her addled brain.

When he pulled his head back questioningly, she rephrased. "Two places both down to the wood."

"You got any shingles?"

She knew a person had to be practical and couldn't look a gift horse in the mouth, unless the gift was from the Greeks, as Vivian was fond of telling her. Claudia understood that to mean you should take whatever God gives you in the form of help but always be aware that some assistance, which seems to be genuine, may have strings attached, such as expectations of reciprocation, or may just not be a real gift but a subterfuge like the Trojan horse. She was so confused lately she didn't know how to respond. She reverted to practicalities.

"We bought more when we built the loafing shed for the new cattle. There should be enough." Already she was in mid-stride down to the shed to survey how many there were. They calculated about how many would be needed. She never really asked him for help, and he never really offered. He just left saying, "I'll be back tomorrow after chores." And he was.

He had her ladder up against the side of the house by eight the next morning. When she followed him up the ladder, he had the nerve to protest, but she set him straight with one look. By noon they had woven the shingles into the existing ones. Claudia was content with silence. She and her father often didn't talk during the day. They were each doing their separate tasks unless something required two sets of hands, and then they spoke only as needed. Hank stopped hammering and leaned forward to point to his sleek chestnut filly down in the corral of Claudia's barnyard where he had left the filly when he arrived.

"You see that horse." Claudia sat hammer in her lap and listened. "She could've been a race horse. I saved her from becoming dog food. She kinda fell into my lap." Hank proceeded to tell Claudia how he'd met their neighborhood cattle jockey who had a customer with thoroughbred racehorses. The customer had a mare that got bred by mistake and had troubles. They wanted to save the mare at all costs, so when she dropped a bitty filly of bad breeding, the owner told the cattle jockey to haul it away for glue.

"Pure chance that I met him on the road leaving the farm," Hank recounted as he resumed weaving new shingles in between missing ones and nailing them in place. "I gave him the dollar the renderer would've paid. I bottle-fed that little thing because she had something about her that snared me the minute I looked in the back of the cattle jockey's truck." He paused and waited for Claudia to turn her brown eyes to him. "She lifted her head and those big doe eyes appealed to me." He turned his gaze away, and Claudia almost missed his next comment, "I wanted to unravel her mystery or at least corral it." He didn't quite hear her so he asked, "What did ya say?"

"Your filly. She reminds me of our foals. Molly's filly died after she started eating hay. My father thought the hay was tainted by pigeon droppings. We had a problem until we got chicken wire tacked over the opening the birds had found." She rested a moment against the roof's slant.

"What ever happened to Dandy's foal?" He stopped tacking for the moment.

"He was healthy as any horse could be." She sighed. "We sold him. We didn't need a single horse. Molly and Dandy were our team." Claudia resumed her hammering.

Hank picked up another asphalt shingle from the pile between them, wove it into the others, and hammered it into place with wide-headed zinc nails from the pocket of the leather apron, which was similar to but larger than the cloth one encircling Claudia's waist. They worked side by side all morning. Only once did she need to lie down, her back against the shingles, focusing her eyes on the overhanging oak branches to stop her head from spinning.

"You wanna go down, start lunch? I'll finish up here." She considered the few shingles left to be tacked and backed down the ladder without a word. When he finished, he returned the tools to the shed, hung up the nailing apron, replaced the remaining shingles on the pile, and washed up at the pump outside.

Claudia hadn't expected them to have anything to talk about other than farming. If asked a week ago, she would have disclosed they had nothing in common except their farms. But she wasn't thinking. She was numb and overwhelmed, so the conversation just happened.

Toward dusk as she was working in the garden, she thought of how the talk had started. Maybe his story of the filly, or his concern for his mother, or his desire for a woman's opinion. However the conversation began, they talked for two hours. The dishes were washed. He dried. Several cups of coffee later, he left, and she realized the time had flown.

The next night a dance was to be held at a local tavern. Thomas had returned to New York after their argument. She didn't know if or when he was coming back, and she wasn't sure she cared. When Hank called on her Friday morning to go to the dance that evening, she accepted the invitation. The day had been difficult. She'd gone through her father's information on their cattle, roughed out a letter extolling their attributes, and written out several copies leaving the name blank, waiting for a response to her ads so she could send the letters to those interested. Unfortunately, agonizing weeks would pass before she would hear any response from the ads. In order to pay some on overdue property tax, she'd sold two of her steers, not to their regular cattle jockey but one out of Amery. A dance would be a good break.

The evening started out well. "Wow, you look great," he blurted out, appraising her up and down, more up than down as he was now a bit shorter than she was in her wedge-heeled Sunday shoes. When they got to the dance, he held the front door of the tavern open and gestured with a sweeping arm for her to enter before him. The music was already in full swing. Several couples were oscillating around the dance floor to a polka. The guitar player sang country western tunes with the heartache of a rejected, penniless cowpoke. When the banjo player's turn began, he plucked out toe-tapping bluegrass pieces and ballads. When the drummer played, he wailed on his drums heedless of a melody. Hank went up to the bar and got two glasses of beer for them. He had taken off his feed cap and had on his dress cowboy boots which,

214

she noticed, he had polished. He was a tolerably good dancer and enjoyed himself. He was self-confident and led her around the floor with assurance. She relaxed into the evening, liking the familiarity of being with a man of patriarchal manners similar to her father.

All in all, the evening was delightful, so much so that when he saw her home and wanted to kiss her goodnight, she let him. He kissed her hard with his mouth wide and wet, only once, but more than enough for Claudia. She jerked away with such vehemence that he appeared startled, then angry.

"What's the matter with you? I thought we were having fun."

"I thought so too until now."

"You just don't have any experience. It's okay. Trust me." He leaned into her, hand cupping her buttock. She pushed him away.

"You shouldn't be so picky." He scrutinized her slowly, holding her attention. Quietly he cautioned, "You're no spring chicken."

Without a word she stepped into her kitchen, still keeping her focus on him, and closed the door.

Early the next week Claudia was pleasantly surprised when Hank stopped with a partial wagonload of wood.

"Hey, we had a few downed hardwood trees after that wind storm last week. Dad wanted me to get 'em cut up and stacked between first and second crop of haying. Our rack was full. This was surplus, so I thought I'd bring some over. I noticed yours was looking sparse when I was here the other day." He parked their team of Percherons next to her wood rack, hopped down from the seat, and began unloading.

Claudia jumped up on the back of the wagon and handed cut-to-stove-size arm loads of wood to him that he'd already split.

"This is very thoughtful of you," she acknowledged remembering the less than friendly ending to their dance evening. "Thank you." She handed wood down, and he stacked until the load was empty, which took all of a quarter of an hour.

"Do you want to come in for coffee?" she asked in gratitude. After another pleasant quarter of an hour, he left but not before securing her agreement to attend the town fair with him on Friday.

The town fair made for a fun afternoon sandwiched between chores. The Johnsons won ribbons for their dairy cows with superior udder conformation and a sheaf of green corn stocks of exceptional height and maturity for this early in August. Mrs. Johnson received a blue ribbon for her lemon chiffon cake. They ate hot beef sandwiches with dill spears washed down with fresh cold milk served at the church booth under a canopy held up by poles.

Saturday morning Claudia was cleaning the chicken coop when she saw the hen scrunched into herself, compressed accordion neck, eyes shut. Bright red spots littered the perch around her. Claudia slowly picked up the listless hen who opened her eye to stare at Claudia. The hen's back end was bloody. Claudia wondered if the blood was from laying an egg too large or from the other chickens pecking her. Probably the result of both, she decided.

She set the manure fork aside and held the black-and-white speckled bird in the crook of her left arm and gathered two eggs with her right hand. One of the eggs was very bloody. Claudia stopped, held the hen, smoothed her feathers, and felt her breathing begin to slow. Claudia set her in a nest box at the end of the top row, one that was rarely occupied. She offered water but the hen was motionless. She put feed in front of the hen, but she didn't peck. Claudia figured she was probably too far gone to care to eat.

She continued to stroke the black and white feathers until the bird's legs collapsed and she lay with her head resting on the edge of the nest box. Claudia held her hand on the hen as the other chickens paraded in.

Claudia worried the hen would die within twenty-four hours. Many years ago, a similar situation had occurred, and that hen, despite being put in a shed with food and water to recover, had died. She had wanted to bring the animal into the house, but Papa would not permit that. "Don't interfere in the normal course of life, Claudia."

She had no predator-free shed available now anyway, and she had to finish cleaning the coop and cut hay as soon as any dew was off. Claudia hoped the hen would recover quickly or die peacefully. She was resting with eyes shut when Claudia left with the manure fork, bucket of droppings, and the two eggs. She would check on the chicken again after doing a few repairs to that old shed. Maybe then she'd have a place that was safe for this kind of situation.

She felt her animals' pain but couldn't allow their discomfort to be too close or the sorrow would collapse her. She needed to stay on her feet. Everything depended on her. Thoughts flew like ravens through her head. Should she wring its neck and put her hen out of misery or let nature take its course? She worried maybe this hen was too old, no spring chicken, and should have been butchered when she had done the others. Maybe she had made a mistake.

She remembered a story her father had told her after she had brought home an orphaned baby bunny only a couple inches long, which she wanted to keep.

"A man had a sow with a litter of piglets which included a runt. His young daughter begged her father to keep the runt, and against his better judgment, he gave into his child's pleadings. She was too young to bottle-feed the piglet so the man had tried to put the runt to a teat whenever he passed by the pigpen. The piglet never gained, and while his siblings thrived, he, by comparison, got smaller and smaller. One day his daughter came running in screaming helplessly. 'Papa, Papa they are eating their brother, and the mom is not stopping them.' The father followed his daughter to the pigpen where now the sow was chewing on the tiny head of the runt. A farmer's gotta let nature take its course. Only the strong survive."

At the time Claudia thought that reasoning made sense, but she remembered thinking *when I am in charge I will take the runt and feed it in its own pen until it is big enough to fend for itself.* But she had been very young then, and she was older and busier now.

Her father knew that when the likelihood of survival was slim, an animal's discomfort was better ended quickly. "To prolong an animal's agony is inhumane," he'd cautioned her. "The father wanted to please his daughter, but that hurt the girl worse." And that is where her father had left the discussion and the baby bunny—in the thicket only yards from where she'd found its dead mother in a snare trap. She fleetingly wondered what Thomas would have done. She felt she knew that Hank would be like her father, practical.

The rhythm of the work, the beat of hammer pounding, the back and forth motion of the saw, and the click, click of the sickle mower kept her body so occupied on Saturday and Sunday that she only had room to think about finding the necessary materials and how best to perform the job. Only when she couldn't find where her father had stored the pieces of metal did she realize she was angry at him. She needed assistance but wouldn't ask.

She did not want Hank bossing her on her own farm. If he kept coming to help, in a matter of time he'd start taking over, making decisions. And Thomas? He wouldn't boss her if he were around, but he had an opinion. He got that look that warned her she might be doing something he thought foolish.

Claudia resorted to what she always did—work. She wasn't even sure if the work was worth doing. The old, ramshackle shed on the corner of the property was decrepit. The small out building held a broken leather sewing machine that could be useful for parts, maybe, some discarded wooden barrels, and a box of mixed nails and bolts that had been collected after a barn-raising that still held floor sweepings and curls of wood from the planes and chisels.

Her plan had been to re-side the dilapidated shed with some leftover siding from several projects ago. The galvanized sheets were unwieldy, buried under other piles of lumber. Most of the pieces were bent at the corners, and some had old nail holes. She and her father had collected some of the sheets out of the swamp where a storm had blown them. She remembered now that many had been peeled back by the wind and were left curled up on the wall of the milk house. She and her father had struggled with a crowbar to pry off the remaining attached sheets. Her father had decided to re-side the milk house with a more modern material.

Thoughts churned as she had stomped on a board placed across the dished metal. If flattened, the sheet could be nailed to the wall of the shed. The metal sprang back and slit across her leg, cutting through her jeans and into her skin. *Why am I doing this?* She abandoned the idea of using the metal. She harnessed Molly, hooked her to the sickle mower, and cut the rest of the wild hay. She needed every blade she could get, even if she ended up selling more of her cattle. She was still waiting to hear from the ads. The need to sell anything of value weighed on her. She'd sold some of her father's tools in Amery where word wouldn't be as likely to spread. She'd paid some on the property tax but didn't know what to sell to pay the balance or how to make the loan payment.

By the time Claudia finished cutting hay, she needed a kerosene lamp to close the chickens in for the night. She'd missed church service. Her hen was lying on the ground in a corner of the chicken yard, dead. She had been pecked at where she had bled. After digging a shallow hole, Claudia covered the corpse, washed up, and went to bed.

Claudia walked out into the Monday morning mist feeling the pull to return to the cocoon of her bed and the escape sleep could give, maybe. She had two broody hens who sat daily in the nesting boxes trying to hatch nonexistent eggs. She collected eggs at least twice a day, yet these two persisted in sitting all hunched up and irritable ready to peck her when she reached under them. Without thought she cooed to them, telling them to go outside and get some fresh air, that this was the wrong season to be setting on eggs. *Would summer never end?* She almost welcomed the thought of winter even though she didn't have enough wood or hay made to get her, her horses, and cattle through a tough winter.

Her chickens, like her, were doing things that they had done forever and for a reason that made sense at one time. Animals followed instincts and patterns that had worked for them. Maybe the unusual weather—hot then cool—messed up their instincts. She too was going about a routine that had lost its logic. Normally she followed her instincts. But innate behavior, hers and her hens', had gone haywire. Instead she and these foolish hens were persisting in an unproductive activity that they stubbornly wouldn't change. They had gotten mixed up and couldn't break the cycle. Was it the unexpected falling in love with Thomas? Or the equally unexpected feelings of familiarity stirred by Hank? Or was the weather to blame? Dust storms, the unexpected quick rain, then dust again. One day was in the mid-nineties; the next morning frost lay on the ground. She didn't know whether to keep her long underwear on or remove them; whether to wear a cotton T-shirt or a flannel long-sleeve.

She crawled back into bed after setting the milk in the icebox and the basket with two eggs in the cool back pantry. The day was misty but no rain. As she pulled the coverlet made by her mother over her head, she pulled a thought over her, justifying her reluctance to be productive: *It is rainy. I can't work in the garden, anyway. The repairs to the shed will have to wait. Besides, I am exhausted. I shouldn't have worked past sunset both nights especially without taking time to eat properly. I can't face RT or a banker today.*

She nursed her wounds, hoping no one would stop and find her not working.

24. Randy's Gang

Back in the middle of July, Randy Rottman had stared out his upper window at Claudia Nelson, who'd left his office in a huff. He knew that Francis had taken out the loan to help his lady friend Nora expand her restaurant. He also knew that for Claudia not to know was unusual. When Claudia was little, she often sat in the mortgager's office half listening and quietly drawing on a pad of paper or reading a book while the men discussed and came to an arrangement on terms, rates, and timelines. He had thought that this time she would've seen reason and been ready to make a deal. He had time. He could wait, but she couldn't. But he had to be careful not to tarnish his image as he negotiated this deal.

Randy knew the profit that lay beneath Francis's crop land. He'd thought on more than one occasion how sweet if Francis was unable to make good on his loan. Francis had always been proud of his daughter. The two men had crossed paths on community projects and farm financing. He and Francis had exchanged glory stories on more than one occasion. Randy had listened patiently when Francis bragged of thirteen-year-old Claudia's initiative and the Belgians' help in rescuing a snowbound family she'd come upon stranded on their return from town. A beautiful, clear day had taken a sudden turn causing the family's father to send them home while he finished getting supplies. The snowstorm increased in severity which caused the young Claudia to hitch the team to retrieve her father who was also in town. But Randy had minded Francis's casual dismissal of Andrew's athletic achievements, especially his all-star performance at the state football championship.

After his meeting with Claudia, Randy came home to a wife who was anything but pleasant. She could hold a fleet of men enrapt at a cocktail party, but get her at home alone and Randy felt she was a wild cat—unpredictable and moody. She was not old enough for the change, but by the Almighty she was changeable. Today she was worried about the party they were going to host, the Fall Festival Fundraiser. She was concerned that Andrew, their less-than-perfect child, who she bragged in public was the most adoring and accomplished of sons, would not stand up to the "scrutiny of routine conversation."

Penny pounced on Randy the minute he walked in the door. She didn't even give him time to get a cocktail. "We cannot have Andrew at home for the party. Can't you keep him busy in another city or send him on business to visit a college friend back East?"

"I have bigger fish to fry than figuring out how to keep our son out of the limelight," he declared while clinking ice loudly into his glass and pouring two fingers of Scotch. "Why did we pay big bucks for an education at one of those vine-covered schools if they can't guarantee him an Ivy League job?"

"If you paid more attention to your son and wife than every dirt farmer, you would realize they can only do so much. He does have a father who, everyone assumes, will guide him. I cannot spoon-feed him the Bible, keep your business associates and their wives happy, do the community and church work, and raise an adult son."

"I thought that was your *job*. You are his mother, aren't you?" Randy hated dealing with what he considered her business. It burned him up that the haranguing could go on for hours until he felt forced to slam the door of one of the most expensive houses in town and go to the club or stop to see one of his "friends" who understood a hard-working man. He expected his wife to back him up, not question him. What he did and where he went was a man's prerogative.

He had had to tell her more than once, "You are not my mother."

She'd exclaim, "Then quit acting like my child." He'd then admonish her, "Does Andrew pay your jewelry, shoes, and clothing bills?" That usually shut her up. Penny's job was the house, entertaining, and Andrew. Randy's job was to keep the money flowing and to keep finances strong to cultivate the image they desired.

After his graduation with the top science prize from MIT, Andrew worked at Western Electric at the Hawthorne Works in Chicago for less than three months, and each month his complaints became more emphatic. Andrew declared to his parents that the boss had a personality conflict with him, the other employees couldn't handle that he was more gifted than they were, and finally that the company was demanding that he, the new and inexperienced guy, work longer hours.

When Andrew moved back in with his parents in Rice Lake, he explained, "I was fired because I wouldn't work for unappreciative people in that hostile environment. They were using me. Western Electric is supposed to be so innovative, but that place was killing my creativity. For my own sanity, I'm glad to be out of there."

Randy called his contact at Western Electric to chew him out and discovered that Andrew had quit because he was out of his depth. The owner of the prestigious Chicago company contacted Randy the next day. "We hired your son believing he was as gifted as his college transcript indicated and evidenced by the science prize award. The only quality he seems to genuinely possess is being a tolerably good athlete. Andrew's modest knowledge and extravagant charisma could no longer carry him here. We advised him in July that we would have to let him go if he didn't start working up to his potential. Andrew became indignant that anyone could think he wasn't good enough to work for them. At the beginning of this month, he informed his supervisor that he didn't need to work where he wasn't appreciated and quit."

Randy hoped the operator wasn't listening in on this long-distance call.

The owner of Western Electric continued, "Clearly, your son was getting credit for someone else's work. We'd like to hire the man that actually constructed and executed that science project to be on our team. If you get us the information on the individual, we won't contact the school or cause any trouble for your son."

Later that day while Penny was out shopping, Randy confronted Andrew.

"You evidently got help at college, which is to be commended, but not to keep your head above the fray is careless. With the extravagant cost of that help, I would have expected you to handle yourself more adeptly."

Andrew gave Bennett's name and address to Randy.

He assured his son, "You can work for me. I can keep an eye on you and you can learn the ropes, but we'd better keep this between ourselves. No need to involve your mother. Tell people the company didn't suit your qualifications."

After Randy relayed the information to the company, his colleague there sent him a letter in which the associate revealed they had contacted Bennett's parents to offer their son the prized job but were informed that he had died alone in a hunting accident less than a week before the call.

Randy's stellar son had fallen to Earth, and Randy didn't like the sound of the meteoric crash. Maybe, he thought, another person's fall from grace, like Claudia Nelson, would distract everyone and give his son time to mature and take his rightful place in society next to his father. Randy believed Andrew just needed a few life experiences under his belt, and then his son would come to appreciate the status and position they had fought so hard to achieve for their family.

He'd done his part by getting Andrew out of his jam, but Randy couldn't tell Penny that. When she returned from the shops and was settled with a cocktail, he met her in the lounge where she'd had her work for the Fall Festival Fundraiser spread out for weeks.

Penny had been preoccupied with the semi-annual event at their place, so her fuse was a little short. Randy hadn't heard from Claudia and needed Penny to help him get what he wanted from Francis's daughter, so he bit his tongue and changed tack. They were both women, so Penny would have an idea on how to get the uppity, old maid to do what he wanted.

He understood the kind of pressure Penny was under, and he respected her ability to hold the whole shebang together so well. Everyone wanted to be invited to the Fall Festival, the most popular event in two counties. The food was catered by a chef Randy brought up from the Twin Cities. For music Penny insisted on a fifteen-piece band in white suits. Randy would've liked guitars and drums and less classical music, but when the most successful people of the county were coming, the hosts have to play the part.

Penny had the invitations printed on stiff linen paper edged in gold with black script lettering. Randy had disclosed to Bill that deep pockets were required for linen with gold borders. Even if times were tough, being chintzy didn't get donors to dig deep and shell out big bucks. If a business was in a slump, the owners were not on the guest list. Penny removed people from the list if their clothes were not from one of her catalogues or from Chicago or New York or if they were wearing last year's leavings. If a person did not respect themselves enough to try to keep up with their neighbors, they did not make the list.

"That's what's driving this Country to rack and ruin… people who just don't care. There isn't room for everybody." Randy had made that clear. "That's why God gave some of us brains and others brawn and broad backs. Those of us with brains are divinely charged with making those with muscle productive." A person had to be worth the cost of an invitation and the investment of ten bucks a head, which is what Pen had figured was the cost to host the shindig. Randy insisted Penny take anyone off the list who was not likely to produce or give a good return on the investment. Technically, the money raised went to charity, and the profit did, but Randy believed in the Bible verse that stated a laborer was worthy of his hire, and God did not expect him to work for free. Randy did enough gratis work for the community.

Everyone was looking forward to this year's event, so Penny's solution was simple. "We need to invite Claudia and her friend."

"Friend?" Randy scoffed. "You mean that wuss from out East that's been sniffing around her?" But she was right. If he couldn't get that woman to cooperate with him, maybe Penny could work her magic.

"Put them on the list," Randy instructed her. He needed a hedge against his bets. Francis was an independent cuss, and his daughter was going to be a tough nut to crack. Too independent for a woman. Too opinionated for her own good. She could get into trouble.

Randy was reassured that nature followed its course when Francis had used his valuable land to back Nora's marginally successful restaurant. Even though Francis had not made a payment since the first of the year, neither the banker nor the mortgage man had notified the farmer. After Francis's death, Bill and Randy had allowed the debt to accumulate, and then they filed the mortgage with the register of deeds, making the lien public record. He'd given Claudia notice that she had a week to clear the mortgage, an impossibility. Legally they could proceed to collect on that debt by seizing chattel, equipment, and property for repayment. Randy had been hoping Francis would default on that loan and be forced to sell land. His death had been a godsend. Randy felt that was literal. The debt had been accumulating at sixteen percent interest and Francis had only made interest payments, nothing toward principle, which meant that the mortgage amount was now greater than originally.

"Nature has a way of leveling the ground," Randy reassured his business cohorts. For someone who understood the process, a profit could result.

A shoemaker in town had not been able to keep up the payments on his shop. People who could not afford feed for their animals did not buy new shoes. When fixing their old footwear became a necessity, they had the cobbler mend them. Crafting, assembling, and producing new footwear wasn't in demand. Repairing shoes only put bread on the table. That scant income was not enough for the shoemaker to pay the property tax or the land payment. The shoemaker had been foreclosed. His shop and home were put up for sale. They were evicted to the street by a middleman, a stranger from out of town.

In private Randy confided to his friends, "That's God's way of weeding out the weak. I'm just God's instrument."

The Rottmans never blamed a poor soul whose investment did not perform well or failed to generate the expected income. But the curve of Randy's smile and the tilt of his knowing head disclosed that the Midas touch was not there. With more time and work, anyone might be able to contribute as much money as the Rottmans and get a building or field named after them. Randy had learned his art at the school of hard knocks, and he was never going to be whacked down again.

He understood the influence women possessed in the bedrooms that determined the decisions in the husbands' boardrooms. His Penny was performing the same dance of courtship, currying men to choose to align themselves with that wonderful Rottman couple. If a man was deciding where to invest his company's capital or who to handle his finances, then Rottmans were the smart choice. Didn't everyone want to be as successful as the Rottmans? To have a house as luxurious and a car as fast? To have his tailor or her seamstress?

Once Randy had been accused of being a common criminal. He did not protest but smiled. He was not a villain with a black top hat and sweeping moustache or wart-ridden face doing dastardly deeds. Some people were blindsided by anger at God's plan of preordination. He thought of himself as a hero similar to Hoover when he was Secretary of Commerce or when he first became president while the stock market was thriving. They both had worked in the name of God and for the good of the Country. The Crash wasn't Hoover's fault any more than a bank foreclosure was Randy's.

25. Secrets

Claudia hadn't seen Vivian since the threshing, which was almost a month ago, and hadn't been to the store in the two weeks since her recent trip to New York. She arrived moments after the store's opening and laid the parcel containing the tissue wrapped borrowed items—gloves and the satin shoes and the beaded purse—on the counter.

"You're here earlier than usual. Most farmers are still at chores, and it's Wednesday." Vivian looked up to the bead-board wall where a large white-faced clock with stark black numerals hung. Tacked below was the colorful Great Northern Railroad wall calendar that this month featured the warrior Clears Up sitting cross-legged, hands in his lap. He appeared relaxed, unlike Claudia, but as serious as she felt. "I wasn't able to sleep. I had to roust my animals for chores."

Vivian reached into the gilded cage, and Percy climbed onto her finger. She stroked the parakeet. Claudia wished she had the life of ease Vivian had. "How was your trip?" asked Vivian. Claudia had dealt with the storm, roof, shed, hay, and garden, but she did not want to deal with the speculation about being seen with Hank at a dance and the fair. She was sure Vivian had been pestered by gossips' questions. "I thought she was sweet on the mortuary man. What happened? Why is Hank good enough for her now?" She stuck to the topic weighing on her heart.

"The concert was wonderful, but the next day our trip fell apart. He's been living a lie with me. I've been so stupid." Claudia sat dejectedly on her customary cane-backed chair. "I thought he was different, but Papa was right. City folks have no connection to land and animals to keep them grounded. They live to please themselves."

"What did this horrible man do?" Vivian's voice sounded sarcastic, but when Claudia glanced up, Vivian was pulling a bolt of cotton fabric straight, and Percy was perched on her shoulder.

"He had a girlfriend with whom he was intimate. He claims it was only once, but if he lied about her, why not lie about how often, and maybe he sees her when he goes back to 'work' in New York." Vivian's hands had stopped smoothing the cloth and studied Claudia. "I don't want him in my life anymore. I don't need him or anyone." She slumped in the stiff-backed chair, clothes as crumpled as her spirit, hair as wild as her thoughts. She couldn't bring herself to confess that Thomas had been engaged while seeing her and that he thought the girl was pregnant with his baby. She'd sound like a radio soap opera. She'd been such a fool. Last night the memory of his touch and smell haunted her sleep.

"The trust is broken. Papa wouldn't want me to be with him. Papa is probably looking down disappointed in me." She spoke stridently as if she were convinced.

"You think you know what your father would think, but none of us can know what's in another person's head or why they do what they do." Vivian sat on her high-legged chair with Percy perched on her shoulder like an ostrich feather clasped to a *Vogue* model's hat. She reached up and Percy jumped to her finger where she scratched his head as she talked.

"There was this widow, Boniface, who took a shine to Francis, but he wanted nothing to do with her. She brought him casseroles after your mother's death, and years later, she was definitely interested in him, but he spurned her. I don't think he thought she was good enough. As time went on your mother became more ideal in his memory. He'd declare, 'Helen was a saint.' Take no offense, but your mother was no saint; no human is. Well, Bonnie married Mr. Xavier after he moved to town and started to court her. She was happy, but Francis was bitter and regretful."

Claudia was shocked. "I never knew Papa liked Mrs. Xavier. He was never very pleasant to her or she to him. I wondered why Papa was cool to her. They had lots in common. I always thought they should be good friends."

"I think your dad would've been happier married again. He could have given you another mother. His life would've been easier with a woman to help, but maybe he didn't want to be disloyal to your mother's memory." Claudia wondered how much more there was about her father that she didn't know.

She began to reveal to Vivian her belief that her father had had a relationship with a Rice Lake woman and put their farm at risk. Tawdry and incomprehensible, her father was not the man she'd thought, but maybe Vivian could make sense of the inconceivable. "While I was in Rice Lake I met…"

When Mrs. Gilbert opened the screen door, Claudia and Vivian exchanged glances.

"Good morning, I need some pearl buttons for a blouse I'm making for Wilna."

The Gilbert's jewelry store was the next door down, and both women were aware of Mrs. Gilbert's penchant for juicy particulars. Claudia's love life and current partner would be prized currency.

Claudia picked up the first thing at hand, a loaf of bread, from the counter. "Put this on my bill, would you, Vivian? I better get back to work." Mrs. Gilbert stepped back toward the door blocking Claudia's escape.

"Don't leave on my account. Actually, I am glad I met you here." Mrs. Gilbert fiddled with her cross-stitched handbag that hung from the crook of her arm, opened the clasp, pulled out a hankie, and wiped gingerly at the tip of her nose. "I was wondering how things were going for you all alone out there on the farm. Whether or not your good neighbors are rising to the call to help one another?" Her voice raised, expecting an answer.

Claudia couldn't get out without squeezing between Mrs. Gilbert and the door frame. Claudia raised her forearm to her face and made a show of sneezing into her plaid shirt sleeve.

"Sorry, I'm afraid I'm coming down with something and wouldn't want you to catch whatever I've got." With that she turned sideways and slipped out the door brushing against Mrs. Gilbert, who covered her entire nose and mouth with her lace hankie.

"I wonder why she came into town if she's not feeling well," huffed Mrs. Gilbert, turning to leave.

"Don't you want those buttons?" asked Vivian.

"Pardon?" Mrs. Gilbert, eyes wide, turned back to Vivian. "I'll get those another time. Thank you."

Claudia snickered to herself at the trail of gossip that circled their community. Everyone knew everyone else's business. She felt fortunate not to have confided to Vivian the details of Thomas and Macy. Better for Claudia to be known as fickle than foolish.

When she got home, she picked, baked, and canned the squash whose vines had dried prematurely. She could've kept them whole in the cellar, but this way she could make soup quickly. She picked up the windfall apples, cut out the bruises, made sauce, and canned that also. She had finished chores just as the sun was setting and was waiting to pull the last of the applesauce jars out of the hot water bath when she heard the frantic knocking on her door. She pulled the canner off the heat and answered the door. The oldest O'Brien girl was breathing hard. "Ma said you gotta come quick. We lost our brother."

26. The O'Briens

Farm folks joked about having to pick two crops a year on a place like the O'Briens' home place. First was gathering the crop of rocks that appeared each spring regardless of the diligence of last year's picking or the covering of those too big for an ox and man to muscle free from the field. The farmer, ox, and stone boat traversed the field back and forth for a dozen trips each way, stopping at the fence line to unload, then back to the field. Sometimes the farmer had to pick rock before he could plow, but usually he would plow first, then collect rock.

The O'Briens had a parcel of kids to help harvest rock. The family came from good Irish Catholic stock and had seven children under the age of twelve as testimony to their faith. When they arrived in the mid-1920s with Mr. Obrien's elderly father to the Bear Creek area from the western part of Minnesota, they searched for land they could afford, and this was what was available—a hillside and some fields with a sparse border of white pines at the base of that hillside. The loggers either tired before clear-cutting all the trees, or maybe they didn't like the prospect of felling the scrawny pines on a steep hillside. For whatever reason, this little wood of white pines appealed to Mr. O'Brien. In addition, his affable father got along well with all the locals.

He built his log home from the pines he cut down to clear the spot. Using the ox that he had brought with him, he dug into the south side of the hill and placed their home on a spot he flattened and cleared. The north wall of the cabin was partially covered by the dirt. Mr. O'Brien thought that would protect them from the fierce north winds but failed to consider that the wooden logs would rot quicker hugging the soil, and his aging father had no experience in building to give constructive advice. Mr. O'Brien's decision would be one of several well-intentioned but ill-thought-out choices he made. He failed to consider that a soft wood like pine would rot faster, and that leaving the bark on the logs would harbor decay and insects. Mrs. O'Brien was too busy keeping children fed and clothed and caring for her father-in-law to question her husband's choices. The spot was pretty enough and had a spring of water not far down through some swampy lowland.

They lived in their canvas-covered wagon for the first spring and summer until the one room cabin was built. They hadn't found a Catholic church yet, but heard at the store that regular services were held at the Lutheran church. After a few services the parishioners, who kindly didn't point out Mr. O'Brien's poor choice of building material, came out and helped him finish his home with a sod roof, and the family settled into their new life. They had a home and water. Mrs. O'Brien worked up a garden and planted seeds she had carried from Minnesota. She loved peonies and irises and found a corner for the few bulbs and tubers she'd brought from their old place.

The children ran wild among the fields and woods surrounding their eighty acres and sometimes helped as their mother hauled wood and water into the house, worked in the garden, and washed clothes in the backyard in a tub. They also walked to Bear Creek to fish and swim.

They enjoyed their humble, demanding life for several years until their home crumbled around them, Mr. O'Brien's aging father died, and Mr. O'Brien became crippled while clearing a field of a boulder that rolled back onto his leg. Their simple life grew in complexity, and they couldn't pay their bills. The O'Briens needed a place to live. Randy Rottman obliged by purchasing their farm, which was being auctioned off for unpaid property taxes. He obliged further by renting them the Meiser home and a large garden plot in the fall of 1932. They were grateful not to have to face a winter in their wagon. They were grateful for Doc and the mortuary man who came out to clean and dress the wound their ten-year-old son got when he pulled a pot off the stove and burned his arms with a hot mash of potatoes and cabbage.

The lost child was Mrs. O'Brien's second youngest who was not yet five-years-old that fall. Mrs. O'Brien dispatched her eldest, a twelve-year-old girl, to the neighbors for help when she faced a crisis beyond her ability to fix. Her face frantic, the girl arrived at Claudia's door out of breath.

"Ma said to come get you. We need help, we can't find our little brother. We've been looking for hours. Can you go to town to ask for help?" Anxious to be of immediate assistance, Claudia stopped briefly at the Johnsons to urge Hank to recruit help from town while she and Doris gathered up food and proceeded to the O'Briens at the Meiser farm. Mrs. O'Brien had collapsed on the ground clutching her youngest child, a two-and-a-half-year old girl, and rocking back and forth. Claudia and Mrs. Johnson bent down to the woman, whose face was streaked with tears and sweat and dirt, and pulled her upright, still clutching her daughter, who alternately attempted to get herself free and allowed her mother to confine her like a kitten caught in a toddler's loving grip. Prying Mrs. O'Brien's fingers open, the women permitted the child to slip away into the house, while they supported the mother's weight between them.

Mrs. O'Brien poured the story out as if throwing up a tainted bowl of stew. "Why didn't I remind them to stay together. They should know better. I shouldn't have to tell them. They'd finished their chores. Being Sunday, we need to keep holy the sabbath. Despite his crippled leg, Mr. O'Brien and me, us all, been looking since we noticed the young'un was gone. They was all playing in the swamp grass since the meadow's been cut. Oh, God, please don't let him disappear in the swamp! You know those kids. They jump swamp humps. If he fell off and got stuck and sucked down into the swamp, Jesus, Mary, and Joseph. We'll never find him! What will I do?" She leaned heavily into the two women.

"Let's go into the house so you can sit down, and we can get you something to drink," Claudia urged. Mrs. Johnson supported a cloth-covered basket on her arm, which Claudia knew had to be heavy.

"Dear Lord, we hadn't had dinner. He'll be hungry," Mrs. O'Brien wailed. They carried the food they'd brought and the woman into the house where they saw no one, not even the toddler.

"Are all of them out searching?" asked Claudia.

"All except Sharon," the distraught mother looked around for the daughter she'd been holding. "I kept her with me after I got back here. Mr. O'Brien said I should come home in case Aaron came back. He'd get scared with no one here. Sharon?!" Mrs. O'Brien hollered, then saw her youngest peek around the corner of the front room.

Outside they heard the Johnsons' pickup pull into the yard. Through the window they saw half a dozen men and a few women get out and start to form into groups. The women came into the house with baskets of bread, cheese, and meats. The eldest O'Brien girl came running out of the swamp when she heard the truck approaching. Her mother sent the twelve-year-old Siobhan back out to show the men where the rest of the family was searching. The men began to walk toward the swamp and woods carrying unlit lanterns. Dusk was approaching and they would need illumination soon.

As dark descended the O'Brien children returned and dropped off their younger siblings. The three oldest grabbed a lantern, a sandwich each, and their jackets and returned to the search. The women fed the younger children, threw grain to the chickens, slopped the pig, and sat down with sighs to hot coffee and Mrs. O'Brien's nervous chatter and waited.

An hour after the sun had set, the women, huddled in the kitchen, heard the voices. By the uplifted sound they knew the almost five-year-old had been found. Sweat-chilled men stomped their mud-caked feet and stuffed the house. The O'Brien parents slept upstairs in one bedroom under the eaves and two middle-aged boys slept in one under the other eave. Three single beds crowded the front room. Two of the youngest slept in one, a bigger boy got a thin bed to himself, and the eldest girl shared the bed against the wall with the youngest, the little lost Aaron. Claudia never knew you could sleep so many people in such a small space. In order to get into their beds, the children stepped onto and across the other beds. Once fed and washed, they crawled under their quilts and listened to the adults as they filled their growling stomachs and rehashed the evening's events.

Mr. O'Brien didn't have much to share by way of refreshments, but he had a small jug of hard cider that he passed among the men. He hobbled from one to another shaking hands and passing the jug with grateful thanks.

"These old shambling legs canna' stomp through the swamp like before. I canna' thank ya enough."

"Where was he?" begged Mrs. O'Brien. The story flowed like water from a primed pump—full, broad, replete with details.

Mr. O'Brien began, "The children said they'd been playing hide-and-seek and didna' see that none of 'em had been watching Aaron. Sharon scuffed her knee and our eldest, Siobhan, were tending to her. She'd last seen Aaron with his brothers. Events get a bit muddled after. They tried looking for him but got scared and come home to get us.

"Aaron told me he were playing hide and seek and when no one found him, he come out. With everyone gone, he went to look for 'em. He got tired and found a tree to crawl into and fell asleep. The tree were a ways from where us family were looking, but he mus'n't of heard us. With more folks we covered more ground. He popped out of the dark like one of the wee folk or a mischievous ghosty steppin' out of a tree. Its rotten base were dug out on one side by some animal. 'Tweren't a big space, but he could fit in and were hidden. When he woke, he said he got scared by the voices. The sound weren't familiar and sounded angry, so he kept hisself hidden. Aaron told me he heard his name song and seen the fireflies that comed to lead him home. Patrick confessed that as he searched he took to singin' Aaron's name like Ma did to soothe the young'un when he were a wee bairn. Aaron wanted to catch one of them fireflies. Must've seen our swinging lanterns. Patrick and several of you can back me up. Aaron come out of that tree crack—singing his name song and reaching out to grab a firefly."

Well past supper and chores, the neighbors, who'd left their responsibilities for a few hours, returned to their farms and to town to do their own chores and put their own children to bed. Under her own quilt alone in her own bed, Claudia thanked God that they weren't alone. They had each other in spite of all the hardship that pursued their town and township. Together they could manage.

27. Thomas Talks with Ernie

After Claudia had chided Thomas, stating she never wanted to see him again, he escaped to work out East. The specter followed him on the train from Wisconsin to New York, haunting him for three weeks as he worked at the Hagstrom's Furniture and Mortuary, and then hounded him on the train from New York hustle to Wisconsin quiet. Upon his return to Turtle Lake, the wives scrutinized him and whispered to each other. The men outside Ernie's got quiet when he stepped out of his uncle's shop.

Thomas didn't have anyone with whom to talk. He considered that as Ernie had known Claudia all her life and worked with Vivian, Claudia's closest friend, Ernie might have insight and advice. Thomas hoped verbalizing his confusion might bring clarity. He walked from his uncle's mortuary to Ernie's store. When he saw Vivian was gone, he started to explain to Ernie.

"I didn't want to tell Claudia. I wanted to forget it had ever happened. I tried to explain on the day I helped her repair her henhouse to keep the weasels out. I thought she understood and it was okay. Then when we fought after our second trip to New York, she acted as if she never knew about my friend."

"What happened?" Ernie asked and plopped his generous bottom on a keg of nails, smoothing his snow-white apron across his Santa belly. Thomas started to sit in the chair Claudia usually occupied when she talked to Vivian, stopped, and searched for an alternate spot. He chose to upend and sit on a box stamped "Iron Hinges" in black block print. Ernie had pulled a quart jar of amber liquid from under the counter when he had seen Thomas stride in looking like death warmed over. Ernie lifted two pint jars from the shelf behind him and splashed a couple of tablespoons from the quart jar into each pint and handed one to Thomas, who held the jar without noticing the contents.

"The trouble began when I came to Wisconsin to help my uncle whose health was failing, and he couldn't keep up. I went back to New York when they needed me. I'd met a sweet woman, Macy, in March. I continued to see her but then she was always busy with family. The beginning of May she informed me she was pregnant. I was never really sure what happened that night, just what she told me. But I know the situation had gotten out of hand. The middle of May I received an unexpected letter from her telling me to 'Take your time, no need to rush back,' and I didn't. Initially, I intended to go back to New York and marry her or maybe bring her here. I've been saving money to buy out my uncle." He gazed down and seemed to notice for the first time that he was holding something. He stared at the jar cupped in both hands.

"I wasn't sure what I should do. I was falling in love with Claudia. I was realizing I didn't really love Macy. I kept going back to New York to help the old firm, but I had more reason to stay in Wisconsin and take over my uncle's business like he wanted. I was reluctant to make the change at first. I felt guilty for leaving Macy back in New York alone. Then she seemed too busy to see me."

"All of us've done things we wish we hadn't done," Ernie confided as he took a sip from his jar and sighed gazing out the window and reflecting on the past.

"That one night I drank too much. She stated the baby was mine. I went back to tell her I would take responsibility for the child but could not marry her. Then she was with that other man, clearly not a relative, at the theater and clearly not pregnant." He set the untouched jar on the counter.

"That's a pickle of a predicament." Ernie nodded and shifted on the keg, resetting his ample legs, and laid his round arms across his belly like a Buddha.

"I know that was cowardly." Thomas stared at his feet then up at Ernie intently, "I'm ashamed of it all, but I can't be married to a woman I don't love. I never realized there could be a woman as independent, beautiful, intelligent, and passionate as Claudia. I can't let her go. She would be wasted married to a farmhand. I am sorry, Ernie, but George's boys are country bumpkins. Either she would shrivel up or become bitter. I cannot let that happen, but she won't talk to me. What do I do?"

"That there is the prize question, my friend. Let's have another jar to wet my whistle while I put on my thinking cap." Ernie tipped the quart jar of amber moonshine into Thomas's untouched jar and into his own. "There's no pleasure like the pain of being loved, and loving." Ernie shook his head knowingly. "My wife and I were lucky. We stumbled upon each other and stuck together like cockleburs. I used to recite to her as we lay falling asleep. There's a poem, "The Dying Raven,": 'Mutual love brings mutual delight— brings beauty, life; for love is life, hate, death.' It's all mixed together, you see. Like a stew—you can't get the gravy out without eatin' some of the onions and rutabaggie. We all hanker for the meat and potatoes."

"I like so many things about Claudia. And I can tolerate her need to do things her way, but if she refuses to talk to me? I don't know how to proceed."

"'It's better to have loved and lost than never to have loved at all' is what one fella said."

"I know. That's from Tennyson."

"I can tell you I've seen war, killing, death. People doing stuff to each other that no man should see. Sometimes I wonder how we made it at all. I thought coming here to this New World would mean leaving old, worn-out ways behind. I thought "new" meant better. Seems people are people no matter what." Ernie watched Thomas hang his head lower. Ernie lifted his jar of amber liquid and admired the moonshine.

"Did you hear the one about the guy that took his girl out for dinner? He lifted his glass to the girl and said, 'How about a little toast?' The girl said, 'Toast for dinner? I never heard of such thing. I want a regular meal.'" Thomas forced the corners of his mouth up for a few seconds. Ernie continued a bit louder and faster. "You probably never heard this one in New York as your restaurants are too high-class, but a waiter says, 'Here's the menu, ma'am, what do you wish?' The old lady says, 'Dear me, I left my glasses at home.' The waiter says, 'We furnish glasses, but you can drink out of the bottle if you want to.'" Thomas stared past Ernie out the window.

The sky outside the large front windows was getting dark, but Thomas was in no hurry to go anywhere. He was rudderless. Believing Claudia did not want to see him, he stayed close to town except when needed for work. In Wisconsin he was with his uncle making caskets. In New York he was working for his old firm. He felt hollowed out like a jack-o'-lantern with gaping mouth and nothing of substance within, everything of value scooped out. Thomas closed the door slowly behind him.

Ernie emptied his jar, and, as Thomas had left his untouched, Ernie shrugged and finished that jar as well. He swung his round legs, jumped off the keg, wiped the pint jars, and returned them to the shelf. He set the quart jar of liquor under the counter next to a box of receipts, safe from judging eyes yet ready for the next poor soul seeking comfort.

Ernie's quart jar was found the next day by Vivian who wrinkled her nose but stuck the moonshine back in its spot behind the receipt box. She was bent down when she heard Percy start to chatter and straightened to see the sharecroppers outside the window in their old International pickup with stake sides full to bursting with mattresses, bed frames, sacks, and kegs tied down with hemp rope. Grandma was in the front seat of the rusted heap, but the two children and their young aunt were tucked into a fold of a thin straw mattress. Their two chairs were tied upside down on the top of the pile.

Vivian watched the mother and father get out of the truck and enter the store. They nodded to Vivian and gathered a gunny sack of beans and another of rice. The mother opened her coin purse to pay while her husband shouldered each sack in turn and wedged them into the corners of the bed of the already full truck.

"Looks like you are leaving us," Vivian stated.

"We've got nothing to keep us here. There's no work to be had and without our vegetables, well…" She studied her family through the window. "We heard they need fruit pickers in California. It's warm there. Even if we have to sleep outside, we'll be okay." Outside the window, her husband was pulling a large, well-used tarp over the majority of their shabby belongings with the help of their son. The two women watched as the father and son secured the tarp to the stakes sticking up from the sides of the truck. They left a cave opening between the two chairs under the tarp where the children were now settled.

"Thought best to head out before the snow flies. We think we can make it south before the weather gets too cold. Maybe pick cotton down there before we head west." She stuck her coin purse back into the front pocket of her rounded skirt and tightened her kerchief on her head.

"I'm sorry to see you leave," Vivian offered feebly. "Sorry about the situation."

"We got that tarp and each other." With that the wife walked out and joined her husband and mother in the cab. After several attempts, the truck finally started. Vivian watched as exhaust filled the air, and they were gone.

28. Dandy Speaks

We could feel the difference in her hands. Something was changed. Something wasn't right. She was always calm and even. Unlike her father, she was predictable. We always knew what to expect with her. Since we first knew her when we were all inexperienced, trying to get a feel for each other, she was patient and learned easily.

As a foal I became impatient with her; she held the reins like her father—tight. I jerked my head, pulling to get them to loosen up, then he'd pull back on my mouth and startle me with that sharp voice.

Molly just stood. She was of a mind to think, "Pull all you want. I'm not moving until the three of you—man, girl, and pasture partner—figure this out."

They had us out in the pasture alone. Our mothers were gone. We knew the basic routine. Being tied next to our mothers, we'd seen it all. We just weren't interested. Being in harness after running free was boring. After a while she finally figured how to let us know what she wanted from us. She came up to us in the pasture, talked quietly, and scratched where she knew we couldn't reach.

Once they brought us through the swamp on the way to the woods. He was driving. Remember, Molly? You knew we were in trouble. I thought we could do it, but you held back, and he slapped the reins down on our backs as he commanded, "Step up, girls, you can do it." Molly gave in, and we broke through the mud humps, which sucked at our legs and feet, then we hit a hole or something. I was scared. I flicked my ears and was breathing hard, trying to lift my feet, but they were pinned in the mud. I felt like I was sinking.

I looked at Molly, and she was now up to her chest in mud. She'd been struggling like I had, and I could see she'd settled into a fearful waiting, so I did the same.

I felt the girl beside me whispering. Stroking my face. Next to my ears. I hated direct touching of my ears. Normally when she stood between us, so tiny, we had to be careful because we couldn't always feel where she was, much less see her. The blinders let us see only directly in front. We more felt her presence. She held her hands on the outside of each of our faces as she stood between us. Our heads bent to hers. Her head was at our head—level with us. She must have been standing on a swamp hump.

We felt the harness fall as he unhooked us from the heavy bobsled. She stayed between us the whole time whispering as he held the reins. He clicked his teeth more quietly than ever before, and she stood between us, her arms stretched to their full length holding our bridle by our cheeks. We went step by step, slowly so as not to step on her. We kept moving forward with her between us. We pulled ourselves free of the mud-sucking swamp. We walked out of that mud hole between frozen cattails and swamp grass. Once on firmer ground, we waited. The man hooked us to something unfamiliar, but she was right between us, arms stretched up to our faces. When he urged, "Step up," we stepped, bearing forward. "Step. Step. Step," he continued in a low strong voice.

Soon we felt the load far behind us give. As she encouraged us, we put our backs into each step until we felt the bobsled pull free, and we could walk easily again. With the blinders on we couldn't see what he was doing, but we could feel him re-hook us to the bobsled. I was glad we didn't go out into the woods that day but back home to the barn. Molly and I got rubbed down like usual. We weren't tired from pulling logs out of the woods like a normal winter day, but our insides were tired. I ate the first mouthful of oats quickly, then left the rest. Molly ate two mouthfuls before she turned her head aside. We had no stomach for food. We wanted the solid space of our enclosed pasture.

Tonight, Molly and I are restless. There are flashes of light in the sky, and she is putting us inside our stall, which feels comforting. But something's not right. We can feel the difference in her hands.

29. The Turning

A rosy glow out the window caught Claudia's eye as she was getting into bed. The September sun had set hours ago. The barn was on fire. She ran, her mind racing.

Her mind had been preoccupied. She must have forgotten to check that the lamp wick was completely out. *Careless!* Earlier there was the threat of a storm. Heat lightning had split the dry sky. It was dark when she put the Girls away. *Mistake?* Just the three of them and Shep. She had been agitated and in a hurry. The fight with Thomas haunted her, the unresolved debt nagged her, distress with weather and work overwhelmed her. She was alone. She had wanted to be done, to go to sleep.

Now she had to get the horses out. Before they burned alive. She closed the door on Shep and ran to the barn knowing she couldn't get them out alone. Horses for some unfathomable reason were drawn back into a barn on fire. She rushed in with her nightgown neck pulled up over her nose and mouth and ran to where her trusted companions stomped with fear. She had overheard speculation that smoke in their nostrils confused them, made them hug the familiarity of their stalls. Daisy almost ran her over as Claudia opened the heavy wooden barn doors. A stub of smoldering rope hung from the frenzied animal's neck.

She pulled back the latch and swung the stall gates wide. Other old-timers believed smoke prevented horses from seeing. She tried to talk above their frantic whinnying and stomping. But her voice was as frantic as theirs. When hitched up, horses wear blinders so they aren't spooked by a fluttering leaf that seems as big as a sheet or a puddle of water that seems as deep as a pond. Who could say what this smoke appeared to be to them.

Her windmill arms tried to feel for their bodies to grab their manes to lead them out, but the confined space was a flurry of flying hot ash, flailing horse hair, and stomping hooves. She felt the flank of one horse then the neck of the other, but their fury of agitation prevented her from getting a hold on both, and she was frantic to hold both of them. The smoke from burning straw and wood was choking her.

She was disoriented and confused. Why wasn't Thomas here to help her? They could each grab a mare and together herd them to safety despite their smoky confusion. But she had insisted she did not need nor want his help, and now the barn was on fire. The building and its contents would be ash before anyone could get there to help her. Even the Johnsons were out of immediate reach. Her eyes were stinging, her chest contracted against the invasion of smoke, her hands reached blindly for her companions but touched red hot wood. She was pushed by thrashing, scorching-hot hide.

She did the only thing she could. Nothing. Coughing, she stumbled out the barn door and fell, her lungs contracting, her eyes burning. Even the nearest neighbor's house was almost half a mile away as the crow flies. The first smell made her flinch, remembering she'd failed to eat. When she realized the smell was from her dear Dandy and Molly, she bent over in the dust and dry-heaved until her throat tasted bile and she fell.

She felt his presence, then heard his familiar voice. *Relief.*

"Claudia! Are you alright?" He was beside her, holding her shoulders, "Can you get up?"

She opened her eyes. Hank. Several metal buckets were beside him. Behind him she could see flames reflected in the chrome bumper of his truck. Her eyes burned. She struggled to her feet with his help.

"We've got to get them out!" She glared at the blazing barn doorway, a curtain of fire, and back at Hank. He thrust a bucket at her and grabbed the other two and ran to the horse trough. They threw water into the roaring mouth of flame. When the two basic elements met, the fire evaporated the water ravenously. Soon George and Ethan were there with more buckets, trying to slow the spread. Claudia could hear them shouting, "Wet this. Maybe we can save this section."

Her arms ached, her head pounded, and still the four of them flung buckets fruitlessly into an ever-enlarging cavern of fire. Finally, they heard the fire trucks and men shouting over the roar. Claudia allowed Hank to pull her back from the inferno.

He sat her on the ground by the horse trough. "Stay here, Claudia. Your eyebrows and lashes are singed off. Thankfully, your hair and clothes didn't catch on fire." She stared blankly at her nightgown, as he left to help the others. Burn holes, some as big as a nickel, spattered across the flowered cotton were turning her nightgown into a macabre burst of polka dot stars.

Claudia stumbled among the debris looking for something. She wasn't sure what. She knew something was gone for good. *Not good! Forever not good!* In four months, she had lost what her great-grandparents, grandparents, and parents had taken four generations to build. But it was more than that. Something she could never get back. *What was it?*

To the east, the sun was cresting the dark horizon, a luminous egg rising from a cast iron skillet. To the west the fire had consumed the barn and burned itself out. The pigsty, chicken coop, and shed were left untouched, as was the house. Forlorn, she stood at the charred remains of the barn. Shep had been let out of the house by someone, but even he skirted her. With a long stick, she was trying to pull anything of value, a piece of leather harness, the tines of a manure fork, from the smoldering embers with a long stick. She saw Hank, the first one to the fire after he'd called the fire department. He was in front of her, considering her face. She looked away, ashamed.

Ash and charred bits floated in the air. Her nightgown was spattered gray and black. Even the jacket someone had put on her was marked, ash clinging to where firemen's spray had landed. She pinned her eyes to the ground. She didn't want to inadvertently catch sight of that pile. The pile that Hank and Ethan and George had pushed out of the barn and over to one edge. That pile whose smell made her retch. She had nothing left to expel.

Her limbs quivered, her fingers were numb, unable to grasp anything anymore. Men she knew, but whose names she couldn't remember right now, were still pumping water and spraying smoldering lumber, throwing to the side what could be salvaged for reuse.

She also wanted to find something to set off to the side, to preserve, but she couldn't think what was left to salvage.

"Claudia, I'm so sorry."

She'd heard similar words and the shouts of, "Over here! We need water here!" all night but this time the words were from someone who she'd told recently, "Leave. I don't need or want you here. You don't understand; you never have." She'd made a mistake. Her words weren't true. She'd made so many mistakes.

The speaker approached her cautiously from the side, not from behind, so she could see him. When she looked up, she saw Thomas. He glanced toward the large pile of bones, hide, and burnt flesh that yesterday had been her horses. She turned away and dry heaved again. He held her bent body, and she didn't fall. She desperately wanted to dissolve and be absorbed by the earth.

He was New York, music, and ease. Was that what she was looking for amidst the charred fragments?

Dazed, like a child who has learned that loved ones can die within moments, she collapsed into his arms. For the first time since her father's death, she cried uncontrollably. Deep, hard, wet sobs that shook her exhausted body.

Those who had come to help, picking and sifting through the still-hot rubble, had respected her silence. Now they left, speaking in whispers. What could any of them do, anyway. Even if she did rebuild, construction would take months and winter was fast approaching. The wreckage needed to be cleared and lumber found and cut, or purchased, if she could somehow find the money. When Hank caught her interaction with Thomas, he left with an overzealous slam of his truck door. The next day from her window she would witness Hank's Farmall with the manure bucket carrying to a far corner of the yard, not manure, but the pile he was going to bury.

The bystanders here or those in town spoke with certainty about what she should do. She would hear the words' echo later.

"Now, she'll see the wisdom in quitting this nonsense of thinking she could farm alone."

"She should either marry Thomas and move back East where things are easier or marry George's boy who has always taken a shine to her, settle into a farmer's life."

"She's too stubborn. She'll never be happy being told by him or any man what to do. She's more like Vivian, a born old maid."

Thomas guided Claudia to the house where Vivian had been making sandwiches for the people who came to help. Vivian had told Bruno and Pete Mevissen, "I know bacon and eggs would be more to folks' liking this early in the morning, but I'm not the domestic type." She kept slicing bread and adding things between the slices until people quit coming into the house.

When the others had left, Vivian set the table, put a clean dishcloth over the plate of sandwiches, put the pitcher of milk back in the icebox, and went into the front room to lose herself in the latest novel she had brought along for just this purpose. That is where Claudia and Thomas found her, curled in Francis's chair. The couple sat next to each other on the sofa in deathly silence in the room meant for living.

The wind that had fueled the fire had died down during the early hours of the morning. The air was so dry and the sun so bright that it looked like a great day to be a farmer.

30. Claudia Dream-Sleeps

I'm inside a snow globe. This can't be real but seems real. The snow flutters around me and I see the cats I am petting. I hear their purrs, feel their nudges, their fur too soft to be solid, the snow too delicate to be cold. This must be a glass bubble. If I were to feel, to face the burned barn ash settling on their bodies, I fear the earth would give way. You can't be swallowed up if you are in a snow globe. I know. The one on my shelf that Papa gave me is heavy and the bottom solid, unlike the ground under me today.

The Christmas I got the farm snow globe, little painted animals surrounded the tiny farm yard, with a snowman and child in the yard and an angel perched on the roof, all safely encased in a glass globe. I controlled the amount and ferocity of the snowfall. I could tip the glass world and watch flakes fall for hours or, frustrated, I could shake and watch the storm I created.

Am I safe within a snow globe? Today, I feel I'm inside something, but without control. There are no sides, no top or bottom, only this falling. If I could be safely contained, resting on a shelf, I could have peace. I long to be the child inside that globe playing with a dog, my loving parents inside the miniature house. A family of horses, a cow, and cats resting peacefully inside the barn with roosting chickens and a pig. All as life should be. Not as it is now.

31. Claudia Supposes

Today, Claudia resolved, would be different, better. Even the weather wasn't as harsh. A September wind blew but no dust. She tied her recently acquired horse to the post outside the mortuary. Even though today was Sunday, she could hear someone inside. Old Glue was a tired, Standardbred gelding that she had kept from going to the glue factory. He got her from here to there and for that she was grateful.

"Hello," she glanced around the shop. "Thomas not here?" She wasn't surprised to see the uncle slowly, steadily at work. All days were the same to him and he seemed content with that.

"He's gone ta church then to help tend that fireman that got his hands burned, out ta yer place." The uncle returned to his work. *Another mistake.* She should've gone to church; they could've talked afterward.

"Mind if I wait for him in the house?" She didn't want to hear any more about the harm she'd caused by her carelessness. He nodded, and she walked around the back to the compact whitewashed home where Thomas and his uncle lived. She glanced around for something useful to occupy her time; morning dishes were done but the wood box was only half full.

She decided to get wood from the pile in the backyard. The wind had picked up and the temperature had dropped. She searched for something to put on her head. Next to the door under a row of pegs for coats was a box of mittens and a heavy wool scarf. She reached deep into the box and absentmindedly pulled out the softest item her fingers touched—a knit hat of soft brown yarn almost too delicate for a man and trimmed in a random pattern of blue stitches. Scrutinizing the hat, about her size, she wondered how it could be large enough for Thomas. His uncle wore a red-and-black plaid visored hat with flaps that pulled down over his nearly deaf ears.

The soft woolen hat, which smelled sweetly floral, was not the precise, solid, stitched knit typical of the farm women of Wisconsin but a less fastidious, looser working. As her fingers stretched the edges to fit her head, she poked through a missed loop. The name Macy flashed in her mind. Claudia's fingers pulled and unraveled the hat before her brain registered any connection. As far as Claudia was aware, no known bond existed between the hat and Macy. She did not register what her fingers were doing. She had no conscious association of her feelings for Thomas and those for Macy. She reacted, feeling only the yarn, pulling apart. She reflexively balled up the hat scraps and shoved them to the bottom of the box. *If he kept a hat made by her, he must still have feelings for her!*

She had wanted to be useful while waiting for him to return. She left without filling their wood box. She had come on an impulse—to reconcile their differences, to apologize for her words of anger to him a month ago. She untied her horse without going in to speak to the uncle, who she hoped would forget to mention her visit. She left, glad she had not wasted her time doing anything for Thomas. No one could be trusted—not her father, not Thomas, not even herself and her judgment. *What is wrong with me?*

Claudia pushed the old riding horse too hard. Motion felt numbing. The faster the better. The wind whipped Old Glue's mane and her hair, but the thoughts could not be whipped away. The ride to her farm was long enough for her fearful, overactive imagination to create a picture of deception. In her mind she envisioned Macy stopping to see Thomas at the Hagstrom's Furniture and Mortuary Emporium in New York. She visualized Thomas being beguiled by a sophisticated, feminine woman discussing literature, opera, and composers.

She created a companion that matched Thomas in culture and genteel elegance. Clever and even erudite, she thought, just not very adept at knitting. At her farm she stepped off the horse and into a pile of horse manure. Shep's wet nose and cockle-burred fur pushed at her hand for attention.

After unsaddling the old horse without brushing him, she turned him into the sparse pasture, grabbed the curry comb, and attacked the burrs in Shep's fur. Grumbling about not being able to trust anyone about anything, she tugged the comb through the black-and-white Border Collie's fur and dropped prickly burrs on the porch. He sat patiently observing her, his eyes pools of milky brown. He must be getting cataracts, she thought. She stopped when she realized she had been yanking the serrated circles of steel through his matted hair, and the old canine had not whined or yelped once. She put her nose to his, dropped the curry comb to the dirt at the foot of the steps, and caressed the smelly, bristly face in her hands.

"Sorry, old boy. I don't mean to include you." Later she remembered the incident with the she bear. She admitted she could not depend on Shep, either. He was too old, too deaf, and nearly blind. She could not rely on anyone but herself. She was alone. No one's fault. Life was what it was. She had better accept that and move on.

Days were both free and full. Not having to be aware of what her father needed next left Claudia with time for small projects she had always wanted to get to do. One day, soon after her father passed away, she fixed boards on the barn to keep the snow out. Another day she clamped and glued the leg back on a kitchen chair, removing the wire her father had wound around the cross piece as a quick fix. When she had protested over a year ago that visitors might break their necks, he had dismissed her, gesturing toward the shed, saying he'd mend the thing as soon as he could. Well, now the chair was fixed.

Other days she roamed from room to room picking up tasks, setting work down unfinished, so unlike her. She had no focus, no point upon which to turn, and no one with whom to react. The force, the magnetic pull of her father's mere presence had determined meals, work, even down time. Now she could go days without a proper meal. She felt alternately free and fulfilled, then scattered and directionless.

Before, she always knew what she wanted. The little free time she had was claimed by several desires jostling for attention. After he was gone, she wondered what was her purpose and where was she going. She only felt useful when she was busy with the animals or repairing something. With the loss of Dandy and Molly and the land at risk, she questioned the importance of any of her efforts. Neighbors raised animals, garden produce, and milk which she could buy, eat, and drink, and someone else could fix harnesses. She did not need to stay here where there was more work than time. She could rent a room in town and not even own a horse.

Maybe she should get a job where someone else just told her what to do. She had skills that could be valuable to someone. If she moved to the city, she could have a small home that was easy to manage, less to think about. Get up in the morning, go to work, come home, cook and eat, maybe get a chance to read at leisure again. That scenario actually did not sound too bad when she phrased the circumstance like that.

But at night lying awake, she thought how tedious that would be and how she would miss her farm, the daily interaction with her animals, and tending to her garden. She would not be there to pat the trees she and her father had planted and watered. She loved being on the farm, even when losing the battle with woodchucks, weasels, and stubborn bulls. Even if life continued without her family of Father and Dandy and Molly. But at what price? What good was a farm, if the life of the farm burned in front of you?

32. Macy and Her Doctor

Macy was affected by the cost of her decisions just as Claudia paid a price for her choices. Macy first saw Richard in mid-May when Thomas was in Wisconsin for the second time. She was attracted to Richard's perfect dress, so sharp and clean. He stood very tall and shook everyone's hand. Talking came easily to him. Everything came effortlessly to him. She wanted comfortable, and living in a backwoods in Arkansas was not. Thomas the mortician and Richard the doctor were both tall. While Thomas was plain and simple, Richard was refined and exquisite.

She had noticed Richard's shoes, which were always shiny. She carried an old hanky to keep the dust off hers. He appeared to never bend down. The only time his head was lower than his waist was when he was lying on the bed.

They had a whirlwind romance. She had had the company of two men for two months before she and Richard married in July. Before they were married, Richard brought her small gifts—a book of poetry, a bottle of perfume, and a lacy nightie. He rarely fell asleep without his arm protectively across her.

He had a stable of horses and a groom to keep them perfectly cleaned and trimmed. He owned a silver Rolls-Royce Phantom and employed a mechanic like the boy Macy left in Arkansas. The mechanic kept the car at the top level of performance. Richard maintained that high standard with his wife as well. Macy went to the hairdressers regularly and occasionally had to return the same day if they hadn't arranged her coiffure the way he preferred. Being taken to the seamstress for return visits to get the fitting exactly to Richard's taste was an extravagance she'd never experienced before.

At first Macy and Richard's life seemed idyllic to both of them. He had her study music, and escorted her to the opera. Then he had his tennis coach give her lessons, and they played mixed doubles. She was entrusted with the keys to the larder, which increased the tension between her and the cook, who'd previously had complete control. They took breakfast at 7 a.m. before he went to the surgery. They ate supper at 7 p.m. sharp, and if cook didn't have everything to his taste, Macy was scolded for not keeping her on time and task.

"Everything ran as smooth as clockwork before, and now that you are here as mistress of the house, you should be able to keep the staff at peak performance. That is your job. My job is to keep you happy." He smiled down at her.

She paid close attention to her dress, taking great care with every detail that first month because he wanted her "to be impeccable for supper whether we are entertaining guests or dining alone." She tried to anticipate his needs and desires to avoid his disapproval and disappointment. Being small and helpless in her hick town had been an advantage with men stumbling over each other to please her, but Richard demanded compliance when she was with him and "confident assurance" when they were out.

"I wasn't raised to know how the rich do things. I can learn. Teach me," she begged him when he'd instructed her in which utensils and glassware to use and when.

"You're working at a disadvantage because of your poor breeding. Like with horses, you'll have to work harder." He'd encouraged her that first month.

"I'm sorry that I make mistakes. I'll try harder." And she did.

A month later at a dinner party, she'd kept her fork in her right hand and put the meat into her mouth after cutting the steak with the knife in her left. On the way home he chastised her, "If I had known how poor your breeding was, I would never have married you. No amount of beauty can make up for poor breeding."

"I want to be a good wife." She spoke quietly.

One night she started to get up to use the commode in their tiled indoor bathroom featuring a white enamel, claw-foot tub. But his arm held her down. She tried to wiggle out from under him, without waking him. The more she squirmed, the firmer he gripped her. She lay with her ankles crossed and tried to fall back to sleep, but after a while her need exceeded her fear of waking him.

She waited until he began to snore. She started to slide out from under his arm, but as her leg tentatively extended over the side of the bed, he reached out and grabbed her. Startled, Macy's bladder let go.

He jumped up, eyes blazing, "Clean up that mess. Not even an animal soils its own bed."

"But I tried to get up, and you held me."

"I can't prevent you from doing what you have set your mind to do. You should have relieved yourself before bed like civilized people do, and then you would not need to disturb our slumber in the middle of the night. Sleep is the most important thing for your health next to small regular meals."

"I know. You know what I should eat and when. You're educated and I'm not. I know you instruct me for my own good. You know best. You're the doctor."

She was so ashamed.

"Get up," he scowled. "You'll have to strip this bed yourself. We can't have the household know you are incontinent like an old woman." With that he whipped their good satin coverlet back and threw the light-as-a-cloud eiderdown to the floor. He grabbed her wrist, put her hand on the corner of the bed sheet, and forced the cover up and away. The sheet with its wet spot flew like angry black birds knocked from their nest. "Like a good husband," he smiled. "I will help you." And he let go of her.

Ships become unmoored, and a wagon is like a ship on land. Macy's parents had been travelers, gypsies enjoying freedom, variety. With a baby on the way, they'd parked their wagon in Arkansas, blocked the wheels, and got jobs in a restaurant. The itch hit Macy's dad shortly thereafter, and he scratched by hitting the road, alone. Her mom quit hoping and got a divorce when Macy was six.

Her mother's response was sharp when Macy asked about a real house. "I got you this far. It's up to you to get the house." At various times in her life Macy stayed with her Aunt Iris. The first time was when Iris lived in Arkansas. When Iris moved to New York with her husband, Macy was sent to get some culture and give her mother a break. Iris welcomed her pretty, little, blond niece and felt sorry for the poverty in which her younger sister lived and the environment of a succession of boyfriends and husbands that Macy saw as father figures.

When Macy was twelve, her mother's second husband liked to hold her on his lap. One day Macy's mother came home from work early and saw the inappropriate touching.

"Get off, Macy. Go to your room." There was loud arguing for hours in the small trailer before the tinny door slammed. When Macy finally ventured out, her mother was packing a bag.

"Momma, you're not leaving? It won't happen again. I didn't want to but he told me if…"

"Don't say a word!" Her mother went into Macy's room and put clothes into the cloth bag that Macy would use as a suitcase on her trip to her aunt's.

"You can't help if you look mature for your age. But I can get you out of the way. Steve and I are having enough problems without you as a distraction."

The trip for Macy came abruptly, but Aunt Iris and her husband were understanding. Aunt Iris's husband was kind to Macy, but rebuffed her inappropriate overtures to get attention. He and Iris talked about their suspicions of Macy's current stepfather's possible proclivities. They understood, as few childless couples could, that Macy sought a father figure, financial stability, and maybe a bit of status. They saw Macy's act of being frail and weak as her way to obtain a man's protection. "Unfortunately, Macy feels the only way to get a man is to outwit him and use her feminine wiles to woo him," observed Iris's husband. They had watched her change over the years in Arkansas and New York. She was like a chameleon who adapted to whatever was required. But some lizards tried to escape the backwaters of their birth.

Aunt Iris enrolled Macy in dance class and hired a tutor for her to catch up in school. Bouncing back and forth between her mother's home in Arkansas and her aunt and uncle's in New York was disruptive. Where Macy lived was determined by her mother's need for reassurance when she was without a man or for space and time when she was with a man.

When nineteen-year-old Macy met Thomas, she saw her ship arrive. Her mechanic boyfriend in Arkansas confessed he loved her, and she loved being loved. They were intimate, and although they had not set a date to marry, marriage was understood. She went to New York after her uncle died. She stayed to woo Thomas. She suspected in late April that she might be pregnant and seized the chance to marry her way up the social ladder by seduction. She was frantic after dumping the Arkansas kid and discovering Thomas was going to Wisconsin, another backwater. When she miscarried early in her pregnancy and met Doctor Richard, she thought an ocean liner, not just a ship, had docked in her port.

Claudia and Macy both lost a parent when they were six. Both wanted to please the men in their lives. Before either of them reached her eighteenth birthday, Claudia would've only traveled within the sixty-mile radius surrounding her home, but Macy would've journeyed like the spokes of a wheel through countless states in a wagon, a train, a trolley, and endless vehicles. Neither would get a formal education past high school. They would never meet, but each would be influenced by the choices the other made.

What are the chances that these two seemingly disparate women would have their fates affected by one mortuary man, who bridged their two lives across half of the country? The triangle of distance separating the two women as they grew up was over three thousand miles, but they would be connected, unknowingly, by one man who would alter his destiny and theirs by acting on a series of dissimilar impulses and urges.

Thomas was between Wisconsin and New York but on a path similar to Macy's. Each had worked to improve the hand they had been dealt then later wanted to trade in the hand they had made for one they hoped would serve them better. Neither thought they were breaking any rules.

33. The Pig Man and Luella

They all needed each other. Why were some people so reluctant to allow others to give them a hand? Vivian stood at the window considering the diabetic farm wife, who had declined help getting the much-needed groceries into the back of the wagon. Luella Eggert's trips to town had become scarcer. Thomas had gone to the farm to treat her. When Vivian had inquired after Luella's leg, she'd shown Vivian the healed wound with a clean scar. The farm wife rarely left her house since her husband Herbert had taken a turn for the worse three years ago, a martyr to the cause in Vivian's view. She was not clear about what cause, exactly, but one thing was for sure, Luella appeared two decades older than her seventy-two years. Vivian watched the diabetic woman shuffle around to the side of the wagon, place her boot on the flat metal disc and gingerly step up; her leg seemed sturdy. She clasped the reins in her hand. With the woman in the wagon, the horse plodded slowly down the street. Vivian noticed Luella glance up and followed her gaze to a dirty, shaggy figure coming from the outskirts of town. While she cast her eyes back down to the horse in front of her, Vivian stared.

A basically barefooted man of indeterminate age wearing ragged, dirty dungarees and a tattered shirt was churning up the dust from the street. Even in a farming community, the sight was unusual. A fat miniature pig in a twine string harness and lead was being guided by the man. The contrast between the two was startling. The pig held his head high. He was perky, pink, and plump. He fairly pranced on his ballerina toes. The thin man hung his head distractedly between the limp arms at his sides. His hair was tangled, matted, and dirty brown. He shuffled his feet, which were bound in strips of leather.

He stared at Luella as her wagon passed and started to extend his empty left hand, then let it fall. At the general store window, Vivian saw him notice her, straighten himself, and lift his head. As he approached, Vivian noted he was not as old as she had first assumed. She pushed the door open, and he walked in. She winced at the pungent odor of unwashed flesh. She was used to the smell of sweat from all the farmers coming in their work clothes for parts. Even the bachelor Swedes, who lived out east of town and were known to live in their long underwear from October to May, had a strong smell, but this was different. A sweet, rotting smell like apples in a barrel with a small, hidden, moldy one spoiling all it touched. The bachelors had a dusty, dry-sweat smell.

"Can I help you, mister?" She couldn't bring herself to say "sir." She noticed she hadn't given him her usual, "So what can I get for you today?" As she turned her head away, she could see Luella's wagon getting smaller and wondered what awaited her at home. Vivian hoped Herbert would be alert enough to notice the little celebration Luella had planned.

At the edge of town with the horse headed for home, Luella thought about their fifty-fourth wedding anniversary. She hoped Herbert would be aware enough to taste the applesauce cake she planned to make. Maple frosting was his favorite. She would open that jar of cherries she had been saving for something special. Even though Doc had cautioned her against sweets, she decided a small piece would be okay. Being married to the same person for fifty-four years was not an accomplishment everybody could claim.

Luella knew something was wrong before she even stopped the horse. Stubble-faced Ned came out of the house when he heard the wagon approaching. Her son hooked his thumb toward the house, and she could see he could not speak. His brother Carl was working on the back forty and not expected until evening. Not that her sons were much for words anyway. He gently extracted the reins from his mother's hands and helped her down, got the boxes of groceries out of the wagon, and set them on the ground as she hurried inside. In a few seconds she was back outside and surveyed Ned, who mumbled about the barn and things needing to be attended to. She pulled herself back up onto the seat of the wagon.

As she turned the wagon around, the thin, patient horse swung his head back toward his mistress and pulled up short, waiting. Uncharacteristically, Luella slapped his back with the reins. Startled, the horse resumed his stumbling gait back to town.

She pushed the thoughts of the figure in her home now devoid of life out of her mind. She tried to think of other things. As she'd approached their farm yard moments ago, she'd scanned the clutter of rusted machinery that most folks would call a junkyard. She didn't usually pay much mind to the jumble. That was the men's business, hers was the house. She understood the why behind the untidiness.

When anyone needed a part for some old relic of machinery, they would stop by the Eggerts and try to convince one of her boys to sell them the part decaying away on a "dinosaur" hidden among the weeds and saplings growing up, around, and between. Usually the Eggert men would shake their heads with "I might need that if'n mine breaks." Or "Never know what might happen. Gotta be prepared. Pa always said, 'Waste not want not.'" The farmer, desperate to get back to his own field work, would say, "But you're not wasting it. You're helping a neighbor." The neighbor wouldn't say, "Your pa would've sold that piece," because that wasn't necessarily true. Luella didn't much care if men were poking around for a part to fix equipment, but her menfolk minded.

She'd heard folks speculate, "How'd those Eggerts even find the part they needed amongst all that piled machinery?" But her menfolk always did know where to find what they needed. After a bit of poking and prying, there the part would be like a long-lost kin waiting to be rescued. Occasionally their boys would part with some old piece, just often enough that people kept coming out when they were desperate enough and persuaded the boys to part with a relic of similar year and make to theirs for a more than fair price.

In town Vivian had been watching the stranger drift among the barrels of nails, jars of pickled eggs, and bolts of cloth. She cringed every time he lifted his dirt-caked hand to touch something. She had already instructed him to tie his pig up at the horse post as the health people wouldn't allow for a barnyard animal to traipse into a store with food goods for sale. Seeing the pig, Vivian recalled that Claudia was going to butcher her pig within the next week. Vivian had inquired, "Why aren't you waiting until after the first frost like usual?" Claudia had been evasive.

Vivian noticed Luella's buckboard coming from the edge of town. She wondered if some of the fixings for the anniversary cake had gotten left. She turned back to her counter and saw no cake ingredients sitting there. She thought of Luella's counter and remembered the clutter in that kitchen at her last visit.

Several weeks earlier Vivian, who had not seen Luella in town for weeks, had walked out to the Eggert place. In May Luella had injured her leg, which hadn't healed quickly. The Doc and Thomas had tended the wound until the flesh closed over. Vivian wanted to check on Luella and decided a walk for exercise gave her a reasonable excuse. Vivian knocked at the door, then entered. "Hello? It's just me." Vivian noticed a paperback romance on the table and rags that smelled of bleach hung on the backs of three mismatched chairs. But the bleach could not mask the smell of bowel movement, which was not the same as the cow manure smell that hung in most farmhouse entryways where barn jackets and coveralls hung on hooks or here at the Eggerts on eight-penny nails.

"I'm so sorry." Luella grabbed up the drying rags and stuffed them under the enamel-clad cast-iron sink. The coffin-sized sink was surrounded on the bottom with cloth curtains that hung slightly open and were gray where a hand pushed between the flaps to reach for soap, a dishpan, or a piece of steel wool to clean a stubborn pan.

"I can't get Herbert down the front or side steps and out to the biffy. I have to lift him onto the dishpan." She set the dishpan in the sink with a graying dish towel as a cover. "The boys usually are in the fields or barn."

Out of politeness Vivian turned her attention away from the sink area where Luella had "hidden" the rags and the makeshift bedpan. Vivian focused on the table, touched the circle of lace under a pot of artificial flowers. "I always admired your handiwork. You have a way with tatting and crocheting." Luella blushed at the unexpected compliment. "Haven't had much time for any of that, not since Herbert's episode."

When will they see this was not an episode, Vivian had thought. The man will never get back on a tractor but needs round-the-clock care and ought to be taken into a facility. Vivian knew that was not how things were done out here in the country or even in town in the Midwest. Vivian had heard the protestations often enough. "We take care of our own." "I'm not putting my hubby into some place for strangers to look after him. I promised to care for him for better or worse, in sickness and in health." And no more was to be said. That was that. Vivian had heard as much from Luella that day they had visited at her farm. The smell of this pig man in the store brought to mind those rags at Luella's.

Scanning past the smelly pig man, Vivian recognized Luella's wagon drive by the large store windows.

Recently Luella had fetched Doc for Herbert. She had birthed those two boys out on the farm with no one to help her. She did not have much of a social life, because she always felt a bit conscious of the "clutter" the menfolk had scattered in the front, sides, and backyards that "they were just fixin' to get to" or had "just been workin' on and then had to get to them chores" or that "bit a field work." No one disputed they stayed busy all day. But at what? Digging around for a scrap part to fix a piece of junk. But that was Vivian's speculation shared by most women and quite a few men around town. She had heard the talk in the store but mused that a person's life was more complex than what appeared on the surface. Look at Luella.

Vivian stepped closer to see Luella's wagon bouncing her poor arthritic bones around and stop, but not in front of the store. When she realized Luella had halted in front of the undertakers, Vivian knew. No doctor this time.

She tried to step past the pig man, who was explaining how hungry he was and did she have anything he could do to get just a bit of bread. She was wondering how a man could be so stupid as to lead around meat on a string with hunger in his belly. Pigs were a food factory, the garbage-into-meat machine, the miracle, staple animal on a farm. Pigs got fed all the vegetable ends, spoiled bits, leftover oatmeal, and stale bread that wasn't enough to make into bread pudding. If scraps weren't fed to the chickens, they went into the pig's slop bucket. Vivian extricated herself from the man, stepped over his pig tied to the rail but straining toward the man, who was young and fit enough to get a job.

She was intensely angry. "Here you are walking with food on a string wanting help, and you don't have the gumption to help yourself." She stopped short, and he nearly fell into her.

She twisted the front of her dress and stared where Luella stepped heavily down from the wagon.

The pig man began to follow her toward the undertakers. She turned abruptly. "God helps those who help themselves." She could not be bothered with him. She needed to think of words of comfort for Luella.

On this bright fall day Luella should be home mixing up a celebration cake for her husband, who could not remember who she was much less that today was their fifty-fourth anniversary, but Vivian knew a celebration was imperative for Luella. She halted steps from the undertakers' door, stared at the boardwalk, and paused.

Earlier this morning Luella had been reminiscing to Vivian of that day fifty-four years ago when she and Herbert had stood before the preacher, she in her best dress and him shaved with hair slicked back, smelling of barber shop and the food she had prepared for both their families. The wealth of a bountiful harvest, a barrel of beer, and a couple jugs of moonshine carried their spirits into the evening before they all had to leave to do chores. By the time the wedding couple got out of their finery and into barn clothes, the cows were bellaring, but the couple milking them whistled. Vivian had smiled as Luella relived her wedding day joy. No whistling today.

Vivian debated if she should step forward and help Luella open the door of the undertaker's or respectfully remain back. Then she realized what must be going through Luella's mind standing on the threshold of the mortuary. Forever on this day Luella would remember that she had not been with her husband when he died. The anniversary of their new life together would now be the anniversary of the death of that life together. Luella looked up, took a breath, and walked into the mortuary.

Vivian followed her and heard her tell Thomas's uncle, "My beloved Herbert has left me."

Vivian put her hand out to help Luella into a chair. "What will I do without him? I did all I could, but it wasn't enough. Why did he leave me? I was only gone for a short time."

Quietly Vivian reassured her, "Maybe this was Herbert's last gift to you. His anniversary gift. To die and free you from the labor of caring for him."

The look in Luella's eyes was clear: she wanted to return that gift.

34. Andy Saves the Day

Late in August before the weekend, Andy went to his father's friend Bill with a proposition he was sure would surprise his dad and get him back into his father's good graces.

After bolstering his resolve from his father's liquor cabinet, he walked into Bill's bank, one of the few still operating, and was shown into Bill's office separated from the main bank area by a large window and windowed door that the teller closed behind Andy.

"Good afternoon, Bill," Andy grasped the banker's extended hand. Bill resumed his leather cushioned seat and gestured for Andy to take the matching but cloth-clad arm chair opposite. "Dad and I were talking. You and he are considering moving a piece of property that has a creek and small pond." Bill nodded, leaned back, and interlaced his fingers over his belly listening while Andy continued, "I've got a friend from college. Our fathers are friends and his dad is looking to retire on a small acreage."

"I didn't think Randy was ready to push that person right now." Bill sat forward.

"We've looked into the particulars. Forty acres of prime land was purchased by the father in 1902 in exchange for eighty acres of his original quarter section that was rocky and poorer. That high forty, which is on a separate deed, could be broken off the one hundred twenty to satisfy the delinquent portion of the debt, the accumulated interest, and the taxes. The other eighty acres on another deed could be sold later to take care of the balance." Andy adjusted himself, reached into his pocket, and popped another peppermint into his mouth.

"Sounds like you've done your homework. I'm ready if your father is. I can take care of the transfer next week. We'll just need to pay the fee and have the conveyance registered." Bill leaned forward intently.

"I've got the checkbook to take care of the fee today." Andy rose, pulled out the leather-clad booklet of blank checks and stubs.

"Fabulous," exclaimed Bill who hoisted himself up from his desk and vigorously shook Andy's hand. "You're a man of action." Bill studied Andy. "Your father seemed hesitant. Glad to see he's stepping up to the plate. The apple fell straight down in your family. The process may take two transfers, but I'll get the conveyance taken care of in the next week or so." Andy wrote Bill a check. They talked briefly about sports occurring this weekend before Andy left to find a few friends with whom he could celebrate his victory.

When he crossed paths with his father Monday midafternoon, Andy was a little worse for wear. "You look like you were ridden hard and put away wet," Randy observed. Andy adjusted his shirt, re-tucking the back, blinked his aching eyes, and remarked, "Just ironing out a few wrinkles on a prospect."

"That's good to hear. Glad you're settling in. Your mother and I haven't seen much of you the past few days. Being noticed at Sunday service with us wouldn't hurt you." Andy shrugged and Randy returned to his office and the papers on his desk.

The following Monday Andy talked with Bill to confirm the transfer had occurred. With a clearer head, Andy strutted into his father's office smiling. "You'll be glad to hear that your concerns over that property you wanted have been handled." Randy regarded his son questioningly then returned the smile. "Oh, you mean Meiser's where the O'Briens are renting. Glad you got that paperwork sorted. Our next project will be putting the pressure on the old maid." Andy stretched taller and threw his shoulders back. "That's the one I'm talking about. The transfer has been filed. I took care of everything last week."

"Francis Nelson's place?" Randy pushed up from the chair, placing his hands on his desk. "Which piece? How much? You don't mean the piece with the house and barn?"

"I don't know if the land includes the house and barn. They aren't worth much. I drove by and looked. I didn't concern myself with that. I thought you were interested in the good ground. I told you my buddy's dad was looking and hot to buy at $30 an acre. I already told him the land was as good as his and now it is."

Randy circled around to the front of his desk where his son stood holding his ground. "Is it the forty-acre piece that is separate or the eighty from the original quarter section? People in Turtle Lake and Bear Creek won't be happy to hear we evicted one of their founding families from her homestead. We've got to be aware of our reputation. Didn't you think to talk to me first?"

Andy scowled. "You're always extolling the virtues of initiative. I thought you'd be pleased."

"Don't get me wrong." Randy backed away then proceeded again. "A man needs to strike out and make his mark. But, there are ramifications to weigh."

"Aren't there always? We can't please everyone," Andy retorted.

"Yes, but there are considerations of which you aren't aware. Things that have been going on for years." Randy pressed forward again, "Certain assets not immediately visible, particulars better kept close to the chest." Randy had been circling his son until his son's back was up against the front of Randy's mammoth desk. Andy pushed off the desk and nearly knocked his father over as he stepped into the space beyond his dad.

"Maybe I should've been informed?" Andy spat out.

"How can anyone please you!" Randy shot back.

"Nothing I do is good enough." Andy slammed the door behind him. At the startled receptionist's expression, Andy smiled and strode down the steps and out to the street.

Upstairs Randy watched his son retreat and dialed Bill. Randy discovered that the forty acres already transferred was not the marginal land with the mineral deposits, but prime agricultural land that overlooked the pond and creek that Bill was pleased to say would be ideal for a retirement home for Randy's friend.

Without disclosing that he hadn't been informed of his son's intent, Randy inquired after the land containing part of the mineral deposit vein running through Polk and Barron Counties.

"I wasn't able to transfer that piece yet. That eighty acres, which includes the house and outbuildings, will need to go through foreclosure."

"Maybe best to hold off at present. Slow things down a bit." Silence followed on the other end of the line. Randy thought they may have gotten cut off when he heard Bill announce, "But we've got momentum. Without that forty acres of cropland, she'll feel more pressure to sell the balance. With land prices at twenty to thirty dollars an acre and interest rates at sixteen percent, her entire eighty could be ours for a song. If you want her to keep the house, we can take the marginal forty with the minerals, but she'll still owe sixteen hundred on the debt. She'll be left with only forty acres. Without the crops and pasture, she won't be able to feed her cattle."

"I know." Randy steadied his voice. All the township farmsteads had originally been quarter sections, one-hundred-sixty-acre parcels. He knew that Francis had sold eighty acres of marginal land to the north from the original for the purchase of forty of prime crop land to the east when he assumed the farm after his parents' death. That prime crop land was the property now slated to become a recreational retreat for his son's friend. Randy had favored a plan that allowed him to purchase the entire parcel or for Claudia to keep her home forty. He wanted the land with minerals that lay to the west of Claudia's home, but he did not like how this scenario would play out to his customers in Bear Creek or Turtle Lake. He continued with more confidence than he felt. "But our Christian duty is to look after our neighbor."

Again, there was a long silence on the other end of the line. "If that's what you want."

"Yes. I'll get back to you. Soon."

35. Quentin—No Way Out

Almost two weeks since the fire and almost a week since Thomas had left, Claudia went to church September 11th looking for solace. Before service started she heard the couple in front of her exchanging judgments. Vivian walked in and sat next to Claudia during the discussion.

"He took a baseball bat and bashed in the cemetery stones. He's reprehensible," the husband declared.

"I was told by Mrs. Gilbertson who heard the story from the constable that they found a hunk of pipe. That delinquent defaced and destroyed church property," the wife stated confidently.

Vivian leaned over to Claudia. "I chalk his actions up to dissatisfaction and frustration. Quentin had to quit school to work at the railroad loading and unloading cars of grain. No wonder he's gotten so gaunt."

"If the boy's father had stiffened his backbone and set boundaries, acted like the head of his family, she may have been more moderate. But the more he gave in to his wife, the stronger her resolve grew. She wanted to make something of the men in her family," the woman in front of them continued.

"If he'd been firmer with her, she could have eased up on the rest of the family," the man asserted. "The longer they were married the weaker he got until he couldn't hold an opinion without her arms lifting it."

"The more Caspar Milquetoast he became, the stricter she had to get." The woman shook her head and clicked her teeth.

"I'd have to agree that Quentin's mother dried up and his father became more reticent until no affection or care was left in that family." Vivian lamented, shifting in the pew.

Into this family Quentin had been born, the eldest of two. He occupied the slot each Sunday between his stone-faced mother and wooden father, who held his toddler sister. When she turned seven, her mother had placed the thin girl next to her and apart from the men.

Claudia leaned over to Vivian's ear, "But I never saw or heard any signs of violence in their family. Quentin was always so quiet and polite. At the barn-raising, he brought the lumber and unloaded the timbers as reliably as any young man and played his guitar later. He seemed okay to me."

The church buzzed like a hive of wasps around Claudia and Vivian until the preacher ascended the pulpit.

In this church for years Quentin's mother had been praised for her dedication to the rules of religion, the dictates of decency, and her adherence to social norms and appearances. Her somber frugality and economic constraints were admired. Her husband, who lacked that fortitude, had valued those Puritan virtues when he married her. They never missed church, occupying their regular pew halfway back on the right.

Claudia was distressed to see Quentin appear so thin and ragged, cowering between his mother, whose head was held high, her back flat, and his father whose body was bent around their daughter. For the moment the rules of relationships and proximity had changed for the obviously distressed little sister in her Sunday dress. The parents leaned away from each other while Quentin sagged like an old, uninhabited barn. The minister used the circumstance to give a sermon on our responsibility to others.

"We don't live alone. All of our actions affect others. We can't be thoughtless, godless people. This is a world dependent on all, especially our youth, being responsible citizens." The pastor who was normally quite reserved felt justified in banging his fist on the pulpit.

"Lawlessness cannot be tolerated. We need to respect each other and care for one another. The Gospel is there for us; John 15:12 commands us to love one another as God has loved us. How do we show that solidarity? By our actions! We are saved by faith alone but our actions demonstrate our conviction and belief in God's love and forgiveness."

At first, Claudia couldn't add up the particulars. Quentin was a sweet, if melancholy, young man. He always nodded to her on the street. He'd worked diligently at the railroad and the barn-raising.

After the service Claudia walked to the small cemetery behind the church to see if understanding would come to her, if the facts could produce a sum that made sense. He hadn't broken her father's stone. Several tombstones had corners broken, and two headstones were decapitated with only the date of birth left standing. She understood irritation and anger. She understood the young man's need to relieve his pent-up frustration, to do something extraordinary. If he didn't take out his exasperation on an inanimate object, he could turn on someone, maybe himself. But she also understood the damage he had caused to those who had scrimped and saved to erect an eternal memorial where they could come to grieve. No one had the funds to replace the destroyed markers. Now, she reflected, each time a family member would come to pay their respects, they would think of the anger enacted on their loved one's grave.

Claudia read the promise on one of the damaged tombstones, "Never Forgotten, Always in My Heart," broken in half. The destruction saddened her, but the effect on quiet Quentin, the cause, disturbed her. She noticed the gravestone of old Mrs. Elmer, whose granddaughter had gone to elementary school with Quentin. The two outcast youths had been friends before Quentin was forced to quit and work at the railroad. Vivian joined Claudia on the grassy hill of the cemetery. "Mrs. Gilbertson heard from the constable that the vandalism occurred Friday night," remarked Vivian, staring at the angel on Mrs. Elmer's gravestone. The angel's head and the tip of the left wing lay on the ground next to the robed body and feathered wings. Next to the angel was an old tin bucket partially full of tar, a crusted brush sticking out.

Claudia could imagine the scene that caused the devastation. This ruin was not caused by a gang of boys filled with herd fever. No one was boasting with bravado, just Quentin wordlessly bashing headstones without reason. Excitement would have coursed through his arms, heedless of anything except smashing, breaking. Claudia knew the desire. She had often wanted to throw a glass or a plate against the brick behind the woodstove when everything seemed out of her control. She never did. She would have had to clean up the mess and try to replace the broken dish. She bet his arms ached as he wielded the pipe.

"He would have had to run the few blocks home to get something to repair the damage." Claudia regarded the bucket and brush.

"That's how he was caught, attempting to tar the angel back together. A couple of men coming home with a skin-full grabbed him and hauled him to the constable. I guess they were bragging yesterday in town how they were glad to put the 'wussy guy's kid' in jail for vandalism," Vivian shook her head sadly, "But that's not the worst. The constable woke Quentin's mother in the middle of the night to inform her but wouldn't release the boy."

"Why not? What's to be gained having him sit in that iron-barred room all night?"

"That's what I just said to the constable after service." Vivian put her hands on her bony hips. "He disclosed if she had to walk back Saturday morning and her husband, who normally would be sleeping after working the night shift at the creamery, had to stay awake to care for their girl, the boy would learn the consequences of breaking the law. The parents might learn a lesson to teach to their children. Can you believe such claptrap?" Vivian shook her gray curls vehemently.

She viewed the scene where he had vented his inexpressible dissatisfaction, alone. She wanted to know who was responsible to be there for Quentin, to listen to him? To love and forgive *him*.

Claudia ruminated on her way home from church. *Life used to be simple.* If she wasn't happy, the cause was because their animals or her father weren't okay. She just had to figure out what she had to do to get them back to equilibrium. Life would then return to normal. She liked predictability. She had done the expected childhood schoolwork. Around the daily routine of chores, she had carved out some time for reading and listening to the radio.

Her father's rhythms and routine were predictable and familiar. He did his things. She did hers. They saw each other at meals and across fields, much like the picked fields surrounding her on her ride home from Sunday service. If she needed time away, she and Vivian would take the train into Cumberland or Amery to shop or pick up a delivery for Ernie's store or her father. They may have a bite out and window shop or go to the library or walk along the lake. The light reflecting off the lake and the lapping of waves against the shore had always soothed her.

Now she didn't know what to expect. Her father was gone. Thomas was gone. She missed brushing Dandy and Molly. That repetitive rhythm always soothed her. Brushing the gelding had become another chore that had to be done. Her Dandy and Molly were gone. Forever. As the gelding tripped along with his unsteady gait, Claudia closed her eyes and longed to be draped languidly over Dandy's broad back allowing her to take the two of them home, Dandy's steady, rhythmic clop, clop tapping away any worries. Maybe Quentin had no soothing outlet as counterbalance.

She felt disquiet. Unsettled. Like the hens when they wanted to set and hatch out eggs, but she wouldn't let them because the time of year was wrong and she needed eggs, not more chicks. If she could determine what was causing her frustration, she could figure out what to do to correct the problem. For the life of her, she couldn't figure out who to be upset with or to blame. She turned Old Glue into the desolate pasture. In the house she splashed water across her face to remove the dust and walked across the fields and road to the Johnsons. The exercise loosened her muscles, which had stiffened while holding onto the boney back of the gelding on the ride from church.

36. Claudia Can't See, Does God?

Farmers from the area had gathered at the Johnsons after church services to discuss the problems in enforcing the agreements between cooperatives and milk processors over the classified pricing plan. A decade ago George with three hundred and twenty acres and Francis with a hundred and twenty acres had worked on the plan together, which gave farmers more say over a consistent, fair price for their milk. After the October 1929 crash, milk prices dropped and instability followed. As Francis's daughter, Claudia was expected to attend. She wasn't milking cows, but she was hoping for information. Without her horses and pig, she'd hoped she had enough feed to get through. More and more her cattle were bellaring, no grass in the pasture. After she picked her corn, she could fence the field and turn them in to forage for whatever corn the picker had missed.

A half dozen or so farmers were situated around the Johnsons' kitchen table. Those seated were part of the local cooperative, but some farmers, like the one directly to the north of her and the one south of the Reuters, were not in attendance and had undercut co-op prices just to sell their milk.

Pete Mevissen was not happy. "Do they think that we all aren't in the same boat! We have to stick together. That's why we formed the co-op in the first place."

Matthew Reuter protested, "We can't go on being paid less than the cost for us to produce our milk and butter. The expense to produce eight pounds of milk is well over the forty-three cents a gallon the city consumer pays."

"I don't see the rates for vet visits, seed, or machinery

parts going down," added Mr. Andersen. "I can't afford to vaccinate the calves. I had several die cuz of that." Silence followed. They thought of the farmer to the south of Matthew who wasn't at the table who'd burned his wheat in the field because he no longer had cattle to feed, no gas for harvesting, and would've lost money with the cost of shipping. A bushel of wheat in 1919 brought $2.16 but sank to $.49 in 1932, yet the cost of a loaf of bread made from that wheat had not gone down.

George removed the cigarette from his mouth. "We formed co-ops and opened cheese factories in Turtle Lake, Clayton, Clear Lake, Almena, Amery, Joel, and Comstock to turn milk into a product that had a longer shelf life and was not as susceptible to daily changes in milk prices. We can't get discouraged." Claudia had attended the meeting but hadn't spoken. Hank was reticent, too. She wasn't sure she had anything to offer, even though the drop in crop prices and rising costs affected her.

"We gotta do something drastic." Mr. Fournier, usually so reserved, slapped his open hand onto the tabletop, not loudly but coming from him the gesture got their attention. "The radio reported cooperatives are dumping their milk in the streets in protest. They're calling the demonstration a milk strike. Maybe we need to do the same."

Matthew spoke again. "I say we force-feed our calves as much milk as they can take without giving them the scours. Let our pigs gorge on unshipped milk. I'd rather the missus fed us custards and pudding at every meal than see my milk wasted as street wash, even if doing so would settle the dust."

Doris Johnson, who hadn't uttered a word but kept an eye on coffee cup levels, spoke in the ensuing silence. "And that's getting nothing for your hard labor, sixteen to twenty hours a day, seven days a week." Shortly after Doris served them apple crisp, the group had dispersed with a promise to write to the milk processors demanding they stick to the agreements with cooperatives and expressing dissatisfaction with their non-compliance, but no one expected any real change to occur. Claudia went home as dusk settled. Hank had offered to walk with her, but she'd expressed her need to think.

Wisconsin dairy farmers, like those gathered in Bear Creek Township, had thought, after the initial crash, that they were in for a period of calm. But the fallout from The Crash continued as every aspect of farming was affected.

Claudia had heard on the radio that a share of American Gas, which a few years ago would've been purchased for $42, was now worth only $5. That tidbit was followed by a newsman's quip, "Want to know what I'd do if I had all the money in the world? Apply it on my debts as far as it would go."

Talk of debts prompted Claudia to blame Randy Rottman for her dissatisfaction. She had plenty of reason to be upset with him even if the current economic crisis wasn't directly connected to him. She trudged home thinking back.

Months ago, the February 18th edition of the *Turtle Lake Times* printed in its "State Capital News" column an article about a possible job insurance program, but that would only affect a few of the thousands of unemployed in Wisconsin. Shell Lake had held an unemployment meeting later that month where a free lunch was served. The Forestry Department was going to hire laborers to build fire lanes up north for twenty-five cents an hour. For an hour's wages a man could buy one quart of bottled milk or a partial pound of coffee or three loaves of bread or a pound of meat or eighteen eggs. Gas cost seventeen cents per gallon and a used Model T car cost several hundred dollars if one could be found for sale. Tires, a week's earnings, constantly got punctures and an old car could burn through a quart of oil, an hour's wage, like it was gas. A man could chop trees, haul, and burn brush all day to buy a frying pan, then work another day to afford the food. But he'd have to walk to get the groceries and cook them over an open fire as a stove cost $8, almost a week's wages.

Hearing or thinking about the situation made Claudia's head spin. At least she had her meager garden, her five hens, and her twenty head of cattle. She needed to keep them watered and fed. She'd had to butcher her pig early because she lacked feed. Her chickens were subsisting on bugs and a scattered handful of grain. She couldn't have revealed to the men gathered at the Johnsons that she didn't have enough feed to grind, the scanty corn hadn't been made into silage but remained unpicked except what she'd gathered by hand, and she had only several bushel of oats, not enough to feed twenty head of stock this winter and keep some for seed. She felt overwhelmed.

Thousands of people were without jobs while others were doing more for less money. The weather heaped insult on top of economic injury. Ernie had read aloud all week from that same newspaper to anyone coming into the store of two events: the death of a twenty-five-year-old Grantsburg man on crutches caught out in a blizzard after his car stalled and the following letter from an Oklahoma man to his debtors.

"It is impossible for me to send you a check in response to your request. My present financial condition is due to the effects of federal laws, state laws, county laws, corporation laws, by-laws, brother-in-laws, mother-in-laws, and out-laws that have been foisted upon the unsuspecting public. Through the various laws I have been held down, held up, helped up, walked on, sat on, flattened out, and squeezed until I don't know where I am, who I am, what I am, or why I am.

"These laws compel me to pay a merchant tax, capital tax, stock tax, income tax, property tax, gas tax, water tax, light tax, cigar tax, street tax, school tax, syntax and carpet tax.

"The government has so governed my business that I do not know who owns it. I am suspected, inspected, disrespected, examined, re-examined, until all I know is that I'm supplicated for money for every need, desire and hope of the human race, and because I refuse to fall and go out and beg, borrow or steal money to give away, I am cussed, discussed, boycotted, talked to, talked about, lied about, held up, held down and robbed, until I am nearly ruined; so the only reason I am clinging to life is to see what the h--- is coming next."

In February Claudia worried about others as she listened to Ernie but hadn't offered a comment. She had whispered a prayer in her head for the boy who died. In September she worried about her own debt but didn't know whom to blame. There was no white blizzard of winter yet but often a gray one of dust. In February her father had been here, but now in September she was alone. At home Old Glue with his neck stretched over the top of the paddock fence was reaching for nonexistent grass. She ambled over to him and stroked his head, but her heart wasn't engaged. She hadn't even been able to offer him grain before turning him into the barren pasture. She strolled toward the thin trickle of a crick that snaked through the tough swamp grass where the skinny cattle pulled at greenish brown clumps knee-deep in what used to be the swamp. She'd cooked the last of the beef and would have to decide if and when she'd butcher one of her steers to replenish her supply. Beef was bringing less than four dollars per hundred weight, which barely paid to ship them, but she needed money for tractor gas.

Like the urgency accompanying the sale of the two steers she'd hoped to fatten and ship when prices rose, she couldn't wait. She hadn't been the only one paying delinquent property tax in the township, but she hated being grouped with the destitute when the Mevissens, Johnsons, Eggerts, Reuters, and Andersens had never been late. Until this year, she'd counted the Nelsons in with those who paid in full and on time. Nothing of value was left to sell. Since the fire she was making do with junk tools from the old shed. She always had her land.

She pushed her New York's indulgence down and away every time the thought sprang up and bit her unaware. *How did the mortuary business in New York make money and farming in Wisconsin was less profitable? The price of dying remained stable but the cost of farming was precarious.*

She had spent the better part of the last two weeks cutting and gathering the wild grasses growing in every ditch and the swamp foliage dry enough that hadn't been harvested by another farmer equally as desperate for winter fodder. The only hay that had survived the barn fire were a few stacks of wild hay she'd left sitting in the field. When she thought of yesterday's meeting at the Johnsons, which had ended without any clear plan to rectify the quandary, she felt thwarted. She couldn't think about the larger picture. She cared but felt helpless to resolve those problems.

Here she was with more work than God had green apples, and she couldn't motivate herself to do anything more than mindless tasks of harvesting and daily chores. Her father's ideas and dreams were the structure that had prompted their planning. She had never planned alone. Her job had been to help make her father's purpose a reality. She wasn't even sure she had a dream of her own for the future. She wasn't sure she knew what she wanted. Claudia lumbered up the house steps to get ready for bed.

She remembered after Christmas on a clear winter afternoon when she and her father sat together at the table, sun pouring over their shoulders onto marked-up seed catalogues. She'd prepared lists of needs for cattle and equipment repairs, tallied sources of income, and calculated outlays of cash. Her father had been too tired to do more than glance at the catalogues last year, and the year before he'd been too busy, and she had not insisted.

What had seemed his normal stubbornness was a warning sign. She never saw it coming.

The thoughts of New York arose as she was falling asleep. Music, lovely music, carried her effortlessly. Guilt snatched briefly at her stomach. *You should have and you shouldn't have* murmured in her ear.

That last weekend in July in New York seemed like a lifetime ago. Back in July she thought she could cope with the stream of changes. By September change was cascading relentlessly down on her. Sleep was eluding her, just out of reach.

She sought solace in memory. The concert with Thomas in New York was a world away, but she brought the music close to comfort her and pushed the guilt and should-haves back to a far corner, off her property. Earlier in the day she'd heard the radio playing a Sibelius selection.

At the concert that evening the name of one piece on the all Sibelius program, a symphonic poem, should have warned her, *The Wood Nymph: op.15*. But like his *Violin Concerto in D minor op: 47*, she had been taken by surprise. July was hot outside but cool in Orchestra Hall. Thomas and Claudia were close back then. The specter of Macy hadn't appeared between them. The program notes described the tone poem as a man's ephemeral romance with a wood nymph. The opening march gave no indication of the sighing violins to follow.

From their seats to the rear and side, neither in the expensive section nor the crows' nest balcony, Claudia had gazed out over a sea of heads and felt a cool breeze. As she pulled her borrowed silk shawl close, she realized a circulating fan must have come on. When Claudia considered the freshly coiffed women in elaborate gowns seated in the front rows, she felt like a dowdy milk cow in a herd of prize heifers at the fair. Although her clothing and hair were not as refined or sophisticated as the others, she believed her desire to appreciate and enjoy the performance was equal to theirs.

Claudia thought the conductor was like God. He controlled the action without ever directly commanding or touching or forcing any of the participants. Each orchestra member performed and chose how hard or soft to stroke or pluck, blow or strike. But the conductor chose when to begin or end, when to crescendo or proceed quietly. By each member relinquishing control and the need to "direct" their individual part, the performance and the work were fuller and more complex and reached a deeper, richer total because one force—the conductor—held them together. Each member of the orchestra needed to be aware, to listen, and to watch for the conductor's baton. Or, Claudia thought, for God's hand to reach out to them like He did to Adam on the Sistine Chapel ceiling. The musicians must be ready to blow their trumpet triumphantly or pluck their string in the space provided by the conductor's hand or to clash the cymbals that one time in fifteen minutes when called upon to make their contribution.

As Claudia watched, she realized that each player's surrender contained power beyond their singular performance. In the act of letting go of their own wills, they were a part of something more magnificent. The players' relinquishing to the conductor's will allowed the music to flow with varied vibrations into an ocean of complexity. They could concentrate on their individual part, giving themselves over to being the conduit to the whole. She did not notice until later that the analogy applied to her when she was directing and driving Dandy and Molly. The horses could concentrate on pulling, staying in the furrow doing their job; they could relax because she was directing their movements.

The conductor was considering the entire piece with individual movements, sections, and instruments that weren't separate but a whole composition. Similarly, she saw the whole field with hedgerow and swale and knew when to turn her team of horses, when to encourage them to put their back into the task, and when to let the grade of the land work with them.

Claudia wondered how those exquisite sounds, the tickle and tease of violin strings to emit vibrations, could come from a strand of horse hair drawn across four strings of cat gut.

The conductor had stood passively during the solo to let one musician shine. Claudia felt cocooned by the semi-twilight in Orchestra Hall. Each player concentrated less on another player and his peculiarities and personalities and more on the whole performance, more concerned with the comingling of the entire work. Claudia realized that whether constructing a concerto or raising a barn, someone's bad breath or pushy behavior didn't indicate that person's ability to cut, hammer, and swing or hold a tool. An individual's differences did not matter unless one focused on them. Each participant wanted each of the others to do whatever was their forte. Collaboration made them all shine. Even the solo violinist relinquished his first chair position to play with the entire string section, just one of forty violins and dozens of cellos and bass violins. At a barn-raising, the one who excelled at notching logs was as valuable as the one with brawn to hoist the timber or the two who could saw through the beam like butter.

Despite all the chandeliers in the hall, the audience sat in semi-darkness. Claudia wondered if the orchestra members were hot, men all in black punctuated by white shirts and black ties and women all in black.

The conductor wanted more from the musicians. Claudia could tell. He was almost leaping, arms raised and pulling, then he lowered his splayed hands palms down to quiet the emanating sound. Was God, the conductor of her life, wanting more from her? Was she capable of giving more or was she mistaken? Maybe God was actually wanting more from someone next to her and not her. How could the individual know where the baton was pointed and if she was being directed to play more or less, harder or softer?

The solo violin was a sweet bee buzzing in her head like an orchestra of instruments in and of itself. The violin comprised two distinct vocal sounds. A beat of wings, then two notes and all the while a humming higher voice that filled the space within her. God and conductor as two distinct entities. Or not? The music and her thoughts twirled in and around her.

The conductor and God were putting forth as much energy into us, our performance, as we, his performers, are trying to put into pleasing him, to use the gifts given to us by Him. The conductor crouched and leaped up, arms out and then together, down and up.

When I think of God as the great puppeteer, I don't think of Him being pulled to jump and prance upon the stage of life, but there he was. The one in charge of conducting all the others is jumping, crouching, leaping as if jerked by the musicians plucking, stroking, blowing, and striking. The players are controlling the conductor as much as the conductor is directing the players.

Is that the way with us? God moves us and we move Him? Was the breeze in the hall the breath of the Holy Spirit whisking through on occasion to wake me up to the realization of my power through submission of my will to that of the whole and to the conductor? Or was it just the ventilation system? Or does God take his cue from his creatures as the conductor does from his musicians?

Each put their passion, their joys, their sorrows into the movement of arm, head, and body stroking furiously, toes and heels moving. One woman violinist pulled down on her bow with such passion that Claudia feared she would decapitate the instrument she held so tightly, as if the violin were her child.

The cello poised on a needle like a ballerina on point, the cellist's fingers tickled the neck of the instrument, he drew his arm and bow across her middle and she vibrated low and throaty. The piece culminated before Claudia was aware that she was not ready for the music to end. She wanted to remain in the pool of sound vibrating through her.

The maestro walked off, head down, then returned to the stage. He flung his head back as he faced the audience and bowed, threw his head back again, eyes to heaven. *To thank his father in heaven?*

In the midst of all the heartache and work of July, she still had reason, abundant reasons, to be thankful. Her father was gone, but she had her Dandy and Molly and Thomas. At the end of July, she had chided herself not to forget.

She'd almost gone under into sleep when the guilt and should-haves crept in again. So much change had occurred in the couple of months since July that in September she had difficulty remembering the essentials for which she was grateful. She considered all the should haves. *I should have told the hobo to stay and help me. I should not have been so bull-headed with Thomas. I should seriously consider all options. Hank is helpful and cares. Am I supposed to let go of my control like the orchestra members? But who will make sure everything turns out okay, if I don't?*

37. Hank and Claudia Negotiate

The Nelsons and Johnsons had been neighbors for as long as Claudia and Hank could remember. They were friends, fellow farmers, and with a couple awkward kisses, maybe more than friends. Nothing was very unusual when Hank stopped by the early part of September much like he had on that day in August when he had helped with her roof and the day he'd brought wood. Neighbors and fellow farmers would stop if they wanted to negotiate a trade of labor or to discuss a cattle or machinery transaction or trouble with a mutual boundary line. Friends would stop to visit.

She was at the fence reattaching staples to a wooden post where a steer had popped the top staples on two adjoining posts to get at a patch of dried grass in the yard.

"How are you?" Hank asked as he held the wire to the post, and she gripped the staple with one hand and hammered with the other.

"Fine." She could have fenced alone, but two sets of hands required less than half the time. She had welcomed Thomas's help but his hands were back in New York. Their paths did not cross much. Hank was knowledgeable besides helpful. "Thanks." She didn't want to look into his face, fearing he could read on hers the extent of her trouble.

"I wanted to talk to you about your situation," he hesitated, shifting his weight and squeezing his seed cap in one hand, his other hand shoved down into his overalls pocket. *Oh God, please don't let him start in on Thomas or the farm.*

Secrets were difficult to keep in a small town. People had questioned Vivian about the rift between Thomas and Claudia and the social connection between Claudia and Hank. Everyone knew by now of the debt and her need for cash, but a financial problem was a topic people usually kept to themselves. A few people bragged about how much they paid for a piece of equipment or what a bargain they got on an animal. Most folks were too humble and too proud to ask for help. Business between farmer and banker was akin to that between farmer and pastor. But a relationship conflict or a couple's crisis held more juice than a financial setback. People may know of a dilemma, may chew on the intricacies at length with each other, but wouldn't directly mention the predicament to the person with the trouble.

"There's talk that you may be thinking of selling off some land," he offered tentatively.

"I'm not selling anything!" she straightened, clutching the hammer. "Who told you that?"

"Well, I just know that maybe you were needing…" he paused. Her expression blocked the boundary he'd crossed. He set his cap back on his head and shuffled his feet.

"Our farms have always been side by side. Your dad and mine have both milked cows and raised beef. We've always helped each other out."

Yeah, she thought and you and your family have not had a mortgage on your farm since the beginning of time. *Wait, maybe he was offering financial help.*

"What were you thinking of, Hank?" She rarely called him by his given name.

"I have some money I've been setting aside that I don't need just now," he removed his Dekalb seed cap again and pushed the sides together, then open, "that I could lend out to a person to tide them over a rough spot." Fear and hope surged to gain hold, and she forced both back.

Her shoulders relaxed; she let the hammer fall limply held by the end. "What would you expect if you were to lend money? And what if you needed the money you were saving? What then?"

"You know my brother and me will take over our place. Dad has given us each some land we can build a house on." Her face hardened at that suggestion. He gazed over her shoulder out into the fields. "I'm not interested in building a house now. I like where I'm at. I'm just saying some day. But, if you needed an investor for a period of time, well, I'd be willing."

"What would be in the bargain for you?" She asked bluntly. She'd been advised before that she came off abrupt and harsh. She wished she knew how to be softer without feeling vulnerable and uncomfortable.

"You mean besides helping a neighbor and friend?" He spoke the last word quietly. She let the hammer fall to the grass. "There could be worse things than our two farms being in partnership." To which he added, "A partnership of sorts." She thought about that day he had helped her with the roof. The way they were with each other and how similar to the interaction with her father. *I could do that kind of a life.*

Her first thought was relief. She considered her life with him as financial partners. She would not need to marry him or live with him. She could stay in her house and farm her land the way she always had. He could stay in his house with his dad, mom, and brother and farm their land. The thought flickered, then died, that he might not be satisfied with that arrangement. She assured herself that she could begin to pay him back when she sold the calves of their Scottish Highland heifers. She would need to keep a couple and she would need time to find the right market for this breed of beef. With Hank's help she would be able to buy feed and pay off the taxes. Maybe if he was willing to wait to be paid over a period of years, there would be no need for her ever to have to marry him. She was not sure he would be satisfied merely being her banker. *Besides, there could be worse men to be paired with.*

She was quiet for so long he began again. "I don't know how much you need, but I have enough set by for a small house, and I have cattle that I raised up from calves with my money, and I can sell those. I'm looking at the big picture." He waited. Her face softened. She could feed her animals and keep her land and no one need know the particulars. He added, "Down the road."

"Thanks, Hank." She stooped to retrieve her hammer. "I appreciate the offer. Your suggestion is very generous. I'll need to think about it." She never answered yes to anything right off, and this had implications she wanted to consider.

"Whatever." He pulled his cap down by the visor. She could tell he was angered by her words. He swung up onto his filly. Claudia was concerned he may want to break her will like he'd tamed his filly. He nodded to Claudia. She did not want to be stuck in a house raising kids like his mother had, content being a farmer's wife. His face had relaxed. She nodded back and smiled. She didn't want to be foreclosed on or bankrupt, either.

That night as she was frying up potatoes, onions, and bits of the last of her beef, she thought about the prospect of marrying Hank. She knew he had had a crush on her in high school when she was a senior and he a freshman, but she had never had much time for socializing. He had been too young and she had towered above him in high school.

Why hadn't he married one of the other farm girls in the area or even one from town? He had dated a couple. The surrounding farms didn't include a lot of girls Hank's age. She could only think of chatterbox Sandra Andersen, who would drive Hank nuts with her constant jabbering. Wilna, the pretty and sweet jeweler's daughter, was too refined to live out on a farm.

Maybe he had hoped all along to marry her. Claudia thought joining with Hank in a financial and social relationship might be reasonable, if he considered the arrangement an engagement, and she deemed the plan a trial period. They could date on a regular basis. He could give her the money to pay off the loan. She could tell RT she was not going to attend his Fall Fundraiser, which she had been dreading but thought imperative to attend to convince him to extend her credit.

If Hank had enough money to build a small house that might cover the mortgage or if not, then maybe he would sell some of his stock or take out a loan on his little parcel of land to make up the difference. She didn't want to sell her home. Her ad for the Scottish Highland heifers had yet to produce a response. She refused to sell them as meat on the open market at the same price as any old beef cow, which would be less than half of what they were worth.

Oh, Lord, why would Hank want to sell his stock when I don't want to do that? Only if he gets me in the bargain, she surmised.

Seated alone at the table she ate her dinner with the cat curled on the windowsill and Shep splayed out on the rug. She found Hank attractive but also a bit too down-to-earth. Claudia was attracted to Thomas in a visceral way but also tactile. Being with Thomas reminded her of the first time she'd stepped into a house with all electric lights, startlingly bright, almost surreal. Being touched by him was exciting and conversations with Thomas were comfortable.

Life with Hank would be the daily work of chores, going to an occasional barn dance, taking in a movie, and attending the county fairs. She understood that life with him would involve being his physical wife, which she anticipated could be assertive. She could temper that quality in him over time, especially if she started now. Another consideration was Hank had offered to help; Thomas had not. She did not think an undertaker in a small town could make much money, and she did not know how good he would be as a part-time farmer. She had to be practical. She needed to use her brains and not let her emotions carry her off. As she sat at the oak table imagining the two paths her life could take, she tried not to think of her father. Besides, Thomas was probably back with a sophisticated, young woman and not even interested in Claudia.

If she were able to marry Thomas, would he want to live in New York? Would his professed love of the farm endure the daily tedium? Maybe he would leave. She liked New York, but she did not want to live there. The city was too big and too crowded. How could she survive where people lived on top of each other, had to go to a park to be surrounded by trees and flowers, and bought all their food at a store? The city air was so full of factories and smoke that she could not smell the seasons.

She carried a gristly chunk of beef to the cat on the sill and stroked his head. Shep snored on the rug. Back at the sink, her hands in the basin of soapy water, she stood washing the day's dishes. Predictable is what her life with Hank would be, but with Thomas? She could not imagine.

Once Thomas mentioned to her he had been setting money aside to purchase his uncle's business. She did not imagine that could be enough for her, even if his uncle would wait to be paid off. Even if Thomas had half of what she needed, that wouldn't get her out of the debt with the bank. She would still have to sell land or cattle. Besides, he had not offered so that was a moot point.

After chores, lying in her single bed with the cat purring at her feet, she thought of her father. What would he advise her to do? Would she even listen if he were here? None of the other farmers in the area thought his novel Scottish beef cattle that fed primarily on pasture was the answer. Claudia had never seriously doubted her father's judgment, but she was not sure tonight which he was—ahead of his time or foolish.

Years ago, Francis had set up the local creamery as a co-op so farmers had more power and say-so in the production and sale of their milk. He made the change from raising wheat to oats right before the wheat market was flooded. He changed from milking cows to raising beef stock at the time when the price per pound of milk fell and the price of feed rose. He helped start the cheese factory in town. Claudia believed her father was successful because he was ahead of his time, but she wondered if she had missed something. Claudia could not help but compare their one hundred twenty acres to the Johnson's three hundred sixty acres. Outside her bedroom window the moon was cloaked in cloud and the wind quaked the oak leaves.

The Johnsons weathered the recent farm crisis because they milked Holsteins, which were volume producers, and had three times the number of cows most farmers had been milking. When Francis had dairy, he milked Jerseys for their high butterfat and gentle natures. While he had one grainery, the Johnsons had several, including one for wheat and one for oats. Francis had one short stone silo but the Johnsons, whose family settled here before the Nelsons, had two, tall, concrete-stave silos. The Johnsons raised all their own feed, enough to sell in good years. The three Johnson men worked from sunup to sundown. Although the family lived frugally, they bought the best equipment, believing "it was only expensive once," especially if you took care of your possessions, and they did. Hank would not be reckless or extravagant.

Occasionally, Francis took a risk but was never rash. He seemed to know what was going to happen in the market. He read all the news on agriculture. Claudia had blindly trusted his instincts. How could he have been so wrong about his backing Nora and her remodeling work? Was he blinded by emotion? She could not allow that to happen to her. Or was his hunch right? Maybe enlarging Nora's restaurant would bring success. The moon had moved out of her window's frame and the wind had increased. The leaves rattled and branches crackled against each other. Claudia scooted down under the cotton sheet.

She wasn't sure which path she should take even if a path with Thomas were an option. She couldn't continue the way she was going. She could approach Nora about the loan, but how could she come up with that much money without selling? Claudia wouldn't force Nora to lose her livelihood. If Claudia did, her father would be upset with her. She admired Nora's pluck. Why had her father died and left her alone! Claudia did not want to lose her farm or her independence. She fell asleep with visions of cattle and men riding across the prairie. Dirt devils rose out of nowhere, swirled up around her, her head full as a black slate. In her dream she was struggling to keep up, trudging behind the others with a sack of seed across her shoulders and a pail of water in her hand.

38. A Family

The next morning while doing chores Claudia remembered a relaxing Sunday evening earlier this spring. She and her father were sitting on the porch after supper as the sunlight transitioned from day into night. The horses grazed out in front of them. They had churned ice cream, a treat they enjoyed frequently but not so much lately. Francis seemed withdrawn, not unhappy but distant. Shep was curled under the cool porch and Tabby was at Claudia's feet. The cattle cropped grass in the pasture, Daisy was in the barn, and the pig was sleeping in his sty.

Claudia wanted to discuss her father's cattle plans. The Highland heifers they'd bought as calves had been bred to their old bull and would be calving soon. She'd assumed this time they'd breed them to the three-year-old Highland bull calf. He already was a mammoth beauty of shaggy brown hair almost to the ground and a massive head crowned with a four-foot span of horns, which curled up into graceful points. Was her father thinking of breeding their Hereford cows to the Highland, too? After their old bull had bred the heifers and their cows, he'd pushed through a fence. Francis had sold him. "We don't need more trouble. He's getting bullheaded." She needed to know what their plans were.

Claudia didn't like to interrupt or bother her father. She was used to him quietly spending time on the creamery cooperative business or on the church board paperwork or reading his farming magazines. Often, he would chew over an idea with her. But not tonight. Lately he stared silently into space, drifting in thought and not concentrating on a specific issue.

At such times she could be waiting for his mind to "come

back" to the farm, and the moment might pass before he'd look up, as if suddenly aware of where he was, and mutter, "I think I'll turn in. Good night." And the opportunity to discuss what to do about his new and old cattle had passed; the discussion and decision would have to wait for another day.

The occasion hadn't happened as of this April evening. As she contemplated their Belgian draft horses munching the grass surrounding the house, she felt too peaceful to try to broach the subject.

The setting sun threw the horses in silhouette. They were so close to the porch that she could smell their sweet grassy breath as their teeth pulled the tufts and chewed. Occasionally one of the Girls would blow a slow puff of air out her nostrils. A similar sigh of contentment would often follow from one of their human companions. They were eating teaspoonfuls of strawberry ice cream, Francis's preferred flavor, from her mother's everyday creamy white Buffalo-ware bowls. The bowls rested in the palms of their hands as if molded to fit them, heavy and smooth. Her father's hand completely enclosed the bowl. His hands were as brown as the earth he loved to rub between them. His fingers were long and sturdy and unadorned during the work week. Each Sunday he put on his thin, gold wedding band. As Claudia considered her father's hand, she noticed he wasn't wearing his wedding ring. Had he had it on earlier at church service? She couldn't remember. She couldn't remember seeing the band on his finger for quite some time. Maybe the ring had become loose and lay on his dresser so it wouldn't get lost. His chest didn't seem as full in his shirts. But she hadn't seen him without a shirt for so many years, she couldn't remember the last time the heat had caused him to strip to his sleeveless undershirt.

Dandy's head came up and she snorted, which drew Claudia's attention to where Dandy was looking. Molly had pulled another mouthful of grass, this tuft from under Dandy's neck, before she lifted her head slowly, continued to munch, looked to see what had drawn the attention of her two friends. Francis continued to stare out at the deepening skyline. A currant red-orange pink stain spread across the western horizon.

Then the humans heard the cold-shivering sound. To the southeast. A deep, low, long howl of a wolf silhouetted against the amber-burned sky on the only hill visible to them from the porch. Shep, who had been under the steps in the cool, loose dirt dragged himself up and croaked a response from his hoarse throat, then turned to Claudia as if to apologize but also with an air of how could he be expected to know an intruder was there when his ears were feeble and his good ear had been pressed against the earth in sleep.

Francis scraped the sides of his empty bowl, then stood. "I suppose we best be getting in." Claudia handed her bowl to her father. He nestled the bowls together and opened the screen door.

"I'll put the horses into the barn for the night instead of out in the pasture," her voice rising slightly in question. Her father, as was usual lately, didn't respond.

She wondered if she was being overly cautious. Dandy and Molly wouldn't be taken unaware and heaven help any single predator who tried anything with the two of them. Looking out the front room window on a sleepless autumn night, Claudia witnessed the horses in the pasture. She noticed a crouched animal creeping slowly toward them. She was about to grab a broom and go out when she saw both horses kick at the animal, which had foolishly slunk into striking distance.

What followed was a ferocious flurry of legs kicking and tossing the animal in an orchestrated movement, as if rehearsed, so that neither horse struck a blow to the other. She realized a premeditated plan was impossible, but they were so used to each other that they knew where and when each would strike, like when she and her father worked the two-man buck saw. The Girls' coordinated rebuff took only a minute or two to send the intruder, which howled once and fled, tail between its legs, into the woods.

This April evening Claudia decided to be safe and put the Girls into the barn. Shep followed her but Tabby had remained on the porch. She unhooked the single wire they strung up around the yard to let the horses know where the boundary was. She joked to her father once that she believed they could just draw a line in the grassy dirt and tell the Girls please stay within this space and they would until they ran out of grass. Then they, who were obviously more attentive than their human companions, would eat outside the lines as any intelligent being would.

After leading Dandy and Molly into their box stall next to the open area where Daisy spent the night, Claudia went back out to coil and hang the wire inside the barn door for the next time. That night with the sun safely beneath the horizon, her horses securely within their barn, and her father comfortably preparing for sleep, she felt confident that everything in her world was right. Nothing could go wrong if a body paid attention and didn't do anything reckless. Never did she think chaos lurked in the natural world around her, and she was capable of creating her own whirlwind of drama.

Less than six months from that evening she was on that porch with a gray sky overhead, without the comfort of a bowl of ice cream or a distracted father, but worse, without her beloved horses. Those thoughts made the guilt sweep over her and hover like howling ghosts scolding her for being ungrateful to miss her horses more than her father.

But the pain of being without the daily tactile contact of her warm, breathing companions was a sickening, hollowed-out void never to be filled. Not by Thomas, not by Hank, not even if her father were still here. She could climb up on Dandy or Molly's back and drape her arms down their neck, and they could trot or munch or reach their head back for her to stroke their nose. They were hers, and she was theirs. They would always be hers, or so she had arrogantly thought. And that conceit, that alone she could handle everything, had caused her to lose them forever.

Was forever going to be the length of time that she would have this cavern within her? At an opera or a concert with Thomas, she could temporarily forget how much her loss hurt. Dancing with Hank distracted her from pain. During Ernie's ridiculous story, she hadn't thought of her grief, only her embarrassment at being teased in front of others. In the whole scheme of things, what did her discomfort in front of her neighbors matter? But the loss of Dandy and Molly, could anything obliterate that? Intellectual talk in her head didn't relieve the ache of loss.

She wanted to dig a hole, crawl in, and drag the dirt over herself. She wanted to escape into nothingness, but the pull was occurring less often than in the beginning of the losses. Did loss come in groups of three? Her father's death was the first, her loss of Thomas as best friend was second, then the coup de grâce, the worst, the loss, *my forfeiture*, of Dandy and Molly. Was she safe now? At three strikes was she now safe?

Or as the strange woman from town had proclaimed, "It's hard to lose someone, but it gets worse. Much worse." This was offered to her as words of comfort.

39. Death Comes Knocking

Yesterday after Hank had made his offer and left and the fence was mended, Claudia couldn't stop thinking about what options were open to her and what she should do. This morning she'd finished hanging the well-salted hams and sides of the pig she'd butchered last Wednesday. They were in the attic, being cured by the smoke from the wood stove that was exhausted into the space before curling out under the eaves.

When the sacked, ground feed had burned in the fire, she'd had to use what little oats she'd gotten from the threshing and a few handfuls of corn stripped from the stalks to keep the chickens and pig fed. She had enough for seed for next year, but not much more. Now that the pig was cut up, her next jobs would be to do lard, make sausage, work on the corn picker, and pick the field before the racoon and deer decimated the crop. In her garden the next evening she was watering the spindly plants that were trying to put forth fruit on their scrawny stems. The heat was so intense that if she'd had time she'd have jimmy rigged a shade arrangement to keep the vegetables from drying out completely. In a normal year she'd have mulched with old straw or hay unfit for feed or bedding. This year even newspaper was in short supply. She had nothing to keep the weeds, which seemed to flourish without water, from overtaking the tomatoes. Her second planting of lettuce and spinach had headed out in seed before she had even had one meal of greens. The beans would have to be picked even though they were small, or they would be so tough they'd only be edible in soup.

"I feel like your leaves look—shriveled." Claudia was on

her hands and knees placing the pulled weeds around the base of the tomato stems. "Soon it'll be dark and we'll both get a break." The water she'd poured had soaked immediately into the ground next to the small basket of wrinkly green beans. The anguish cry startled her. She upset the bucket spilling the remaining water onto the cracked dirt. The sound of an animal in distress was coming from the north. Shep roused himself from under the cool of the back stoop and began howling in sympathy. Walking to the back of the house, she reached her hand toward Shep and squinted across her property. To the north lay the poorer eighty-acre piece her father had sold before she was born to purchase their best forty acres.

Listening carefully, she heard a crack like a maul striking a wooden fence post followed by a wail and the unmistakable cry of cows. Shep howled again, his head extended out and up.

The family that lived there had come from the Twin Cities several years ago with little farming experience and had shunned the advances made by their neighbors. The father was seen in Ernie's buying supplies and at the feed mill purchasing grain. The land was so poor their crops couldn't produce the amount of grain needed to sustain their dairy herd. The mother wasn't seen in town and the children didn't attend the local one-room school. When asked, the city farmer humphed a reply about home schooling and exited the store. They were left to themselves. No one stopped to invite the unseen wife to the local homemakers. Their driveway, with a no trespassing sign at the end, was long and uninviting.

At first Claudia worried the sound was people being hurt and wondered about the concealed children and wife. The sound of cows separated from their nursing calves, a necessity, had always saddened Claudia. This was a cry of torment or agony, the keening of intense human grief and suffering but coming from an animal or several. Shep continued to howl. With fingers in her ears, she hollered to

Shep to follow her into the house, but he paid her no mind. Once in the house where the day's heat had not yet dissipated, she paced as the sound penetrated the walls. She had contemplated sleeping on the porch on a cot after a cold supper, but the sound was painful, reverberating in her chest, causing her heart to race frantically. Then as quickly as the anguish had begun, it stopped. She unplugged her ears and pondered the mantle clock. What had seemed like hours had been a mere quarter of an hour. Shep scratched to be let in the house, but Claudia opened the door and stepped outside. Night had descended. Soon the heat would dissipate, but her body felt on fire. What had happened? Something must have been killed, but what? More than one creature suffered in that interminable fifteen minutes. She pressure canned the few beans she'd picked earlier.

Monday, four days later in Ernie's, Claudia learned the answer from those gathered. She sat and listened after getting her spices, more salt, and string for tying off sausage.

"The knacker was out to Andersens to pick up a horse that tangled and broke his leg in barbed wire." Ernie was seated on an upturned box labeled "Hinges." "Mr. Andersen said the knacker had been contacted by the city farmer to haul calves away, but the knacker told him he'd have to charge him per calf, as he wouldn't get nothing for 'em and gasoline wasn't free."

Klive, who was leaning on the counter scratching his chin added his bit, "I was at the feed mill on Thursday, the day it happened. They told me they'd had to refuse the farmer any more credit. The bill was months overdue. He hadn't got feed for over a month."

"The creamery foreman came in on Friday," continued Ernie. "He said the farmer'd had only one can to ship lately and hadn't had any the last two weeks so he hadn't had a milk check in a month." Those gathered shook their heads. Bruno, who'd gone to Doc for an infected hand, entered the store with his left hand wrapped in gauze. He relayed the last piece of the puzzle.

"I went out to the farm the day after the commotion. I was curious as Pete Mevissen said the racket had upset his cows, and they wouldn't let down their milk. I found the city farmer burying three calves in a corner of that rocky pasture." Bruno shook his head in Claudia's direction. "Your father hated that pasture. He claimed the land grew worse rock than grass." Claudia listened to the men but didn't offer a comment. "He never looked up, just kept on digging. I pulled a pick ax from the back of my truck and began loosening the gravely dirt." Bruno cradled his bandaged hand, "I cut my hand trying to pull a chunk of shale loose. After thirty minutes of silence, he finally stopped. Sweat was running down his face and his shirt was soaked. I went to the truck and wrapped a rag around the cut. I had some of Ernie's moonshine and offered him the jar."

Vivian scowled. "You should've dumped the moonshine on your hand. Would've done more good."

"Well, he didn't want none, but he did take a long swig from my canvas water bag. After that we leaned against the truck and the facts came out." Ernie seemed content to let his buddy spin the story. "He began by trying to kill a newly born calf with a sledge hammer, but it didn't die right away, and smelling blood the scraggly cows went into a panic. His wife begged him to shoot the other two animals, but he told her he couldn't afford to use the shells. He needed them for shooting the wild game that put food on their table."

Mrs. Gilbertson had come in during Bruno's recitation after seeing so many gathered at Ernie's. "Why bury them? Why didn't the family eat the calves?" She asked from the doorway.

"A wild rabbit foraging in the woods had more meat than on those bag o' bones newborns. He hadn't thought to lock the cows in before he started. They'd run themselves ragged in the stubbled dirt of their overgrazed pasture before his wife got the underfed things closed in the barn," explained Bruno.

Mrs. Gilbertson walked out shaking her head. She'd heard enough. The three men wandered to the back of the store, leaving Vivian and Claudia in the front.

Vivian stared quizzically at her. "Are you feeling okay?"

"Yes." Claudia gave her an expression she hoped would end any further inquiries. "Listening to the slaughtering of those calves was horrible." Claudia had shifted to her usual chair which Klive had vacated. "People shouldn't be coming out here dumb as stumps thinking they can farm when they've never raised anything before and don't know their arse from their elbow. They should've stayed in the cities."

Vivian slowly wagged her head at Claudia. "Everybody that's here came at some time from some other city or country, unless you're a Native American like Ernie's wife."

Claudia hadn't considered that they were all immigrants or transplants from somewhere.

Her family had been here for three generations, the Johnsons had been here for four, and Ernie was a first-generation settler. She'd heard RT's family had come over on *The Mayflower* but even that was only three hundred years ago. Vivian was correct. The Indians and Eskimos were the only true natives to the land.

"I just wish people would learn something from so much living and not be so foolish," Claudia retorted before leaving. At home Claudia ground the pork pieces and stuffed them into the intestines she'd prepared for casings. Her week and a half had been crammed processing her pig, gathering every blade of anything with nutrients, and stacking the forage for winter feed for her cattle.

She had not gotten to the corn yet. She couldn't get the machinery to run despite hours of struggle late into the night, and she went to bed with no heart for food. She was sick of the smell of processing pork. The pig hadn't been as heavy as normal, which meant the work was less, but there wasn't as much meat either. She had her canned, stewed hens in the cellar. The week was full of late nights. One she spent rendering the lard, which she'd kept cool in the cellar waiting, without luck, for a cooler processing day. Despite temperatures in the nineties, fear of the fat going rancid forced her to start a fire in the cook stove, put the pork fat in the largest kettle, let it cook down, skim the cracklings off to be used in baking, then pour the hot liquid into jars, secure the lids, and store them in the cellar. The next day she returned to gathering hay and trying to get the corn picker to work. She'd given up making silage as the stalks were too dry.

By the end of the week she awoke hot, sweating, and dizzy. She dragged herself to the cellar and found a jar of beef-bone broth from several years ago. She pulled herself up the narrow steps, jar in hand. The seal on the lid finally released when she held it against the counter and pried, but in the process the glass rim chipped. Some of the broth sloshed to the floor.

She swiped weakly at the wet floor with the dishrag. When she felt the dark descend around her, she slumped to the floor to avoid falling. With both hands she held the jar to her lips carefully, the chip away from her lips, and drank the liquid down, gulp by gulp. When no more liquid filled her mouth, she opened her eyes to see pale light again fill the room.

She leaned against the cabinet, the empty jar between her legs, and realized she was still in barn clothes. Had she not undressed last night after chores? Had she slept in her bed in these? Her head dropped to her chest; her matted hair hung limp. When had she last cut her hair? Or washed it? She didn't have the energy to force her mind to remember. She began to feel anger rise and her stomach ached. No, not anger; hunger. Was she hungry? When had she last cooked? She couldn't think; her head hurt, and she had to do morning chores.

The rooster had woken her. Good thing she hadn't made him into soup the last time he'd grabbed the back of her leg.

Everything on this farm had gone haywire. Animals that previously had acted as expected had lost their sense.

She couldn't do everything all alone. No, she could. She had been doing everything alone. She couldn't help getting sick. *Enough! Get out there and feed and water those animals before they rebel and leave for the neighbor's place. Then the whole dang town will know what a girl you are.*

She hated that term—girl. She was a woman. A woman doing a man's work. She pushed her back against the kitchen cabinet until she stood upright. She placed the jar in the sink to wash later but remembering the chip, she set it under the sink next to the pail for the pig. The pail was empty. She hadn't cooked. There were no scraps to add to its feed.

She shook her head for clarity. The pig wasn't here. She'd run out of feed and the cut up pork was hanging in the attic. She stepped out the door and almost stumbled over a brown feathered bundle lying in a dusting of snow that had fallen last night. That turn in the weather had come a few days late. She chuckled. What a joke God played on her. She'd waited and waited for cool weather then rendered the lard in blistering heat, and three days later snow fell. If she didn't laugh, she'd cry. She looked down at the brown body at her feet.

Slowly she bent down and picked up the limp, warm body of a ruffed grouse. She stroked the soft golden brown and russet back and turned the feathered bundle over; its head fell limp to the side, its lidded eyes closed. She ran her fingers over the delicate down-covered breast and the two slender, cream pantaloon-covered legs. The scaly feet, three curved toes grasping nothing, ended in black claws that could prick a pie crust or could be used to clean the crusted dirt from beneath her fingernails. She shook her head again. *What was she thinking!*

The bands of stripes and chevrons across the wings and tail reminded her of Indian blankets. The iridescence that glinted when she first picked up the feathered bundle was already beginning to fade; the life and sparkle had gone out of the animal. She regarded the breast and neck. No visible wound. No cat in sight. Her eyes cast about for an explanation. There was a spot in the snow with the faint imprint of wings like a snow angel, then another a foot away but more lopsided. *Had the bird hit the side of the house, fallen, and then attempted to get up to fly?*

She turned back into the house, sat in a chair, and methodically plucked the feathers and set them to the side to be used later. Soft down for pillows, the stiff longer feathers to take to the Rice Lake millinery shop. She'd pin the opened tail to a scrap of wood. A fan. Then she made one small cut at the base of the breast and gripped the feathered skin and pulled gently up to the neck like removing a pullover sweater. The breast was pink and so warm she resisted the urge to put the warm flesh to her cheek.

She stripped down the legs and cut around the breast, releasing the muscle from the backbone. She fingered the slender bones. *So delicate, slight. How could a bird fly? Yet that is exactly how—weightlessly.* She wondered what flight would feel like with hollow bones, soaring across the pines and over the hedgerow. This morning in bed she'd felt ungrounded, drifting above her bed, but that had felt wretched. Setting aside the breast and legs in a bowl with water, she shook in some salt and set the contents on the counter. She cupped the small head in her palm, and the backbone and coiled innards spread across her wrist, the rest feathered her arm.

When she had severed the head from the breast, a cascade of wrinkled red berries fell from the bird's craw. High bush cranberries. He'd been a partridge in a cranberry tree. She smiled and set them aside in a small dish. *Were they poisonous?* She couldn't remember, but she'd ask Vivian to check in her books. *Later.* She sat back down into the kitchen chair, arms in her lap, the bloody hollowed body cradled there. She took a breath, then two.

A beautiful bird dropped from the sky when she didn't have any beef left, an attic full of hams and sausage curing but no stomach for pork. There had been a few eggs, the only protein she could stomach since she got sick. Eggs were easy. With the sudden cold snap, her five hens hadn't laid an egg in two days.

The broth had taken the edge off. Even though her throat hurt and her eyes felt rusty as they moved in their sockets, her stomach didn't feel like expelling its contents as in the past couple of days. She went out feeling like doing chores was possible. The rooster crowed and she blessed him in her mind for waking her, and looked down at the gutted bird, eyes closed peacefully as sleep, and she thanked him for coming to her door. She called, "Here kitty, kitty" and placed the warm remains for Tabby in the dish that sat just inside the shed. Daisy mooed low in anxious greeting.

40. Hank to the Rescue

Before the trees had completely turned silver, gold, and copper, Hank noticed that Claudia's corn crop, like most of those in Bear Creek township, was suffering. Because the Nelson farm had sandier soil than the Johnsons, the drought had impacted Claudia's crops more than Hank's. Since the Johnson corn was taller and denser, the racoon and deer, which were opportunistic eaters, had more difficulty feeding there. They chose to graze the shorter and easier-to-move-through corn of the Johnsons' neighbors. Two years ago, the Johnsons had purchased a newer variety of corn planter that sowed the stalks closer together, which ironically helped with the lack of water because the plants shaded each other and their clay soil held the moisture against the dry winds that stripped the exposed crops of many of their neighbors.

The trees surrounding the Johnson and the Nelson fields helped to mitigate the force of the driving winds that blew across those farms that had sacrificed the tree lines between fields for the ease of cultivating larger plots. Fortunately for the Johnsons and Nelsons, their ancestors had preserved the tree lines that stopped the wind and soil erosion. The tree lines had also provided habitat for pheasant, grouse, and other small game that provided meat for their tables. In years of plenty, some immigrant offspring argued with their parents in favor of removing the natural obstacles to create large areas easier to plant and harvest. The seasoned farmers who'd seen the effect of erosion in the old country held stoically to their ways. The offspring of the Nelson and Johnson immigrants had, for the most part, taciturnly obeyed their fathers, and today Hank was grateful for their obedience.

Several of Hank's neighbors had decided to make their corn into silage before the crop ripened and dried enough to be picked. Harvesting sooner gave the scavengers less time to devour the corn. In the past month the choppers and wagons had filled the fields, and the roaring whoosh of silo-fillers had choked the air. Hank thought that Claudia might choose to do that, but he didn't see any activity to indicate she had been making silage, and the corn was now too dry. She'd be forced to pick the corn, but he didn't see any indication she'd begun that either.

Hank could have been working on their own farm, but his father and brother could handle today's work. After morning chores he let them know he had some business to take care of. His mother looked at him questioningly, but his father with a nod and rumble acknowledged his son and kept smoking, enjoying his morning break of coffee and a sweet roll.

When Hank turned his horse into Claudia's corral where Dandy and Molly should have been, his filly raised her head and smelled the air through flared nostrils, her eyes wide, which indicated to Hank she must be able to smell the remains of the fire or even the lingering carcass odor.

He placed his hand on the filly's neck. "They're not here. You're okay." He walked to the screen door. In years past if the farmer wasn't in the fields, he'd have looked in the barn, but the Nelson barn was a heap of burned rubble with a small pile of singed lumber salvaged from the wreckage lying haphazardly to one side where the neighbors had thrown the pieces. Surprised, Hank had expected the partially blackened boards to be stacked off to one side because Claudia, like her father, didn't like to leave things half done.

He knocked twice on the doorjamb, then walked in, calling, "Claudia? You home?" Her old horse, which she'd gotten after she lost her pair of mares, was not in the corral but could easily have been turned loose with the heifers for companionship. He heard a light thud and some creaking of floor boards. He waited. Finally, she appeared around the corner disheveled, pale, and clutching her housecoat, which was over her work jeans and shirt. He stepped toward her, but she shook her head, and they walked to the kitchen. She sat heavily in one of the kitchen chairs, and he opened the icebox, which held that morning's milk from Daisy and not much else. The back hall had a basket with one small egg, lying on a scrap of cloth. Hank realized as he picked up the egg there would be no straw for bedding, much less cushioning eggs. She'd been sure to get all the good hay and straw, which wasn't much, in the barn for Daisy this winter and any calves born while snow was still on the ground come spring. The only surviving hay, nutrient-poor swamp grass, was in stacks outside. He wondered what she'd do for feed and shelter for Daisy and her horse. How would she feed her cows and bull? The swamp hay he'd seen in the stack could be used as feed or bedding, but not both. How could she afford to buy hay and straw when nobody had much of either? If she could find someone who had extra, the cost would be dear.

While he'd been thinking, he'd turned the knob on her little gas stove. The fire in the wood cookstove was out. He pulled the cast iron skillet off the cook stove top and over the gas flame. With a spoon he dipped some bacon drippings from the jar on the back of the stove into the pan. As soon as the drippings began to crackle, he broke the egg into the pan and reached for a spatula to flip the egg over easy like his mother made theirs. He turned off the gas, slid the egg onto a clean plate from the cupboard, and set it with a glass of milk in front of Claudia. She ate without a word but pushed away the milk, which he returned to the icebox. They sat in silence for a few minutes.

"Thank you," she murmured but didn't meet his eyes. He brought the plate to the sink where he saw several unwashed dishes with hardened egg yolk and a pot with silverware sticking up out of cold, cloudy water. He placed a pan with fresh water on the gas stove and turned the knob again.

When he sat down, he placed his hands on his knees, bent forward, and announced, "I'm going to get our corn picker over here. It won't take long. If I need a hand, I'll get Ethan to unload the wagon into your crib."

He stood to check if the water was hot, but she had pushed herself up and was protesting. "I will help. Don't get your brother." Her body was swaying slightly. He was afraid she'd fall. He wanted to steady her but decided to take the water to the sink and began washing the dishes, which he would not do at his home. His mother did the housework and the men did the barn and field work. Division of labor.

The thought struck Hank like the time he stumbled upon a fourteen-point buck sitting in his wheat field. Both were so unexpected. Claudia must have been doing all the household chores for her dad like his mother did for them plus doing the farm work like he and his brother and father did. She was doing double duty before her dad died and now she was trying to continue but without her dad. What would he or Ethan do if their mom died? He didn't want to do women's work every day, and his dad wouldn't even know the first thing about housekeeping. If his dad died, he and Ethan and their mother would survive, even with the loss. He'd miss his father's experience and knowledge. His father was a repository of information and experiences he had or he had heard from his dad and his uncles.

That afternoon Hank picked the small field of corn and filled Claudia's wagon, which she hauled back to the wood-slatted corn crib with her tractor. She was shoveling shriveled corn cobs into the crib when Hank returned from the field. He noticed she was even paler than she'd been earlier, and when he approached to take over, she turned and let out a cry of pain like a mountain lion, the sound of a woman being hurt slowly. She was doubled over in the doorway to the corn crib, her hands clasped around her ankle.

"What happened? You all right?" He bent over her, which was difficult not just because of her height but her body blocked the narrow opening to the crib.

"I twisted my ankle. Stupid. I turned with a shovel full of corn and my ankle gave out. I don't know what's wrong with me." She was so pale and fragile that Hank wanted to pick her up and carry her to the house, but he couldn't. He pulled; she hopped. With her arm draped over his shoulder, he helped her into the house. After putting her in bed, he chipped a chunk off the block from the icebox, wrapped the ice in a dish towel, which he set on her ankle.

"I'll unload the wagon. Shouldn't take long. I'll run the corn-picker home and be back to check on you."

"I'll be okay." She didn't appear like she would, but he didn't say anything. He left her there with her eyes closed lying back in the narrow bed, a rag doll on a quilt. When he returned, he shut the chickens in their coop for the night, gave Shep the soup bone he'd brought from home, and poured the glass of milk Claudia hadn't touched into Tabby's dish. He knew Claudia was only milking Daisy in the morning as the cow's milk was down. Daisy should have been put with the bull to be bred back and then she would freshen in ten months, but the task was probably low on Claudia's priority list. Daisy's milk would be plentiful after calving, but Claudia would be without milk for the last couple of months while Daisy was dry. He saw the pig was gone. She must have butchered it. She should've waited a couple months when the weather turned cold and the pig had fattened up.

Hank had never thought of how complicated life was for Claudia doing everything alone. Sharing the jobs at home made all of the chores go quicker. He took for granted cows were bred back and meals appeared on the table with predictable regularity.

Darkness had descended when Hank checked on Claudia. His mother had sent a plate of roast beef, mashed potatoes and gravy, string beans, and a thermos of sweet tea. When he went into the downstairs spare room that had been a sewing room and then Francis's office, he found Claudia asleep on the daybed. She woke when he called her name. He sat in the rocker next to the bed while she ate everything and drank most of the hot tea.

The next day he was at her house milking Daisy when she hobbled out the front door, a Y-shaped stick under one arm, her injured ankle dangling and wrapped with another chunk of ice tied up in the dish towel.

41. Claudia's Decision

Claudia lay in the pre-dawn light considering. Hank had been so good to her. Thomas was gone. *Why does he keep intruding into my thoughts?* He was attractive: tall; slender; gorgeous blue eyes; light brown, wavy hair. What drew her to him? Not his appearance, but the way he was with her, his quiet confidence. Hank was self-assured. She had the feeling that after a while, Hank would begin to assert himself, and she would be absorbed into his life just when she had begun experiences that stirred her beyond her ordinary world. She wasn't satisfied with normal anymore. In fact, she wanted out of the daily grind of clearing manure, feeding, guarding, caring for animals, and planting and harvesting crops. Thomas would've never been satisfied with the simple farm life without the cultural events he was used to and that she had come to enjoy. When he had helped her, he questioned her methods and offered his own ideas. With Hank, she wouldn't need to explain anything. Their families did things basically the same. And, she knew he would work from sunup to sundown.

In her head she could hear Ernie's voice. "A man works from sun to sun, but a woman's work is never done." That's what her life would be. That's what it was now. At least with Hank, she'd have a partner. She knew also Hank would expect a meal on the table and he wouldn't want a lot of discussion. He would expect to be the boss. Unlike Thomas who loved to discuss and talk, which prompted her to put her fingers on his lips and urge, "Let's listen to the crickets." *Why keep going back to Thomas? Stop it!* Be grateful for what you have. *This* is your life.

She wished the world could allow her to go to New York whenever she wanted, and the farm would be here when she returned. In June with Thomas, she'd fantasized that possibility. *That* was not reality. Real life was work. The thing was—she loved her farm. Reality was to solve her problem. She either had to accept Hank and his proposal of financial help and then be bound to him in the future or...or what? She did not want to sell land or cattle.

Her head hurt as dawn pierced through the window curtains. She had to get up, but her ankle still ached. She wasn't sure she was worth having. She was a cutter-canner cow, old and worn out, not worth more than to be put in tinned stew.

Hank was like her father. Francis would approve of her joining forces with Hank, increasing their buying power, and sharing the workload. Yes, she thought, that made sense. She'd go tell him after grinding a little of the corn with some of her oats for Daisy and a little to scatter to the chickens.

She was apprehensive as she rode the gelding the short distance to the Johnsons' place. The russet and gilt leaves fell prematurely from the smaller trees dried out by continuous sun and wind. As she gingerly swung off the gelding, guarding her ankle, she held onto his reins and stood in the sun. In the shade of the shed, Hank glanced up from the tractor's torn-apart transmission. A smile crossed his face, and he grabbed a rag and began rubbing his grease-coated hands. He advanced several steps toward her, still wiping his hands on a rag so well-oiled he could have used it to lubricate the hitch pin. "You've seen the sense of my line of reasoning." He sounded triumphant and she felt instantly deflated.

"I've appreciated your help and if you are willing, I'm agreeable." She backed up a step before he reached her. She tripped over her sore ankle, and he grabbed her before she fell against her horse or on the hard-packed ground. He held her elbows in his blackened hands with the rag between her right elbow and his left hand. He leaned forward as if to seal the bargain with a kiss. She backed into the old gelding, smelled the reassuring horse scent, and reached out her right hand.

"Yes, I guess we have an arrangement," she concluded. He stepped back, the smile gone, the rag limp in his hand, but he shook hers with his free one.

"Today's Thursday. If I can't get to RT's tomorrow, I'll go the beginning of next week and make arrangements with him to pay the bank note." His words were flat. She smiled perfunctorily. She knew she could seem cool but being congenial was such an effort. How had her father managed being affable so effortlessly? She mounted and traveled through the coin-colored trees toward her farm.

Claudia rode home slowly. Soon she would be out of debt, the financial pressure off, her land and cattle safe. She didn't feel as lighthearted as she had hoped. As the gelding clopped along the dirt road, Claudia reassured herself the cause of her unease was winter's approach and the need to build up her woodpile and find more hay. She shoved to the periphery how to get money to rebuild the barn, which could wait until the heifers needed a place to calf. The literature she'd found of her father's stated that the Scottish Highland breed could calf in a snowbank and survive. Hank had helped her throw up a makeshift shelter, a roof and one side off the south end of the small shed as a loafing barn for the heifers and calves. There wasn't enough space for the cows and bull, but they could make do with the aspen, oak woods, and the row of pines as protection against the north wind. Daisy and Old Glue had been sharing the low-ceilinged shed space. Not ideal but serviceable.

42. Thomas Learns

After three weeks in New York Thomas, back in Turtle Lake, walked from his uncle's shop to Ernie's store to see if the nails, which his uncle had ordered, were in. His uncle, despite feeling poorly, continued to build coffins for his business and Hagstrom's. Thomas was helping with the construction work he'd obtained for his uncle.

"Thomas!" Ernie declared with more than his normal enthusiasm. "How's New York?" Ernie, about head level with his friend, was standing on a short stepladder stacking cans of tomatoes, turning the bright red and green labels to face front on the shelves.

"Cold and busy. I stopped to pick up the nails my uncle ordered." Thomas drummed his fingers on the counter slowly.

"The nails aren't in, but Vivian has his woodworking catalogue that came in this morning's mail. You can take that to him." As Ernie stepped gingerly down from the ladder, Thomas met the eyes of the short, round storekeeper for the first time since entering.

Wiping his hands across his generous belly to smooth his apron, Ernie queried, "Did you hear the one about the judge interrogating the prisoner?" Thomas shook his head. "The judge says, 'What did you hit the man with?' Prisoner replies, 'With a tomato, sir.' Judge looks at him in disbelief. 'A tomato? Why he's been in the hospital three months.' Prisoner says sheepishly, 'Well, your honor, the tomato did have a can around it.'"

Laughing, Ernie started to hand the uncle's catalogue to Thomas but didn't let go right away. "You heard that Claudia won't need to worry about her debt with RT."

"No," Thomas's voice rose, inviting further explanation. The last time he was in Turtle Lake he'd heard about the debt and Claudia's impossible situation. Just before he'd left for New York, he'd started to go out to talk to her, but he turned back as her words rung in his ears, "I never want to see you again!"

The unthinkable entered Thomas's thoughts.

"What happened? Is she going to sell her land?" Ernie released the catalogue which Thomas slapped on the counter. "Not to RT!"

"No…" Ernie dragged the word out. As Thomas opened his mouth to inquire, Ernie rushed ahead.

"Hank Johnson has taken care of everything. Went to the bank and paid them."

"But…how? What is he doing that for?" Thomas knew Hank had feelings for Claudia. He knew the Johnsons had enough resources to come up with the cash. He rolled the catalogue tightly in his hands. Ernie smiled expectantly as if a joke crossed his mind but the smile went limp and he remained silent.

"Well, I guess that's that." Thomas left the store.

Back in the mortuary, Thomas couldn't settle himself. When his uncle looked up Thomas stated, "The nails weren't here but your catalogue was. Did you know that Hank Johnson paid Claudia's debt?"

"Well, I heard he went to RT and paid some on it but there's some complication or other." His uncle went back to staining the top of a rich, walnut coffin that would be fitted with brass grips and ready to hold a dead senator or city lawyer.

"I could've paid some on it!"

His uncle appeared surprised. "Then why didn't ya?"

"Because when I'd heard the amount, I didn't have enough for that *and* what we'd talked about as a down payment here on your business."

"Don't be handing me none 'a that. Ya know I don't need much, just my expenses, which don't amount to diddly squat." He'd finished the staining and was cleaning the brush with turpentine in an old coffee can.

His uncle's business wasn't lucrative, but Thomas liked country life. A month ago, he'd contemplated life as the area mortician and regularly visiting the big city. He had worked for three weeks in New York with the idea of making enough money to bring that into actuality. He'd believed with the passing of time Claudia would forgive and forget, and he could offer to help her. A lost opportunity, now.

"If you are okay with what we've gotten done, I think I'll go back to Hagstrom's and work some. I can accompany the coffins we've finished. They will be happy we are ahead of schedule." Thomas picked up the screwdriver and finished attaching the metal work on the coffin he'd been working on before going to Ernie's.

Three days later, he returned to New York.

Thomas rode the train, believing Claudia had chosen a life with Hank and feeling he was not good enough for her. Sitting in the upholstered train seat, he watched the changing color of leaves, the change from countryside to cityscape, and the change in his life.

He wasn't smart about farming, but Hank was. He was strong but not as strong as Hank. He was financially solvent but not land-rich and resource-wealthy like Hank. He could understand why she chose Hank.

He couldn't help loving her and wished he had a chance to make things right, but he couldn't see how. He should be gracious and let her go. He didn't want to create more trouble for her. He'd thought they had a serious relationship. She was being capricious. Why?

He pictured her in her home with Hank and a couple of children. Claudia wouldn't want a houseful, but he could see her with a boy and a girl, teaching them about the farm and her father. The Johnson family and her new family would be celebrating Thanksgiving and Christmas and Easter in country fashion with simple, wholesome food, listening to the radio. A life he could have enjoyed, but would not be his. Claudia had made her choice. She'd chosen the man better suited to her.

He looked out the mahogany-trimmed train window as trees, buildings, and the life he'd contemplated slipped by.

43. Hank and Claudia Date

The week after Hank had helped Claudia harvest her meager corn crop and four days after helping her erect a makeshift lean-to, he accompanied her to the Opera House, a large room on the upper floor of a two-story building in Turtle Lake where the town showed movies and people came to perform on the little stage at the front. *Below Zero* and *Hog Wild*, two Laurel and Hardy films, were the double feature that Saturday being projected on the large, pulled-down screen. Sitting in the darkened room on cushioned seats, they saw the Metro Goldwyn Mayer lion roar, heard the organ grinder music, and tasted the buttery saltiness of the popcorn from the bag between them. They both relaxed into timelessness.

The opening scene of *Below Zero* was a screen with the words "The freezing winter of 1929." Skinny Stan Laurel was seated playing his bellows piano with a tin cup to collect coins, and Oliver Hardy, occasionally plucking the bass violin, which was as wide as him, stood in the falling snow. The folks in the theater could relate to the winter that had passed and anticipate the one yet to come. They chuckled to hear the two playing in the snow while singing "In the Good Old Summertime." They couldn't help but laugh when the pair of men on the screen discovered they'd been futilely playing outside a deaf and dumb institute. Laurel and Hardy took their frustration out on each other in a slapstick, with which the audience could identify. When the two men stood over a street heat vent and tried their luck again, the farmers and small business owners present could admire their opportunism and pluck. A woman leaned out of her upstairs window and asked the musicians, "How much do you make?" to which they replied, "Fifty cents a street." The audience roared with laughter when she threw them some coins entreating, "Here's a dollar. Move two streets down." Claudia let the laughter cocoon her. When her hand and Hank's met in the oily bag for another handful of popcorn she felt relaxed, companionable. Yesterday she had fenced the picked cornfield. Today was untroubled.

The irony of the situation on screen, the capriciousness of nature in their daily lives, and the fickleness of fate hit everyone when a man with dark glasses, a cane, and a neck sign saying "Blind" picked up from the snow a coin that Laurel and Hardy had missed.

Their musical instruments, their means of making a living, were physically destroyed by an irate woman and a passing vehicle, but also by the two men's pride. Innocent Hardy inadvertently got snow in her milk bucket so she crushed his bass over his head and body and when well-meaning Laurel attempted solidarity by tossing her pail of milk into the street, she tipped his piano into the path of an oncoming truck. The movie watchers identified with Laurel and Hardy's endeavors to make a living in spite of bad luck and their attempts to deal with circumstances beyond their control. The audience hooted heartily, as crying was the only other option, and that would have been a waste of water.

Hank crushed the finished bag of popcorn, dropped the oily paper to the floor, and caught Claudia's hand. Claudia resisted her impulse to pick up the discarded bag and dispose of it and welcomed the comforting connection of Hank holding her hand.

When the two penniless men on the screen found a wallet of cash in the snow and around the corner a cop chased off their would-be robber, they invited him to lunch. As they went to pay, the policeman recognized his lost wallet and ordered the two miscreants to pay for their own lunch. Claudia shook her head at Laurel's dismay but Hank chuckled at Hardy's bravado. The audience could relate to being without the means to accomplish what they'd like, but at least their circumstances weren't as dire as those of the two on the screen. And the situation got worse. Hardy was tossed into the street, and Laurel tipped into a barrel of ice water, which he drank, then was waddling like an inflated, pregnant elephant. How could any of the audience not laugh at someone who was obviously so much worse off than any of them?

After an equally hilarious second film, Hank escorted Claudia home and set up a date for the following week when they attended an exhibition in Cumberland. They ate hot dogs and candied apples and talked about all the interesting things they saw. One weekend they cut and hauled wood with the Johnsons' team of Percherons. Claudia was content to let this pattern of work and distraction continue until Thanksgiving.

44. Fire and Loss

The first winter after her father died was unusually cold for the last week of October. Claudia was used to cold winters. Routinely she and her father had dressed according to the weather and did what needed to be done. Throughout the night, the temperature had dropped. The next morning, the frost hung heavy on windows and frames. During the night she pulled the quilts and wool blankets up over her head, unrealistically willing her father to get up and put another log on the fire. She knew without lifting her head from under the covers that the fire had gone out. By the cold penetrating through her wool socks and gloved hands, she knew restarting the fire was going to be unpleasant even huddling under the blankets pulled from the bed.

After coaxing the matches, paper, and wood into a cool yellow life, she went back to bed to try to warm herself before getting out of her nightgown and into coveralls. Breathing in her own hot breath in the circle of space under the covers, she realized why all the old bachelor farmers put on their long johns in October and didn't take them off again until May or June. On this day the meticulous Claudia did not change her long underwear or her underpants but slipped off her nightgown and pulled on her flannel shirt, sweater, blue jean pants, wool pants, and coveralls over the top. She plucked off her nightcap and tugged on the heavy knit hat she wore outside doing chores. Normally she'd wear the soft, worn wool, skull cap inside while making breakfast and change hats before chores. Not today.

She headed outside without a decent breakfast. She ate a chunk of leftover bread made from vegetables, fruits, and nuts and washed down with a ladle of water that had not completely frozen in the reservoir next to the stove. She couldn't remember a time before this when the water reservoir had formed ice. One person couldn't keep up with the chores that two normally did. She was grateful for Hank's help. But she'd claimed she was doing fine and he needn't check on her. She didn't like his unexpected swooping in to "save" her.

She admonished herself to get it together for the Lord's sake. She was getting lazy, not even enough gumption to get up in the night to stoke the fire. Next thing she knew she would be like one of those old guys they found frozen in his cabin come spring. She pulled on the double-knit gray woolen work mittens, wrapped the brown scarf double around her neck, and bent her head into the wind of the coldest morning in a long time.

Seeing the glow in the eastern sky, she thought how beautiful. Then she saw the smoke and realized there was a fire in town. More than one person had tried to coax more heat out of a wood stove that night.

Claudia rushed through chores. In town out of the way of the volunteer firemen, she left her gelding in an empty stall at the blacksmiths down from the train depot and walked the two blocks to Ernie's store. Claudia pushed past those few folks huddled at the entrance wondering what to do to help.

Everyone was speculating. Ernie had been taken to the hospital in the early hours of the morning. He was lucky, unconscious but alive. People were still standing around watching the smoldering ruins of his home, but the store had been saved. The constable and owner of the Opera House had run to get the pumper truck going, and they had soaked the store. The volunteer firefighters were prying boards off the house side to be sure no embers lurked unseen in the studs comprising the common wall. A couple of younger men from the boarding house were pulling the lumber off to the side where the wood hissed in the snow.

Vivian was standing in her winter wool coat behind the counter helping people. Many were talking, trying to make sense of a senseless accident that was all too familiar in small towns throughout the plains in the winter. Fires were a necessity but so unpredictable. Actually, fire was quite predictable, needing three things to live—oxygen, fuel, and heat. Without oxygen, a match set to a log would not burn. If there was no fuel, such as wood, oxygen and heat alone would not produce a flame. But a hunk of wood out in the air would combust like magic if it got hot enough. Claudia had seen the phenomenon happen to the side of a shed fifteen feet from where a man was burning a large rubbish pile. The wood lap siding started to smoke. She couldn't get her words out fast enough to alert the adults caught up in conversation, leaning on their shovels and rakes. As Claudia opened her mouth, she had heard a man's voice shout, "Fire!" and she was astonished that that low, commanding voice had come out of her mouth. They had doused water on the shed before the smoking siding burst into flame, but the blackened wood was still there as a testament to the fickle ferocity of fire. That shed wall had been charred like the wall of Ernie's store, which Claudia stood looking at wondering where Ernie would live.

Conversation in the store was as fast as the help had been to arrive to extinguish the fire and save Ernie's store and surrounding buildings. The phones in town had all rung one long continuous ring. No party line code to say who the call was for. This call was for everyone. The volunteer fire truck had come immediately and now, a couple hours later, the men were winding up the hoses.

Mr. Gilbert posed the question to the crowd at large. "You think he was burning wood that was too dry?" He had come from his home eager to help and worried that the fire might spread quickly. His jewelry shop was right next door. He had pulled pants over his blue-and-white-striped pajama bottoms. His matching pajama top was visible under his coat, which was stained in a line across his front and in the crook of each elbow where he'd held the sooty fire hose.

"Ernie's no fool. He knows better than that," replied the blacksmith who was tacking up some boards to span the area where a few burned studs had been pulled down.

"He did have some pine that was pretty dry. Maybe in the dark he got that by mistake," offered another volunteer firefighter who was holding the other end of the boards and nailing them to the remaining wall studs.

"I'd bet good money the fire started with that old wood burner he had in the back," speculated Bruno, his friend who'd spent a lot of time with his feet propped up next to that wood stove.

"There's a chink outta the cast iron on the door," contributed Klive. "Told him to order hisself another one. What's the sense a owning a store if ya don't take use of having it. Get hisself the best stove if"en he wanted."

"Not Ernie. A wadded-up piece of steel wool wrapped in tinfoil he'd shoved in the hole said held fine," continued Bruno.

"Ya know what happen'd, don't ya? Bet ya that the strength got outta it. Heat an' all. That there steel wool was gone. Got sucked up the flue," added Thomas's uncle, hunched in his full-length coat and a night cap, watching and shaking his head.

"He's lucky he's not gone."

"Poof like smoke, fire'll take ya. Why, I know'd a guy had a friend that there happened to," one of the young boarders offered.

"Oh—that kind of talk won't do us no good. Anybody heard how Ernie's doing?" wondered the blacksmith. The charred door between the store and what used to be Ernie's home stood open. Vivian looked up from where she'd been picking up cans, wiping down the shelves covered with ash, and replacing the canned goods.

"Doc came back after getting him to the hospital. They had to cut off burned skin on his hands where he'd tried to pull the stove and chimney out the back door. His hands are all bandaged and he breathed in lots of smoke, but Doc says he'll live."

Claudia considered how a tragedy to one in their community made her own daily drudgery or worries recede into pettiness. None of them were standing in long bread lines, nor did their hard work go down in the stock market crash. They had their share of trials and tribulations, but a person's own troubles sat in the back seat when a neighbor needed help. A disaster pulled life into sharp focus. Claudia picked up a rag and started wiping down soot-covered surfaces.

Two days later, Claudia heard the knock on her kitchen door just as she was sitting down to her leftover potato salad. At 1 p.m. on a Wednesday in late October, who could possibly be bothering her at this time of day in midweek? She saw the sheriff's car but hadn't heard the engine over the whistling of the tea pot. Shep was asleep under the woodstove. Who could need her help that they'd send the sheriff?

"Sorry to bother you at dinner time, Claudia, but I wanted to catch you at home. I don't fancy traipsing across half frozen fields trying to find you." The sheriff was apologetic but irritated.

"Come on in," she offered the words tentatively, wondering what would bring him out here. She motioned toward a kitchen chair and waited. He remained standing in his coat and hat and regarded her, his eyes level to hers.

"You gotta get your cattle off that cornfield." His words were plain enough but made no sense.

"What cornfield? Did they get out? Why didn't the neighbor call me?" Claudia tried to think in whose cornfield her cattle could be. She'd fenced her little field and had checked on the steers where they were busy cleaning up every stalk and missed cob. She'd soon have to find something else for them to eat.

"I got a complaint. They brought in the deed that shows a man from Chicago owns that property." He looked away as she felt her face blanch. "That field you picked. That forty acres to the east of here." She felt her face flush.

"I don't understand." She sat down in the chair she'd intended for him.

"I don't know the particulars. I asked, but was told to mind my own business, just enforce the law. I'm sorry." With those words left hanging he nodded and walked out the door.

"Wait," she called after him from the doorway. "Who can I talk to? Someone made a mistake."

He turned back toward her, shrugged his shoulders. "I don't know any more than what the banker showed me and the statute he cited, which I looked up, and he's right. You gotta get them cattle off of there, now."

She sat trying to unravel the sequence of events. She and Hank had been out to the pictures Saturday, October 1st, after the Thursday when he'd assured her he'd take care of the debt with RT. She'd fenced that week and put the cattle out that Thursday. They'd been to the exhibition that Saturday and cut wood together the following Saturday, and he'd never uttered a word about any trouble. She'd assumed he'd done as he promised and paid off the three-thousand-dollar debt. She put her untouched plate of boiled egg, potato, and bacon in mayonnaise into the ice box. She'd have to saddle the gelding and talk to Hank.

She couldn't see anyone around in the barn or sheds so she went up to the house. Doris Johnson answered, wiping her flour-covered hands on her apron.

"Claudia, what a nice surprise." Then she frowned. "What's the matter, girl?"

"I need to see Hank. Is he in one of the fields? No one was in the barn or the sheds." She looked past Doris into the house as if he might be resting in an armchair. Doris placed her body to block the view into the front room.

"Mr. Johnson is having a lie-down. Ethan's gone to call

on Rachel, and Hank mentioned at dinner that he had an errand in town. I suppose he's there. Come into the kitchen and visit while I finish up my bread." Doris opened the way toward the kitchen, but Claudia backed away.

"No. Thank you. I need to talk to him," she emphasized.

"You can, dear. I'm sure he won't be long, an hour or two, three at the most. The boys were going to make wood this afternoon. This forenoon they got the saws sharpened after milking and feeding. They were hoping to cut for a couple hours before supper and evening chores. Come in and have a cup of coffee, and in an hour, we could have some hot cinnamon rolls," Doris began to walk toward the kitchen but glanced back when Claudia didn't follow.

"I can't. I'm sorry. I've got to go," Claudia could see the disdain flash across Doris's face before being replaced by coolness. She'd put her foot in her mouth again, not saying and doing things the right way. She left.

As she rode to town, she wondered if she would catch Hank. Unless he planned to run another errand in a different direction, she'd see his truck on the road returning and could talk to him. Why hadn't he paid the debt as he'd agreed or why hadn't he at least told her he hadn't? *Men are so egotistical.* He probably couldn't come up with the money and was too proud to tell her. If he could only pay part, why didn't he just say so? How was she going to feed her cattle without that prime forty acres? She couldn't. She was right where she didn't want to be. She leaned forward, clicked her teeth, and tapped her heels against the old gelding's sides to spur him on.

She heard the whistle as she approached town and saw the steam and smoke rise from the train just in from out east. She stopped at the creamery first, thinking that may be where his appointment was. They informed her that he'd stopped but went over to the boarding house to meet with a representative. She tied up her old gelding in front of the boarding house on Main Street next to the mortuary and walked to the dining room where she assumed the two men would be.

Hank was sitting in clean overalls and a sturdy blue shirt with a man in a black suit and tie with a briefcase open on the table and papers spread out between them. The representative was pointing to a diagram and Hank was bent over examining with great interest. Claudia's head swirled with phantoms of doubt and accusation, but she decided to sit out of direct view and have a cup of coffee. By the time her coffee was cooled and almost gone, the representative put his papers into his briefcase, rose, as did Hank, and they shook hands. Claudia approached Hank as the man left. Hank smiled and put his arm around her waist. There were three other boarders sitting and talking at the few tables in the room.

"What an unexpected surprise." Hank pulled the chair out for her.

"I have to talk to you." She spoke as calmly as she could, aware of the other people in the room.

"Okay, but what couldn't wait that you came to town? This isn't Monday." He smiled at his reference to her predictability, and she chaffed at the intimacy of the remark and the glint in his eye. He had his chair pulled close to hers and still had his arm touching her, now across the chair rail and against her back.

"The sheriff came out to my place to tell me that I don't own my property." She hoped her words weren't so defiant as to draw any notice to their conversation.

"What are you talking about?" Hank asked and put his hand up to touch her face. "I can see you are distressed." Just then there was a loud voice behind them.

"What's going on here? At the boarding house where everyone in town can see?" Thomas was towering above them in his traveling clothes with his suitcase at his feet. He must have come in on the train.

"What concern is it of yours, mortuary man?" Hank

pulled Claudia closer to him with his arm. Claudia couldn't stand and felt trapped.

"I think I have a right to be concerned about the reputation of this woman." Thomas blurted.

"We're having a private conversation that doesn't concern you," Hank retorted.

"After six months with this woman, I am concerned that her character isn't sullied by the likes of you." Thomas glared at Hank.

Hank pushed his chair back. He was shorter than Thomas by six inches. Hank threw back his shoulders and thrust his chest out. "Me? You're worried about me wrecking her reputation? What are you? Funeral man, dead people. Six months? I've known her forever. Known her!" He articulated the last inference with a defiance and a smirk that Claudia did not like. People had turned to stare at them. She was now free to stand. She turned first to Thomas.

"Hank and I have business to discuss which does not involve you. I appreciate your concern, but I can take care of myself." The words sounded firm. She hoped she sounded steady even though she felt unmoored. Thomas regarded her and his kind blue eyes showed such caring and distress that she had to glance away. She turned to Hank who stood hands clenched on his hips, his brown eyes ablaze with defiance at Thomas.

"We will need to continue this but not here or now." Claudia put her hand on Hank's arm and felt him relax. She had to get the truth but did not want to be the topic of gossip or pity.

Thomas nodded to Claudia, held Hank's glare, then picked up his suitcase and left. Hank began to sit again but Claudia remained standing so Hank waited. His body had relaxed but his facial muscles were twitching, and Claudia fought with herself. She wanted to find out what had happened to her land and to figure out how to rectify the situation, but she was unsure where or how to discuss the problem. She hated doing everything on her own and yet realized when she relied on others that didn't work either.

"Hank, we need to talk. Can we go outside of town a bit and talk in your truck?" A little outside of town, Hank pulled over. They tied the gelding to the truck and Claudia got into the passenger's side of the Ford.

"What's got you worried?"

"The sheriff said my east forty has been transferred to some Eastern executive. I thought you'd taken care of the debt with RT." Claudia's voice got rushed and higher as she spoke, sounding almost desperate. She cleared her throat, "What happened?"

"You tell me. I went to RT and he said no one had made a payment since January and the interest and principle were higher than the current value of the farm so they had to liquidate part so you didn't lose your home." He sat against the corner where the truck door met the seat, arms crossed in the space formed by his cocked right leg and this left foot on the brake as the truck idled, the heater blowing onto them, and the windows fogging.

She did not want to disclose to anyone, especially her successful neighbor, that she'd let her family's reputation down after her father had let her down. What would the Nelson name become if her neighbors knew she was grinding her seed oats and corn for feed and had paid her taxes by selling off some of her stock before the market had stabilized and before her steers were ready. She couldn't be blamed that land values had decreased from fifty-two dollars an acre in 1929 when her father acquired the loan to less than thirty dollars for an acre of prime agriculture land in 1932. The interest had increased from six percent to sixteen percent so even with his monthly payments that covered interest only, the mortgage amount had increased. She'd recently discovered these facts from his papers which had become haphazard and a jumble the last two years. Hank would probably understand if she confessed the facts to him, but she couldn't.

"I didn't know," she replied, which sounded weaker to her than the truth, but her ignorance was the truth until recently. "Do I own my home? Did you pay off the balance of the loan? Who will I owe?"

"Your home is safe as long as payments continue to be made. The market isn't right for me to sell my stock. Land prices are too low to sell. Also, I need to keep the piece of land my dad gave me." His eyes had softened as he talked. But she saw them become clear and cold as he said, "My family has always paid their debts as we go and never borrowed what we can't repay." She felt ashamed and glad she'd not confessed to grinding seed as feed, another no, no.

"I made the payments for you through the end of the year and for January and February of '33." Hank sat in his corner squared off to her. She had pushed herself into the opposite corner of the Ford and was shivering despite the heater running full bore.

"Thank you, Hank. I'd better get going. Your mother said you were going to be cutting wood, and it's almost supper time." She opened the car door and felt his arm draw her back. He pulled her close to him so that her back was against his chest and his arms wrapped around her. He breathed in deeply of her stocking-capped hair.

"It will work out fine. It is not perfect but it will be fine." He kissed the top of her cap and she didn't feel anything like comfort or relief but rather a vacant dullness. She gathered herself together as she supposed her father must've done when dealing with unpleasant situations.

"Thank you." She slipped from his arms, turned her head, smiled, and closed the Ford's door. She rode the gelding through the cold and frosty late afternoon wiser for the information she had but sadder for the truth that came with it.

45. Giving Thanks

Claudia hadn't been into Ernie's since the sheriff had been to her house with the awful news. Her train to Rice Lake would leave in half an hour, but she stopped to check on Ernie.

"How is he doing?" Claudia asked Vivian as she got down from the ladder where she'd been stocking shelves. She was performing Ernie's jobs as well as hers after he had gotten out of the hospital.

"He is fair to middling and partly cloudy," quipped Vivian, which made Claudia smile.

"You're beginning to sound like him." Claudia was standing in front of the November calendar page turned to the glum, wrinkled Morning Gun, a Blackfoot Indian in a Western white Stetson with a feather; she felt like he appeared—old, tired, and out of place in his Western hat.

"I'm going to see RT. I suppose you heard that some of my land was taken. I'm hoping to straighten out the mix-up." She kept her gaze from Vivian, who was standing next to her, but concentrated on the pages of the calendar as if studying the images of the familiar Blackfoot Nation. When Vivian didn't say anything, Claudia turned and examined Vivian's face that showed too much knowledge of people. Claudia cast away her glance. "Well, my train will be here soon. Just wanted to check on Ernie. Tell the bachelor boys hello from me," she offered in what she hoped was a lighthearted tone.

She pulled her church woolen coat around her, wound the knitted scarf around her neck, and with face tucked between scarf and hat, she started down the plowed street but cut through between Doc's and the closed bank to the depot.

Even though she'd have to wade through snow, she wanted to avoid the mortuary. She didn't know if he was in town or not, but she didn't want to talk to anyone, least of all him.

In Rice Lake she shed her coat in RT's reception area and waited to be called into the "inner sanctum." His secretary opened the door for her in less time than she ever had before. Claudia was surprised to see RT standing, waiting for her on this side of his desk.

"Why don't we sit over here." He motioned to two leather arm chairs under the window. Snow, beginning to fall, sifted a powdered sugar coat on the trees and street below. Mechanically, she slumped where he indicated and he relaxed at an angle to her with his elbows on his knees.

"You had an unexpected visitor. I didn't realize, or I'd have contacted you." He actually appeared regretful.

"I don't understand what happened, and I'm hoping to unravel it today." She couldn't muster her past anger. She wanted to be forceful, but she couldn't garner the energy needed.

"The land had to be repossessed to settle the large delinquency." He seemed earnest but she returned a questioning face. "When your father took out the three-thousand-dollar loan, interest rates were six percent, and he made a calculated decision to pay only the interest for the first year as he'd invested in the Highland cattle and needed the cash flow. He thought as soon as the herd was productive, he'd make double payments to compensate. Unfortunately, after the first year, interest rates had climbed, so he could only afford to continue paying the interest and nothing to reduce the principle." He leaned back in his chair. Was she supposed to understand now? Was she ignorant? Did everyone else understand? Maybe she was a failure?

"Please, I don't understand." She attempted to keep any pleading out of her voice.

"He'd borrowed the money to finance the restaurant in town. I think he believed the economy would turn around, and the restaurant could help pay back the loan. He was an optimist at heart, a man of his word, and believed in the good in everyone. If The Crash hadn't occurred right after he'd committed the funds to Nora or if he'd sold off the Highland cattle to fund the restaurant…all speculation. Your father just gambled the wrong way or backed the wrong horse."

He sighed. "Your neighbor Hank Johnson has given you some breathing room. A payment isn't due until March of next year. Your father's actions may not make sense to you, but you have your house, and if you need money, I can buy that worthless forty to the west of your house. That could help ease the strain." She looked up abruptly. What? She wasn't going to sell any more of her land! She stood. He stood.

"So, I can do nothing to save the forty that was taken?" Her voice had normal strength again.

"No. But as I said we can get you a little cash that I'm sure you could use, and you can keep the house." His voice had become less certain.

"I appreciate your offer, but I'm not selling any land." She turned to leave and saw his hand extended toward her.

"I'm always here to help if you need me," he imparted and his look had softened once again.

"I'll keep that in mind," she acknowledged and left his office. The secretary had taken Claudia's coat from the rack and helped her arms into the sleeves. She must have heard the exchange and anticipated Claudia's exit. *She was the fly on the wall.*

The train ride back to Turtle Lake with a transfer in Barron was quiet but Claudia couldn't manage to think. She wanted to be angry at her father but couldn't. Back in town, she picked up her horse from the stables and rode home. The day had elongated from chores to chores. Almost dry, Daisy was milked once every other day, there were no eggs to collect, but everyone needed to be watered. The cattle in the pasture had finished the stack of wild hay she'd forked to them. They'd need more tomorrow. She didn't have the wherewithal to uncover a stack of wild hay for the cow and horse. From a bale Hank had put in the shed when she'd been sick, Claudia threw some of the good hay to the gelding, Daisy and the five hens. She went for what was easy and better quality feed. She'd worry later, about later. *Oh, my gosh! Is that what my father had felt?*

All fall Claudia had allowed Hank to talk about his plans for the future, ideas he had for a herd of milk cows and her beef cattle. They had held hands at the movies and tapped their shoes to the singers and musicians during a show, but Claudia had been bothered by Hank's habit of rubbing her hand and arm until she felt he'd wear a hole in her skin. His goodnight kisses were wet, full-lipped affairs that she didn't enjoy the way she did Thomas's light butterfly kisses. Claudia rarely saw Thomas in town, and she wouldn't know how to talk to him after the incident at the boarding house. Anyway, he probably had a steady, sophisticated woman friend by now. Besides, Hank and Claudia worked well together at farm tasks, but ever since the sheriff's news and her trip to RT for confirmation, she felt gutted. Between the loafing shed and wood with which Hank had helped her, her animals and she had shelter, but without more feed and hay, the cattle could starve. Regardless of the nominal price she'd get, she had to sell animals soon. To the single inquiry she'd received, she sent one of her letters filled with persuasive facts about Highlands. She'd worry about next year, next year.

The week before Thanksgiving, Mrs. Johnson invited Claudia to spend the holiday with them. A handful of relatives would also be there. At first Claudia declined, but after Hank's "Why miss a great meal to eat fried eggs with Shep and Tabby?" she'd agreed. The day was unseasonably warm after weeks of cold and dreary. She helped peel potatoes and stew cranberries. The smell of roasting turkey filled the large, country kitchen when Mrs. Johnson opened the oven door to baste the twenty-pound, browning bird that had been raised for this day. The men smoked and discussed the election of Franklin D. Roosevelt and whether his talk of a New Deal would solve the Country's problems. Hank's uncle and dad argued whether the *Farmers' Almanac's* predictions for a hard winter would prove true.

Thanksgiving with Hank's family was warm and filled to bursting with good things to eat for his family of four, herself, and a visiting uncle, aunt and their children. Hank introduced Claudia to his cousins as his fiancée. With relatives all around, she didn't object, but seated in his truck in front of her house later that evening, she brought it up.

"What do you mean?" he warned her. "Why do you think I gave you that money? Why do you think we've been fixing at your place?"

"Because we are friends and neighbors." As she uttered the words, they drifted without substance out the truck's cracked-open window.

He had his arm around her and now held her more forcefully. "We are more than friends."

She thought of the night they spent kissing for so long he had tried to put his hand up her shirt. She had squirmed away saying she was tired and wanted to go to bed. He had hinted that that would be just fine with him. She had kissed him, "Goodbye, I'll see you tomorrow," and gone into the house.

She was beginning to realize she needed to set clearer boundaries. She turned her head to face him more directly in the confined truck.

"We've got a business arrangement," she asserted.

Hank clarified. "No, a banker has a business deal with a customer. You and I have a relationship, an understanding." She realized she really had made a mistake. She had heard of girls that were teases or even women who were gold-diggers, and she was beginning to wonder if she had slipped into a role she hadn't intended. An autumn of bittersweet with Hank was becoming a winter of exasperation. Hank was frustrated with her, and she was conflicted over feeling free of the immediacy of debt repayment and being bound by Hank's expectations. She felt especially indebted to him and vulnerable, without options. She told him she needed to think and left without their customary kiss goodbye.

November ice slid to December snow. Animals' feeding and care required constant attention. She sold another steer to pay the balance of the property taxes. One less to feed. Hank was busy at his farm and Claudia kept to herself. One day at the end of November, Pete Mevissen arrived unexpectedly with a small wagon load of baled hay and straw that he and his son stacked next to her shed and covered with a tarp.

She sputtered and blushed, but Pete raised his hand. "I'm paying old debts." She thanked him. That night she cried into her pillow with relief and disquiet. What would her father say? Whirlwinds swept her thoughts as she fought for sleep.

So many firsts this year. She had accepted outright charity. Her father would be mortified. Everyone in town would know she wasn't coping. Worse, she'd lost one third of their farm, the best third! She avoided town, fearful of the looks or questions. Her first Thanksgiving without her father would soon slide into the first Christmas without him. The holiday would disappear without them exchanging simple homemade gifts. No special treat to take out to Dandy and Molly. Last year she had knitted wool throw blankets with ties to go under their bellies front and back as added protection when the worst of the subzero winds blew. The few animals she had left would not have a warm barn or calorie-rich feed to fight off the cold. Vivian and Ernie wouldn't be invited to the Johnsons as they'd been invited to the Nelsons in previous years. Claudia and Francis would have made a little something special for their single friends to open, but not this year. She didn't even care if the holiday came.

If she could just hold on until spring. The new heifers and her cows had been bred to the Highland bull. What would she do come spring to feed them? She had to get money. She needed to begin to pay Hank back. This messy, complicated relationship couldn't continue. The few times they had been out on a date alone made that clearer and clearer. She'd heard of arranged marriages in the old country. She could understand how those women must have felt like chattel to be "awarded" to the young man of the family with the best prospects without regard to the woman's wishes.

That night Claudia dreamt she was a deer lying in the dust gutted. Vultures picked at the deer's flesh and she winced in her sleep as if the birds of prey were pulling her apart. The dream became mixed with Thanksgiving at the Johnson house. The house in her dream didn't resemble Hank's spacious home but more like the Meiser house. On the Meiser's scarred, bare table a Thanksgiving turkey carcass lay with its ribs picked of vital muscle. In her dream the carcass became the Meiser barn. The arched rafters forming a heavenly haven for animals and their caregivers had become bare and broken. She tossed and turned in her sleep. The curved wooden spurs resembled opened, elderly hands with fingers spread to the exposed sky, begging for what? She felt she knew those weathered hands, but whose? What were they begging for? Food for those standing in bread lines? Jobs for those seeking the dignity of work?

Not a begging hand grabbing but a hand outstretched, wanting to be helped up. Somebody or some beings needing someone willing to stand shoulder-to-shoulder to assist them in pulling out of the ditch of despair and up onto the road again to continue the journey. A deer, a turkey, a barn, her body, timeworn hands—they swirled like dervishes in her dream. *What did it mean?*

46. Thomas Talks to Hank

Thomas was not thrilled to come back to Turtle Lake, but as so often happened in the winter, an elderly man had passed away, and Thomas's uncle needed him. Thomas had been doing everything he could to earn more money. This fall he had persuaded his New York employer to purchase his uncle's coffins for less than the cost of their previous supplier. Local lumber was inexpensive and his uncle was a craftsman. Thomas had solicited several other Eastern mortuaries and received the go-ahead to provide coffins for another starting in January. The challenge was his uncle couldn't keep up with the demand, and Thomas had to help him more and more.

Thomas returned to Turtle Lake distressed and dejected. He had seen Claudia in town looking very sad after Thanksgiving. He went into Ernie's store, which had returned to a semblance of normalcy except for the blackened door leading to the area that used to be his home.

"How's Ernie doing?" Thomas asked Vivian.

"He's moved in with Bruno and Klive. Only his right arm and hand are causing him trouble. You just missed him. He's not working as many hours. Did you just get back into town?"

"The conductor commented that I'm making the trip back East almost as often as those businessmen who take the train from the Twin Cities to Chicago and New York. I've been working three weeks then coming back to help my uncle for a week or two. I help Doc sometimes. I haven't been back since the end of October." Thomas fiddled with the flannel shirt folded on the counter, thinking of that encounter at the boarding house with Hank. "How's Claudia? I saw her leaving town on her old gray gelding, and she looked like the world rested on her shoulders."

"Today is the first in a month of Mondays that she's been in. She misses her father and her horses, and she hasn't felt comfortable with the debt arrangement. I don't know if your uncle has told you, but she lost the best part of her farm." At his alarm, she added, "She didn't lose the house. She still has that eighty acres, but it's hard for her. Can't imagine what she's feeding the animals, although a few neighbors have been helpful, but she's so stubborn." Vivian cast her eyes to the overhead tin ceiling.

Thomas shook his head. "I knew Hank Johnson couldn't be trusted."

"No, that forty had been repossessed to pay the overdue amount before he could pay down on the debt."

"How could they just take her land without informing her? Did she confront RT?"

"Oh, she went to RT alright. She gave him the first degree. Unfortunately, her father had secured the loan with all his land and that forty was on a separate deed and RT had a friend who wanted it so that was that. She felt so humiliated that her father hadn't confided in her."

"I hate that she has to feel indebted to someone else. Her spirit will be broken, if it hasn't already. First RT, now Hank," protested Thomas. "Wish Ernie the best for me, would you? I'll see you later." Vivian nodded solemnly and Thomas opened the door into the cold December air.

At the mortuary he told his uncle he'd be gone for several hours, started his car, and drove down snow-packed Highway 8 toward the Johnson farm.

He had enough money saved from his New York earnings to save Claudia from being tied to Hank. He wished he'd done something sooner.

He'd have a quiet word with Hank. Maybe they could come to an agreement. They were two adult men who both cared about Claudia. They could come to an arrangement. Thomas felt optimistic.

He pulled up to the farm in his Packard. Through the

opening of the machine shed, he could just see Hank's legs sticking out from under a piece of machinery. Thomas slid back the heavy door. The shed housed several pieces of machinery that Thomas assumed Hank was maintaining in preparation of spring planting. Hank rolled from under the corn planter. He looked surprised, then down at his dirt-stained coveralls and his lined canvas coat with patches on the elbows and knees that his mother, presumably, had sewn to reinforce them. Thomas realized how out of context he was in his church pants and white shirt under his winter coat.

"What can I help you with?" Hank demanded with an edge of defiance, holding a grease gun in both hands. "I don't think you're needed. Nobody's died that I know of."

Without being deterred, Thomas plowed ahead. "I've come to see if you'd be interested in sharing the responsibility of helping Claudia." Still clutching the grease gun, Hank lunged toward Thomas who stepped back, surprised.

"What? Do you think your big city money is better than hard earned dollars from milking cows and shoveling manure?"

"No! I merely thought if we combined our resources we could relieve her of the constant strain of worry. I have about a thousand dollars that I could put toward the debt."

"That's not even half of what she owes," Hank smirked. Thomas did not remind Hank that he hadn't paid the entire debt, either.

"I could pay the balance off over a period of time," Thomas offered.

"Why should I? Why should you want to help a woman who's not even interested in you?" retorted Hank. Thomas considered that Hank really couldn't understand why anyone would want to help someone when there was no visible, immediate gain.

"I think you are out of your depth here, mortician man."

"I know I'm no match for what you can offer," Thomas conceded. "I also know Claudia likes her independence. This arrangement would give her that."

"Too much independence can get a woman into trouble. Like all spirited animals, women need a steady hand to guide them, help them through rough spots." Hank pushed the nozzle of the gun up to a zert on the machinery and shot a wad of grease into each of the receptacles. He had his back to Thomas who decided to make one last attempt.

"Would you at least consider my offer?"

"Lemme do some thinking and I'll get back to you." With that Hank slid back under the piece of machinery to shoot the grease gun's contents into every zert, crack, and crevice he could find. Thomas closed the shed door behind him. He had to give Hank credit. He worked hard and at the rate he was greasing, he wasn't going to have any problems with stiff gears come spring. Everything would be in working order.

47. Shifting Triangles of Affection

Shooting grease into the last of the farm equipment, Hank announced aloud to no one, "There, that's as it should be. Everything taken care of. 'An ounce of prevention is worth a pound of cure,' as Dad would say." Surrounded by the tools, buildings, and animals of his daily bread and butter, Hank wondered about the wisdom of joining with someone who could put the land, their livelihood, at risk. Claudia hadn't made her loan payments, had been delinquent in paying her property tax, and had let a third of her land be lost. Why was he spending so much time trying to marry a woman who was so much work? Hank considered the machine shed full of equipment he kept in peak performance. He'd thought Claudia could help him succeed in his dream to take over the farm someday. Now he questioned that logic.

His brother had been stepping out with a sweet, petite girl from a nearby town. At the last movie he and Claudia had attended, they had seen his brother and this girl Rachel in a group of young people their age. As Hank put away the grease gun and oil can, he thought of the times he'd been around his brother and his brother's friends when the pretty, auburn-haired girl was there. She was easy to be around, laughed at the joke he'd made, and listened to him without offering an opinion like Claudia did.

He ruminated that without too much effort he could coax her away from his younger brother. As Hank threw the rag onto the hooks on the shed wall, he contemplated throwing in the towel with Claudia, good riddance to her. She didn't know a good thing when it bit her in the butt. He pulled the shed door shut and walked to the house. Let Thomas have her, Hank declared, but like the dominant dog in a pack he insisted to himself, "No. Even if I don't want her, he can't have her."

Hank hung up his barn coat in the entry and walked into the warm kitchen where his mother's pork roast with potatoes, onions, and carrots was sitting on a platter next to a large bowl of applesauce and a smaller bowl of peas. His father was already seated at the table. Hank stood next to his twenty-one-year-old brother, Ethan, at the sink as they washed up. His brother, who was shorter and not as handsome or confident, stepped aside to give his smiling older brother the room he desired. Hank considered for a moment. Thomas wasn't much of a threat when he could only come up with half the money. If Hank decided he liked the red-haired girl better, then he would want the money to build a house and set up a family. Maybe accepting Thomas's offer would be the wise thing to do. Ethan was a likable kid and could always get another girlfriend. His brother and the girl weren't even really going together, but always in a group with an easy, carefree relationship.

The annual dance held between Thanksgiving and Christmas attracted many young people from the surrounding small towns. Claudia had never attended, and Hank saw no reason to ask her this year. Hank went, not with any specific thought other than to have fun. He saw a group of giggling girls several years younger than him dancing together in a circle with the lovely red-haired girl among them. Hank hadn't paid a lot of attention to the younger girl before, but ever since his relationship with Claudia hadn't been going as expected and he'd seen Ethan enjoying this girl's company, his interest had been ignited.

The holiday dance was held in the Richardson's pavilion outside of Clayton and Turtle Lake and south of Bear Creek. The space was ideal for a variety of social events that included exhibits and dances. Claudia and Hank had been there to view the local fair exhibits in September. The big, open Quonset building had a concrete floor and a wooden platform at one end where a group played instruments and sang. A bar was set up to the side with refreshments, sandwiches, and squares of different dessert bars. A man at the door collected two bits per person to help pay for the costs. Hank observed his brother and his gang of buddies making their way toward the group of girls. Hank strutted up to the girls, gallantly grasped the red-haired girl's hand, and pulled Rachel from the circle to a separate portion of the dance floor where he could dance and talk without the other younger people around.

Only once did Rachel insist that she dance with her group of friends, and the song was raucously fast so that the girls danced together without the boys. The girls teased her and glanced over at the older, more handsome of the Johnson boys. Hank immediately captured Rachel for the slow dance that followed. He heard one of the girls proclaim, "Hank will get the farm when his folks can't do the work anymore."

As he held Rachel close and danced away from the group of eighteen- to twenty-year-olds, Hank checked for Ethan over Rachel's shoulder. Ethan had looked sullen and withdrawn and hadn't danced to the first couple of songs but had perked up by the third song and asked a couple of girls who seemed very happy to oblige him. Hank noticed Ethan was slow-dancing with a dark-haired girl, not as pretty as Rachel but very pleasing with her long, shiny mane.

That evening on his way home flushed with excitement, Hank wondered why he was bothering with Claudia. She was a lot of work. He had put her on too high of a pedestal for too long. He was twenty-four years old. Time was ticking by, time to settle down to a married life with benefits. This petite, young lady was uncomplicated, fun, and enjoyed his attention.

The next day in church he saw Rachel sitting with her parents, and she looked back at him, saw he was looking at her, and smiled. Hank decided to uncomplicate his life and to stop on Monday to see the mortician.

He drove right to the mortuary after chores and walked in with a nod and "Hi ya." He wanted a short meeting so he didn't do his customary small talk. "When can we take care of this business proposition?"

"Right now." Thomas glanced at his uncle who sighed and began to take his coat off the hook. "Wait. Uncle, could we meet in your house for a few minutes?" The uncle nodded and shuffled back to sit down and take up his tools.

"Follow me." Thomas led Hank out the back door. Their breath immediately sent up clouds around their heads. That's when Hank saw her. Between the buildings her slump-shouldered form in a bulky wool coat holding a small brown-paper, wrapped parcel held in heavy worn knit mittens, Claudia trudged over the snow hills at the edge of the street. She must've been at Ernie's. *Cripes, today was Monday, Claudia's town day*. He'd been so anxious to get on to the next stage in his life, he'd forgotten. He stepped out of the line of vision, so he couldn't see her and she couldn't see him.

Once inside the tiny house, Hank blurted, "You can have her and her debt. Give me the thousand you said you have. I've paid nine months of overdue payments plus last month and this month and January and February of next year. Pay me monthly payments at the current rate of sixteen percent interest on what I've paid off for her. I'll give you a year to repay me. You'll have to deal with her and RT on the balance."

"How many months are left to pay to RT?" Hank heard Thomas's words and shook his head. *That was not the question to ask. The question was how much was left and, more importantly, how much could you pay per month.* Relief that he wouldn't need to worry much longer and thoughts of a pretty, petite girl dancing in his kitchen relaxed his attitude.

"The amount owed RT on the principle was not much less

than the original loan. The repossession of the best of her property, the east forty valued at just over a thousand, took care of the interest that had accumulated and the taxes on that piece. At the current rate of interest and if you only made the least payment, it could take almost forever." Hank did not say, *That's why you don't want to go into debt during these times,* but he didn't want his own almost fatal error in judgment to alert Thomas. Let the smart city man figure it out on his own.

Thomas assured him, "I'll contact my bank and wire the money transfer to your account."

They shook hands, and Hank left after checking that Claudia wasn't in sight. In his truck on the way home, Hank dreamed of the compact but modern home he'd build for him and Rachel. He could begin this spring using lumber he and Ethan had slabbed from trees downed in the storm. Maybe he'd marry Rachel this coming summer. In a year when they had a family, he would use the rest of the money from Thomas's repayment to add on to their house and expand his herd.

In the three weeks since he'd decided to drop Claudia to pursue Rachel and a week since he'd been to the mortuary, he hadn't revealed anything to anyone. He'd talked to Rachel twice, once at her place and once at church. He looked forward to when they could date.

Every time Hank heard Claudia make an excuse why Christmas wouldn't work for her to be with his family, he was relieved. But his mother kept assuming Claudia would be there. He heard his mother prattle to Claudia on the phone, which he'd convinced her to put in after he found her sick in bed. His mother went on at length about the gifts under the tree and how excited she was for Claudia to open one in particular. He'd wrapped the gift he'd gotten Claudia, never thinking his mother would make a big deal out of the size. Now he wished he'd gotten her something less suggestive.

One morning after breakfast, his mother corralled him. He hadn't escaped out the door before his brother and father.

"Dear, convince Claudia to take time away and come Christmas Day. She works too hard. We will just be family. We should all be together." His mother held his elbow and looked pleadingly into his face.

"If it's that important to you," he mumbled. Hank didn't like disappointing his mother. He had a feeling displeasure was inevitable, but he didn't want to spoil her Christmas by announcing that he was no longer interested in their stiff-necked neighbor. He could let both women figure it out in time. When he phoned Claudia, she told him that she'd had a response to her ads and would hopefully have a buyer for a Highland cow and calf.

"That's nice. But will you be here? You being here would mean a lot to my mom." Claudia agreed.

On Christmas Day the weather was cool and icy. When Mrs. Johnson answered the door, a red-faced Claudia muffled in wool stood like a statue, the queen of frost. Hank wished the female at his door was the sweet, little Rachel nestled in her dark green coat standing there, waiting for him to unwrap her and seat her next to him by the wood stove.

"You didn't walk, did you?" Doris glanced behind Claudia, drew her into the room, and closed the door.

"The road was so slippery, I left my horse at home." Claudia held four wrapped gifts.

"Hank, take these from Claudia and put them under the tree." She scanned the tags, and handing the one with "To Hank from Claudia" to Hank, she smiled. "Put this one next to that little one of yours." She grinned at Claudia, then at him.

His mom was a good cook, so dinner was great, but Hank was eager for the family event to hurry up and be over. Upstairs was a gift he hoped to deliver to Rachel later today. His father sat in his overstuffed chair smoking Lucky Strikes, and Ethan sat at one end of the sofa. Claudia had chosen the curved back chair with a flowered cushion, so Hank sat at the other end of the mohair sofa.

Hank's mother motioned to the spot between him and his brother. "Wouldn't you be more comfortable on the sofa?"

"Thank you, but next to the stove feels good." Claudia held her hands out toward the Round Oak stove with the chrome top and bumpers. Hank liked that stove and even though he thought he'd put an oil burner in the basement of the house he was going to build, he'd have a Round Oak stove in the parlor with a large carpet. He and Rachel could have matching armchairs. His daydream was interrupted by his mother.

"Claudia should be the first to open a gift, as she is our guest." His mother smiled broadly as she added, "Hank, you get your little package for her to open. We are all excited to see what it is." Hank felt Christmas wasn't going to escape without letting down his mom.

When the small box Claudia unwrapped held a compass on a chain, Hank could see the relief on her face and the excitement turn to disappointment sour his mother's.

"In case you're ever in the woods and can't see the sun." He offered, avoiding his mother's surprise.

"Thank you. How very thoughtful." She handed him her gift. He unwrapped a pair of leather gloves that he'd seen at Ernie's store.

"These are great. I can always use gloves. They're great." He put them on and held his hands for his mother to see, but she was fussing with her holiday apron.

After all the gifts were finally opened, his mother suggested, out of the blue, "Maybe we could sing a few carols?"

His father scowled as if she'd suggested they all jump up and hug and kiss each other. "Why would we want to do that?" he asked. Hank stifled a laugh and noticed Claudia was equally as horrified at the suggestion.

"I thought singing might raise our spirits," his mother responded quietly to her hands in her lap.

"There's nothing wrong with our spirits that a beer wouldn't cure. Ethan, go down to the cellar and bring up three bottles of beer and two of sarsaparilla for the women." His father flicked his cigarette into the round glass ashtray cupped in its wooden pedestal.

After the drinks and strained small talk were finished, Claudia made her excuses to leave.

"Thank you for everything, but I'd better get home to stoke my fire and do chores."

"Hank, you take Claudia home. It's too cold and icy for her to walk back." His mother had that smile back on her face and he felt crestfallen, but then realized she'd given him a perfect opportunity to "stop by" Rachel's on the pretext of running an errand for his mom.

"Sure!" His voice was eager and his mother looked hopeful. "I'll be right back." He ran to his room, got Rachel's gift from under his socks, and stuffed the wrapped locket into his pocket.

"Ok. Let's go." He gripped Claudia's elbow and led her down the steps. "I'll see you after a little bit," he stated over his shoulder to his mother.

"Don't hurry on our account," she encouraged, beaming.

The ride was short and silent.

"Thanks," Claudia uttered.

"Yeah, no problem. See you around." Hank sighed and backed out of her driveway toward what he hoped would be his shining future.

48.Changing Partners

Midweek between Christmas and New Year's Day, Claudia got a call from Hank.

"I just wanted to let you know that I'm going to be busy with some buddies in town bringing in 1933, so if you were expecting to see me New Year's Day, I won't be around."

"Very thoughtful of you to call. I had no expectations. I'm glad you called because I wanted to tell you that I got a response to my ads. There's a farmer in St Croix County with whom I've shared several articles of my father's detailing the advantages of Highlands over the conventional Angus, Hereford, and white face that most farmers are raising." She waited for him to reply. When he didn't, she continued, "He's going to buy two of my bred heifers. He'll be picking them up as soon as the weather and roads look good."

"That's fine." He sounded distracted and not very enthusiastic. "Well, Happy New Year." Click and he was gone.

She was relieved to be alone. New Year's Day was another first alone for Claudia. She was sad but relieved not to have to put on an "everything is fine" face in front of Hank or his family when she felt like the end of the world, not the beginning of a new year. The positive outcome of this windy, cold fall and winter had been that she had gotten a response to her ads, written numerous letters, and had contacted several farmers. The one from St. Croix County was one of two farmers this winter who decided to take a gamble on cattle that were hardy in the extreme cold and could live on the toughest of roughage and gain weight without grain.

By the time February arrived she had almost a hundred

dollars to give Hank toward the fifteen hundred he had used to bail her out with RT so she didn't lose her home. She was excited for the first time in a long time. If she could sell a couple more head, she'd be able to make the March payment of interest and maybe pay some toward the principle. She'd been grinding her seed corn and oats and would have nothing to plant come spring. But, she didn't have any good land on which to plant either crop. With only a dozen head of cattle to feed, what difference did it make?

Once again, she got on her old gelding and trotted across the still-frozen spring ground to talk to Hank and hand him the cash she had put into an envelope. He was out in the machine shed getting his disc and spring tooth harrow ready for when the snow melted and he could get into the fields.

"What's this?" he asked when she extended her arm with the envelope.

"A down payment on the money I owe you." She thrust the packet at him, anxious to have him take the money so she could feel less indebted and freer. He kept his arms to his sides.

"I don't want that."

"I'll be able to pay you back, slowly. If you're willing I can try to get a bank loan once the banks start lending money again, and I don't owe quite so much." He smiled half-heartedly. She extended her arm further toward him, puzzled, her face questioning.

"Forget about it." He slouched against the tractor next to the disc. "I've already got everything taken care of."

"What do you mean, taken care of?" Her arm with the envelope of money in hand dropped to her side.

"Your New York friend paid off most of what I had invested in your debt." Claudia scrunched her face quizzically at Hank, but as he continued she felt her face heat up. "He paid me an initial down payment of two-thirds of the money, and he's been paying me so much a month since then. In less than a year he'll have me paid off. He never told you?

I wonder why?" He didn't seem upset by her discomfort. Only once did his face flinch. The pain she felt at the loss of her father, her horses, her control over every aspect of her life fell into the void within her. On top of that fell the confrontation she would now be required to have with the man she felt the strongest push-pull attraction, the new owner of part of her debt. She stuffed the envelope of money into her jacket pocket and returned home. A week later she used the cash to buy some feed and to mail the March payment of interest to RT.

Just as Claudia had begun to get a handle on taking care of the debt without needing to bind herself in marriage to a man she'd rather not be tied to, she was indebted to a man she hadn't even spoken to for an entire season. She felt betrayed by her father, tricked by RT, maneuvered by Hank, and now Thomas had taken over the debt without even consulting her. *How dare all these men think they could bully and manage her like some piece of chattel! Her father had appreciated her independence! Why couldn't they?*

49. Tables Turned

Even though March's interest-only payment had been sent early, Claudia hadn't had any more inquires on the Highland cattle and the prospect of being able to make April's interest looked bleak. The market for her few remaining Herefords was still terrible. Making interest-only payments was like throwing money down a rat hole. Now, she had to make payments to RT and Thomas, she had to buy seed and gas for the tractor, and soon she had to purchase more feed. She needed a miracle.

Feeling sullen and hopeless, Claudia trudged slowly up the stairs to beg RT for more time. Walking through the open door, she saw no secretary in the reception area but could hear voices in RT's office beyond. She glanced at the wall clock—12:15. The secretary must be at lunch. She debated whether to return when the secretary was back and half turned, deciding to come back later, when she heard her name in RT's voice. "Claudia Nelson isn't aware of anything on her property."

She halted, then continued her quiet walk across the reception area toward RT's office door. Claudia stepped toward the wall, out of the line of vision, but closer, to hear. She knew by the sound of their voices that the two men, RT and Bill the banker, were close to RT's billiard-sized desk out of sight behind the partially opened door. Claudia could see the two stuffed chairs under the window, which overlooked Rice Lake's main street below.

Bill's voice came forcefully, "I say we move fast, strike while the iron is hot. We call the balance of the loan in now and offer to take the entire eighty off her hands to clear the debt." A mumbling of lowered voices could be heard from the inner sanctum. Claudia crept closer to the opening. RT's dropped tone sounded like a petition or plea. She tipped her head down and extended her ear toward the door, willing the words louder.

RT's voice was quieter. "I'm just considering…there's a way that … make this a win–win… garner community's sympathy… get the property." Claudia extended her head as far forward as she could without being in the doorway. RT continued, "If we take everything and leave her with nothing, not even the house, we're perceived as the bad guys." As RT talked, his voice became louder and Claudia glanced up to see him at the window, his back to her but in plain view. She flattened against the wall but wouldn't be concealed if he turned. There was nowhere to hide. On her toes, she turned and tiptoed toward the reception room door, hoping to escape or appear as if she'd just arrived. Bill's voice became clearer and his words easier to discern so she ascertained, without glancing back, that Bill had joined RT at the window.

Bill queried, "I thought you wanted those minerals. We've got Meiser's and the vein goes straight through. We need to get excavating." RT hadn't responded. There was quiet. She turned. As she did, she thought she saw a head movement from RT. Had he seen her? No. He was peering out the window. Bill began again. "Nothing stays secret long in small towns. Your boy knows the particulars. What if he lets the cat out of the bag over a bottle? I say move today!"

Claudia, safely at the outer door entrance, took a breath and knocked on the jamb, "Excuse me," she announced loudly. The men turned. "Am I interrupting?" She stalled while her mind raced, piecing snatches together.

"Oh," uttered RT. "What a surprise." But he didn't sound surprised. RT opened the door to his office wider. Bill's astonishment turned to a grimace then progressed to bluster. "What are you doing here?" He demanded accusingly.

"I've come to make a deal." Claudia proceeded into the

room of polished wood and imported carpets and sat at the window in one of the stuffed leather chairs between the two standing men. Seated, she was almost at Bill's eye level.

His eyes squinted as he pressed forward. "What do you mean, a deal?" He paused, then his eyes glinted. "You've come to see that you must sell all your cattle and land to settle your debt. Wise choice, young lady, to recognize when you're in over your head." Claudia lowered her head to pick nonexistent lint from her sleeve. She needed to put the words together to get what she wanted. What *did* she want?

RT turned to Bill and motioned to the other comfortable chair. "Bill, you take the other seat. I'll pull up my desk chair." RT gave her the time she needed, unknowingly she thought, as he rolled his mahogany and leather chair to face the window and to sit in front of and between the two of them.

"I've been doing a bit of work, well… research really." Claudia's voice was calm but her palms were clammy. She resumed, "My land has value."

"What? Who said that?" Bill began to get up from the chair he'd taken as requested by RT.

RT extended his arm towards Bill, who sat heavily back down. "Let's hear her out." RT turned his attention to Claudia, "Yes?" He seemed pensive not as predatory as Claudia was used to with him.

Claudia began, "I'll sell my agriculturally poor, but minerally rich, forty acres and keep my home forty acres in exchange for clearing the remainder of the debt."

"How do you know it's rich in minerals?" Bill scrutinized RT angrily. "That's just forty acres of rocks."

"How isn't the question. Are you going to buy my forty or do I sell to someone who can appreciate the treasure hidden beneath?" She knew all she had was a bluff, and if they called her on the ruse, she'd lose everything and would have to leave like a dog with its tail between its legs. But she felt okay, not angry or scared, just playing the current hand she'd been dealt.

"But that land is not worth twenty dollars an acre on the open market. You're asking two, three times," the banker faltered then plowed ahead, "what it's worth."

"Maybe to you. But there are farsighted people willing to take a risk." Claudia took a deep breath, without looking at them and brushed her jacket front nonchalantly wiping the sweat from her palms. Motion steadied her shaking hands. "But if you gentlemen are not those people, I'll take my forty acres of 'just rocks' to a geologist." Claudia studied Bill, who had the appearance of a beet freshly pulled from the dirt. She turned to RT and thought there was a glimmer of a smile lingering in his eyes.

"Well! I never!" Bill struggled to his feet and confronted RT.

RT shook his head. "Me either. But I think this line of thought deserves further consideration. Some ruminating on our part, Bill." They were all standing. RT had his hand on Bill's shoulder. Claudia was midway through the door arch when she turned and paused. Her head almost reached the top of the door jamb. She put her forefinger to her cheek and waited. When both men stared at her expectantly, she pronounced the words slowly, not as if they'd just come to her, but as if she was considering whether to give the two men an unexpected opportunity or not.

"This is an offer for today only, gentleman. I have friends who know people who… Well… Let's just say, let's make this a win-win situation and do the deal today." RT did have a smile in his eyes, but he kept his mouth straight and reached out his right hand. "Deal."

RT turned back to his desk followed by a controlled but exultant Claudia and a befuddled Bill. The relieved money man got out a legal transfer form from his desk and wrote up the necessary agreement signing over Claudia's forty acres of not prime farmland in exchange for the lien release on her home forty. In his hand RT held the promissory note her father had signed over three years ago.

"I'll get the papers recorded today." He tore the promissory note into four pieces that fluttered to the waste basket. "And that takes care of this." He held out his hand to Francis's daughter. "A pleasure doing business with you, Claudia." Claudia grasped his hand, which she shook heartily.

"Yes, yes," muttered Bill, as he squeezed by the other two and exited the room.

Claudia rode the train home lighter than she had felt in months. She'd just signed away half of her remaining farm but she was debt-free. She slept the whole way home, only waking when she heard, "Turtle Lake. Next stop Turtle Lake" from the uniformed conductor.

50. Confronting Ghosts

The ground hadn't thawed yet when Claudia began to prepare her equipment to work up her few fields on her home forty in preparation for planting. She had used some of the cash from the sale of her cattle to buy enough seed to plant her mediocre seventeen tillable acres into a little corn and oats. Her hay ground had been seeded down three years ago and was doing okay. Last year she had forty acres of excellent cropland, forty mediocre, and forty less usable but was able to support almost two dozen head of cattle, horses, chickens, and a pig. This year she had forty acres total—seven acres of hay, six for corn, four for small grains, thirteen acres in woods and pasture and the remaining ten contained the house, outbuildings, corral, barn foundation, swamp, and creek. She could barely pasture eight animals if the year was above average and the pasture grew well. Her gelding, Daisy, and her hens counted as two of those. She had twelve head of adult cattle remaining. She wanted to get another pig, which wouldn't cost much but had to be fed and counted as three-quarters of an adult bovine for feed consumption. Adult cattle required two to three acres each so she could reasonably sustain only a few head without buying most of her feed. Without cattle to breed and raise what would she do to pay taxes and live?

She hadn't talked to Hank in over two months. She'd kept herself to herself. She suspected from what Vivian had hinted after the new year that Hank had horned in on his brother's girlfriend. Vivian had also mentioned Thomas was in town working at his uncle's regularly. In the month since she got the news, she hadn't mustered the nerve to approach Thomas about his assumption of her debt.

Claudia had avoided town for most of the winter except once a month when absolutely necessary and today was a necessity. She had lived out of her cellar, and the store of canned goods would be used up soon, except for pickles which still filled a shelf in the cellar. The pork she had smoked and preserved in September would carry her through fall, but if she wanted pork past Christmas she'd have to buy a small feeder pig this spring. She should get more chickens to raise for meat, too. Just as she'd debated on slaughtering a steer, one swallowed a piece of metal exposed by melting snow and choked. Last week she butchered the animal and spent the greater portion of the week pressure canning the meat. She'd run out of canning lids and salt and wanted to order some baby chicks. The thought of property taxes, gas for the tractor, and how to repay Thomas had her worried. At least she didn't need to think about any more payments to RT. She'd checked him off her list of concerns.

From the feed mill she ordered two dozen chicks, which would arrive in April, then she trudged the two blocks through slush to Ernie's store, which seemed no worse for wear. Among all the people to whom Ernie had extended credit, there were plenty of neighbors willing to make a meal or change a bandage while Klive and Bruno provided a place to live and companionship. Ernie was stocking shelves, and Vivian was balancing the books and making out orders for the upcoming month.

Stomping snow from her rubber boots, Claudia entered sheepishly. "Hello. How is everyone?"

Vivian glanced up from her perch on her chair and set down her pencil. Percy, sensing his human's mood, began to chatter, and Claudia recognized Bruno and Ernie's voices in a congenial disagreement. "Well, well, and the dead shall rise." Vivian muttered, went over to the parakeet's cage, and put her hand in to scratch him. Ernie got down from the ladder and went to give Claudia's hand a shake, but she hesitated.

"Is your hand entirely healed?" She inquired, very aware of Vivian who was not paying heed to her but giving attention to Percy.

"Of course," Ernie blustered and shook Claudia's hand with both of his. "Haven't seen you in an age."

"I have a list of a few supplies." She handed the sheet torn from a newspaper and written on a blank portion— "coffee, sugar, canning salt and lids, yeast," and a few other items which he didn't recite aloud but turned to gather from the shelves. He began to hum "Between the Devil and the Deep Blue Sea" to himself, but Claudia knew he was listening to every word the two women spoke.

"I've been busy. A steer died suddenly and I didn't want to waste the meat," Claudia offered.

"Oh," was Vivian's curt reply. "My pretty boy," she cooed to the yellow budgie, "you're such a good boy. Content in your cage, talking to me."

"I said I've been busy, Vivian. I couldn't stop every Monday."

"Who said anything about *every*?" The wiry little woman retorted. "Word was you bought seed at the feed mill last week and paid your bill."

"I sold another steer and settled my debt with RT by selling another forty." Claudia rushed guiltily ahead. She hated to air dirty laundry in front of anyone, even Vivian. She'd felt a failure losing or selling off her livelihood this past year.

"I heard." Vivian sounded aloof, curt. Claudia couldn't look at her.

Claudia sighed. "Besides, they didn't always plow the roads and the gelding isn't as stable on his feet or as reliable as…as Dandy and Molly were." Her eyes turned toward the tin ceiling, and she forced the tears to fall back into her lower lids. With her composure regained, she glanced at Vivian who'd placed Percy in his cage and had moved toward her. Ernie observed the two women and stepped into the back room and began to make some superficial noise that provided them privacy.

"I'm sorry," Claudia offered.

"No need to apologize, you've had plenty on your plate for quite some time." Vivian stood close to her. Claudia dipped her head to stare into her friend's gray eyes and marveled at how peaceful Vivian's eyes always were.

"My life has been complicated and I think I caused some of my problems." She and Vivian selected their customary seats as if no time had passed between them. They took up where they'd left off. Claudia related briefly about her meeting with RT, and Vivian congratulated her on it. Claudia confessed to her misuse of her friendship with Hank and her quandary on how to deal with Thomas and her indebtedness to him. She admitted, "I don't know how to pay him back. I don't want to make the same mistake twice."

"Once burned, twice shy." They heard Ernie's voice from the back room. The two women stared at each other stunned, then laughed.

"I think the easiest thing is to talk to him. He's been in town most of January and February and now March." Vivian put her hand out across the counter and held Claudia's. They sat together allowing the space that had developed between them to evaporate completely. With the intimacy of flesh touching flesh, Claudia realized that, except for Ernie's hand shake a few minutes ago, she hadn't been touched by another person since she'd been out with Hank at Christmas, and she hadn't held his hand since October almost half a year ago. Her body craved contact. She remembered a year ago next month when she had met Thomas and only a month after that, she had allowed him to know her body and she'd explored his. She blushed deeply.

"Is he in town now?" Claudia inquired. Vivian nodded. "Does he know about RT and my loss of another forty?" Claudia hoped to avoid another retelling. Vivian nodded again. "I'll be back to pick up my supplies," Claudia called to the back room.

"Okay," Ernie, unseen, replied. "I'll have them ready." Vivian gave her a wink.

Past the Gilbert's jewelry store and the vacant shoemakers, Claudia proceeded to the mortuary. She wiped her boots on the mat and walked through the front area. "Hello?" she called. When she saw Thomas her mouth, as if trapped by past behavior, blurted out, "What do you mean by intruding in my business?"

Thomas was in the workroom helping his uncle make a coffin. He'd returned to New York once in January and once in February to insure smooth delivery of caskets. He set the finishing hammer onto the lid of the partially completed coffin and wiped his hands on the work apron tied around his slender torso. The ironed blue shirt, which draped his broad shoulders, echoed the azure sea of his eyes. The smell of shaved cedar and the speckle of pine dust motes connected the space between them. Claudia noticed Thomas's stooped uncle peer up from where he'd been planing the edge of another coffin resting on saw horses. She blushed for her rudeness.

The uncle gave a slight nod in greeting and farewell, "Claudia." He stepped through the back door, into the cool, frosty air toward the little house he now shared with Thomas.

"Certainly is a challenge to help somebody like you," remarked Thomas. She bristled at his judgment of her. She felt her anger dissolve into being flustered. Her chest was rising and falling under her yellow cotton shirt, partially visible under her heavy, flannel-lined jacket. She remembered this was the same blouse she'd worn the first time they'd seen each other the day her life turned a summersault.

"You are the most independent woman I have ever met." He spoke quietly, the way she had spoken so many times to steady her horses when they became skittish. She was confused—*Was that a compliment or a condemnation?*

"Well, you aren't the easiest to understand either," she countered. "Where have you been?" They knew she wasn't referring to a physical location. The words hung in the air with the cedar and pine specks between them.

"Are you looking a gift horse in the mouth?" He commented kindly and gently. "You of all people, Claudia, have told me that is like gazing up a dead horse's arse."

To hear him say "arse" wasn't like him or a New York expression. Her laugh burst from her with the force of a dam's release. All that she had held back flooded out and over her. Her father's sudden unexpected death, an unwanted union with Hank, money distress, the loss of her Dandy and Molly, the loss of two-thirds of her land, her awareness of her need for Thomas, and her discovery that even if she could do everything herself, she didn't want that. She laughed uncontrollably, great guffaws that bent her double and sounded choked.

Thomas reached for her, anguish on his face. His genuine distress at her hysteria broke open the fence into which she had corralled her spirit. Her laughter became great gut-level sobs, and he held her bowed body. She sat where he guided her, to the coffin he'd been working on, which rested on the floor. An oak coffin, a hard wood to work but gorgeous.

"What do you want from me?" They were eye-to-eye. "I can pay you back, but over a long time." Claudia, fearful that everything she felt would be revealed in her eyes, cast them down.

"I don't mind. I want to take over my uncle's business and will pay him slowly. He's fine with that. Turtle Lake feels like home. I'll always go back to New York City, but they have new graduates this spring who can take my place at Hagstrom's. Everybody is seeking work. I'll help them train someone." Claudia peeked up for a moment; he had knelt next to the coffin on which she sat. Her finger followed the tight, even, grain lines and the gentle eddies that punctuated the surface.

"This is oak, isn't it?"

"Yes. Bur oak, one of the hardest oaks to work. My uncle

says that sometimes the most challenging of woods produces the best results, lasts forever, and gives the greatest satisfaction when treated with patience and appreciation." Thomas held her chin in his hand and gazed into her eyes. "They, hard woods, are just beautiful, plain and simple."

He moved to sit beside her on the bur oak coffin, which was much like the red oak one she'd picked out for her father. "I don't want to be in debt to you," Claudia had offered, hoping for a short conversation, not a long, drawn-out discussion.

"I understand, but isn't a repayment relationship with me better than a contrived marriage with Hank?" Thomas countered.

"But what do you get out of helping me?" She questioned shyly, her barricade no longer relevant.

"I get to see you happy, not the weighted-down woman from an Edgar Allan Poe tale."

"I don't know how I'm going to maintain a livelihood. I don't have enough land to support my animals, few as they are. I can't sell enough to repay you what you've paid Hank. I only have the Highland bull and two cows and their calves left; the rest are Hereford mixes. I had to sell the Highland bred heifers. They were the only ones to bring a fair price." Claudia felt the talk was all vacuous leading nowhere.

"Isn't the reason your father, then you, couldn't get ahead of the increasing debt because only the interest was being paid, interest rates kept going up, and the interest was compounded?"

"Yes!" She blurted with an exasperation that came out as anger. "Sorry, I mean, of course, but I'm caught in a vicious cycle. My only source of income is cattle. Even if I could get a fair price of forty dollars a head and sold all of them, that amount is a drop in the bucket of what I owe you."

"First, quit worrying about paying me. I don't care about any interest. Right now, I'm living quite contentedly with my uncle and don't have the theater or New York expenses. Let's focus on what is the best for you to do with the land and animals you have. What if you were to sell the other Highland cattle? You'd have fewer animals to feed."

"No! That's the only thing left of my father's dream. I can't sell them." She started to pace the room, swerving among the in-progress coffins sitting on the floor, resting on saw horses, or leaning against the walls.

"Okay. Keep all the Highland and the ten Hereford mixed," Thomas declared following her. She stopped and interrupted him, "Nine. A steer choked last week." "Nine," he repeated patiently. "Keep all nine and the Highlands, use all your land for pasture, and purchase all your feed." When she resumed her pacing, he seated himself by the plain desk at the shop's front. She went into that part of the room to stand next to his chair.

"What? How is that going to work? I'll have no land for crops and I can't buy feed without an income." She stared hard at him.

"Claudia," his voice was soft. "You can't have it all, land and animals. That option is gone. That choice left when your father didn't reduce the principle, then missed payments, and you, not knowing that fact so I'm not assigning blame, didn't make payments. The loan was in default and with sixteen percent interest which kept compounding, the loan increased such that you lost a third of your land to cover the delinquency, and then you miraculously saved your home by sacrificing another third of the land you love." She was gazing into his face and his fingers reached out tentatively and touched hers. "Do you realize how wise and quick you were to have saved your home forty by exchanging the balance on the debt for the poorer forty?" She couldn't look at him. She didn't feel wise or quick. His voice rose as if eager. "What if you sold your home forty and all of your cattle? You could end up with a thousand dollars, maybe more? You could buy a little home in town?" Thomas rose and held her calloused hands in his large comfortable ones. He didn't appear excited when she stared into his eyes.

"But, I love my farm." Tears that had welled up as he spoke tumbled like rock from a wall weary of keeping animals in and intruders out.

Thomas held her in his arms, and she allowed her head to rest on his shoulder.

"What do you want, Claudia?"

You! was her first thought, but what came out of her mouth was "the impossible." He paused then proceeded slowly.

"Is the remaining land and your home more important than the animals?"

To have the definitive choice defined so clearly and stated so plainly drew her loss into sharp focus. She was pierced to her core. Any remaining haze vanished. She'd already lost the animals that were part of her, her equine companions. Maybe her father had had a deep connection to the Highland, she couldn't be sure, but she didn't think so. She'd lost her Dandy and Molly and didn't want to lose Thomas.

"I want my land. I can part with the stock." Her voice was a whisper but he heard the clarity and assurance and smiled.

"Yes! Let's keep the land. Think about whether to sell the Highland bull, two cows, and calves or the *nine* Herefords. I'll continue to pay Hank off. You work on selling more livestock. You can use the income to pay the taxes and purchase feed for whichever animals you decide to keep." They felt a draft as the back door opened and frosty March melt wafted the dust motes toward the ceiling.

Thomas's uncle cleared his throat, "You two got them differences solved?" Thomas and Claudia contemplated each other and nodded.

As she and the old gelding with her supplies tied up behind them headed toward home, she reviewed her options. She didn't have to sell all her cattle. She could sell the Herefords and keep the Highland as breeding stock if Thomas was willing to wait to be paid and wouldn't charge her interest. *Can I allow him to give me that gift?* She breathed deeply of the winter air that held the icy promise of spring even if the assurance of warmth was months away.

She'd have to seed the six acres meant for corn into clover and alfalfa with oats or wheat as a cover crop, but next year that acreage would be hay. At two to three acres of pasture and hay needed per head and buying all her feed, she could keep Daisy, the gelding, chickens, the three adult Highlands and the two calves, and get a pig. She wouldn't be able to live off farming like she and her father had, but maybe Thomas and his uncle could use a hand making coffins. After this year of less field work she would have more time next year with no planting to be done or crops to harvest, other than hay. She wouldn't mind working with the two of them, if they didn't.

Could she allow herself to depend on Thomas to be there? Was she giving up her independence? Her control? As she and her gelding plodded along, Dandy and Molly trotted into her mind. She was a teenager holding the reins loosely trusting her friends to cultivate between the corn rows, and they were trusting her, knowing if something unexpected arose she would tighten her grip and guide them safely. Ernie's voice from earlier in the day "Once burned, twice shy" echoed. She didn't want to live like that, fearful. She didn't blame her father or regret their life. A life with Thomas in the picture wouldn't be better or worse, just different.

Not until she and the gelding reached the turn off from Highway 8 did she replay the conversation with Thomas. He had said, "Let's keep the land" as in "let us" plural. She smiled to herself. He loved her. He planned to stick with her. She sang to the snow tipped trees and Old Glue "Will the Circle be Unbroken?" As she approached home, she passed her lost forty acres with some corn stubble left sticking up through the snow that her cattle could have eaten, but the food wasn't hers to give to them. Then she came to her home forty and surveyed the creek, the hill that would fill with berries, the small field she'd plant in hay next month, the fenced corral, and the cozy home nestled in the trees and shrubs. She observed as a stranger would, not knowing that the snow-covered mound had been a barn to shelter her friends. She could live here, have a garden, a pig, a milk cow, raise a steer, some chickens, and a few Highland for breeding. She didn't even have to marry, if she didn't want to. She could get a job in town. *Yes, let the circle be unbroken.*

51. Christmas on the Farm 1933

Last night snowflakes began falling. Once their friends had arrived, the snow fell in bundles like cotton. More than Claudia could ever remember, except when she was a child.

In those days snow fell from the roof into piles that huddled on the sides of the house. Papa cleared a path from the door and around the windows. She never saw snow around other neighbors' houses like around hers. Now she understood the wind had blown the snow away from the buildings and swirled drifts between outbuildings. Her father had planted trees to act as a windbreak and snow-catcher. But when she was little so were the trees, and the snow had been magnificently deep and cozy, blanketing the house. Now her home was protected and the snow drifted respectfully away from the door and at the feet of the evergreens and lilacs her father had planted at the edge of the yard.

When the snow piled high and the frost snowflaked the glass, she watched for Saint Nicholas, imagining that his sleigh was like theirs—dark wood curved in large swirls like a duck's tail feathers. The runners, rimmed in metal to slide slickly over hard-packed or powder-light snow, ran up the front and ended in a curl as the head of an animal that reminded the young Claudia of the Canadian geese that gathered in great Vs to fly south for the winter. When they stopped to admire the fall phenomena, her father had always related the same two stories.

"Did you know that geese mate for life? Everyone talks about a birdbrain and for chickens I can see why, but a goose is a different bird. When a goose finds another that it's attracted to, they mate and stay faithful for life. I've seen a lone goose, honking forlornly, look for her gander until she finds him. Once I watched a male stay with a wounded mate until the water on the pond was frozen completely except for the small patch he kept open for her. The rest of the flock had left weeks before. He stayed while she recovered from a broken wing. Probably the result of a careless hunter who shot poorly. They sat together the first year and raised a brood of five to become adults. They started that spring with twelve goslings. The turtles ate some, and several were lost to fox. By fall there were five left that flew off to winter in warmer weather. I recognized the same couple the next year because her wing had healed a bit crooked and still hung down more than normal. Every year they made a nest on our pond until one year she came back alone and honked mournfully every morning then flew away. I think she joined up with the rest of the flock to feed for the day in the field and river. Every night I'd go do chores and see her return and every morning I'd hear her mournful, persistent honking. The next year she was gone."

The other story about geese he related to the young Claudia was how they worked together for the common good, efficiently and economically.

"Did you know that geese take turns when they fly? A V is the most efficient way for a group to fly. Like an arrow, the formation breaks the air and decreases the drag on each individual bird. Watch them in the sky and you'll see the one in the lead will cut the air and the rest fly in two legs behind. When the lead gets tired the goose falls back and the wing bird just to the right or left of the lead takes over and breaks the wind for the rest of the flock. They keep relieving each other. One out in front taking the brunt of the wind and doing the hard work while those off to the side and out to the back have an easier time until their turn. I've often wondered if they have any slackers—like humans do."

Claudia watched the sky on this snowy day with flakes that had started as big, slow-falling cotton clumps. They had turned from pretty to treacherous in hours. The wind had picked up and the seven inches that had accumulated over the past several days was now being tossed with the vengeance of adolescent schoolboys trying to outthrow each other and prove themselves. Only when someone got an icy ball in the face or a child came into the schoolroom with snow-crusted hair and bloody lip did the teacher traipse out to stop the storm of snowballs and prevent further damage. Unfortunately, there was no teacher to stop the storm of snowfall from raging here.

What if Thomas left when the weather was good and was caught in this, unable to turn back because the distance would be as far to travel as to continue to home? Would he stop at some house to spend Christmas with a neighbor and wait out the storm? Knowing Thomas, the neighbor's holiday would be the richer for his stories and good humor. He would be handing out the candy, which he bought for her and their guests, to the distant neighbor's children. She reminded herself to be thankful that in her home she had Ernie, Bruno, and Klive, besides Luella and her two sons, and their laughter. Ernie's jokes prompted merriment from even Luella's taciturn boys.

"Did you hear 'bout the lady who says to her man, 'You're looking swell' and the man replies, 'Thanks, sweetheart. Sorry I can't say the same about you.' And she comes back saying, 'You could if you lied like I did.'" Ernie assumed the pallid laughter was a cue for more and better.

"Wait, I got one more. A chronic grouch never goes where he is told to go until he dies." A few groans. "Did you know I was unconscious for ten hours?" Several quizzical looks were cast at Ernie, who had recovered from his burns a year ago but bore the scars on both arms as a constant reminder of the tenuousness of life.

"I had a fall." Ernie appeared downcast.

Good old Ned bit the bait. "Where did you fall?"

"Asleep. Get it? I fell asleep." Luella liked that one and

laughed heartily, which caused both Ned and Carl to chuckle to see their mother's mood lighten. She hadn't laughed since her husband died a year ago.

Ned prompted, "Ernie, you should quit eating beans; they talk behind your back." Then everyone laughed to hear anything, much less a joke, come from Ned.

Ernie couldn't be outdone. "Vivian got so tired of my jokes she told me one day, 'Did you hear about the terrible robbery in the backyard last night? Two clothespins held up a shirt.'" They glanced toward the kitchen where they could hear Vivian talking to the ham she was basting with peach juice from the jar Claudia had opened earlier to make cobbler.

Vivian, not much of a cook, was safe basting the ham. Claudia wondered if the mumbling she heard was Vivian coaxing the ham not to burn or more likely threatening. She could smell the squash cooking in brown sugar and the sweet smoke as Carl put another log into the stove. She turned when a draft of cold swept through as Bruno stamped his feet free of icy snow and entered with an armload of logs to top off the already full wood box. Ernie dipped a bit of bread in honey, as was the Bohemian custom and brought the gift out to the pregnant Daisy to insure a plentiful supply of milk in the upcoming year. Everyone wanted something to do. This was the first real Christmas since Francis had passed. No one counted that first Christmas. The shock was so fresh, they hadn't gotten together, and Claudia spent the day at the Johnsons. Claudia seemed to be doing so well. No one expected her to be quiet this year.

Each of them thought of Christmas seasons before, taking sleighs to each other's homes. The ringing of sleigh bells on harnesses had been the only sound in the muffled peace of a snowy ride through the woods or along the hedgerow of trees between fields. Everyone looked forward to a visit to Francis Nelson's. He was always prepared with hard cider for the men and sweet, pressed apple juice mixed with elderberry juice for the women and children. Or the women might be offered his dark elderberry wine or the golden dandelion wine that "snuck up on you from behind like a tall dark dandy," as Vivian was likely to say of her favorite choice. "I like a small glass, but then I always feel a bit reckless."

December was a time to snuggle in, repair clothes, and maintain, strengthen, or mend friendships with visits and shared treats.

If visitors stopped at the beginning of December they might be around for a visit from old Saint Nick, who typically arrived on the sixth of December to fill children's shoes with nuts and an orange. The peel would be kept to be candied and used in Christmas baking or to decorate the tops of holiday breads. In the shoe children might discover a bright red apple, a store-bought item shipped from California. Unlike the wrinkled-skinned, mottled green, yellow, and red apples in barrels in the fruit cellar, these store-bought beauties were firm and crisp.

"Not so good for pie or baking," the women would say, "but they are a joy to bite into." Yesterday, Doris Johnson had delivered several icing-topped loaves of cinnamon swirl bread dotted inside with walnuts and raisins and decorated on top with candied peel and glazed almonds for Claudia's guests to enjoy today. Doris had unwrapped seven colorful dish towels, one for each day of the week, which Claudia had embroidered for her neighbor. Without all the fieldwork, even with helping Thomas and his uncle doing woodworking, she was able to return to her embroidery.

The women in their neighborhood each had their own specialty of baked goods. Sophie Fournier was known for her crepes, which she rolled after filling with the berries they raised or gathered from the thickets or hillsides. Mrs. Andersen served hot coffee thick with cream and sugar accompanied by rosettes, a fried-batter cookie dusted with powdered sugar. At the Reuter farm Matthew supplied warm, dark, home-brewed beer and Anna offered a slice of apple strudel or pumpkin pie. On bread-making day, which was almost daily, she may have pulled some dough aside to make flemisers, a fried-bread delight rolled in sugar. Mrs. MacNaughton served dark tea with thick cream or lemon or, as Claudia preferred, with honey from the farm's bees. Depending on the day and what Mrs. Mac was baking, she might serve scones dotted with dried cranberries or buttery shortbread, Claudia's favorite.

Over the years Vivian had tried to make the fruit-nut bread Claudia's mother had made from gathered hazel nuts, her dried cranberries, walnuts, and pecans shipped up from Alabama, plus store-bought dried dates, raisins, and apricots. Francis had enjoyed Vivian's attempts with the young Claudia to re-create that Christmas treat her mother had lavished so effortlessly on them. Claudia loved the sweet yet tart combination baked together with only eggs and a smidgen of flour. Using Helen's hand-written recipe, Vivian and the young Claudia measured, mixed, and baked together. After a few seasons Claudia was obviously a natural and better at making the bread and preparing her mom's B & B pickles than Vivian, who didn't have the patience for fussy work. That's why she didn't tat, embroider, crochet, or knit. Yet she could sit for hours reading and not budge.

Each of the people gathered at Claudia's farm this Christmas Day had their own thoughts swirling in their heads as the snow continued to circle outside the doors and windows and frost etched the glass and drifted in through any crack. Each smoked or chewed or scratched or basted or stirred or grunted in thought, but the words that came out had nothing to do with the thoughts they were thinking.

"Matthew said he's gonna raise a newfangled cow they brought in from Ireland. Somethin' called a belted Galloway. You ever heard of such a thing? Supposed to do real good here 'cause they're used to cold and wind. Can't see as he'll make a go of it though. The shipping alone will kill any profit." Klive repeated what he'd heard at Ernie's store and didn't even think to consider the similar risk Francis and Claudia had taken.

"Did you see that Julia is coloring her hair? She's been pulling gray hairs for some time. Recently she came back from Rice Lake and there's not a blade of gray anywhere to be found," added Luella, who couldn't care less about where to get gray hair colored but wanted to add something to the quiet in the room.

In their minds they remembered stockings hung on a mantle to be filled by a parent with a small, carved toy horse or soldier, a hair ribbon or corn husk doll, and a stick of white and red peppermint or a handful of hard, multicolored, ribbon candy. No children were here so no stockings were hung. The O'Briens had been invited, but that was before the storm had started. The parents with their brood of eight children wouldn't venture out in this, especially with the new baby. Claudia imagined they'd be inventing games and clustered around their wood stove where Mrs. O'Brien would have a kettle of rabbit, potato, and carrot stew cooking and fresh bread. Claudia had only put up a tree because of Thomas. He was in Almena checking on a family whose children had chickenpox. If a tree had been up to her alone, she wouldn't have bothered. Now she was glad she'd taken the trouble to find, cut, and decorate this feathery white pine. With their friends gathered, the tree was festive. Ernie and Vivian had attended previous Christmases here. Bruno and Klive came as Ernie was their house guest. Vivian had mentioned in passing that Luella was a bit blue being released from her husband's care so Claudia invited her and the boys. Maybe one day Claudia would invite Nora to join them. She breathed deeply. *Something was missing.*

Thomas couldn't call even if he was at a home with a phone. Heavy snow had taken down the phone lines and shortly after the electricity had gone out, too. The kerosene lamps that hung on the walls through all of Claudia's youth were lit as they were whenever the lights went out. Her father had always kept them filled and the wicks trimmed and the chimneys cleaned for just such an outage.

"Always be prepared," he'd cautioned. "There's no excuse for being unprepared. Just laziness in Sunday dress."

They gave up waiting for Thomas to arrive even though the snow had stopped. No one said anything, they just set the table and Claudia pulled the ham out. She sent up a little prayer of thanks to the pig she'd fed through last year. She asked Ernie to carve. Vivian handed each of them a bowl to carry to the table before they sat down. Bruno carried a bowl heaped with bright orange carrot slices. Luella held a smaller bowl of sweet peas that had taken hours to shell. They would be eaten in minutes but with the appreciation of the time and effort the womenfolk had put into this delicacy. Klive brought in the large crockery bread bowl full of steaming mashed potatoes. Ned held the gravy boat in one hand and the cranberry salad in the other, while Carl carried a pitcher of water. The table already held the basket of rolls, hot and brown under a linen napkin similar to those that lay at each place setting. The dishes, which normally were plain, heavy, white were today, in honor of the Christ child's birth, replaced by delicate bone china rimmed with a single gold ring—a luxury Francis had given his wife on their fifth anniversary only a couple of years before she died.

When they were all seated, Vivian reached out for Ernie's hand even though she didn't believe in God. She knew the ritual retained after the loss of Claudia's mother at this household. If truth be told, even though she pretended to put up with the whole rigmarole, she loved the tradition of holding hands at this table and praying to each other, for that's how she looked at the belief, for their thankfulness. When all hands were joined and heads bowed, Claudia did what her father had done since she could remember.

"Bless us, oh Lord, and these thy gifts which we are about to receive from thy bounty through Christ our Lord. Amen." She paused and Vivian could hear the quick intake of breath before Claudia continued, "Dear Lord, we thank you for these friends and family and those unable to be with us." Almost as an afterthought she added, "Be with us all. Hold us safely in your hands." Everyone thought of someone lost, departed, or too far away. There was silence. Then Vivian completed with "Amen." An echo of "Amens" followed. They didn't look at each other but reached out and began to fill their plates with ham, cranberry salad, and vegetables. As meat, potatoes, and gravy filled plates and bellies, tongues loosened and memories filled the room.

Luella remembered a comb and brush set her Herbert had given her, which she had admired being displayed in the jeweler's window one spring. Unknown to her, he'd gone in and made arrangements with Mr. Gilbert to pay so much a month until he had paid for and given the extravagant gift to her that Christmas.

"The comb, brush, and mirror with a bird and floral design still sit on my dresser. I use them and think of him brushing my hair at night." Ned and Carl exchanged glances. They had trouble imagining their gruff father brushing their mother's hair. Wonders never ceased.

"We would go tobogganing down the Indian mounds when we were first married like I'd done before I met my bride," offered Ernie. "My wife's family put a stop to it. I didn't know any better, and that was the steepest hill in the area. But when you know better, you do better. Later we strung the toboggan behind the sleigh on a long rope. You get the horses going on the packed road, and you can take a parcel of folks on a dandy ride." Conversation continued after dishes were done. They moved into the front room where the woodstove was crackling and popping.

No one but the dog heard him come in. Shep didn't bark. He was just glad his friend had finally made the party. Even if the dog had barked, because there was an unfamiliar smell behind his familiar friend, no one would've heard with all the ruckus. They were playing charades, acting out Christmas carol titles. Lumbering Bruno had just pretended to punch Klive for the first word of a three-word song. He about shouted out the title after he walked the hall gesticulating and rubbing the walls for the third word when Thomas blurted out, "Deck the Halls." They turned and laughed. Relief and superfluous abundance spilled out and filled every corner of the room.

After Thomas and his companion were relieved of their snow-crusted coats and boots, they relaxed on the sofa with mugs of hot coffee, the party looking on. Claudia knew the delicate coffee cups and plates from dinner would feel uncomfortably fragile to the two shivering men. Two mugs of hot coffee and two solid plates of food were dished up and the two men ate in silence for a few minutes. Ernie could wait no longer and asked, "So, what's the story?"

"I was well on my way here from Almena when the storm came up out of nowhere, from the southeast of all places, blowing at my back, but Jasper and I just kept coming." He reached out to put his hand on Claudia's knee.

"I didn't want to miss Christmas here." He gazed at her with those eyes the color of a glacial stream she'd seen in a *National Geographic* magazine. "The wind shifted direction, putting us straight into the storm. I decided best to stop and wait it out. Poor Jasper's eyelids were freezing shut, and his nostrils were so ice-crusted I had to stop to break the icicles from both of us several times." He held the coffee to his lips and drank long.

"I couldn't remember where the closest house would be. I was a bit disoriented. I decided to head into some woods for a little protection. Purely by accident I came upon a little shanty tucked into the woods and..." Here Thomas reached to his other side to touch the shoulder of his shabbily dressed companion.

"Jack was good enough to welcome me into his humble home. He had a bit of a fire going and a hunk of blanket I could use to rub the circulation back into Jasper." With the pink returning to his cheeks, the man, who at first had appeared to be ancient but was only about Thomas's age, hung his head shyly.

"The storm let up after an hour, and when I discovered Jack was spending Christmas alone and we were less than ten miles from here.... Well, I knew you all would be glad to have me bring him along to share in our festivities." Later, putting their empty plates in the kitchen, he shared with Claudia the poor condition of the shanty and the lack of any real meal for a Christmas dinner. After Thomas and Jack had eaten and they were still busy with dishes and talking, Claudia pulled the tag off one of the gifts under the tree that she had wrapped for Thomas, socks she had knitted in soft, gray wool. She would make him another pair. At the opening of gifts, she knew when she saw Jack's surprise and Thomas's glance that her instincts had guided her well. He fingered the socks like pearls, delighting in the texture.

"I never seen such." His barely audible response was one of two or three things he uttered all night.

"Thank yer fine lady for me," he indicated to Thomas. Everyone else had opened their gifts. The women held carved animals or bits of purchased doodads. They all sat festooned with nubby knitted scarves or donned heavy tight woven caps bright with newness. Fruitcakes, fudge, and containers of homemade treats sat in the laps of men who would taste the fellowship of Christmas each bite until they licked the crumbs from the insides of tins in the days to come.

Vivian, with the exquisite cameo brooch Claudia had given her pinned to her lace collar, sat at the piano while the others clustered around her as puppies around a dish of milky mash. Ernie's bass and Thomas's tenor set off the rest, who wiggled their notes up and down and around in merry off-key to "Jingle Bells." Ned and Carl uncased their fiddle and squeezebox to join in. Thomas held the carols together, just as he did the hymns in church, with his voice coming in strong as the others struggled to hit the correct note, or he provided the word for which they fumbled. Where they were sure in the song, Thomas sang softly and they swayed with their security and held each other's notes and words together as a beautiful crazy quilt, loud and haphazard, warm and wonderfully different from any other. Claudia's alto and Vivian's soprano were as different as the two women. Claudia sang mostly in reserve but true and clear. Vivian's voice warbled high, delightfully sweet but loud and unabashedly imperfect. The storm had ended hours ago but they continued to sing well until the moon rose, revealing a glistening coverlet of snow peacefully laid.

Ernie curled up on the sofa under the crocheted quilt he had received as a gift this night, and Luella and her boys hitched up their sleigh, guided by the full moon's light, and glided home on fresh snow to stoke and bank their own fire and tuck into their own beds. Thomas put Jack to sleep in Francis's bed where Thomas usually slept when he stayed. The next day, sunny and clear, Jack would set off for his home in the woods with a sled laden with enough Christmas left overs to last him weeks. Klive and Bruno, not much interested in singing, had left earlier. Vivian was sitting on the piano bench, fingering the keys and playing a rough rendition of "Silent Night." Next to her sat Thomas, with his arm around Claudia, who was holding a small box, which held amber-and-sterling earrings she could appreciate without reopening the box. Nestled next to the earrings was a sterling-silver cross with a drop of amber in different hues on each end, all hung on a thin chain of delicate silver links. The piano trio looked like three sleepy Magi slumped on a camel after travels afar and adventures anew. Soon even they would find a loveseat and a bed in which to fall until the rooster called them all to another day.

Epilogue

Angels Guiding and Guarding with Music

This April evening as the winter of 1933–34 ended and spring warmth held promise, they were lying in bed listening to the recording of Brahms on Thomas's gramophone. Brahms was romantic emotion. Claudia could understand what Thomas meant when he'd admitted he'd gone to the concert instead of eating.

"I ate bread and cheese for a week so I could feed on the music," he'd confided to her when they first went to hear live music. The Bible states "Man does not live on bread alone." God meant music. Music was another bread of life, Claudia thought. Jesus Christ is the word of God who speaks to my soul through music.

"People are God's instruments on earth," the preacher extolled at church last Sunday. God is giving me a glimpse of heaven tonight with Thomas, she mused. Seraphim and cherubim—those angels aren't just guiding and guarding us on earth; they are singing people to heaven's gate, like bees surround plump grapes and as apples hang ripe with summer's heady sweetness. The room and their bodies smelled and tasted salty sweet like loamy soil—rich, musky, and fertile.

The heady pluck of strings was like the taste of champagne at the concert they'd attended months ago in January when he'd proposed and she'd accepted. That night Claudia noticed that all the musicians were a mass of black and white. Tonight, three months later she and Thomas lay in flesh tones of tan and pink. Did the orchestra members purposefully attired themselves in black and white because a feast of the ears gorging on sound could not accommodate the eyes? Could eyes only tolerate two colors—black and white? Could a feast of fingers and tongues only tolerate tan and pink? Would she burst from the flooding of color because her ears were bleeding sound into her veins through her soul?

She felt that she was riding a wave of rainbow-hued sound strung together like soap bubbles. She didn't think what to do for the future but only what felt good now. This was so different from the way her normal days had been up until the last few months since their relaxed wedded routine had become customary. Her daily schedule of chores, which remained physical, had become less demanding, since the sale of the Herefords, and pleasant. She felt exhilarated using her body, like when she was younger.

Once again she felt capable around the farm; she and her father had cared for the fields and animals. She still cared. This was lighter, freer but only if she could keep her father's voice out of her head. But her father hadn't been who he seemed to be, so what had been true? What had been good? Did her realization of his fallibility, his being at times foolish, make him less of an honest, sincere farmer and community man? Did his imperfection undo his fatherness because he hadn't lived up to her belief of who he was? Did all their time together become a lie because he had lied? She wouldn't believe that. She remembered their talks, their companionable silence, and their working together as equals. He had respected her and her work. He relied on her and she remembered his smile when he saw her with Dandy and Molly. She knew he had loved her even though he never spoke the words out loud. Her father was unlike Thomas, who told her often how much she meant to him, that he loved her. She leaned on him and he on her and that interdependence felt okay, even good and necessary. Like rafters in a barn or people on each end of a saw, they needed to lean on each other. A rafter or a person could stand alone but without someone close by, either would fall if the weather got rough.

Claudia and Thomas lay in their house, the farmhouse of her life, and she couldn't sleep. Not because of unease but because of her joy. She loved her life, she loved Thomas, she loved her farm, and she would love the daughter she would one day conceive and bear. None more or less than the others. Each differently. She didn't love the piano more than the violin or less than the French horn or drums. She loved the variety, the diversity, the sumptuousness of so much abundance and range in their lives. Even the saxophone and clarinet when Thomas had taken her to the jazz club. She closed her eyes. The wind blew outside. She fell softly into sleep in the arms of the man who loved her, to music twirling in her head.

The End

Endnotes

Parenthesis indicate page number of the novel where the first reference can be found.

1. George W. Powers, *Handy Dictionary of Poetical Quotations,* New York: Thomas Y Crowell Company Publishers 1901 was used for Ernie's quotations. I think he picked up the volume somewhere and liked to read to his wife from the little red-cloth, hard-covered volume. (p.5)

2. Twinkies were invented in Schiller Park, Illinois on April 6, 1930 by James Alexander Dewar for Continental Baking Co. The filling was banana cream until WWII when they changed to vanilla. Wikipedia (p.15)

3. *National Music Reader* vol. 2 circa 1800 (*Third National Music Reader* (in same volume) is by Luther Whiting Mason 1871.) (p.16)

4. Flemisers were a bread dough treat that was made by pulling a piece of risen dough to form a flattened circular piece that was put into a shallow cast iron fry pan with an inch of hot lard and fried. When one side was brown the puffed-up dough was flipped to brown the other side. When both sides were browned the flemiser was turned out onto clean rags, brown paper sacking, or paper toweling to dry then while still hot was placed into a brown paper sack with several tablespoons of sugar (or cinnamon and sugar) then removed and eaten hot with lots of milk. These were made by my German maternal grandmother. I never saw the word written only heard her and my mother call them flemisers. I can't find anything on the internet to indicate an origin. (p.22)

5. Soybeans information from NC Soybean Producers Association. In 1851 soybean seeds were distributed to farmers in Illinois and the corn belt states and in 1870's farmers began planting for forage for livestock. In 1919 the American Soybean Assoc. was founded. Henry Ford's used soybeans to make plastic knobs, buttons, window frames,

pedals, casings, and assemblies for his automobiles. By 1935 Ford was using one bushel of soybeans for every car he manufactured. By the 1940s farming soybeans was ubiquitous. USDA prices nation-wide for soybeans in 1932 averaged .50/bushel and corn .25/bushel. (p.33)

6. Local information on crop prices came from a daily diary kept by Lars Bjorkman, who listened to the radio reports. On Oct. 31, 1932 hogs 2.85/cwt, bulls $2/cwt, top notch prime $4/cwt, corn .04/bu. and .08 for shelled corn Iowa, wheat .43 in Chicago, oats .13 in Minneapolis. He paid .25 for 50# of potatoes, $7.85 for a car tire, $1.35 for car tube, and received $1.50 for an old tire. Prices for products and weather from Lars Bjorkman's hand-written journal 1930–1933 resides in Turtle Lake, Wisconsin at the TL Museum. (p.48)

7. Ernie's jokes came from local newspapers of the time. (p.66)

8. The general information about trains in the area came from (Tom Belter at) the Spooner train museum and train schedules. The specifics of those running through Turtle Lake came from the Turtle Lake sesquicentennial book *A Tribute to the Time Turtle Lake, Wisconsin 1898-1998* published 1998 by Halco Press, Turtle Lake, WI. Additional information came from the *Amery Centennial 1887-1987* book published in 1987 by Amery Free Press, Amery WI. (p.95)

9. In 1926 a Wisconsin referendum to amend the Volsted Act (which outlawed the manufacture and sale of alcohol) to allow for the manufacture and sale of beer with 2.75% alcohol was passed by popular vote but declined by the governor. Beer of 0.5% was legal to produce, sell, and drink, but many folks made their own high alcohol content beer. By 1929 voters had repealed the Wisconsin prohibition enforcement law, the Severson Act. I chose to use the term low alcohol content beer to mean 3.2% even though that beverage didn't become popular in use until 1933. (p.139)

10. As I was unable to find the date when the practice of a silent auction first began, I fictionalized that could be 1930's. (p.140)

11. Stout Island, twenty-seven acres with luxury log dwellings, was owned by the Frank D Stout family who called it the Island of Happy Days. After Frank died in 1927, his wife continued to enjoy the island until her death in 1949. He was very protective of his private island, even though they entertained many guests. I took the liberty to imagine Mrs. Stout as donating a weekend stay as her contribution to the nearby Rice Lake Fall Fundraiser. (p.145)

12. *Chapbook A Garland of 10 Polk balance hi* Middlebury College Press 1941, Middlebury Vermont. This soft-covered volume is the source of Ernie's Hog–Thorny Bear ballad, of which I imagined he heard an oral version on his travels west to Wisconsin. (p.149)

13. The term Ivy league school is attributed to sports' writer Caswell Adams in the 1930s in reference to a football game which would've interest Randy. (p.221)

14. I have taken the liberty of giving the vagabond man a smaller pig as a "pet" similar to the potbellied pigs which were developed in Viet Nam (for food) in the 1960s. (p.262)

15. "The Evolution of Milk Pricing and Government Intervention in Dairy Markets" by Eric M Erba (Ph D student) and Andrew M Novakovic Professor of Agricultural Economics at Cornell University is a publication of the Cornell Program on Dairy Markets and Policy ARME Dept. Ithaca, NY (p.280)

16. Prices from numerous sources (see #6 above, *1932 Yearbook* Seek Publishing, *1932-1933 Price List* Mooresville, Indiana, and *Turtle Lake Times* 1932 issues) (p.282)

17. *Turtle Lake Times* February 18, 1932 Halco Press (p.282-284)

18. In the 1930s phones were operated using a main switchboard operator and each phone had a distinctive ring

on a party or shared line so homeowners would know if the call was for them. Individuals sharing that line could pick up and listen in on a call meant for another home. In the case of the fire department, this system could notify numerous phone owners in a community of the immediate need to respond. (p.331)

Even though Turtle Lake had several stores, a pool hall, a separate post office, two feed mills, hotels, a bank, and several churches in the area and was "dry," no legal alcohol, I chose to simplify the town. Just as Bear Creek Township doesn't exist but is modeled after Beaver Township, the Nelson farm doesn't exist but is similar to several farms in the township in 1932. In 1932 a grist mill stood west of Beaver Township in Joel, but that town no longer exists and its mill has not been operational for decades.

Regardless of the fact that the majority of farmers were dairy farmers in the 1930s, Francis quit milking cows and raised beef, which was, not unheard of but, definitely ahead of his time. He was old-fashioned in other ways, e.g. preferring to stay on the farm, having a close connection to the land, and preferring not to travel very far.

Interviews, histories, diaries, letters, newspapers, and various other local sources were used to verify and collaborate my story.

Although the Dust Bowl (and Black Sunday in 1934) refers primarily to the southern plain states of Oklahoma, Kansas, Colorado, New Mexico, and Texas, the consequences of severe drought and farming practices that were heedless of conservation affected other states including the Midwestern states of Wisconsin, Minnesota, the Dakotas, and Michigan. The four drought waves occurred in 1930–31, 1934, 1936, and the last was in 1939–40 with sustained record-high temperatures occurring throughout the United States during the last two waves.

Even though wheat was the primary crop in the southern

plains and cotton in the south, the Midwest primarily produced corn, potatoes, tobacco, oats, hay and hay seed, spring wheat (winter wheat production decreased by 1932), and barley. (WI Coop Crop and Livestock Reporter vol XI, no.7 p.2 1932) There was an increased production in feed crops and a decrease in cash crops. Soybeans, raised originally in the south, were grown experimentally in the Midwest and used initially for plastics (Ford Motor Co. used them in their automobiles). Only later were soybeans grown for feed. In 1922 soybeans were $1/bushel. USDA prices nation-wide for soybeans in 1932 averaged .50/bushel, which was better than corn which locally was .08/bu. and nationally averaged .30/bushel. Crop prices overall fell below subsistence levels in 1932.

Following closely on the heels of the Great Depression, the Dust Bowl wreaked havoc on the country. Help to farmers began with seed subsidies by President Herbert Hoover but significant aid and legislation wouldn't arrive until President F.D. Roosevelt's government took office.

About the Author

Grief and gratitude sparked the conception of *Aria for a Farm: Lean Together or Fall Alone* about a small Wisconsin farming community in the 1930s. Life-changing health concerns and the loss of loved ones fueled the author's writing. The abundant goodwill of townsfolk and city friends who populate the pages as composite characters from her community ignited her desire to capture the sometimes annoying but usually redeeming compulsion of neighbor to help neighbor in trying times.

Victoria Brenna was born in Hastings Minnesota, a Mississippi River town, and moved to an abandoned farm in rural Turtle Lake, Wisconsin where she has been a farmer, executive director of a federal low-income home-building program, co-owner of a residential construction and remodeling company, teacher, and writer. In addition to milking Jersey cows, raising pastured pork, Highland beef cattle, and poultry—she has done every aspect of producing crops.

She is a wife, mother of two adult children, and grandmother to four fabulous young people. She started a not-for-profit child-care center and a natural food co-op buying group and is active in her church as a lay leader of prayer, chorister, and sacristan.

Victoria graduated magna cum laude with a bachelor of science degree in Broad Area English, Theater, and Communication Skills from UW-River Falls and attended Bread Loaf School of English in Vermont. She has published several nonfiction pieces and writes children's stories, poems, and memoir selections. *Aria for a Farm* is her first novel.